About the Authors

Ellie Darkins spent her formative years devouring romance novels, and after completing her English degree she decided to make a living from her love of books. As a writer and editor her work now entails dreaming up romantic proposals, hot dates with alpha males and trips to the past with dashing heroes. When she's not working she can usually be found at her local library or out for a run. You can visit her blog at elliedarkins.com

After completing a degree in journalism, then working in advertising and mothering her kids, **Robin Gianna** had what she calls her awakening. She decided she wanted to write the romance novels she'd loved since her teens, and now enjoys pushing her characters toward their own happily-ever-afters. When she's not writing, Robin's life is filled with a happily messy kitchen, a needy garden, a wonderful husband, three great kids, a drooling bulldog and one grouchy Siamese cat.

Jacquelin Thomas' books have garnered several awards, including two EMMA awards, the Romance In Colour Reviewers Award, Readers Choice Award, and the Atlanta Choice Award in the Religious & Spiritual category. She was nominated for a 2008 NAACP Image Award for Outstanding Fiction in the Young Adult category. Jacquelin has published in the romance, inspirational fiction and you

D1351765

Unexpected Surprises

Unexpected Surprises:
A Forever Family

ELLIE DARKINS

ROBIN GIANNA

JACQUELIN THOMAS

MILLS & BOON

First Published in Great Britain 2022
By Mills & Boon, an imprint of HarperCollins*Publishers,* Ltd
1 London Bridge Street, London, SE1 9GF

www.harpercollins.co.uk

HarperCollins*Publishers*
1st Floor, Watermarque Building,
Ringsend Road, Dublin 4, Ireland

UNEXPECTED SURPRISES: A FOREVER FAMILY
© 2022 Harlequin Books S.A.

Newborn on Her Doorstep © 2015 Ellie Darkins
The Family They've Longed For © 2018 Robin Gianakopoulos
Return to Me © 2018 Jacquelin Thomas

ISBN: 978-0-263-30400-8

Printed and Bound in Spain using 100% Renewable electricity at CPI Black Print, Barcelona

NEWBORN ON HER DOORSTEP

ELLIE DARKINS

For Rosie and Lucy

CHAPTER ONE

LILY TUCKED HER pencil behind her ear as she headed for the door. She almost had this website design finished, with a whole day to go before the client's deadline. She was privately amazed that she'd managed to get the thing done on time, given the chaos in her house. Even now she could hear chisels and hammers and God knew what else in her kitchen, as the builders ripped out the old units ready for work on the extension to start.

The ring of the doorbell had been welcome, actually. When she'd glanced at her watch she'd realised that she'd not taken a break since settling down in her home office at six. She was overdue a cup of coffee— and no doubt the builders would appreciate one, too.

A glance through the hallway window afforded a glimpse of a taxi heading up the road, but she couldn't see anyone waiting behind the frosted glass of the front door. Strange… she thought as she turned the key and pulled the door open.

No one there.

Kids? she wondered, but she'd lived in this house almost all of her life, and she couldn't remember a single case of knock-door-run.

She was just about to shut the door and head back inside when a kitten-like mewl caught her attention and she glanced down.

Not a kitten.

A Moses basket was tucked into the corner of the porch, out of the spring breeze. Wrapped tight inside, with just eyes and the tip of a soft pink nose showing from the yellow blanket... A baby.

Lily dropped to her knees out of instinct, and scooped the baby up from the floor, nestling her against her shoulder. Making sure the blanket was tucked tight, she walked down to the front gate, looking left and right for any sign of someone who might have just left a baby on her doorstep.

Nothing.

She moved the baby into the crook of her arm as she tried to think, her brain struggling to catch up with this sudden appearance. And as she moved the baby she heard a papery crackle. When she pulled the corner of the blanket aside she found a scribbled note on a page torn from a notebook. The writing was as familiar as her own, and unmistakable.

Please look after her.

Which left all the questions she already had unanswered and asked a million more.

She walked again to the gate, wondering if she could still catch sight of that taxi—if she had time to run and stop her half-sister before she did something irreversible. But as much as she strained her eyes, the car was gone.

She stood paralysed with shock for a moment on

the front path, unsure whether to run for help or to take the baby inside. What sort of trouble would her half-sister have to be in to do this? Was she leaving her here forever? Or was she going to turn up in a few minutes and explain?

For the first time Lily took a deep breath, looked down into the clear blue eyes of her little niece—and fell instantly in love.

His feet pounded the footpath hard, driving out thought, emotion, reason. All he knew was the rhythm of his shoes on the ground, the steady in-out of his breath as he let his legs and his lungs settle in to their pace.

The sun was drying the dew on the grassy verges by the road, and the last few commuters were making their way into the tube station. The morning commute was a small price to pay to live in this quiet, leafy part of London, he guessed.

He noted these things objectively, as he did the admiring looks from a couple of women he passed. But none of it mattered to him. This was the one time of the day when he could just concentrate on something he was completely in control of. So, no music, no stopping for admiring glances—just him and the road. Nothing could spoil the hour he spent shutting out the horrors of the world—great and small—that he had encountered in his work over the years.

Tomorrow he'd be able to find a solitary path through the Richmond Park, but this morning he was dodging café tables and pedestrians as he watched the street names, looking out for the address his sister had texted to him. She'd been taking furniture deliveries for him before he flew home, and had left the keys to his new place with a friend of hers who worked from home.

He turned the corner into a quiet side street, and suddenly the fierce cry of a newborn baby ahead skewed his consciousness and he stumbled, his toe somehow finding a crack in the footpath.

He tried to keep running for a few strides, to ignore the sound, but found it was impossible. Instead he concentrated on counting the house numbers—anything to keep his mind off the wailing infant. But as the numbers climbed he felt a sense of growing inevitability. The closer he drew to the sound of the baby, the more he wished that he could get away—and the more certain he became that he wouldn't be able to.

The rhythm and focus that had always come as easily as breathing when he pulled on his running shoes was gone. His body fought him, sending awareness of the baby to his ears. Another side street loomed on his left, and for a moment he willed himself to turn away, to *run* away, but his feet wouldn't obey. Instead they picked up their pace and carried straight on, towards a dazed-looking woman and the wailing baby standing in the porch of one of the houses ahead.

He glanced at the house number and knew that he'd been right. His sister had sent him to a house with a baby—without a word of warning.

'Hi,' he said to the woman, approaching and speaking with caution. Lily, he thought her name was. 'Is everything okay?' He couldn't help but ask—not when she was standing there with a distressed baby and looking as if she'd just been thunderstruck.

Her blonde hair was pulled back into a loose ponytail so shiny that he could almost feel the warmth of the sunlight reflecting off it. Her eyes were blue, clear and wide—but filled with a shock and a panic that stopped him short.

She stared at him blankly and he held out his hands in a show of innocence. 'I'm Nic,' he said, realising she had no idea who he was. 'Dominic—Kate's brother. She said to drop by and pick up my keys?'

'Oh, God,' she said. 'I'd completely forgotten.'

But still she didn't move. Her eyes did, though, dropping to his vest and running shorts, moving as far down as his ankles before her eyes met his again. There was interest there, he could see, even behind her confusion and distress.

'Is everything all right?' he asked again, though everything about her—her posture, her expression—told him that it wasn't.

'Oh, fine,' she said.

He could see the effort it took to pull the muscles of her face into a brave smile, but it wasn't enough to cover the undercurrents of worry that lay beneath. There was something about that contrast that made him curious—more than curious—to know the layers of this woman.

'*My* sister...' she said, boldly attempting nonchalance. 'She never gives me much notice when she needs a babysitter.'

Which was about five per cent of the truth, if he had to guess. He found himself looking deep into her eyes, trying to see her truths, all the things that she wasn't saying. Was there some sort of trick here? Was this something Kate had set up? Surely she'd never be so cruel, never willingly expose him to so much pain?

But he wanted to know more about this woman, he acknowledged. Wanted to untangle her mysteries.

Then he could ignore the screams of the baby no longer, and knew that he mustn't even think it. He should turn and walk away from her and the little bundle of trouble now. Before he got drawn in, before wounds that had taken a decade to become numb were reopened.

But he couldn't, *wouldn't* walk away from someone so obviously in trouble. Couldn't abandon a child, however much it might hurt him. He'd discovered that on his first trip to India, when he'd seen children used as slave labour, making clothes to be sold on British high streets. He'd not been able to leave without doing *something*, without working to improve the shattered lives that he'd witnessed.

Now, ten years later, the charity he'd founded had helped hundreds, thousands of children from exploitation or worse. But that didn't make him any more able to ignore this single child's cries.

Distressed children needed help—whoever they were, wherever they were living. He finally forced himself to look at the crying baby—and felt the bottom fall out of all his worries. He was in serious trouble, and any thoughts of walking away became an impossibility. That was a newborn baby…as in hours-old new. Completely helpless, completely vulnerable and—by the look on Lily's face—a complete surprise.

The baby's crying picked up another notch and Lily bounced it optimistically. But, if he had to guess, she didn't have what that baby needed.

'Did your sister leave some milk? Or some formula?'

She looked up and held his gaze, her eyes still a complicated screen of half-truths. There was something dangerously attractive in that expression, something drawing him in against his better judgement. There was a bond growing between himself and Lily— he could feel it. And some connection with this baby's story was at the heart of it. It was dangerous, and he wanted nothing to do with it, but still he didn't walk away.

'She asked me to pick some up,' she replied, obviously thinking on her feet. 'Thanks for stopping, but I have to get to the shop.'

He chose his next words carefully, knowing that he mustn't scare her off, but seeing by the shocked look on her face that she hadn't quite grasped yet the trouble that this newborn baby might be in. Who left an hours-old baby with a relative who clearly wasn't expecting her? There was more, much more, to this story, and he suspected that there were layers of complications that neither of them yet understood.

'That's quite a noise she's making. How about to be on the safe side we get her checked by a doctor? I saw that the hospital round the corner has a walk-in clinic.'

At that, Lily physically shook herself, pulled her shoulders back and grabbed the baby a little tighter. There was something about seeing the obvious concern and turmoil in her expression that made him want to wrap his arms around her and promise her that everything would be okay. But he was the last person on earth who could promise her that, who could even believe that it might be true.

'Maybe you're right,' she said, walking away from the open front door and through the garden gate.

'Kate's keys are in the top drawer in the hall. Can you pull the door closed on your way out?'

And then she was speed-walking down the street, the baby still clutched tightly to her, still wailing. He glanced at the house and hesitated. He needed his keys, but he could hardly leave Lily's house with the door wide open—the woman hadn't even picked up her handbag. Did she have her own keys? Her wallet? So he had no choice but to grab her bag and his keys and jog in the direction of those newborn wails.

He just wanted to be sure that the baby was going to be okay, he told himself.

'I'll walk with you,' he said as he caught Lily up.

The words were out of his mouth before he had a chance to stop them. However much he might wish he hadn't stumbled on this little family drama, he had. He might be wrong, but gut instinct and not a little circumstantial evidence told him that this child had just been abandoned—which meant, of course, that both mother and baby could be in danger.

He tried to focus on practicalities, tried to put thoughts of what might have been had he and Lily met on any other sunny day out of his mind. He should call Kate. And maybe the police—they were the best people to ensure that the baby's mother was safe and well. But he couldn't ignore the fascination that he felt about Lily. There was an energy that seemed to pull him towards her and push him away at the same time— it had him curious, had him interested.

CHAPTER TWO

LILY EYED NIC, where he leaned against the wall by the door—a position he'd adopted almost as soon as they'd been shown into this room. He looked at the door often, as if reminding himself that it was there. That he could use it any time. So why was he still here?

Under normal circumstances she'd say that an attractive man, background-checked by her BFF, somewhat scantily clad, could involve himself in her life at any time he chose—as long as she had the option of checking out those long, lean thighs. But he really had killer timing.

She didn't have time to ogle; she didn't have time for his prying questions. All she could think about was her sister, Helen, and the baby, and what she needed to do to take care of both of them.

She paced the room, glancing over at the baby and wondering what on earth they were doing to her. Had they found something wrong? If everything was okay, surely someone would have told her by now. She hadn't wanted to hand her over to the doctors, but she'd had no choice.

It was becoming a pattern, this letting go, this watching from afar. She'd lost her father before she was born, to nothing more dramatic than disinterest and a lost phone number. Her mother had died the year that Lily had turned thirteen, and it seemed her sister had been drifting further and further from her since that day. All she wanted was a family to take care of, to take care of her, and yet that seemed too much to ask from the universe.

And now someone had called the police, and her sister was going to be in more trouble than ever, pushed further from her. She tried not to think of the alternative. Of Helen out there needing help and not getting it. If it took the authorities getting involved to get her safe and well, then Lily was all for it.

She started pacing again, craning her neck each time she passed the baby to try and get a glimpse of what was happening.

'Just a couple of tests,' the doctor had said. How could that possibly take this long?

She glanced across at Nic, and then quickly away. How had she never met Kate's brother before? Surely there should be some sort of declaration when you became best friends with someone about any seriously attractive siblings. He'd been abroad, she remembered Kate saying. He ran a charity that tried to improve conditions for child workers in factories in the developing world. He'd recently been headhunted by one of the big retailers that he'd campaigned against, and would be sitting on their board, in charge of cleaning up their supply chain. So attractive, humanitarian, and with a job in retail. There should definitely be a disclaimer for this sort of thing.

But there was something about him that made her nervous—some tension in his body and his voice that told her this man had secrets too: secrets that she couldn't understand. It was telling her to stay away. That he was off-limits. A warning she didn't need.

Nic came to stand beside her. 'Try not to worry. I'm sure that everything is fine—they're just being thorough.'

Lily bit her lip and nodded. She knew that he was right. He gestured her back to a seat and cleared his throat, giving her a rare direct look.

She continued pacing the room, waiting for news—until she heard a shriek, and then she was by the bed, her arms out, already reaching for the baby.

The doctor barely looked up from where he was pricking the little one's heel with a needle.

'I'm sorry, we're not quite done.'

'You're hurting her!'

Lily scooped the baby into her arms as she wiped away the spot of blood from her foot and cooed soothing noises, gently rocking her. Back in Lily's embrace, the baby stopped crying and nuzzled closer. Lily leaned over, instinctively shielding the baby from the doctor who had hurt her, until she felt the little body relax. She kissed the baby's forehead, leaving her own face close for a moment, breathing in her baby smell. Once she was satisfied that she was calmed she looked up at the doctor, and instantly stiffened her resolve at the look of disapproval on his face.

'I'm her aunt,' she stated, as if that were explanation enough for everything. 'Have you finished with the tests? It looks as if she's had enough for now.'

She stared him down until he conceded that they had everything they needed. That was when she spotted Nic, looking grey and decidedly ill by the door.

'When she cried out…' he said. 'I thought…'

Whatever he had thought had scared him witless, she realised, instinctively taking a step towards him.

'She's fine. We're fine,' she told him, in the same soothing tone she'd used with the baby. She turned her towards him. 'Look, she's settled now.'

He breathed a sigh of relief and Lily could almost see the adrenaline leaching from his body, leaving him limp and drawn. She met his eyes, looking for answers there, but instead saw only pain. An old pain, she guessed, one that had been lived with a long time and had become so familiar it was hardly noticed. Until something happened—a baby screamed—and it felt like new again.

For a moment she wished that she could soothe him as easily as she had the baby—smooth those creases from his face and the pain from his body. But something told her that taking this man in her arms would bring him anything but peace. She pressed herself back against the wall, trying to put whatever space she could between them.

'Is everything okay?' she asked.

'Fine.'

Nic's reply was terse, sharper than she'd expected, and she saw the fear and hurt in his expression being carefully shut down, stowed away.

'I need to grab a cup of coffee. Do you want to find the canteen? We've been here for hours.'

And leave the baby alone with strangers? 'I'm fine, thanks. I don't want to leave her.'

He gave her a shrewd look. 'I'll go, then,' he said, pushing himself away from the wall.

He looked better now, as he had in her front garden, all bronzed skin and taut muscles. No sign now of the man who had looked as if he might slide down the wall from fear.

When he returned with coffee and cake his manner was brisk and his eyes guarded. *Good&*, Lily thought. *Guarded is good. If we're both being careful, both backing away slowly from whatever this energy between us is, then we're safe.*

'I've got to go,' he said. 'I promised that I'd meet Kate and she's not answering her phone so I can't cancel. I don't want to leave her stranded.'

And then he was off—out of their lives, and no doubt relieved to be so. She held in her heavy sigh until he'd slipped out of the door with her polite words of thanks.

CHAPTER THREE

KATE BURST THROUGH the door of the treatment room, wearing her air of drama queen as if it was this season's must-have.

Lily smiled at the arrival of her best friend. If anyone was going to help her make sense of this situation it would be Kate, with her remarkable ability to see through half-truths and get straight to the point.

'So I get back from court and pop in to see my brother in his new flat, and he's got this crazy story about your dear sister and a baby and a hospital. I didn't have a clue what was going on, so I thought I'd better get down here and find out just what he's talking about. Explain, Lily! Where's this flippin' baby come from? What are you doing here? And why does my brother look so cagey whenever I mention your name?'

Lily couldn't help but laugh—trust Kate to boil this down to the bare essentials.

'She's Helen's baby. Helen left her on my doorstep with a note. Your brother was passing by to pick up his keys and…and kept us company while we were waiting here.'

It was rare that she saw Kate lost for words, but she dropped into a chair now, silent, and Lily could practically see the thoughts being processed behind her eyes. Her barrister's brain was reading all the evidence, everything that Lily was saying, and everything she wasn't.

'Okay, give it to me again. And this time with details.'

Lily sighed and took a breath, wondering how many times she would have to repeat everything that had happened. But when she came to talking about Nic her words stumbled and faltered.

'Nic turned up to collect his keys just as I'd been left literally holding the baby and was freaking out. He suggested we walk over here and have her checked out.'

'And then he waited with you? How long for?'

Lily glanced at her watch. 'A couple of hours, I guess.'

Kate blew out a deliberate breath, and Lily raised her eyebrows.

'What?'

'Nothing…nothing,' Kate said, but Lily had known her long enough to know that she was hiding something.

'Not nothing,' she told her best friend. 'Definitely *something*.'

Kate looked at her for a long time before she replied.

'Something,' she agreed, nodding, her eyes sad. 'But not my something to tell. Can we leave it at that?'

Lily nodded. Though she was intrigued, her friend's rare sombre tone had pulled her up short and warned her to stop digging.

'So you and my brother, then…?'

'It's not like that.' The denial came to Lily's lips as soon as she realised what Kate was getting at. 'I don't think he wanted to be here at all. He looked like he was going to bolt the whole time.'

'So why didn't he?'

True to form, Kate had hit on the one question that Lily had been searching for an answer to—to no avail.

'I've no idea.'

'I've got one or two,' Kate said with a sly grin. 'So what happens with the baby now?'

Another question Lily had no answer to.

No doubt between the hospital staff and the police someone would be arranging for a social worker to visit her. But she had no intention of letting her niece be looked after by anyone but herself. She knew that she could look after her—she already ran a business from home, and had flexibility in her hours and her work. It was one of the things that she enjoyed most about her job as a freelance web designer—the chance to balance work and home life. She'd manage her work commitments around caring for the baby—whatever it took to keep the little girl safe and with her family.

'She's coming home with me.'

Lily gulped at the baldness of that statement, and backtracked.

'Until we can find Helen.'

'Right. And then you're going to hand her over to a woman who's been living God-knows-where and doing God-knows-what for years?'

'Helen's her mother—'

'And she seems pretty clear about who she wants taking care of her daughter. I'm not saying that taking her home is a bad thing—she's family. Of course you want to look after her. I'm just saying it looks like it might be slightly more commitment than a regular babysitting gig. Are you ready for that?'

Ready for a family? It was what she'd wanted for as long as she could remember. She'd been lucky after her mother had died. She'd been placed with a wonderful foster family who had slowly and gently helped her to come to terms with her grief. She'd certainly been luckier than her sister, who, at sixteen, had decided that she was old enough to look after herself.

They'd exchanged letters and emails, but over the years they'd become less and less frequent, until now she couldn't even rely on a card at Christmas. All she wanted was a family of her own. To recapture something of what the three of them—herself, her mum and Helen—had had before the accident.

She'd even looked into ways to build that family. After her own experience of foster care she'd thought of offering her house to children who might need it.

The old family home had seemed echoey and empty when she'd moved back in when she was eighteen. Her mother's will had protected it in a trust for her and her sister, but it had been lonely with no one to share it with. But she'd never considered she'd ever be handed a newborn baby and asked if she was ready to be a parent.

'We have to find Helen,' Lily said. 'That's as far as I can think right now.'

'There is one slight flaw in that plan,' Kate said.

'Only one?' Lily asked, only half joking.

'Your house. It's currently a building site, and—unless I'm much mistaken—not exactly ready for a newborn…whether she's going to be there permanently or not.'

Lily's face fell. In all the drama she'd somehow managed to forget the chaotic state of her house. There was no way that she could take a baby back there. And if she couldn't take care of her niece that left only one option. Letting social services place her with strangers. Her gut recoiled at the thought of losing another member of her family, of her and Helen and their past being fractured even further.

'Don't look like that,' Kate said. 'This is not insurmountable. We can sort this out—'

'That's really kind,' Lily said, her mind still racing, 'but your place barely has enough room for me to pull out the sofa bed. I'm not sure that—'

'Not *me*!' Kate exclaimed. 'Good God, no. We'd lose the baby under a stack of briefs or something. Nic's place—it's perfect.'

Lily gave a little choke.

'Nic's place? I couldn't possibly impose…'

She couldn't share a flat with that man—not when she felt drawn to him and afraid of that attraction in equal measure. When her skin tingled just from being in the same room as him.

'Honestly, you should see his place. It's ridiculous. A penthouse—overlooking the river, naturally. He told me it was something to do with investing his golden handshake money, and London property prices, and being able to do so much more with the money once he sold up. Personally, I think it might have something to do with sleeping in hostels for the best part of a decade. It's huge, and he's barely ever there.'

Even the thought of a Thameside penthouse couldn't convince her that spending more time with a man who had her wanting him and wanting to run from him was a good idea. But what choice did she have? If she wanted to take care of her niece she couldn't afford to be picky about what help she accepted. And, anyway, what she thought was probably irrelevant…

'Nic would never—'

'Nic will be travelling on and off for the next few months. He's due to fly out again tomorrow, I think. You won't see each other much. And if the man who's preached charity and child welfare at me for the past ten years can't see it in his heart to give an abandoned baby a home for a few months, then I'll disown him.'

Somehow Lily didn't think that was a threat that would carry much weight for Nic.

'*And* trash his lovely new apartment,' she added.

'Okay, ask him,' Lily said eventually. What choice did she have?

An awkward silence fell for a few moments, until Kate obviously couldn't stand the quiet any longer.

'So, does this little one have a name, or what?'

Lily shook her head. 'Helen didn't exactly say.'

'Well, that's just not right, is it? She's had a rough enough start in life already, without ending up being named just Baby Girl. So what are we going to go for: naming her after a pop star or a soap star. Or we could go big and Hollywood?'

Lily raised an eyebrow.

'Okay, so I'm guessing that's a no. What do *you* suggest?'

Lily looked closely at the baby, trying to work out who she was. 'Look at her,' Lily said. 'All pretty and pink and fresh and soft…like a flower. A rose. What about Rosie?'

'I think it's perfect,' Kate agreed. 'Little Rosie—welcome to the world.'

Nic's feet pounded on the pavement as he tried to get thoughts of Lily Baker out of his head—with zero success. Since the moment he'd met her she'd invaded all of his thoughts, forcing him to keep busy, keep working, keep running. But even two days on his body still wouldn't co-operate, refusing to find the quiet place in his mind where he could retreat from the world.

His sister wasn't exactly helping, with her pointed remarks and regular updates on how baby and aunt were faring. Did she think he couldn't see what she was doing? That the strings of her puppeteering were somehow invisible? But he *did* wonder how the baby was. Kate had said that she was doing well, and the doctors hadn't seemed worried when he'd left the hospital, but he knew better than most how precarious a new life was, how quickly it might be lost.

Turning for home, he tried to find his usual rhythm, but his feet carried him faster than he wanted, rushing him.

His mobile rang as he reached his flat, and Kate's latest unsubtle update gave him all he needed to know. No news on the missing sister. Baby apparently doing well in hospital. But somehow it wasn't enough. What did that mean anyway? 'Doing well in hospital.' Surely if the baby was 'doing well' then she wouldn't be in hospital at all. She'd be home, tucked into a cot, safe. And this time Kate had not said anything about Lily.

He hadn't been able to think of a way to ask about

her without raising suspicious eyebrows. He could hardly say, *And how about the aunt? The one with the glowing skin and the complicated expressions and the fierce independence? How's she getting on?*

But he was desperate to know. Lily Baker seemed to have soaked into his mind until his every thought was coloured by her. It was no good. The only way he was going to get this woman and her niece out of his mind was to get some answers, some closure.

He saw her as soon as he walked onto the ward. He should have known that she would have been there all night. Had been there for two nights, he guessed. Her hair was mussed, rubbing up against the side of the chair she'd curled into, but her face was relaxed, looking so different from when she'd worn that troubled, burdened expression before.

He knocked on the door, aware that he didn't want to answer the questions that being caught watching her sleep would give rise to. Lily sat bolt upright at the sound, her hand instinctively reaching for the cot, eyes flying towards the baby. Only once she was satisfied that she was sleeping soundly did she turn towards the door. Her eyes widened in surprise, and he realised how unguarded she was in the moment after waking—how her expression shifted as her eyes skimmed over him appreciatively.

There was no mistaking the interest there, and his stomach tightened in response as he fought down his instinctive reaction. Eventually her eyes reached his, and he saw her barriers start to build as she emerged properly from sleep. Her back straightened and her face grew composed.

The rational, sensible, *thinking* part of his brain

breathed a sigh of relief. He was glad that she was as wary as he was of this energy he felt flowing and sparking between them, the pull that he felt between their bodies. Much as he might find her attractive, he would never act on that. He wasn't the kind of man she needed in her life. When she found someone she'd need a partner—a father for this child and the ones that would come in the future. She would need someone she could rely on, and he knew that he wasn't capable of being that man.

But the part of his brain less removed from his primal ancestors groaned, trying to persuade him to get that dreamy look back on her face, to seduce her into softness.

'Morning,' he said, rather more briskly than he'd intended. 'I brought coffee. I know the stuff here's awful.'

'Morning. Thanks…'

Her voice was as wary as her expression, and he guessed that he wasn't the only one who'd thought that they would never see each other again after he'd left the hospital. He wondered if she'd found it as impossible not to think of him as he had of her. Of course not, he reasoned. She had the baby to think about—there was probably no room in her life right now for anything other than feeding, nappies and sleep.

At the sound of her voice the baby had started to stir, and Lily automatically reached out a hand to stroke her cheek.

'How is she?'

'She's fine…good. They've said that I can take her home today.'

Home. So that settled it, then. Kate had been right

the other day—Lily was going to look after the baby as her sister had asked. And that meant he'd been right to fight off this attraction. Because if there was one thing he was certain of it was that he could never get involved with someone who had a child. He could never again open himself up to that sort of hurt.

Even if Lily's sister returned, he couldn't imagine that Lily saw a future without children. He'd seen the melting look in her eye as she'd gazed down at her niece—there was no hiding her maternal instincts.

'That's good. I'm glad she's okay.' Now that he had his answer he felt awkward, not sure why he had come. No doubt Lily was wondering what he was doing there, too. Or perhaps not. Perhaps his real interest was as transparent to her as it had been opaque to him.

Perhaps he had imagined this energy and attraction—imagined the way her eyes widened whenever her skin brushed against his, the way she flushed in those rare moments when they both risked eye contact. Maybe she saw him as nothing other than the Good Samaritan who had happened to be there when she'd needed someone. If only she knew that when someone else had really needed him, when they'd relied on him to be there for them, he'd let them down.

He glanced up at the name plate above the crib and realised that the little girl was no longer Baby Baker.

'Rosie?' he asked, surprise in his voice. Kate hadn't mentioned that.

'It seemed to suit her,' Lily said with a shrug. 'It's not official yet. If Helen doesn't like it...'

'It's pretty.'

'Look, I hate to ask this when you're already doing so much for us...'

Lily glanced at the door and Nic guessed what was coming. Instantly he wished himself anywhere in the world but here. But Lily was still speaking, and he knew that it was too late.

'...just for fifteen minutes or so, while I grab a shower. I know the nurses are listening out for her, but I hate the thought of her being alone. I know I can trust you with her.'

A lump blocked his throat and he couldn't force the word *no* out past it. He'd not been responsible for a child since the morning he'd found his son, cold and still in his crib. But the look on Lily's face—the trust that he saw there—touched his heart in a way he hadn't realised was even still possible. And more than anything he wanted to know that the baby—little Rosie—was going to be okay. That was why he'd dragged himself down here, after all. Fifteen minutes alone with a sleeping baby—surely he could manage that, could ensure that she was safe while Lily was away?

He nodded. 'Sure, go ahead. You look like you could do with a break.'

Her smile held for a moment before her face fell. Oh, God, that wasn't what he'd meant at all. He'd all but said, *You look awful,* hadn't he? What was it about this woman that made it so impossible for him to function anything like normal?

He started back-pedalling fast. 'Sorry, I didn't mean it like that at all. You look fine. I mean—I just meant you've slept in that chair two nights in a row, and I bet you're tired. You look great.'

This wasn't getting any better. But Lily grinned at him, probably enjoying his discomfort, and the fact that he didn't seem at all able to remove his foot from his mouth.

A disconcerting noise and a very bad smell halted Nic's apology in its tracks, and as he caught Lily's eyes they both laughed.

'Well, perhaps if you change her I might find it in my heart to forgive you.'

Before he had a chance to argue she was out of the room, leaving him alone with the baby. This was not at all what he'd expected when he'd reluctantly agreed to watch a sleeping baby for fifteen minutes, but he reached for the nappies and the cotton wool, acting on instinct.

He narrowed his eyes, trying not to see Rosie's little pink cheeks or her tiny fingers. He just had to concentrate on the task in hand, and he could do that without really looking at her, without thinking about the fact that this little body was a whole new life—maybe a hundred years of potential all contained in seven pounds of toes and belly and new baby smell. Without thinking about his son.

He had nearly finished the nappy when Rosie began to fuss. As he fastened the poppers on her Babygro and washed his hands, he silently pleaded with her not to start crying. But her face screwed up and the tears started, and her banshee-like wail was impossible to ignore. He shut his eyes as he scooped a hand under her head and another under her bottom and lifted her to his shoulder, making soothing noises that he hoped would quiet her. He tried not to think at all as he bounced her gently, waiting for her tears to stop, tried not to think of the first time he had held his son, Max.

Or the last time.

The memory made him clutch Rosie a little tighter, hold her a little safer, knowing how precarious a young life could be. Eventually her cries slowed to sniffles as she snuggled closer to his shoulder and started looking for a source of food. He looked around the room, wondering where he'd lay his hands on formula and a bottle. He could ask the nurses, he supposed.

He transferred Rosie to the crook of one arm, only flinching momentarily at the remembered familiarity of the movement, and headed for the door. As it opened he was greeted by the sight of Lily, fresh from the shower, with no make-up and her hair pulled back, and it took his breath away.

Any chance of kidding himself that his interest was only in Rosie's welfare was lost. It was more than that. It was...*her*. He just couldn't stop thinking about her. But that was the problem. If he'd met Lily just one day earlier, before her sister had turned up with a baby, he wouldn't have hesitated to explore this connection between them, to imagine Lily looking as she did now— all fresh and pink and polished from the shower. But the shower would have been in his flat, and she'd have just left his bed.

Everything about her fascinated him. But she'd taken in her sister's child without a thought. And because of that he knew that they could never be happy together. He could see from her every look at Rosie that Lily was born to be a mother. She wanted a family, and he could never give her that—nor could he ask her to sacrifice it for him. There was no point considering a brief fling, either: a taste of her would never be enough—and if he started to fall for her then how would he make himself stop? And all that was even without the added complication of his sister's unspoken threats to hurt him in a *very* sensitive place if he messed with her best friend.

'I was just going to try and find her a bottle.'

Lily waved the bottle of formula she was carrying. 'No need. I see you couldn't resist a cuddle? I don't blame you—she's very squeezable.'

'It's not like that,' he replied instinctively. 'She was crying, that's all. Here—take her.' He almost shoved the baby at her, alarmed at how quickly he'd adapted, how natural it had felt to hold her.

'What's wrong?' Lily asked, her eyes wary. 'I don't mind you holding her.'

'I know.' Nic breathed slowly, trying to fight the urge to run from the room, knowing that he should explain his harsh words to Lily. Hating the wary, guarded look that had just entered her eyes. 'I'm just not good around babies.'

She glanced down at Rosie, who looked happy and content. 'Seems like you're pretty good to me.'

An awkward silence fell between them, and Lily looked as if she was trying to find the right words to say something. Suddenly he wanted out of the room. Her face was serious, and he wondered if she had guessed about his past, or if Kate had told her about it. His heart started racing as he remembered all the times he had failed at that in the past. All the broken conversations, the broken relationships that had followed.

'Nic, I don't know how to thank you for being there for us the other day. And Kate told me—'

Before he knew it he was reaching for her, wanting to stem the flow of her words. He didn't want to know what Kate had told her of his failings as a father and a partner.

He'd do anything to stop her speaking.

His lips pressed against hers as his fingers cradled her jaw, and for just a second he wondered what would happen if she opened her mouth to him, if her body softened and relaxed against him. If this kiss changed from a desperate plea for mercy to something softer, something more passionate. But he pulled away before it had the chance.

'I'm sorry,' he said, shutting his eyes against the confusion on her face and heading towards the door. 'I shouldn't have done that.'

Lily stood shell-shocked in the middle of the hospital room, the baby in one arm and the bottle held loosely in her other hand. What on earth had just happened? She'd been about to thank him for letting them stay with him—just until the work on her house was finished. But the cornered look in his eyes had stopped her words, and the kiss he'd pressed against her lips had stopped her thoughts.

It had been difficult enough to see herself living in his apartment. How was she meant to do it now, with this kiss between them, dragging up every fantasy she'd been forcing herself to bury? If she'd had any other option she'd have jumped at it. But Kate had been right. This was her only choice—kiss or no kiss.

She wondered at the expression on Nic's face, at the way he had cradled Rosie in one arm as if it was the most natural thing in the world. He'd obviously been around babies before. Had he been a father once? Was that what was behind the fear and the pain she saw in him? She couldn't imagine that anything but the loss of a child could draw such a picture of grief on someone's face. He carried a pain that was still raw and devastating—so why on earth had he agreed to let her live with him?

She spun at the sound of a knock to the door, wondering for an instant if it was Nic, back to rescind his invitation, to tell her she wasn't welcome anywhere near him. But instead of Nic it was her social worker standing in the doorway, case file in hand and a smile on her face.

CHAPTER FOUR

LILY LEANT AGAINST the wall of the lift as it climbed to the top of the building and snuck another look at Rosie, sleeping in her pram, not quite believing that she was really going to do this. But Kate had promised her that Nic was okay with it. He would be away on a business trip for the next week at least, so she'd have plenty of time to settle in and find her feet before she had to think about him. Or that kiss.

What had he been thinking? Perhaps the same as her—nothing. Perhaps the touch of their lips had banished all rational thought and left him as confused as she was.

At least all the paperwork and everything in officialdom was ticking along nicely. It was just a case of getting the right legal papers in order, and making sure that Helen had the medical help—both physical and mental—that she needed to get and stay well. There had been no talk of prosecution for abandonment—only concern for Helen and Rosie's welfare.

A stack of half-opened parcels littered the hallway, making the apartment look less bachelor sophisticated and more like a second hand sale. Kate must have beaten her here and picked up all the internet shopping that Lily had done while she was in the hospital with Rosie. They had some work ahead of them to get the apartment baby-ready—that was clear.

She peeked into the living room and was tempted to shiver at the abundance of black leather, smoked glass and chrome. Everything in the room shone, and Lily wondered if Nic was quite mad for letting them stay here. One thing was for sure: even with Rosie on her best behaviour it wasn't going to be easy keeping the place looking this show-home perfect.

'Kate?' Lily called out as she stood in the living room with Rosie in her arms, her eyes drawn to the glass walls with a view out over the river. 'Are you here?'

A voice sounded from the end of the hallway.

'In here!' she shouted. 'I'm just doing battle with the cot.'

Lily followed the sound of Kate's swearing and found herself in a luxurious bedroom. Between the doorway and the enormous pillow-topped bed Kate's curly head was just visible between the bars of a half-built cot.

'Are you winning?' Lily asked with a laugh.

'Depends on who's keeping score,' came the reply, along with another string of expletives.

Lily covered Rosie's ears and tutted.

'Sorry, Rosie,' Kate said, finally dropping the screwdriver and climbing out from the pile of flat-packed pieces. 'How are we doing?' she asked as she crossed the room to give Rosie a squeeze and Lily a kiss on the cheek.

'She's fine,' Lily told her. 'Clean bill of health. Thanks so much for getting started with this.' She waved a hand towards the cot.

'Don't be daft. It's nothing. Now, are you going to put the baby down and give me a hand?'

'Let me just grab her carrycot and I'll see if she'll go down.'

As Lily walked back into the hallway she jumped against the wall at the sight of a man's dark shadow up ahead of her.

'Nic…?' she said, holding Rosie a little tighter to her.

As Nic took a step forward his face came into the light and she could see the shock and surprise written across his features.

'Lily, what the hell—?'

'Kate!'

She wasn't sure which of them shouted first, but as it became apparent that Nic had had no idea she was going to be there Lily felt flames of embarrassment lick up her cheeks, colouring her skin. Oh, Kate had some explaining to do.

Kate at least had the good grace to look sheepish when she emerged into the hallway.

'What the hell is *she* doing here?'

Lily's gaze snapped back to Nic at the anger in his voice and she felt herself physically recoil. She was as surprised to see him there as he was to find them both in the flat—Kate had promised her he would be out of town for at least a week yet—but the venom in his voice was unexpected and more than a little offensive.

'Nic!' Kate admonished. 'Don't talk about Lily like that. I promise you, I can explain. You're not meant to *be* here.'

'It's my home, Kate. Where else would I be?'

'Well, India, for a start. And then Bangladesh. And Rome. And...'

'And I decided to spend a few weeks in the office before I go abroad again. I pushed some of my trips back. Not that I need to explain myself—*I'm* not the one who's in the wrong here.'

He threw a look at Lily that was impossible to mis-interpret.

'Look...' Kate was using her best lawyer voice, and Lily suddenly felt a pang of sympathy for Nic. When she took that tone there was little doubt that she was going to get her own way.

But it didn't matter how Kate was planning on sweet-talking her way out of 'stretching the truth', as she was bound to call it. There was no way she could stay here—not with the looks of pure anger that Nic was sending their way.

'This is how I see things: Lily needs somewhere to stay. Rosie can't go back to Lily's as it has no kitchen, no back wall, isn't warm or even watertight. You have a big, ridiculous apartment that was *meant* to be empty for at least the next week, and which even when you're here has more available square footage than most de-tached family homes.'

Nic opened his mouth to argue, but Kate held up a hand, cutting him off.

'You, Mr Humanitarian, having spent the last de-cade saving the world one child factory worker at a time, have the opportunity to practise what you preach here. Charity begins at home, you know.'

Lily rolled her eyes at the cliché, and from the cor-ner of her eye caught just the hint of a smirk starting at the corner of Nic's lips. When she built up the courage to look at him straight she saw that the tension had dropped from his face and he was smiling openly at his sister.

'Oh, you're good,' he said. '*Very* good. I hope they're paying you well.'

'And I'm worth every penny,' she confirmed. 'Now, seeing as you're home, I don't want to step on any toes.' She thrust the screwdriver into his hand and Nic had no choice but to take it. 'I'll leave you two to work out the details.'

And before Lily could pick up her jaw from the floor Kate had disappeared out of the front door, leaving her holding the baby and Nic staring at the screwdriver.

'I'm *so* sorry,' she said, rushing to put Rosie down in her pram and take the screwdriver from Nic's hand. 'She told me that you'd okayed it, but I should have guessed…I'll pack our stuff up and order a cab and we'll be out of your hair.'

Nic gave her a long look, and she watched, fascinated, as emotions chased over his face, first creasing his forehead and his eyes, then smoothing across his cheeks with something like resignation.

'Where will you go?'

'Oh…' Lily flapped a hand, hoping that the distraction would cover the fact that she didn't have a clue what her next move was. 'Back to mine, of course. It's not that bad. I'm sure I can come up with another plan.'

Nic rubbed his hand across his forehead.

'What plan?'

'A hotel,' Lily said, improvising wildly. 'Maybe a temporary rental.'

He let out a long sigh and shook his head slowly.

'Stay here.'

'Nic, I couldn't—'

Lily started to speak, but Nic's raised hand stopped her.

'Kate's right. You need a place to stay. I have loads of room here.'

A warm flood of relief passed through Lily. For a moment she'd thought that she might be out on the streets—worse, that she wouldn't be able to provide Rosie with the home she so desperately needed. And it was the thought that Rosie needed somewhere safe to stay that had her swallowing her pride and nodding to agree with what was almost certainly a terrible idea.

'Thank you. I promise we'll keep out of your way.'

Lily stood in the kitchen, coffee cup in hand, surveying the vast array of knobs and buttons on the espresso machine built into the kitchen wall. She'd already boiled the kettle, intimidated by the levers and chrome of the machine, but in the absence of a jar of good old instant coffee she was going to have to do battle with this beast. She tried the sleek-looking knob on the left— and jumped back from the torrent of steam that leapt from the nozzle hidden beneath. Thank God she'd left Rosie safely sleeping in their room.

A lightly haired forearm appeared over her shoulder and turned off the knob, shutting down the steam and leaving her red-faced and perspiring.

'Here,' Nic said, taking the cup from her hand. 'Let me.'

'Thanks.' Lily handed over coffee responsibility gratefully, and leaned back against the kitchen counter.

Embarrassment sat in the air between them, and Lily's mind couldn't help but fly back to that kiss in the hospital. The way that Nic's lips had pressed so firmly against hers, as if he was fighting himself even as he was kissing her. He'd known that it was a bad idea at the time—she was sure of that. And yet he'd done it anyway. Now they were living together—and apparently they were just going to ignore that it had happened. But even with them saying nothing, it was there, in the atmosphere between them, making them awkward with each other.

She wondered whether she should say something, try and clear the air, but then she heard a cry from the bedroom.

'You go and get Rosie. I'll sort the coffee.'

Was that an invitation? Were they going to sit down and drink a cup of coffee like civilised adults? And if they did would he bring up the kiss? Would she? Surely they couldn't just carry on as if nothing had happened. It was making her clumsy around him, and she could never feel relaxed or at home unless they both loosened up. Maybe that was what he was hoping for. That he'd be able to make things awkward enough that she'd have no choice but to leave. Then he'd get his apartment back without having to be the big bad wolf in the story.

Lily had returned to the kitchen with the baby in one arm, and set about making up a bottle for her. Nic watched them carefully, knowing that a gentleman would offer to help, but finding himself not quite able to live up to that ideal.

'It's good we've got a chance to sit down and talk,' he said as he carried their coffees over to the kitchen island. 'I wanted to apologise for the other day. The...

the kiss. And the way I left things. I know I was a bit abrupt.'

'It's fine—' Lily started, but he held up a hand to stop her.

The memory of the confusion on her face had been haunting him, and he knew that if they were to live together, even if it was only temporarily, he had to make sure she knew exactly why that kiss had been such a mistake. Why she shouldn't hope for or expect another.

They had only known each other for a few days, but after that parting shot at the hospital he wouldn't be able to blame her if she'd misinterpreted things—if she'd read more into that kiss than he'd ever wanted to give. She deserved better than that…better than a man with his limitations. And with Rosie in her life she was going to have to demand more. Demand someone who would support her family life whatever happened. He'd already been tested on that front and found wanting. It was only fair that Lily knew where they both stood.

'Please,' he continued, 'I want to explain.'

A line appeared between her brows, as if she had suddenly realised that this was a conversation neither of them would enjoy. The suggestion that she was hurt pained him physically, but he forced himself to continue—for both their sakes.

'There's no need to explain anything, but I'll listen if you want me to.'

She glanced over at the counter, her edginess showing in the way she was fidgeting with her coffee cup. The anxious expression on her face told him so much. She'd guessed something of his history. Guessed, at least, how hard it was for him to be around Rosie. Had she seen how impossible it would be for them even to be friends?

Not that *friends* would ever have really worked, he mused, when the sight of her running a hand through her hair made him desperate to reach across and see if it felt as silky as it looked. When he'd lain awake every night since they'd last met remembering the feel of her lips under his, imagining the softness of her skin and the suppleness of her body.

He kept his eyes on Lily, never dropping them to the little girl in her arms, not risking the pain that would assault him if he even glanced at Rosie or acknowledged that she was there. The way Lily looked at him, her clear blue gaze, gave him no room to lie or evade. He knew that faced with that open, honest look he'd be able to speak nothing but the truth.

'There's something I need to tell you…' he started.

His voice held the hint of a croak, and he felt the cold climbing his chest, wondered how on earth he was meant to get these words out. How he was meant to relive the darkest days of his life with this woman who a week ago had been a stranger.

'I know there's something between us—at least I know that I've started to feel something for you. But I need you to know that I won't act again on what I feel.'

He kept his voice deliberately flat, forcing the emotion from it as he'd had to do when faced with people living and working in inhuman conditions. And he looked down at the table, unable to bear her sympathetic scrutiny. Or what if he had read this wrong—what if there was nothing between them at all? What if he'd imagined the chemistry that kept drawing them together even as it hurt him? It wasn't as if he'd even given her a chance to return his kiss. He risked a glance up at her. Her lip was caught between her teeth and the line had reappeared on her forehead. But he wasn't sure what he was seeing on her face. Not clear disappointment. Definitely not surprise.

'It's fine, Nic. You don't need to say any more.'

'I do.'

He wanted her to know, wanted to acknowledge his feelings even if just this once. Wanted her to understand that it was nothing about *her* that was holding him back. And he wanted her to understand him in a way that he'd never wanted before. He'd never opened up and talked about what had happened. But now he had been faced with the consequences of the choices he'd made so many years ago he wanted to acknowledge what he had felt, what he felt now.

'I want to explain. For you to understand. Look, it's not you, Lily.' He cringed when he heard for himself how clichéd that sounded. 'It's…it's Rosie. It's the way that you look at her. I won't ever have children, Lily. And I know that I cannot be in a relationship—any relationship—because of that.'

'Nic, we barely know each other. Don't you think that you're being—?'

He was thinking too far ahead. Of course he was. But if he didn't put an end to this now he wasn't sure how or if he ever could. What he had to say needed to be said out loud. He needed to hear it to make sure that he could never go back, never find himself getting closer to Lily and unable to get away.

'Maybe. Maybe I'm jumping to a million different conclusions here, and maybe I've got this all wrong. But the thing is, Lily, I'm never going to want to have children. Ever. And I don't think it would be right for me to leave you in any doubt about that, given your current situation.'

He allowed himself a quick look down at Rosie, and the painful clench of his heart at the sight of her round cheeks and intense concentration reminded him that he was doing the right thing. It was easier to say that it was because of the baby. Of course that was a big part of it. But there was more—there were things that he couldn't say. Things that he had been ashamed of for so long that he wasn't sure he could even bear to think of them properly, never mind share them with someone else.

'Well, thanks for telling me.'

She was fiddling with her coffee cup again, stirring it rapidly, sloshing some of the rich dark liquid over the side. He'd offended her—and what else did he expect, just telling half the story? All he'd basically done so far was break up with a woman he wasn't even dating.

'Lily, I'm sorry I'm not making much sense. It's just hard for me to talk about… The reason I don't want children…I was a father once. I lost my son, and it broke my heart, and I know that I can never put myself at risk of going through that again.'

And if she was going to take this gamble, raise her sister's child with no idea of what the future held, then she needed someone in her life she could rely on. Someone who would support her with whatever she needed. Who wouldn't let her down. He hadn't been able to do that when Max had died, hadn't been the man his partner had needed, and he'd lost his girlfriend as well as his son.

A hush fell between them and Nic realised he

had raised his voice until it was almost a shout. Lily dropped the bottle and Rosie gave a mew of discontent. But Nic's eyes were all on Lily, watching her face as she realised what he had said, as the significance of his words sank in.

She reached out and touched his hand. He should have flinched away. It was the reason he had told her everything, after all. But he couldn't. He turned his hand and grabbed hold of hers, anchoring himself to the present, saving himself from drowning in memories.

Now that he had told her, surely the danger was over. Now she would be as wary of these feelings as he was. He just wanted to finish this conversation—make sure that she knew that this wasn't personal, it wasn't about her. If Rosie had never turned up...if he'd never had a son... But there was no point thinking that way. No point in what-ifs and maybes.

'Nic, I'm so sorry. I don't know what to say, but I'd like to hear more about your son. If you want to talk about it.'

He breathed out a long sigh, his forehead pressed into the heels of his hands, but then he looked up to meet her gaze and she could see the pain, the loss, the confusion in his eyes.

'It won't change anything.'

She reached for his hand again, offering comfort, nothing more—however much she might want to.

'I know, but if you want to talk then I'd like to listen.'

He stared at the counter a little longer, until eventually, with a slight shake of his head, he started to speak.

'I was nineteen and naïve when I met this girl—

Clare—at a university party. We hit it off, and soon we were living in each other's pockets, spending all our time together. We were both in our first year, neither of us thinking about the future. We were having fun, and I thought I was falling in love with her.'

Lily was shocked at the strength of her jealousy over something that had happened a decade ago, and fought down the hint of nausea that his tale had provoked.

'Well, we were young and silly and in love, and we took risks that we shouldn't have.'

It didn't take a genius to see where this was going but, knowing that the story had a tragic end, Lily felt a pall of dread as she waited for Nic's next words.

'When Clare told me she was pregnant I was shocked. I mean, a few months beforehand we'd been living with our parents, and now we were going to be parents ourselves... But as the shock wore off we got more and more excited—'

His voice finally broke, and Lily couldn't help squeezing his hand. There was nothing sexual in it. Nothing romantic. All she wanted was to offer comfort, hope.

'By the time the baby was due we'd moved in together, even started to talk about getting married. So there I was: nineteen, as good as engaged, and with a baby on the way.'

His eyes widened and his jaw slackened, as if he couldn't understand how he had got from there to here—how the life that still lit up his face when he described it had disintegrated.

'The day Max was born was the best of my life. As soon as I held him in my arms I knew that I loved him. Everyone tells you that happens, but you never believe them until you experience it. He was so perfect, this tiny human being. For three weeks we were the perfect little family. I washed him, changed his nappies, fed him, just sat there and breathed in his smell and watched him sleep. I've never been so intoxicated by another person. Never held anything so precious in my arms.'

His face should have glowed at that. He should have radiated happiness, talking about the very happiest time of his life. But already the demons were incoming, cracking his voice and lining his face, and Lily held her breath, bracing herself.

'When he was three weeks old we woke one day to sunlight streaming into the bedroom and instantly knew that something was wrong. He'd not woken for his early feed. And when I went to his crib...'

He didn't have to say it. All of a sudden Lily wished that he wouldn't, that he would spare her this. But *he* hadn't been spared; *he* hadn't been shown mercy. He'd had his heart broken, his life torn apart in the most painful way imaginable. She couldn't make herself want to share that pain with him, but she wanted to help ease it if she could. She'd do just about anything to lift that blanket of despair from his face.

'He was gone. Already cold. I picked him up and shouted for Clare, held him in my arms until the ambulance arrived, but it was no good. Nothing I could have done would have helped him. They all told me that. They told me that for days and weeks afterwards. Until they started to forget. Or maybe they thought that *I* was forgetting. But I haven't, Lily.'

For the first time since he'd started speaking he

looked up and met her gaze head-on. There was solid
determination there.

'I can never forget. And when I see Rosie…'

It all became clear: the way he turned away from
the baby, the way he flinched if he had to interact with
her, the stricken look on his face the one time he'd had
to hold her. Seeing Rosie—seeing any baby—brought
him unimaginable pain. There could be no children in
his future, no family. And so she completely understood why it was he was fighting this attraction. Why
he pushed away from their chemistry, trying to protect himself. Knowing that there could never be anything between them didn't make it easier, though. The
finality of it hurt.

But there was one part of the story he hadn't finished.

'And…Clare?'

He dropped his head back into his hands and she
knew that he was hiding tears. It was a couple of minutes before he could speak again.

'We were broken,' he said simply. 'We tried for
a while. But whatever it was that had brought us
together—it died with our baby. She needed… I
couldn't…I saw her a couple of years ago, actually, in
the supermarket, of all places, by the baked beans. We
exchanged polite hellos, because what else could we
say: *Remember when we lost our son and our world fell
apart and could never be put back together? Remember when you needed me to be there for you, to help
you through your grief, and I couldn't do it?*'

Lily choked back a sob. She couldn't imagine, never
wanted to imagine, what this man had been through.
She wanted to reach out and comfort him, to do any-

thing she could to take his pain away, but she knew there was nothing to be done. Nothing that could undo what had happened, undo his pain. All she could do was be there for him, if that was what he wanted.

But it wasn't.

'So now you know why getting close to Rosie scares me—why getting close to you both can never happen. I can't go through that pain again, Lily. Just the idea of it terrifies me. How could I cope with another loss like that?'

Lily didn't have the answer to any of it. Of course she could say that the chances of it happening again were slim, but she couldn't promise it. No one could. And how could she blame him for wanting to spare himself that?

She didn't say anything when Nic stood from the table, only reached out a hand and rested it gently on his arm.

'Thank you,' she said. 'For everything. And I wish you all the best, Nic, I really do. I hope you can be happy again some day.'

CHAPTER FIVE

THREE WEEKS AFTER her sister had dropped her little surprise off on her doorstep Lily still hadn't heard anything from her. Social services seemed happy that Lily was being well cared for by her aunt, and were trawling through the appropriate paperwork. To begin with she'd thought it must be temporary, that one of these days Helen would call and ask for her daughter back. But so far—nothing.

And barely a word from Nic, either. Not that she had expected much after the way things had been left, but it was strange living with someone who could barely say more than good morning to her. A part of her had hoped, she supposed, that he might rethink things. That he might think that she—they—were worth taking a risk on. And then she remembered the look on his face when he told her about losing his son and knew that it couldn't happen. Knew that he wouldn't risk feeling like that again.

She lifted her head from the pillow and looked over at Rosie, still tucked in her crib, fast asleep again after her six o'clock feed. Lily listened to her breaths, to the steady whoosh of air moving in and out of her lungs. Rosie was the same age now as Nic's son had been when he died. After three weeks together, Lily could no longer imagine life without Rosie—couldn't imagine the pain of being torn from her.

So what would happen if Helen wanted her back? How could she keep mother and daughter apart, knowing how much it hurt to want a family and have them disappear from your life?

She collapsed back into her pillows and threw her arms over her face, blocking out the world, fed up with the circles her mind was spinning her in. She wanted to make sure that Helen was well and happy, but would that mean handing Rosie over? Accepting the fact that Helen might take off again, leaving her missing Rosie as she missed the rest of her family?

Much as she had tried to remember that she wasn't Rosie's mother, somewhere the line had become blurred. Because Helen hadn't just nipped to the shops, and Lily wasn't just being a helpful aunt: she was almost her legal guardian. It was Helen who had blurred this line, and Lily wasn't sure how she would cope if she suddenly turned everything on its head.

Thoughts still racing around her mind, she swung her legs out of bed and reached for her dressing gown. She'd learnt that if Rosie was sleeping she'd better shut her eyes, too, but this morning that was a luxury she couldn't afford. She had managed to put off a couple of her deadlines when she'd told her clients what had happened—sparing them most of the details—but she couldn't put them off for ever.

She had beta designs for two sites to finish, and while Rosie was sleeping she couldn't justify not working. Then there was the fact that she'd not bothered with the dishes last night, the fridge was looking decidedly bare, and when Rosie woke up she'd want milk, clean clothes and a clean nappy. The round of chores was endless, even with Nic's generosity, and she sometimes felt she'd been walking through fog since Rosie had arrived. A joyful fog, obviously, but an endlessly draining one, too.

She padded into the kitchen and hit the button on the kettle—still too foggy to attempt espresso—knowing that she needed coffee this morning, and wondering how breastfeeding mums coped with the newborn stage without caffeine. She felt as if she was flailing, barely keeping her head above water, and she wasn't even recovering from giving birth.

Over the rumbling of the kettle coming to the boil she heard her mobile ringing in the bedroom and ran to get it, hoping that she could reach it and hit 'silence' before it woke the baby.

When she got to it Rosie was already mewling quietly, and Lily scooped her up quickly before swiping to answer her phone.

'Hello?' she said, as quietly as possible, rocking Rosie in the vain hope that she'd decide to go back to sleep.

When her social worker told her the news she couldn't think of an answer. *Why* couldn't she think of an answer? So many times these past weeks she'd wondered how her sister was, whether she'd ever be ready to be part of a family again, and now here was the proof that she might want that one day. She wanted to see Lily—and her daughter—that morning.

'Okay,' she told the social worker eventually. 'I'll bring Rosie to her.'

As soon as she ended the call tears were threatening behind her eyes. Irrational tears? she wondered. Through the sleep deprivation she was finding it hard to remember what was reasonable and what wasn't. She needed Kate and her no-nonsense way of seeing the world, her way of cutting through the mess and making the world simple.

She dialled her number and waited, rocking slightly on the bed. 'Come on, pick up…pick up…' She walked back through to the kitchen as the ringing continued on the other end of the phone. 'Come on, Kate. *Please* pick up…'

'Everything okay?'

Not Kate. At the sound of Nic's voice she spun around and the tears started in earnest, though she couldn't rationalise why. Too much family drama. Too little sleep.

'Any idea where your sister is?'

'Not sure,' he told her, and she could hear concern for her in his voice. 'But I know that the Jackson case is coming to trial this week. My guess would be chambers or court. Is everything okay? Rosie?'

'She's fine,' Lily told him, though she couldn't stop the tears.

She still clutched Rosie tight against her, her every instinct telling her that she must protect the baby at all costs. But protecting her didn't mean keeping her from her own mother, if seeing her was what she wanted.

'Look, I've got to go out, but please can you find Kate and tell her to meet me at the Sanctuary Clinic as soon as possible?'

He paced the corridor of the clinic, asking himself for the thousandth time what he was doing there. The sense of déjà vu was almost overwhelming. It had been only a couple of weeks ago that he'd paced a similar corridor, asking himself a similar question.

Lily.

She had been the reason then, and she was the reason now. Her voice, so quiet and shocked, but filled with a fierce protectiveness for Rosie. *Find Kate*, she'd said.

But he hadn't been able to. When Kate was embroiled in a case there was no telling when she might emerge for sunlight and fresh air. All she could see was her duty to her client. Just as impossible as getting his sister on the phone was the thought of leaving Lily alone. She'd been so stoic, but he had heard the vulnerability in her voice and been unable to ignore it. The way she'd sounded—those intriguing layers of vulnerability and strength—had made him want to be here for her, *with* her. She could do this on her own, he had no doubt of that, but that didn't mean he wanted her to have to.

He was just relieved for now that Lily's sister was safe and well—he knew how much Lily had worried about her, how much she'd hoped to have her back in her life.

Lily emerged from the bathroom with Rosie smelling fresh, but there was a fearful look on her face. When they were halfway down the corridor, without thinking, he wrapped an arm around her. Holding her close to him, he could feel her body trembling.

'Here—' he gestured to some seats set against the wall '—do you want to sit for a minute? Get your breath? Helen's not going anywhere, and nor is Rosie.'

She sat in a chair and he pulled his arm back, suddenly self-conscious, aware of the line that he had crossed.

'Do you want to talk about it?'

Lily shook her head, but spoke anyway.

'Helen's been staying here since she left Rosie with me. She's not wanted to see us before now, but she's decided she's ready.'

'And you and Rosie—are *you* ready?'

She sat silent for a long moment. 'She's my sister. She's Rosie's mum. She's family. I don't want to lose her.'

'But you're the one making decisions for Rosie. Helen asked you to do that. If you're not ready...'

'*I'm* ready,' she said, with sudden steely determination. 'But I want to see Helen alone first, before I decide whether I'm ready for her to meet Rosie. I can't get hold of Kate and there's no one else. I know that I shouldn't ask. That after everything we've spoken about—'

'It's fine.' The words surprised him. He'd been all too ready to agree that she shouldn't ask, that it *was* too much, that he couldn't... But he'd looked down at Rosie, and he'd looked up at her aunt, and he'd known that this family had touched him. That Lily had touched him. And that much as he wanted to pretend he had never met them, that was impossible now.

It had been impossible from the moment he'd found Lily on her doorstep, babe in arms and already with a fierce determination to protect. It had been impossible when he'd laid out the hardest and most painful parts of his past, hoping that it would scare her off, hoping that the pain the conversation dredged up would be enough to scare *him* off. But it hadn't. He'd spent all that time questioning what he'd done. Wondering how he was going to live life full of the regret that he felt when he thought of Lily. Wondering if he could be brave enough to try and live another way.

And when he had reached out just now and taken her in his arms he'd had his answer. He didn't have a choice. The feelings he had for Lily weren't going to go away. Trying to convince her—convince himself—that they shouldn't do this hadn't made the pain less. It had made it worse. Walking away from Lily would leave another hole in a life that was already too empty.

'I'll watch her for you.'

'Are you sure?'

Her disbelief was written plainly on her face, and when he nodded he thought he saw a flash of hope there, of anticipation. He smiled in response—they had a lot to talk about later.

'We'll be fine. Your sister needs you now.'

Lily hesitated outside the door. She'd waited patiently for her sister to be ready, hoping every day that she would come back into their lives, but feeling terrified at the same time that she might ask for Rosie back, take her away. And then Lily would have lost a niece—almost a daughter—as well as her sister.

She took a deep breath and pushed open the door.

At the sight of her sister in the bed, pale and skinny, all her fears left her. As long as they were all safe and well, the rest of it didn't matter. She'd hoped so many times that she'd have a chance to reconnect with Helen. She couldn't be anything but pleased that she had somehow found her way back again.

'Lily?'

Lily hadn't realised that Helen was awake, but she reached out a hand to her with tears in her eyes.

'I'm so happy to see you,' she told her.

Helen sniffed, her expression cautious. 'I thought you might be angry.'

'I'm not angry—I've been so worried. I'm just glad that you're okay.'

'But what I did…'

'We don't need to talk about that now. The most important thing is to get you well again. Everything else we can talk about later.'

A tear slipped from the corner of Helen's eye and Lily wiped it away with a gentle swipe of her thumb.

'I knew that I couldn't look after her,' Helen went on, her tears picking up pace.

And even though Lily hushed her, told her that they didn't have to talk about it now, she carried on as if the words were backed up behind a failing dam and nothing could stop them surging forward.

'The house that I was living in—it wasn't safe. Not for me or her. And I couldn't think of another way, Lily. I knew that she'd be better off with you.'

'You did the right thing,' Lily reassured her. 'And your daughter's fine. She's doing really well.'

At that the dam finally broke, and Helen's face was drowned in tears.

'I…was…so…scared.' She choked the words out between sobs. 'After I left her with you I realised I couldn't go back to where I had been living, but I couldn't come home to you, either.'

'That's not true, Helen. You can come home any time. The house is yours just as much as it is mine. And I know that we both want what's best for Rosie.'

'Rosie?'

Lily gulped. She hadn't meant to use her name, knowing that she'd taken something of a liberty by choosing one in the first place. But there had been no one else to do it.

'If you don't like it…'

'No, it's perfect. I love it.' Helen's tears slowed. 'It just goes to show that I was right. You're the right person to look after her, Lily. I know that the way I did it wasn't right—just dumping her and running—but I didn't make a mistake. I can't be the one to raise her.'

Lily took a deep breath, feeling the thinness of the ice beneath her feet, knowing that one misstep could ruin her relationship with her sister for ever, could lose her Rosie.

'You've not been well,' she said gently. 'And you don't need to make big decisions right now or all at once. There'll be plenty of time to talk about this.'

Helen nodded, her features peaceful for the first time since Lily had arrived. 'I want to be part of her life—and yours, too, if you'll still have me. But I'm not going to change my mind. You're the best person to look after Rosie. I'm not ready to be a mother, Lily. I might never be. I'm not going to change my mind about this.'

Lily just squeezed her hand, lost for words.

'And maybe I will want to come home one day—but not yet, Lily. I can't do that until I'm really properly well, and that's going to take me some time.'

'I could—'

'I know you want to do everything for us, Lily. But you're already doing so much. I have to get better on my own, and I need space to do that.'

Space? How much space did she need? She'd given her nothing *but* space for years, and where had that got her? Living somewhere she didn't feel safe with a baby she couldn't care for.

'Will you do it? Will you take care of Rosie.'

There had never been any question about that.

'Of course I will. She's here, you know. If you'd like to see her.'

Pain crossed Helen's features for a moment. 'I thought I was ready, but…I'm not, Lily. It would hurt too much to see her. So what do you say? I'm not talking about a few weeks or months, Lily. I need to know that she'll be safe for *ever*. That I can concentrate on getting well without the pressure of… I know it's selfish.'

It wasn't. It might have been the most self*less* thing Lily had ever heard. Because the yearning and the love in Helen's face was clear. She hadn't abandoned Rosie because she was an inconvenience, or too much hard work, or because she cried too much. She'd done it because she loved her. She'd broken her own heart in order to give her child the best start in life, and Lily couldn't judge her for that.

'It's not selfish. And of course I'll take care of Rosie.' Her voice was choked as she said the words. 'I love her, Helen. You don't have to worry. I'll keep her safe.'

Some of the tension left Helen's body, and Lily could tell that she needed some of that space she'd been talking about.

She gave her hand another squeeze. 'I'll come back and visit again when you're ready. Rest now.'

'Thanks, sis,' Helen said, drifting off. 'You were always going to be an amazing mum.'

Back in the corridor, Lily leaned her forehead against the wall and took a couple of deep breaths, wanting to compose herself before she saw Rosie, not wanting her to sense that she had been upset.

She glanced down the corridor and saw that she was no longer in her car seat but on Nic's knee, being fed from a bottle. Lily couldn't help but smile. While she had been talking to her sister she'd almost forgotten that Nic had stayed, and the look on his face when she'd asked him to watch Rosie even though she'd known that she shouldn't. But the fear and the panic that she'd been expecting to see there hadn't emerged. Instead there had been something different, something new, and it had given her hope.

Now, seeing him holding the baby, she wondered what this meant. After everything that he'd said to her back at his flat, the harrowing story of his loss, she'd thought they'd said all that needed to be said about their feelings, their future. But here he was.

'Thank you so much for this,' she said as she reached the chairs and sat beside him. 'I can take her if you want.'

'She's fine. Let her finish her bottle.'

His words suggested that he was comfortable, but his body language was telling a different story. He was sitting bolt upright on the plastic chair, his shoulders and arms completely stiff. Rosie was more perched on him than snuggled against him, but that hadn't stopped her staring up at him with her big blue gaze locked onto his face as she fed.

I wish I could look at him like that, Lily thought. *With no need to hide what I feel, no need to look away when I realise that he's seen me.* How simple life must seem to Rosie, with no idea of the impact her birth had had on her whole family.

'How was it?' Nic asked her at last.

Lily blew out a breath. 'I don't really know—it's not like I have a lot to compare it to. But okay, I think.'

'That's good…'

'It's good that she wants to get better. But I wish she'd come home, that she'd let me take care of her. It's what I've been hoping for for years. But…'

'But you're worried about what will happen to Rosie if she gets well?'

She nodded, the lump in her throat preventing the words from coming.

'You know I can't tell you for definite what will happen.' The tone of his voice was soft and measured. 'But everyone involved will want what's best for Rosie.'

She nodded, still not trusting herself to speak.

At the beginning she had genuinely believed, when she'd said she would look after Rosie, that she was only taking care of her temporarily, until Helen was back and better. Now she couldn't imagine watching someone else sing her to sleep, someone else comfort her when she was upset. She was a little jealous just watching Nic giving her a bottle.

'So, are you heading home?' he asked when Rosie had finished.

'I thought I might walk through the park first, as the sun's out. I think me and Rosie need some fresh air. The smell of hospitals…'

'I'll walk with you, if that's okay?'

CHAPTER SIX

WALKING THROUGH THE PARK, just the three of them, Nic couldn't shake the feeling that he had wandered into someone else's life. To anyone else they would look like a family—a loving husband and wife, perhaps—taking a stroll with their baby, talking together, making plans for the future. This had been his life once, and it had left him so scarred that he had sworn he would never let himself come close to it again.

Until he had met Lily and been unable to forget her. And now was the moment he had to decide. It wasn't fair on Lily to keep pushing her away and then changing his mind. If he was going to take this chance, he had to commit to it.

'So…' he started as they exited the park. 'Have you got plans for dinner?'

She looked a little panic-stricken for a second.

'There're a few bits and pieces in the fridge. I was just going to rustle up something simple. Or maybe order something in…'

He could see the doubt in her eyes as she finally looked up at him, and he cursed himself for the confusion he must have caused her over the past days. He was more aware than anyone of how hot and cold he had blown. He wanted to reach out and smooth the lines of concern from her face. Instead he offered an encouraging smile, urging her to take a risk—as he had—and invite him in.

'We could order something together?' she suggested at last.

'I'd love to,' he agreed, opening the gate for her.

Back in the apartment, Nic reached across for another slice of pizza and asked the question that had been nagging at him since they had left the hospital.

'So, did your sister say anything about what her plans are…with Rosie?'

'It's still early days. I don't think she's really in a position to decide anything yet.' Lily took a long drink of her cola. 'But…'

'But?'

'She said that she wants me to take care of Rosie permanently. If I don't want to, or can't, I don't know what will happen. She'll go into care, I suppose.'

'And how do you feel about that?'

'About Rosie going into care?' She fought off a wave of panic and nausea, reminding herself that the social worker had told her that they tried their hardest to keep families together. That Rosie being taken away completely would be a last resort. 'Honestly, the thought of it makes it hard to breathe.'

Nic looked at her closely and she dropped her eyes, not enjoying the depth of his scrutiny, feeling as if he was seeing all too much of her.

'There must be a lot of fantastic foster parents out there. And couples waiting to adopt. All you ever hear on the news is the horror stories, but every type of family has those. I'm sure that Rosie would find a happy home if that's what you and Helen decide is best.'

Lily shook her head, not trusting herself to speak for a moment. After a long breath, she chose her words carefully. 'But she should be with her family. I *have* to look after her.'

'Why do I feel there's more to this story?' Nic asked.

'What do you mean? I just want to take care of my family.'

'It's not all your responsibility.'

He was using his careful voice again, and she read the implication in that loud and clear. He thought she was being irrational, that she needed talking down like some drunk about to lose her temper. Well, if he carried on like this…

'It's okay to admit that maybe sometimes you need help.'

'I don't need help to look after my niece, thank you very much. I'm sorry if that's not what you want to hear. If you were hoping that maybe I'd wake up one day soon unencumbered by a baby. It's not exactly what I had in mind for the next few years, but she's my responsibility and I'm not handing her over to strangers.'

He held his hands palms up and sat back on his stool, surprise showing in his raised eyebrows and baffled expression. 'Whoa! I'm sorry, Lily. That's not what I meant at all. I'm not going to lie and say that Rosie doesn't make things complicated, but I'd never expect you to give her up. I'd never want that.'

'Then what *do* you want? Because I've got to tell you I'm struggling to keep up. The last time we talked you were very clear that I was nothing more to you than a temporary lodger—and not even a very welcome one at that. But now here we are, strolling through the park and sharing dinner. Why?'

She hadn't meant to get mad at him, but he'd already squashed her every romantic and X-rated fantasy, when she'd only just started to realise the feelings she was developing, and it was suddenly all too much. She'd held back before—keeping her feelings at the back of her mind, not questioning his—and she'd had enough. They were both grown-ups. If he was man enough to have these feelings then he'd damn well better be man enough to talk about them.

'Because I can't make myself *not* want this. And I've tried, Lily. I've tried for both of us. Because I'm not the right guy for you. I've tried to keep my distance because I know that this isn't good for either of us—I can't be the person you need me to be. But something keeps throwing us back together and I don't know if I can fight it any more.'

Man enough, then.

Lily froze with a slice of pizza halfway to her mouth. Complete and utter honesty was what she had been hoping for, but really the last thing she'd been expecting. The raw power of his words made her want to move closer and pull away at the same time. He'd just told her that he wasn't sure he was ready. He was taking a big gamble with her feelings and with his, and she wasn't sure that was a game she wanted to play. Had he really thought this through?

'I'm not sure, Nic. I barely have the time or the brain capacity to think beyond the next bottle and nappy-change. I'm not sure that I can even *think* about a relationship. And you know me and Rosie come as a package deal, right? I don't know what's going to happen with Helen in the future. I don't know whether I'll be Rosie's caregiver for the next week, the next month, or the rest of her life. There are no guarantees either way.'

She let out a long, slow breath.

'I'm sorry, but I don't think I can even consider a relationship right now. If you want to be friends, I'd like that.'

He gave her a long, searching look, before sighing. 'Of course. You're right. But friends sounds good. I'd like that.'

'That's exactly what I need.' She offered him a small, tentative smile, feeling her hackles gradually smooth.

'I guess I could take that as a compliment. But how about we leave off over-analysing getting to know each other and change the subject? If we're going to be friends, then talking over pizza and a glass of wine seems like something we should master.'

'Agreed. So, Dominic Johnson, in the spirit of getting to know each other, tell me something about you I don't already know. Please, let's talk about something completely normal for a change.'

She took a bite of her pizza while she waited for him to reply, trying to make her body relax. Instead all it was interested in was Nic—his smell, his nearness, the fact that he was tearing down barriers she'd been counting on for weeks.

'There's not really much to tell.'

His words snapped her attention back, and she listened intently, trying to school her resistant body.

'I grew up with Mum and Dad and Kate in the suburbs of Manchester. Completely unremarkable child-

hood. Kate and I still get dragged back there regularly
for family Sunday lunches.'

'Sounds lovely,' Lily said. She *knew* it was lovely,
actually, and had been up there with Kate more than
once. 'You're lucky,' she told Nic.

He nodded in agreement. 'How about you?'

Lily took a deep breath, realising too late that of
course her question had been bound to lead to this. In
wanting to hear something completely unremarkable
about his life she'd led them to talking about the most
painful parts of hers.

'Uh-uh.' She shook her head as she reached for the
last dough ball, wondering how best to deflect his question. 'I'm not done grilling you.'

She thought around for a topic of conversation that
wouldn't lead back to her family, and her failure to hold
things together at the heart of it.

'How did you start your charity? Why did you decide that you wanted to spend your life improving the
conditions of child factory workers? It seems like a bit
of a leap the suburbs.'

He smiled softly, obviously resigned to being the
subject of her questioning for now.

'It never really seemed like a choice. I travelled
after…after Max, and I was horrified by some of the
things that I saw. I had nothing to come home to—or
that's what it felt like at the time—so I stayed and tried
to do something about it.'

'And was it what you expected?'

'It was worse—and better,' he replied. 'I saw things
that I wish I could forget, and I saw people's lives saved
because of my work. But what I loved most was that it
was so all-consuming. It exhausted me physically and

mentally. It didn't leave room for me to think about anything else. It was exactly what I needed.'

'And now? Is it still all-consuming?' Because there wasn't room for anyone else in what he'd just described.

'It can be on the days I want it to be,' he said, thoughtfully and with a direct look. 'There've been a few of those lately... But usually, no, it doesn't have to be. That's part of the reason I took the job in London. I knew that I couldn't carry on the way I had been. And I knew that my parents wanted me to be closer to home. I've spent the last ten years trying to change these companies from the outside—I thought trying from the inside might work better.'

She watched him closely, wondering whether she had been part of the reason he'd needed a distraction lately. Or was it just his grief he didn't want to face?

She sat back on her stool and rubbed her belly as Nic eyed the last slice of pizza speculatively. 'I'm done,' she declared. 'It's all yours.'

They fell into an easy silence as Nic ate, and Lily smiled up at him, feeling suddenly shy, and also shattered. Rosie's feeds through the night and her early starts were catching up with her, and much as she was loath to admit it suddenly all she could think about was her duvet, her pillow, and the fact that Rosie would be awake and hungry almost before she managed to get to them.

For half a second she thought about Nic being under that duvet with her, about seeing his head on the pillow when she woke in the morning.

Something of her thoughts must have shown on her face, because Nic raised an eyebrow.

'What?' he asked. 'What did I miss?'

'Nothing!' Lily declared, far too earnestly. 'Nothing...'

'Something,' Nic stated, watching her carefully. 'But if you don't want to share that's fine.'

'Good. Because your reverse psychology doesn't work on me.'

Nic laughed. 'Busted. I want to know what you were thinking!'

'And I'm not going to tell.'

He looked triumphant at that. 'Well, then, I'll choose to interpret that look however I want to, and there's nothing you can do about it.'

Lily shook her head, laughing. 'Right, that's enough.' She stood good-naturedly, clearing away the pizza box and their glasses. 'I'm going to bed.'

He walked through to the hall with her, and she hesitated outside her door.

'This was nice,' she said eventually, feeling suddenly nervous, unable to articulate anything more than that blatant understatement.

He grinned, though, his smile lighting his whole face. Maybe he'd heard all the things she hadn't said.

'I'm glad we talked.'

So he could do understatement too. On purpose? Or was he feeling awkward as well?

Lily reached for the door handle, but as her hand touched cold metal warm skin brushed her cheek, and she drew in a breath of surprise. Nic nudged her to look up at him as he took a step closer. The heat of his body seemed to jump the space between them, urging her closer, flushing her skin. She looked up and met his gaze. His eyes swam with a myriad of emotions.

Desire, need, relief, hope… All were reflected in her own heart. But they couldn't have timed this worse. She'd meant what she said earlier. Friendship was all she had space for in her life.

She closed her eyes as she stretched up on tiptoe and let her lips brush against his cheek. Soft skin rasped against sharp stubble and for a moment she rested her cheek against his, breathing in his smell, reminding herself that even if she did drag him inside to her bed she'd be snoring before he even got his shirt off.

Nic's other hand found the small of her back and pressed her gently to him, appreciative rather than demanding. She let out a long sigh as she dropped her forehead to his shoulder, and then finally turned the door handle.

'Goodnight…?'

There was still the hint of a question in Nic's farewell, and she smiled.

'Goodnight.'

CHAPTER SEVEN

HE BARELY HAD a foot through the front door when Lily flew past him. Shirtless and running.

'Everything okay?' he called to her retreating back, knowing that he should drag his eyes away from the curve of her waist and the smoothness of her skin, but finding that his moral compass wasn't as refined as he'd always hoped. There was something about the way the light played on her skin, the way it seemed to glow, to luminesce...

'I'm sorry,' she called over her shoulder as she ran into her bedroom. 'Spectacular timing. I'll be right out.'

Rosie was in a bouncy chair in the kitchen, wearing most of her last bottle, he guessed, and had clearly been hastily and inadequately mopped up by the kitchen roll on the counter. Lily turned suddenly and he threw his gaze away—anywhere but at her. His mind was filled by the image of her bare skin, the sweep of her shoulder, the curve of her...

No. To ogle a shoulder was one thing, but there were lines he shouldn't cross.

Instead he went into the kitchen and looked at Rosie and at the dribble of milk trickling down her chin. With mock exasperation he grabbed a muslin square and started mopping. He kept it objective, detached. There was no need to pick her up, but it wasn't really fair to leave her damp and uncomfortable, either. If he was going to be spending more time with Lily, he couldn't ignore Rosie completely.

Lily emerged a moment later, pulling down a T-shirt to cover that last inch of pale flesh above her jeans.

'Thanks for doing that. I started, but I seemed to be getting messier from trying to clean her up. Seemed one of us should be clean, at least.'

'It's no problem,' he said, holding out the muslin, handing back responsibility. His eyes were fixed just above her T-shirt, where shoulder met collarbone and collarbone met the soft skin of her neck.

And then it was hidden behind Rosie's soft-haired head and he was forced to look away again. He wondered how he could pinch Rosie's spot, how he could get his lips behind Lily's ear, breathe in her smell as Rosie was doing.

For another whole week, while he'd been putting in fourteen-hour days at the office, all he'd had to remember was that brief kiss on the cheek, the press of her soft warm skin against his, the fruity scent of her shampoo and the heat that had travelled from her body to his without them even touching. The long nights had been filled with plans he knew would never be fulfilled: for picking up where that kiss had left off, for having her cheek against his again, but this time turning her, finding her mouth with his, scooping her up in his arms and heading straight for her bedroom, or the couch, or the kitchen table...

'I'm so sorry. I know I said I'd cook tonight, but

I haven't got started on dinner yet,' she said, bouncing Rosie and trying to snatch up tissues and muslins from the kitchen counter and shuffling dirty pots from the breakfast bar. 'I just don't know what happens to the hours.'

Rosie was showing no sign of settling, so he grabbed ingredients from the fridge and tried to fire his imagination.

'You don't have to do that,' she told him, still bouncing and rocking. 'I'll be on it in just a minute.'

'Don't worry—let me,' he insisted. 'I like to cook.'

She looked up at him in surprise. 'Hidden depths?'

He took a few steps closer to her, pulled the muslin from her hand and stopped her rocking for just a minute. For the first time since that too-brief kiss on the cheek she met his eyes, and he relaxed into her gaze.

'There's a lot you don't know.'

She wanted to find out, she realised. She wanted his secrets.

'I'm pretty sure that you'd rather not arrive home to a strange woman in your apartment, baby spit-up, no sign of dinner, and—'

'It's not so bad,' he said with a grin.

It was true, he realised as he spoke. And he wanted her any way she came—baby spit-up and all. Because for this scene to be any different, *she* would have to be different. *Not* the sort of woman who took in a vulnerable child. *Not* the sort of woman who put feeding that child before her own appearance. He wanted her just as she was.

He looked down at the top of Rosie's head, at the way she was nuzzling against Lily's shoulder, the way she'd started to snuffle again since he'd stopped

Lily moving. If he wanted her to be that woman, if he wanted to be *with* that woman, then he was going to have to learn to be patient. If these few weeks had taught him anything, it was how to wait for Lily.

'She needs you,' he said. 'I'll look after dinner. And then, when she's sleeping, we can...'

She looked up again, this time with a blush and a smile.

'We can eat. And talk.'

The smile spread into a grin—and a knowing one at that.

He started chopping an onion, and had to bat away Lily's one-handed attempts to help. Ten minutes later he had a sauce bubbling on the stove, and had to snatch the wooden spoon from Lily's hand as she attempted to stir it.

'Did you never hear the one about too many cooks? Out.' He threatened her clean T-shirt with the sauce-covered spoon until he could close the door behind her.

Finally, after she'd popped her head around the door twice, just to 'check' there was nothing she could do, they had Rosie asleep in her Moses basket and dinner on the table. Conversation flowed easily between them as he shared stories of his client meetings, and told her about his plans for the new product lines he'd like to stock. They talked about what she'd been up to, but she managed to deflect most of his questions.

He wondered how much of it was her trying to protect him, shielding him from Rosie because she knew the baby caused him pain.

He couldn't remember which of them had suggested watching a movie, but now, in the dark, sharing a couch with her, he wanted to curse whoever it had been.

He felt like a teenager again. Even their choice of a comedy, hoping to steer clear of the romantic, seemed hopelessly naïve. And, like the awkward fifteen-year-old he vaguely remembered being once, he was thinking tactics. How to break their silence and separation? Trying to guess whether she was watching the film or if—like his—her line of thought was on something rather different.

They had agreed to be just friends, but his week of long days in the office—giving her the space she needed—had proved to him that keeping his feelings friendly was going to be anything but easy. Especially knowing that she was attracted to him too. She hadn't denied that before, after all. Only said that the timing wasn't right. Well, when was it *ever* right? Had she missed him, too, this week? Rethought their very grown-up and very gruelling decision to keep things platonic?

As he glanced across at her Lily turned to him, lips parted and words clearly on the tip of her tongue.

'I was just going to…to get a drink. Do you want anything from the kitchen?'

Her cheeks were rosy again, and he wondered if that was really what she had planned on saying. But most importantly she'd hit 'pause' on the movie, broken the stalemate. He watched her retreat to the kitchen and relaxed back into the cushions of the sofa. How was he meant to make it through the rest of this movie? It was torture. Pure torture. She *must* be feeling this tension as much as he was. Was she as intrigued by the attraction between them as he?

She emerged from the kitchen with a couple of glasses, balancing a plate of cakes. She'd pulled her hair back, exposing even more of the soft skin of her neck, and it took every ounce of his self-control not to sneak his arm along the back of the sofa until his hand found it, touched it. He knew that if he did his whole experience of the world would be reduced to the very tips of his fingers, and he'd be able to think about nothing other than how much he wanted her.

Her face was turned up to his, and when he breathed in it was all *her*, fruity and fresh. She smiled, and the sight of it filled him with resolve. She didn't want more than this. He would never be everything she needed in a partner, a husband. They were doing the right thing.

But when he closed his eyes he imagined her hand on his jaw, pulling him close, her tongue teasing, him opening his mouth to her and taking control. One hand would wind in her hair, tilting her head and caressing her jaw. He could practically hear her gasp as he pulled her into his lap. He knew the sound would reach his bones.

But even in his fantasy there was something else: a hesitancy, a caution that he couldn't overcome. He opened his eyes to find her watching him from the other end of the couch. He knew that his fantasy was written on his face, and other parts of his body.

'Nic…'

'Don't,' he said, holding up a hand to stop her. 'Nothing's changed since last time we talked about this. Apart from the fact that I've not been able to stop thinking about you… But it doesn't matter. We're doing the right thing. I know that. One of these days Rosie's going to need a dad—or a father figure, at least. You'll meet someone amazing who can give you the family life you deserve.'

He could never be that man.

'It's been a long week,' he told her, faking a yawn. 'I think I'm going to hit the sack.'

And with that he left her, staring after him as he practically ran from the room.

CHAPTER EIGHT

'RIGHT THEN, MISS. Are you going to tell me what's going on? Because Nic is being annoyingly discreet. I don't know what's got into him.'

'And I have no idea what you're talking about.'

'Oh, like hell you don't. The pair of you have been making doe eyes at each other since the day he pitched up on your doorstep. I can forgive *him* not telling me what's going on: he's my brother, and a bloke, and he has been irritating me for as long as I can remember. It's like a vocation for him. But you're my best friend and you have a new man in your life and you're telling me *nothing*. That's just not acceptable by anyone's standards of friendship.'

Lily groaned as she tipped the pram back and lifted it onto the pavement. 'A nice walk in the park,' Kate had said. 'Fresh air and a catch-up,' Kate had said. Since Rosie had landed they'd barely had the chance for more than a hello. It was her own fault for not realising that what she'd actually meant was *I will be grilling you for details about my brother*.

Well, if that was what she wanted…

'Okay, if it's details about the wild, sweaty sex I've been having with your brother you want you should have said. I hope you've got all afternoon free, though. Because that boy has stamina—and imagination.'

Kate's squeal had an elderly couple by the pond swivelling to stare at them and pigeons taking off from the path.

'That is all kinds of disgusting. I don't want details. But the fact that you've been doing the dirty with my brother and not telling me...*that* we need to talk about.'

Lily laughed at the look of horror on Kate's face. 'Calm it down, Kate. There has been no dirty. I'm winding you up.'

'You're— Oh, I'm going to kill you. *And* him. I've not decided yet which I'm going to enjoy more. So there's nothing going on?'

'Nothing.'

It was absolutely the truth. The fact that they were both *thinking* about what might be going on was beside the point.

'Then why are you blushing?'

Damn her pale skin—always getting her into trouble.

'I know that he likes you.'

Lily took a deep breath. 'I know he does too. But it's more complicated than that.'

'You don't like *him*?'

'Of course I like him. You've met your brother, right? Tall, good-looking, kind—all "I have a brilliant business brain but I choose to use it saving the world"?'

'Then what's the problem?'

What was the problem? There was the fact that she'd just become solely responsible for raising a brand-new human without even the usual nine-month notice period. There was the fact that Nic was still so scarred

from losing his own son that he couldn't look at Rosie
without flinching. There was the fact that she fell
asleep any time she sat down for more than six minutes at a time, and the fact that her life was threatening to overwhelm her. It was hard to imagine how
anything more complicated with Nic *wouldn't* push
her over the edge.

And there was more that he hadn't told her. It wasn't
just Rosie he was fighting. When he looked at Lily
she saw something else—doubt. He'd told her that he
wasn't the right man for her, but she failed to see why.
Not wanting a life with a baby in it was one thing, but
there was more to it than that. He warned her away
whenever they got close, as if he couldn't trust himself.

What really tipped the situation over from difficult to impossible was the fact that she didn't want to
care about any of that. That all the time she was walking around sleep-deprived and zombified her thoughts
went in one direction only—straight to Nic.

'We're just friends—it's all we can handle right now.
Honestly, Kate, if there was more to tell you I would.
But we're still trying to work it out ourselves.'

Kate gave her a long look, but then her face softened and Lily knew that she was backing down and
the grilling was over—for now, at least.

'And how are things with Rosie. Any word from
Helen?'

'Nothing more yet—only that she's still at the clinic
and doing well. Social services are happy with how
things are going with Rosie, so it looks like this is it.
Once they've decided Helen's well enough to make
a final decision I guess we'll have more paperwork
to do.'

'And you're still sure you're making the right decision?'

'I can't see what other decision I could make. She's my family. We should be together.'

Kate gave her a long look. 'I know you miss your mum, and your sister, but that doesn't mean—'

Lily stopped walking and held up a hand to stop Kate. 'Please—don't. I promise you I've thought about this. I've asked myself again and again if I'm doing the right thing and I honestly believe that I am. I *want* to do this. I love Rosie, and we're having a great time.'

'Well, she *is* completely adorable. I can't blame you—totally worth turning your life upside down for.'

Lily looked down at the pram, where Rosie had been sleeping soundly for over an hour. When she was like this, how could she disagree?

She'd just got the baby fed, changed and sleeping when the front door opened. She backed out of the bedroom on tiptoes, holding her breath to avoid waking Rosie. Nic was standing in the hall, bearing a bunch of flowers and a grin.

'Hi.'

He bent forward to kiss her on the cheek—strictly friendly—and she sneakily soaked up the smell of his aftershave and the warmth of his body.

'Hi, yourself. You look good. Did you do something different with your hair?'

She knew for a fact that there was milk in her hair, and that she'd pulled on this T-shirt from where she'd tossed it by the side of the bed last night. What a gentleman.

'How was it?' Lily asked as they walked through

to the kitchen. 'Did you manage to clear your desk for rest of the weekend?'

He'd been working and travelling non-stop since he'd arrived back in London, and had declared last night that he was ready for a break. He'd suggested a touristy day, sightseeing, and had volunteered *her* as tour guide.

'All sorted. I'm free till Monday morning. Are you still on for today?' He thrust the flowers at her. 'I'm banking on you saying yes, and these are a thank-you in advance.'

Lily thought about it—a few hours in the sunshine in one of the parks, perhaps the Tower of London or the London Eye to really up the cheesy tourist factor.

'Of course we're still on. Do I have time to change?'

'An hour before the car arrives. Is that enough? I can always call and delay.'

'An hour's perfect.'

She left Nic in the kitchen while she dived into the shower and grabbed jeans and a clean shirt. Rosie didn't stir in her crib, and Lily kept an eye on the clock, wondering when she'd wake for her next feed. She'd been sleeping for an hour already, which meant that she'd be waking up…just as the car reached them. *Not* perfect, then—far from it.

Maybe she should just tell Nic that they needed to leave a little later—but he'd seen too much of her struggling already, and she didn't want to admit that an hour wasn't enough time to get two people ready and out of the house. She'd just have to wake Rosie early from her sleep and feed her before they set off. Hopefully she'd pop straight off back to sleep afterwards.

Clean from the shower, Lily headed back out to the

kitchen, to find Nic immersed in stacking the dish-washer.

'Nic! You shouldn't! Leave those and I'll do them when we get back.'

'It's no problem,' he insisted as Lily gathered up sterilised bottles and cartons of ready-mixed formula, trying to work out how many bottles they would need to get them through the day.

Nic finished the washing up, despite her contin-ued protests, and with twenty minutes to go until the car arrived the kitchen was looking more like a home than a bomb site.

'Right, then—anything else I can do to help?' Nic asked.

'Absolutely not. I just need to give Rosie a quick feed and then we're all good.'

She cracked open the curtains in the bedroom slightly—just enough so that it wouldn't feel like night to Rosie—and then lifted her from the crib, tickling her fingers up and down her spine and over the soles of her feet. When her eyes started to open Lily moved her face closer and smiled at her, holding eye contact.

'Morning, sleepyhead,' she crooned. 'Time for some-thing to eat, and then we're going on an adventure!'

She swiped a bottle from the kitchen on her way, and then settled into a big comfy chair in the living room, where Nic had turned on some music.

'So, am I allowed to know what's in store for us today?' Lily asked once Rosie had started to feed.

'I can tell you if you really want to know, but I thought a surprise...'

Lily grinned. She couldn't remember the last time someone had organised a surprise for her, and after weeks of being enslaved to a demanding newborn, the thought of being spoilt for the day was irresistible.

'A surprise sounds divine. Though I'm not sure how I'm meant to play tour guide if I don't know where we're going.'

'Without giving too much away, let's just say that you don't have to worry too much about that. You're doing enough, indulging my need to see the tourist hotspots. I don't expect you to sing for your supper, too.'

Lily was distracted by Rosie spitting out the bottle, but managed to rearrange the muslin square before she got a direct hit on her clean shirt. She tried to get her to take the bottle again, but she turned her head and pursed her lips. Lily gave a small sigh. Perhaps choosing this morning to try waking her for a feed for the first time wasn't the best idea she'd ever had—it seemed Rosie wasn't a big fan of spontaneity.

She sat her up and rubbed between her shoulderblades, hoping that she just had some wind and could be persuaded to take the rest of her bottle.

'Everything okay?' Nic asked, when she gave a small huff of exasperation.

'Just fussing,' Lily told him, not wanting to admit that her mistake was probably to blame.

'There's no hurry, you know. We can move the car back.'

'It's fine—honestly.' The damage had been done now, after all.

She offered Rosie the bottle again, but she absolutely refused it, and Lily knew that she was being unfair on her when all she wanted to do was sleep. Cursing whatever instinct it was that had kept her quiet when she could so easily have asked Nic to change their plans, she rocked the baby back to sleep and wondered when she'd wake next—when she'd be hungry next. She couldn't shake the feeling that she'd just played Russian roulette with their day.

The doorbell rang just as Rosie dropped off and Lily held her breath for a moment, wondering if the sound would wake her, but it seemed they'd got away with it. She lowered her gently into her car seat and hefted her to the hallway—for a tiny bundle she was certainly starting to feel like a heck of a weight to carry around.

Nic answered the door to a driver in a smart-looking uniform, and for a second Lily was surprised. She'd heard 'car' and thought local minicab, but it seemed Nic's idea of a day's sightseeing might be somewhat different to her own. She glanced down at the plimsolls she'd been about to pull on and wondered whether she ought to go for something smarter.

'Should I change?' she asked Nic. 'I'm in the dark about what we're doing, but if I need to be...'

'You look perfect as you are,' he told her, and she smiled, but still wasn't entirely at ease.

Lily watched out of the window as they headed down towards the river, trying to work out where they were going. They zoomed past a couple of parks, which ruled those out, and by the time they pulled up at a wharf Lily had to admit defeat. She had no idea where they were going.

'We're here?' she asked Nic, and he grinned by way of an answer. 'What are we doing?'

'Wait and see,' he told her with child-like enthusi-asm. 'But it should be amazing.'

She pulled Rosie's car seat out and looked up at

Nic, hoping for some guidance. He nodded towards the water, where a sleek white and silver yacht was moored.

'Are we going aboard?' she asked.

'We are indeed.'

He was practically bouncing now—and no wonder. The yacht was magnificent—all flowing lines and shiny chrome, and decks scrubbed to within an inch of their lives. She could see through the expanse of glass that a dining room had been set with sparkling crystal and polished silverware. It looked as if they were in for a treat.

'Would you like the pram, madam?' the driver asked as he opened the boot of the car.

She glanced at the gangplank and the yacht's decks, and for a shivery moment had visions of a runaway pram rolling towards the railings that edged the decks.

'I think I'll take the sling instead.'

Nic grabbed the changing bag from the boot and hefted it to his shoulder. Climbing up onto the gangplank, he held out a hand to her. As his fingers closed around her palm warmth spread through her hand, and she had to remind herself sternly of the very sensible decision that they'd both taken to remain just friends. But with the fancy dining room and the glamorous yacht this was starting to look more like a date than temporary flatmates hanging out for the afternoon.

'Welcome, sir, madam—and to the little one. You're very welcome on board. Luncheon will be served in thirty minutes. In the meantime feel free to explore the decks or take a drink in the champagne bar on the upper deck.'

Lily smiled at the man as he discreetly retreated

from them, though she couldn't help a little twist of anxiety. Luncheon, champagne bar… She'd had take-away sandwiches in mind when Nic had first mentioned something to eat and sightseeing, and she wondered if he had higher expectations of the day than he'd let on. This was looking less and less like a casual day out and more like a seduction.

She looked up at Nic, wondering whether she'd glean any clue from his expression. But his beaming smile didn't give much away.

'Nic, this is amazing,' she said. 'If a little unexpected…'

'I know…I know. It's a bit over the top. But I wanted to see London from the water, and my new assistant said the food on board was not to be missed. There's nothing wrong with treating ourselves, is there?'

She searched for double meanings, but found none in his words or in his eyes. She was worrying about nothing. It was no surprise, really. After he'd ended up cooking for them both these last few weeks, he wanted a slightly more refined dining experience.

'So, what will it be?' he asked. 'Exploring or the champagne bar?'

Lily thought about it for a second, measuring the rocking of the boat under her feet and the weight of the baby in her arms. 'Exploring, I think,' she said with a smile.

They walked the decks, gasping over the unrivalled luxury of the vessel, the attention to detail and the devotion to function and aesthetics in every line. Polished chrome and barely there glass provided a barrier between them and the water, but as they climbed step after step Lily's head grew dizzier and her feet a little less steady.

When she had to pause for a moment, at the top of the highest step, Nic gave her a concerned look. 'You okay?' he asked, with a gentle arm around her shoulder.

'Fine,' she told him, shrugging off his arm.

It was making it too hard to think, and she needed to focus all her energy on keeping herself on her feet at the moment.

Nic's face fell—just for a second, before he caught it—and she knew that she had hurt his feelings. She'd opened her mouth, without being entirely sure what she would say, when a liveried steward came up the steps behind them and asked that they take their seats in the dining room. With just a quick glance at Nic, Lily shot down the stairs, glad of the moment to clear her head.

It wasn't that she hadn't wanted Nic's support. God knew it had felt good to have his arm around her. But there was the problem. It was *too* good. It would be too easy to forget all the very sensible, grown-up reasons that they were staying friends and friends only. And it wasn't as if Nic had meant anything by it; he'd just been trying to help when he'd seen that she needed it. It was her overactive libido that was complicating things—having her jumping like a cat every time he came near her.

There were about a dozen tables in the dining room, each set for two with a shining silver candelabra and fresh-cut roses in crystal.

'Wow,' Nic said behind her. 'This is…'

She turned round to look at him, not sure how to interpret the wavering in his voice.

Go on, she urged him silently. Because this dining room had 'romance' written all over it, and right now she was struggling. Struggling to see how they were meant to stay friends if Nic was going to spring romance on her with no warning. Struggling to know what he wanted from her if this was where he thought they were in their 'friendship'.

'This is…unexpected,' he said.

The candlelight made it hard to tell, but she was sure there was a little more colour in his cheeks than normal. She let out a sigh of relief. Okay, so she was worrying over nothing. This wasn't some grand seduction—just a lunch that was turning out to be a little more romantic than either of them had been expecting.

Lily watched the other diners taking their seats as they were shown to a table by the window, tucked into a corner of the room. Light flooded in through the floor-to-ceiling windows, throwing patterns and shapes from the crystal and the flatware.

Nic tucked the changing bag under the table as they sat, and Lily reached down to adjust Rosie in her carrier. She'd slept through their tour of the vessel and Lily glanced at her watch, not sure what time she would wake.

Nic looked determinedly out of the window, Lily noticed, and was careful to make sure that his eyes never landed on Rosie.

'Come on, then,' he said, gesturing at the window. 'What are we looking at? I can't waste the fact that I'm out here with a genuine Londoner.'

'How have you never been sightseeing in London?' she asked with wonder. 'Never mind the fact that your sister has lived here for years, you've been to —what?—six different cities in the past couple of months alone. You don't honestly need me to point out the OXO Tower, do you?'

'And in not one of those other cities did I have a tour guide. Or time off for lunch, for that matter. What can I say? Maybe I've packed in too much work and not enough fun.'

'Well, we'll make today all about fun, then. What else have you got planned for us?'

'Nope—still not telling.'

She laughed, and then looked down as she felt Rosie rubbing her head against her chest, a sure sign that she was about to wake up and demand a bottle. She was just going to suggest that they find a way to heat up some formula when the maître d' appeared.

Seemed everybody was ready to eat.

As a team of waiting staff paraded into the dining room, carrying their starters, Lily dug through her bags and found a bottle and a carton of ready-mixed formula.

'Excuse me,' she said to their waitress, once she'd placed their starters in front of them, 'could I have some hot water to heat a bottle?'

The girl shot Rosie a look that was fifty per cent fear of the baby and fifty per cent disdain. It turned out that diners under one weren't exactly flavour of the month on luxury restaurant cruises.

'Is she okay?' Nic asked, as Rosie started to mewl like a mildly discontented kitten.

'Just hungry, I think,' Lily said, rubbing her back and trying to get her to settle.

If only her fusspot of a niece would take a cold bottle—but she had tried that before, with no success. She tried again now anyway, hoping that maybe she'd be hungry enough not to care, but after screwing up her face she spat out a mouthful of milk and Lily knew they had no choice but to wait for the hot water. She really ought to get one of those portable bottle warmers...

The doors to the dining room swung open, and Lily looked up, hoping to see a steaming pot of water heading her way. Instead the waitress was carrying bottles of wine, topping up the glasses on the table nearest the kitchen. Rosie chose that moment to let out a scream, and every head in the room turned towards her—Nic's included.

'I think maybe I should take her out... Just for a few minutes...until she settles.'

'If you think that's best,' Nic replied, his expression hovering somewhere around concerned. 'Is there anything I can do?'

'If you could get that bottle warm, that would be amazing. Sure you don't mind?'

She'd have done it herself—marched into the kitchen and found a kettle—but from the looks she was getting a hasty retreat seemed like the safer option.

'Course. I'll grab someone. Want me to bring it out to you? Or will you come back in?'

She should have an answer to that. But all she could think was, What was he asking *her* for? *He* was the one who'd done this before—*he* was the one with experience of being a parent, having had months to prepare for it and classes to learn about it.

But she couldn't ask him about any of that.

She pushed through the heavy door and went out onto the deck, taking in a deep lungful of breeze and spray. She let the breath out slowly, her eyes closed, focussing on calming thoughts, knowing that it would help Rosie settle.

Could everyone still hear her? She risked a glance at the windows. Whether they could hear her or not, she was still providing the entertainment, it seemed, as more than one pair of eyes was still fixed on her. It was hard to tell, though, what normal volume was with her eardrums about to rupture.

She rolled her eyes in the face of their disapproval. As if none of *them* had ever had to deal with a hungry baby. Smiling, she looked down at Rosie, determined to stay cheerful in the face of her cries. She was still cooing at her when she realised that Nic had left their table, and she only had a moment to wonder where he was before he emerged through the double doors with a steaming jug of water and the bottle.

What a hero. She could kiss him.

Well, actually, that pretty much felt like her default setting these days. But she was more grateful than ever to have him in her life right at that second. She watched him walk towards her as if he were carrying the Holy Grail.

'One bottle,' he declared as he closed the door to the deck behind him and passed it over to her.

She'd expected him to be sprinting back through the doors as soon as he'd offloaded his cargo, but instead he dropped down onto a bench, spreading his arms across the back. Lily sat beside him as Rosie started sucking on the bottle, quiet at last.

'Why don't you go in and eat?' she said to him. 'It seems a shame for us both to be missing out on lunch.'

'I don't mind––'

'Honestly—go and eat. She's perfectly happy now, so I'll be back in soon.'

He hesitated for a second, but then stood and headed for the door. Lily leaned back against the bench and closed her eyes for a moment, letting herself drift with the rhythmic rocking of the boat. At the sound of the deck doors opening her eyes flew open—to see Nic juggling glasses and plates as he fought to shut the door behind him.

'If Rosie's picnicking out here, seems only fair that we get to as well,' he said with a grin.

Lily risked a glance into the dining room and could see that more than one set of eyes was disapprovingly set in their direction.

'Open up.'

A forkful of delicate tartlet appeared in front of her nose and Lily hesitated, meeting Nic's eyes as he offered the food to her. *Definitely* too intimate for friends. But Rosie's weight in her arms reminded her that this wasn't romance, it was practicality, and she opened her mouth, let her lips close around the cold tines of the fork.

Closing her eyes seemed too decadent, too sensuous. But holding Nic's gaze as he fed her so intimately seemed like a greater danger. As balsamic vinegar hit her palate she smiled. With food this good, why let herself be distracted by anything else?

She sat looking out across the water, enjoying seeing the city that was so familiar to her with the unfamiliar smells and sounds of the boat. Nic's arm was still stretched across the back of the bench, but she didn't move away. It was too easy, too comfortable to sit like this, enjoying the moments of quiet and savouring their lunch.

Eventually, when both plates were cleared and Rosie had finished her formula, Nic nodded towards the dining room.

'Think we can risk human company again?'

CHAPTER NINE

NIC LOOKED DOWN at Rosie, milk-drunk and sleepy again.

'I think we should be safe,' Lily said, setting the bottle down beside them, lifting Rosie to her shoulder and starting to rub her back.

'Let me do that,' Nic offered, already reaching for Rosie.

He hadn't meant to: he'd been clear with himself that the only way he could let himself explore this connection with Lily was if he remembered to keep his distance with Rosie. But he could hardly invite them out for the day and not expect to help. It was what any friend would do, he told himself. Friendship wasn't just offering the parts of yourself that were easy. Taking the parts of the other person that fitted with your life. It meant taking the hard bits too, exposing yourself to hurt, trusting that the other person was looking out for you.

They'd agreed that a relationship was too much to take on, but if they were going to be friends he was going to be a *good* friend.

He nestled the baby on his shoulder as they walked back inside, and for a moment he was caught by her new baby smell—a scent that threw him back ten years, to the happiest and hardest moments of his life. His eyes closed and his steps faltered for a second, but he forced himself forward, pushing through the pain of his past and reminding himself that Rosie wasn't Max, and Lily wasn't Clare.

As they reached the table their main courses arrived, and he slid into his seat with Rosie still happy on his shoulder.

'This looks amazing,' declared Lily, looking down at the plates of perfectly pink lamb and buttery potatoes. She reached for her knife and fork, but then hesitated. 'Are you sure you don't want me to take her?'

'You can if you want,' Nic told her, wary of overstepping some line. 'But I don't mind.'

Lily's eyes dropped to Rosie again as she thought for a minute.

'No, you're right. It would be silly to disturb her when she's settled.'

He picked up his fork, wondering how he was meant to tackle a rack of lamb one-handed.

'Here,' Lily said, with a smile and a sparkle in her eye. She pinned the meat with a fork while he cut it, and when she caught the maître d's shocked expression, she laughed out loud. 'I don't think I've ever caused such a scandal before,' she whispered to him.

He laughed in return, relieved to feel the tension leaching from the air.

'I feel like we're doing him a service. His life must have been very sheltered if we're so shocking to him. Maybe we should up the ante? Give him something to really disapprove of…?'

Oh, did he like the sound of *that*. His skin prickled,

his grin widened and he leaned closer across the table. 'What exactly did you have in mind?'

Lily blushed.

God, it was such a turn-on when she did that—when the evidence of her desire chased across her skin like watercolours on a damp page.

'I…I…I don't think I really thought that sentence through,' she said at last with a coy smile.

He laughed again, feeling his shoulders relax, leaning back in his chair as they seemed to find common ground again…as he started to feel the subtle pull and heat between them that had brought them together in the first place.

'Maybe I'll ask you again another time,' he suggested, unable to resist this spark between them. 'When we've a little more privacy and a little less company.'

She looked up at him from under her lashes—a look, he suspected, not entirely uncalculated.

'Maybe I'll give it a little thought this afternoon.'

For a moment the silence spanned warm and comfortable between them, and he held her gaze as gently and sensuously as if he was reaching out and touching her.

A little choking sound from the baby he'd almost forgotten was in his arms drew his attention and he smiled down at her, so exposed from the conversation with Lily that he didn't have a moment to try and defend himself, had no chance of raising any sort of resistance to those adorably round cheeks or her big blue eyes.

'Sorry, little Rosie,' he told her, mopping her up automatically and shifting her to his other shoulder. 'I guess we weren't paying you enough attention.'

Lily gave him a complicated smile, but then with one more bite of potato she dropped her knife and fork.

'That was incredible—truly,' she told him. 'The closest thing to heaven I've ever eaten.'

'Agreed,' he said, looking a little longingly at the lamb still on his plate.

'I'll take her back,' Lily told him, her tone brooking no argument this time. 'Seriously—you'll kick yourself if you don't eat every bite.'

CHAPTER TEN

THE BOAT SLOWED as they approached the wharf and Lily could practically feel the collective sigh of relief from everyone on board. Not that she cared. The three of them had enjoyed another picnic out on deck, when Rosie had been testy again during dessert, and she couldn't help but think that it had been nicer, anyway, to be out in the fresh air than in that dining room, with its candles that spoke of a romance they were definitely *not* going to be pursuing.

Part of her had wanted to explain to the other diners —to confess that she'd thought more than once that maybe if she was Rosie's real mum she might be better at this. She might be flailing a little less at the prospect of a baby whose needs were really pretty simple if only she could work out the code that everyone else seemed to understand. She couldn't really blame them for being annoyed. No doubt they'd paid handsomely for their lunch, and hadn't expected to encounter a crying baby while they enjoyed it. But their silent judgement was cutting nonetheless.

At least she'd had a partner in crime.

Nic had actually taken the baby today. Offered to help and then cooed at her and rocked her until she was calm. Though the ghost of pain and doubt etched into his every feature was enough to show her that, romantic as the setting was, his thoughts were anything but. There was nothing more likely to put him off, she thought, than being reminded of the realities of parenting.

'You okay there?' Nic asked, breaking into her reverie. 'You look a million miles away.'

The car had met them as they'd disembarked and they were crawling through London traffic again, on their way to sightseeing event number two.

The car stopped outside the Tower of London, and she sent Nic a questioning glance. She couldn't hide her deep breath of apprehension. The last time she'd been to the Tower had been years ago, and she'd had to fight her way through crowds, elbow her way into a picnic spot and strain her ears to hear the commentary from the obligatory Beefeater. She couldn't imagine it being any more relaxing with Rosie strapped to her chest.

'We're here,' Nic announced with a smile.

He reached for her hand to help her out of the car, and then reached in after her to take Rosie from her seat. He handed the baby straight over, but she couldn't help seeing a tiny bit of progress.

They were met at the gate by a uniformed Beefeater, and as she passed through the entrance she realised how different it felt from the last time she'd been there. Looking around her, she realised why. The place was deserted. How on earth had he pulled *this* off?

The Beefeater puffed up his chest as he turned round and launched into a clearly well-practised speech, welcoming them to Her Majesty's Royal Palace and Fortress, The Tower of London. 'There's a thousand years of history here, sir, madam: more than you could discover in a week. So what would you like to see? The armouries? The torture display? The Crown Jewels?'

Lily gave an involuntary gasp at the mention of the jewels. The day of her teenaged visit the Jewel House had been packed and sweaty. She'd managed to get stuck behind someone with a huge backpack on the moving conveyor, and had passed through without getting one decent look at a crown.

She looked up at Nic, who laughed. 'Looks like the Crown Jewels it is,' he declared to their Yeoman Guard.

'You're sure you don't mind? I'd understand if diamonds weren't your thing.'

'That look on your face is exactly my thing,' he told her quietly as their guide discreetly moved away. 'And if it's a diamond that gets it there…'

His sentence trailed into silence, but his gaze never faltered from hers. He *was* talking about diamonds? Had he realised what he'd said? Of course he didn't mean a *diamond* diamond—the type that led you up the aisle and towards happy-ever-after. But if he'd meant nothing by it, why wasn't he looking away. Why was he reaching out and touching her face, as if trying to see something, touch something, that wasn't quite there?

His hand dropped gently to cup the back of Rosie's head, then lower still to Lily's waist, pulling her towards him. She closed her eyes as he leaned in for a kiss, and felt the lightest, gentlest brush of lips over hers. For a moment she couldn't move. Not even to kiss him back or push him away. In that moment she didn't know which she wanted more—which she was more scared of. Because this kiss was something different.

It wasn't the desperate press of his lips on hers at the hospital, or that regretfully friendly kiss on the cheek. This kiss was the start of something new. Something more than they'd had before...something more serious...something more frightening.

Rosie let out a squawk, clearly less than impressed at being trapped between the two of them, and Nic backed off a little, his smile more of a slow-burning candle than a full-beam sun.

He called over to their guide and let him know that they were ready.

Rosie started to whimper a little as they headed over to the Jewel House, and their guide slowed a little.

'Aw, is she out of sorts? She looks just the same age as my granddaughter—and that girl has a pair of lungs on her, I can tell you. Do you want to sit somewhere quiet with her for a while?'

'Thank you, but she's just tired. I think if we keep walking she'll send herself off.'

'Of course. Mum knows best,' he told her with a wink. 'Though if you ask me...' he gave her a careful look '...it's probably Dad's turn.'

He carried on speaking, but Lily couldn't make out what he was saying. Her focus was pinned entirely on Nic as his face fell, then paled, and then as he slowly put himself back together. His eyes refocused, and his jaw returned to its usual position.

'Here,' he said, just as Lily caught something about Colonel Blood in 1671 from their guide. 'He's right. My turn.'

He held his hands out for her, and Lily sent him the clearest *Are you sure?* look she could manage without speaking out loud. He took Rosie in his arms and lifted her to his chin, then leaned down and pressed a kiss to the top of her head. He closed his eyes for a moment and Lily knew that he was remembering. But then he looked up at her with a brave smile, grabbed her hand and squeezed.

They followed the guard, and she tried to listen to his stories, tried to take in the information, but really she just wanted to look. And not at the diamonds or the gold or the ancient artefacts. She wanted to watch Nic with Rosie. Wanted to witness the way he was resisting his hurt and his past and trying to endure, trying to move on. And he was doing it for her.

When they emerged from the Jewel House the evening was starting to draw in. Car headlights were lighting up Tower Bridge, and the banks of the river were bustling with tourists calling it a day mixed with commuters heading home.

'A walk along the river before we head home?' Nic asked. 'I had thought maybe dinner, but…'

Lily burst out laughing, remembering how they'd spent barely half an hour of their lunch actually in the dining room. With a few hours' distance suddenly the whole cruise seemed like a farce. For dinner she wanted nothing more than a sofa and a cheese sandwich. Michelin-starred cuisine was all well and good, but you couldn't exactly eat it in your pyjamas. Or with a baby nearby, apparently.

'I think we'd better quit while we're ahead,' she said. 'Lunch was spectacular, in so many ways, but I think Rosie needs her bed. Enough excitement for her for one day.'

'I understand. We should probably head back.'

Lily nodded, suddenly feeling sombre. The prospect

of an evening together in the apartment was suddenly overwhelming. That kiss—there'd be nowhere to hide from it once they got home.

In the privacy and seclusion of the car, nipping through London traffic, Lily's thoughts were heading in one direction and one direction only—behind the so far firmly shut door of her bedroom. She risked a glance up at Nic, wondering whether her feelings were showing on her face. Were they going to talk about this again? Put aside all their good intentions to do the sensible thing? That kiss had promised so much that couldn't be unsaid.

But she stayed silent—as did Nic. Silent in the car, silent in the lift, silent until Rosie was settled in her cot and they were alone in the living room—with nothing and no one standing between them and the conversation they were avoiding.

Nic let out a long, slow breath, rubbing his hand across the back of his neck, and for a minute Lily wondered if she'd completely misread what had been going on between them—maybe he was happy with things as they were? Maybe he was only interested in being friends?

She risked a glance up at him and all her doubts fled. The heat in his eyes told her everything she needed to know about how he felt—and it was a lot more than friendly. She felt that heat travel to the depths of her belly, warming her from the inside until it reached her face as a smile. He pulled gently on her hand, bringing her close to him, and planted his other hand on her hip.

'Is this a good idea?' she asked, knowing the answer…knowing just as well that it wasn't going to stop them.

'Terrible,' Nic answered, dropping her hand and finding her cheek with his palm. 'Want to stop?'

It took considerable effort not to laugh in his face. Stop? How *could* they stop? They'd tried to avoid this. They'd talked about exactly why this was a bad idea. Looking deep into Nic's eyes, she could see that he still had reservations, that he still didn't fully believe this was the right thing to do. But stop...?

'No.'

'Everything we said, Lily—it still stands. I've not changed who I am, what happened...'

'I know. But what are we meant to do—just ignore this? I can't, Nic. It feels too...big. Too important. So let's see where it goes. No guarantees. No promises. Let's just stop fight—'

His lips captured hers before the word was even out, and she knew that they were lost. They'd been crazy to think that they could live here, together, and pretend that this wasn't happening—that their bodies hadn't been dragging them towards each other, however un-willingly, since the moment that they'd met.

With her spine wedged against a console table and her feet barely on the floor, Lily thought how easy it would be to surrender completely. To let Nic literally sweep her off her feet, caveman-style if he wanted, and really see where they could take this.

But as his hands found the sensitive skin at the back of her knees, lifting her until her legs wrapped around his waist, she knew that the easy road wasn't the right one.

'Nic...' she gasped into his ear, not able to articulate more than that one syllable.

But he'd perched her gently on the table and now, although his breathing was still ragged, he pulled back—just an inch…just enough to give her the space she needed to clear her head. His expression held all his questions without him having to say a word.

'Slower,' Lily said eventually, when she'd regained the power of speech. 'That was…I want to see where this will go, but…slower. Slower than that.'

She could barely believe that she'd managed to get the words out, and even as she was saying them she was already half regretting that she wasn't more fearless. But she couldn't be. Just because they had decided to stop fighting, it didn't mean that she had decided to be stupid. There was no happy ending in sight—no easy way to set aside everything they'd convinced each other was good reason to stay apart.

They'd still have to work through it…whatever it was that made Nic's eyes dim at the most unexpected times. It wasn't all going to disappear because they wanted things to be easy. And until they were more sure of each other there was only so far she could take this.

CHAPTER ELEVEN

SUNDAY MORNING, LILY WOKE to sunshine at the curtains and Rosie gurgling happily in her crib. She stared at the wall opposite, trying to picture Nic just on the other side of it, sprawled across the king-size bed she'd seen when she'd sneaked a look at his room. And she could be in there with him now, she thought, rather than be trying to conjure the feeling of his arms around her waist, the warmth of his chest warming her back as she turned on the pillow and drifted back to sleep…

If only she hadn't been so darned sensible last night.

Much as she was cursing herself, she was glad, really, that she'd made the decision she had. Sure, daybreak wrapped in Nic sounded like perfection—but then what about breakfast? Lunch? All the conversations they hadn't had yet? The things that needed to be said before they decided if whatever it was between them could turn from 'let's see where this goes' into something more real, more lasting?

Footsteps padded down the hallway, and as they approached her room she held her breath, wondering whether they would stop—whether Nic wanted to pick up where they'd left that kiss last night. But they faded again, towards the front door, until she heard a key turn in the lock and then silence.

He'd just gone! Without a word! A cold shiver traced her spine. But she forced herself out of bed and into the kitchen, determined not to read too much into it. He often went for a run at this time of day, before the streets were busy. But it was a Sunday—and, more than that, it was the morning after *that* kiss, when she had a million things to say and no idea where to start. Was that what he was avoiding?

She shook her head as she boiled the kettle and scooped formula. Who said he was avoiding anything?

When he strolled into the apartment at half past ten, still in his running gear, she'd just got Rosie down for a sleep and was thinking of following her back to bed. But the sight of Nic's legs in his scantily cut running shorts gave her second thoughts.

'Good run?' she asked, having still not entirely shaken the worry that he'd left early that morning to avoid her. But he was smiling—beaming, actually— as he fiddled with the coffee machine.

'Brilliant—really good. What about you? Good morning?'

'Milk, nappies, sleep. Pretty much standard.' She said it with a smile, and she could hear the dreamy edge in her voice. It might be hard work, but she would be hard pressed to think of another job that was more worth it.

'I stopped by the office,' Nic said as he placed a cup of coffee in front of her. 'Had a bit of a brainwave when I was running...'

Lily's eyebrows drew together.

'What sort of idea?'

'What have you got planned this week?'

She gave it a moment's thought. One tiny design job that she had to finish and email to her client, and other than that more milk, more nappies, more sleep.

'Just the usual.'

'Then come to Rome with me.'

He was still talking, but a crash of thoughts drowned out his words as she tried to process what he'd just said. A trip to Rome with the man she knew she was rapidly falling for? How could she say no? *Why* would she say no?

Nic squeezed her hand.

'Lily? Still with me?'

'I am—sorry. I think that's an incredible idea, but...'

Even as she was saying the words the real world began to intrude.

'But you're worried about the practicalities and about Rosie? I know—of course you are. But she'll have everything she needs. The logistics might not be easy, but they're not impossible.'

'She doesn't even have a passport.'

'No, but she does have an appointment at the passport office tomorrow. *If* you decide it's what you want,' he hastened to add. 'There'd be a skycot on the flight, and a cot in your room at the hotel. Formula, nappies... I've organised a pram and a car seat—the same ones as you have here—to use while we're there. I think I've thought of everything—if not the hotel's concierge is on standby for anything baby-related. We can even organise a nanny, if you want one.'

Lily slumped back in her chair, her mouth agape.

'I don't know what to say.'

'Say *yes*,' Nic said with a boyish eagerness. 'Have you been to Italy before?'

'No, I've never been to Italy…' she said, her words coming out slowly as her brain fought to catch up. 'But I'm not sure that really comes into my decision. I've got to think practically.'

'You can think practically if you want, but I swear it's all taken care of. Instead you could think about Rome: sipping coffee in a quiet *piazza*, genuine Italian cuisine, the shopping…'

'You're a great salesman—very persuasive. No wonder you were head-hunted.'

'What can I say? I'm only human. Now, stop changing the subject. If you need time to think about it, that's fine.'

Would she use the time to think about it? Or would she use it to talk herself out of it? *Rome*. It was hardly the sort of opportunity that came along every day. And the opportunity to take a spur-of-the-moment trip to a romantic city with Nic seemed like a once-in-a-lifetime sort of thing. She'd be mad to say no.

'Okay, yes. I'd love to.' She could feel the smile spreading across her cheeks, feel the warmth in the pit of her stomach rising to glow in her chest and her heart. '*Rome*, Nic. I don't know where to start being excited about that!'

Nic simply sat and watched as Lily enthused about Rome, so pleased that he'd been able to convince her to come with him. He'd had a flash of inspiration this morning and not been able to rest until he'd got the details in place. His trip had been booked for a while— a meeting with a fabric supplier he'd been in contact with several times over the years. And now that he and Lily had decided to see where this chemistry between them might go, Rome seemed like too good an opportunity to miss.

For a brief moment—just a split second—he'd been tempted to call his sister and ask if she'd babysit Rosie for a night. But he'd stopped himself. He wanted Lily and everything that came with her. He couldn't pretend—didn't want to pretend—that Rosie wasn't going to be a part of their life together. He'd made a few calls, pulled in a few favours, and had plans for the trip underway before he'd even got to the office.

'You know, you don't talk about your family much,' he remarked, once they'd exhausted all possible Roman topics of conversation.

'There's not a lot to tell,' Lily said with a shrug, but the shadow that darkened her eyes told him a different story.

'I know how sad it makes you that you and your sister aren't close…'

He wasn't sure why he was pushing the issue. Maybe it was because he wanted to be close to her, to *really* know her. He'd laid bare the darkest parts of his own history, but he knew so little about her. How could they try and be something more than friends to one another if he didn't really know her?

'It does,' she admitted. 'But maybe now… Maybe things will be better.'

'Was there a big falling-out?'

Lily shook her head as she drank her coffee. A drop caught on her lower lip and he watched, entranced, as her tongue sneaked out to rescue it.

'Nothing dramatic.'

'How do your parents feel about it?'

She caught her breath in a gasp, and though she tried to cover it he knew that he'd just stumbled into dangerous waters.

'Actually, my parents aren't around. My dad never was, and my mum died when I was twelve.'

He felt a gut-wrenching stab of pain on her behalf, and at the same time wanted to kick himself for causing her distress. What an idiot he was to go stumbling around in her past. If she'd wanted to talk about her family she would have brought it up. But then he was sure he'd heard Kate say something about her visiting her family. If not her sister or her parents, then who?

'I'm sorry, Lily. I didn't mean to pry. We don't have to—'

'It's fine,' she told him, settling her mug on the table. 'I don't mind talking about her. It's nice, actually, to have a reminder occasionally.'

'What was she like?'

'She was lovely—and amazing. That doesn't seem like enough, but I'm not sure how else…' Her voice trailed off and she rested her chin on her hand, leaning on the table. 'It was all rather wonderful when I was growing up—which, knowing what I do now about what it is to bring up a child on your own…'

She still had no idea how her mother had done it. Every day she spent battling to keep her head above water with Rosie was another day when her respect for her mother grew exponentially. And when she found herself looking at her own efforts and wondering why she found it so hard…

'And I had a big sister to look out for me. But then Mum was in a car accident and everything changed.'

'I'm so sorry.'

He couldn't believe that he hadn't known this about her before now. That she'd let him talk about his loss and his grief while never hinting that there were people she loved missing from her own life.

'It's not as bad as all that,' she said, catching his eye and giving a little smile. 'At the time, obviously, it was horrendous. But I was placed with a wonderful foster family who helped me come to terms with losing my mother. Helped me so that I could remember her with love, remember the wonderful family that we were. I was lucky to find a second set of people to love me and take care of me.'

He marvelled at her composure, but sensed that her sister's story was somewhat different.

'And Helen?'

'Helen's older,' she said. 'She was sixteen when we lost Mum—too old for foster care. Not that that was what she wanted anyway. After Mum was gone it was like she wanted to prove that she didn't need her. She wanted to do her own thing, take care of herself. She was always welcome with my foster family, and we all tried hard to make her feel included, but it wasn't what she wanted. With our mum gone, the "half" part of being her half-sister suddenly seemed to matter more than ever.'

There were only so many times that he could say he was sorry before it started to sound trite. He couldn't fathom the way Lily had dealt with these blows—how she had come out the other side able to smile fondly when she thought about the family she'd once belonged to but which had since fallen apart. When he'd lost his son and then his fiancée, it had been as if the world had changed overnight. As if the warmth of the sun had stopped reaching him. He'd stopped living. Whereas Lily had grieved and then moved on.

'You didn't stay in touch?'

'We tried. *I* tried. I'd write to her—letters at first, then emails. Sometimes she'd reply and sometimes not. Eventually my letters started coming back to me and the emails started bouncing. She'd drop me a line occasionally, but the message was pretty clear. She was happier without me in her life—I think I was a reminder of what she'd lost.'

'But when she was really in trouble it was you she came to. She must trust you—love you—a lot.'

'I've thought about that. A lot, actually. And done a little bit of reading. I'm not sure that was why she left Rosie with me. Perhaps it was just because we're related. Maybe she didn't want Rosie in the care system. Hadn't completely decided what she wanted for her. Perhaps she thought that if she left her with me and changed her mind she could get her back. It didn't matter *who* I was—it only mattered that we had the same mother.'

'Oh, Lily.' He reached for her hand, turned it under his and threaded their fingers together. 'I can't believe that's true. I think she knows just what a special person you are—that you'll take care of her daughter without even questioning it. That you'll give her the happy childhood Helen remembers having.'

'Perhaps…'

Lily smiled, though he could see that there were tears gathering in her eyes.

'So, what's happening with…?' He wasn't sure what to call it. The Rosie Situation? 'With your guardianship? Have you had any update from the social worker?'

Lily explained the situation—that it was looking more and more likely that she would become Rosie's permanent guardian—and he tried hard to pin down how he felt. Tried to judge the proportions of fear, trepidation, excitement and affection that seemed constantly to battle for supremacy in his heart.

He wasn't sure that he could admit it to Lily, but maybe he could admit it to himself. In those early days, when he'd first been getting to know her, despite her fierce protection of Rosie, he'd managed to convince himself that her guardianship would only be temporary. That he could let himself fantasise because one day Rosie's mother would return, Lily would be a simple aunt again, and the baby's presence in her life would fade to the background. Then there would be nothing to come between him and Lily.

Now he knew that wasn't going to be the case. And it was too late—way too late—to stop falling for her. But what would happen when he hit the ground? He tried to imagine that life and it still filled him with a cold dread. He wanted to embrace all the possibilities that a relationship with Lily might bring, but when he allowed himself to think about the certainties of it he was filled with fear.

He watched her across the table and saw how she became shy under his gaze, dipping her eyes and concentrating far more than she needed to on sipping her coffee. She still wasn't sure of him—and with good reason. She deserved a lover who had no reservations, who was ready for a commitment to her, and he wasn't sure that was him—not yet.

For the first time he questioned whether he'd done the right thing in inviting her to Rome, whether that was leading her on—but, no. Rome was different. It was a way for them to get to know each other better, not a promise.

Three days to plan and she was just thinking about waxing her legs *now*? She glanced at her watch. Not a hope. Nic would be back from work in half an hour, her hair was still wet, and dinner was at least an hour off going in the oven. In fact most of it was still in the supermarket. Rosie was overdue a bath and it was veering dangerously close to being past her bedtime.

Where had three days gone? And how was it that she found it so impossible to do something as simple as cook dinner? Since the moment Rosie had turned up all she'd wanted to do was be a good mum…aunt… sister. To make a family for Rosie and for herself. But it seemed as if every time she thought she had it sorted she found herself in the middle of a disaster of her own making. They sneaked up on her and were suddenly right in front of her eyes.

She heard his key in the lock just as she had Rosie stripped off and ready for her bath. Cursing his bad timing, she wrapped the baby in a towel and carried her with her as she went to the door. Her plan had been to have an uninterrupted bedtime routine for Rosie this evening—to have her down and sleeping before Nic got home, so they could enjoy dinner together before heading off on their trip first thing tomorrow. But Rosie had slept late this afternoon. So she'd fed late and played late. And now—almost—she was being bathed late.

And then Nic was there, and in a moment her stress fell away. The width of his smile created fine lines of pleasure around his eyes as he leaned in to kiss her without hesitation.

'Hi,' she breathed, letting her eyes shut and enjoying that simple pleasure.

When she opened them she realised that the man was not only absurdly good-looking and radiating charm, he was also brandishing carrier bags and a bottle of red wine. It was almost enough to have her crying into Rosie's towel.

'I've interrupted bathtime,' he said, pointing out the obvious. 'I thought I'd leave a bit early and make a start on dinner. Couldn't wait to get home to you, actually, kick off our holiday tonight instead of in the morning.'

There were no games, no subtexts.

'You ladies get back to it, and I'll have dinner ready when you're done.'

Lily opened her mouth to argue: she'd promised him dinner and wine on the table when he got home—a small way of thanking him for the holiday.

'You're a hero,' she told him, meeting his honesty with her own. 'A genuine, real-life hero. Are you sure you don't mind?'

'My pleasure,' he said, already opening drawers and cupboards and emptying the carrier bags onto the worktop.

She shut the bathroom door behind her and checked the temperature of the water, smiling to herself when she found it was still warm enough—no time wasted there. She slid Rosie into the bath and soaped her, distracting her with bubbles as she washed her hair and ran a flannel over her face, rubbing away the last few remnants of milk.

And as she went through their bathtime routine her mind strayed to the man in the kitchen, wondering what his expectations were for this evening...wondering how well prepared he had come. Had he replayed their conversations as often as she had? Had he wondered when would be the right time to take their relationship further? When 'slow' would become impossible?

And what would that next step mean?

Of course she was hoping that they would make love, but doing something like that didn't come without strings attached for Lily. For her it would be a commitment—but did Nic feel the same?

She left the bathroom with Rosie all clean and fresh and tucked into her pyjamas, wishing that she looked half as good herself. Unfortunately she knew that she looked little less than crazed. And, while she couldn't *see* any stains on her T-shirt, the laws of parenting probability meant that there had to be one there somewhere.

When she reached the kitchen Nic was cooking up a storm, but everything seemed to be perfectly under control. What did *that* feel like? She tried to remember a time when her life had felt like her own, when she had been confident that she knew exactly what she was doing and that she was doing a good job. Some time in the haze her pre-Rosie life had become, she assumed.

The paradox plagued her. It was the time when she most wanted to pull her family together, to prove that she could be mother and sister and aunt with the best of them, and it all seemed entirely out of her hands. The more she fought to show that she could do this—

be the matriarch, hold it all together—the faster things spun around her.

Nic stopped stirring the sauce on the hob for long enough to steal a quick kiss, and Lily plonked herself on a stool at the breakfast bar, watching him for a moment.

The kettle clicked and she noticed the bottle and tin of formula standing next to it, ready to be made up.

'I figured if the grown-ups are hungry then Rosie might well be too,' he said.

He'd dropped the wooden spoon and now stood leaning against the counter, hands in pockets. Lily looked at him closely, observing the slight change in his posture, the tension that had sneaked into his body and was holding him a little stiffer. Still trying, still struggling, she deduced. But he kept coming back for more. Not only that, he'd come carrying dinner and was helping to make bottles. She couldn't judge him for still finding things hard: he had earned her respect for trying despite that.

'So, what's for dinner?' Lily asked, placing Rosie in her bouncy chair and making up the bottle.

'Not very exciting, I'm afraid. Gnocchi, pancetta, cream sauce, a bit of salad—I've brought a little of Italy home with me.'

'You are the consummate domestic goddess,' she told him with a smile, hoping that it would cover the twinge of—what? Resentment that that had been *her* role, *her* talent, until she was faced with her first real challenge?

He must see how much she was struggling. Must have guessed that she wouldn't be able to put dinner on the table for him. Not that she was even *trying* for

Stepford-wife-style Cordon Bleu cuisine. She'd have settled for managing to get oven chips ready.

Something of her fears must have shown on her face, because Nic pushed himself up from the counter, hands no longer in his pockets. Instead they were reaching for her waist and pulling her into him. Suddenly emotional, Lily kept her eyes lowered, not wanting to look up and show him how upset she was that she was *still* not getting this right.

'I'm sorry if I did the wrong thing,' he said. 'I only wanted us to have a nice relaxed night. I've been looking forward to this, and the last thing I wanted was to cause you more work, more stress.'

He palmed her cheek and she turned into the warmth of his skin instinctively, and then slowly looked up.

'It wasn't a criticism, or a judgement.' He leaned in further, and pressed a quick kiss to her lips. 'You're doing an amazing job with Rosie, and I just wanted to do my bit.'

Another kiss and her limbs started to feel loose and languid, her body like a gel that wanted to mould to him.

Nic pulled away slightly and rested his forehead on hers. 'I've been thinking about that all day. *Every* day, actually,' he admitted. 'The least you can do after keeping me awake three nights in a row is let me make you dinner.'

She smiled. He was good—she'd give him that.

'Thank you,' she said. 'It's a lovely thought. And, for the record, I *might* have thought about you too. Just once or twice.'

He broke into a grin at that, and swooped a kiss onto her cheek.

True to his word, once Rosie was in bed Nic set two places at the dining table, lit the candles, served Lily an enormous portion of gnocchi and filled up their wine glasses.

'This is incredible,' Lily said as she sat down.

'I wouldn't get carried away,' Nic told her with a self-effacing smile. 'It's just gnocchi and sauce.'

'It's gnocchi, sauce, good wine and better company. It's like being in an alien land, and it's divine.'

'Well, I can drink to that,' Nic said, raising his glass in a toast and clinking it against hers. 'So, what have I missed?'

He'd been in the office until late the last couple of nights, making sure that everything was in place for his trip.

'Well, I have two big pieces of news—Rosie lifted her head for the first time today, and then I thought she smiled at me...but it turned out to be gas. It's been hectic!' She laughed, wondering what he'd make of her day.

'I'm sure it *was* a smile,' Nic said. 'Most likely because she's got such a wonderful aunt to take care of her.'

Lily smiled, bashful, acknowledging his praise with a blush, if not his knowledge of development milestones.

'And did you get the work done that you needed to?' Nic asked.

'Only just,' Lily admitted. 'But it's done now. I've not got anything else lined up for the next few weeks so I can concentrate on Rosie. I'm sure I'll miss it soon enough, and want something to challenge me. A *different* sort of challenge,' she clarified, just in case he'd missed the point that Rosie was an Olympic-sized challenge in herself. 'I'm only going to take on small commissions for now, but it's good to keep my eye in... keep my skills ticking over.'

'I'm impressed,' Nic told her.

Lily shrugged off the compliment.

'No, seriously.' He reached out for her hand as she tried again to brush off his words. 'I'm actually in awe—I can't even think how you find time in the day for it all.'

Lily laughed. 'Oh, it's easy. You just forget the laundry, and mopping the floor, and filing your nails, and...'

'And focus on what's important. Like I said, you're incredible.'

Lily held her hands up and shook her head. 'Okay, that's officially as much as I can take. We're going to have to change the subject or I'll become unbearable. What about you? Did you get everything sorted that you needed to?'

'Everything's taken care of. All we have to do tomorrow is get in the car when it shows up.'

And then make some pretty huge decisions about their future.

That bit didn't need saying, but after the careful way they'd spent the last few days she thought they both knew that that was what Rome was really going to be about. About finding out what they wanted to be to each other. What risks they were prepared to take and what hopes they were going to nurture.

They lingered over their coffee, neither of them making a move to go to bed—alone or otherwise.

But as Lily stifled a yawn Nic stood and cleared

away the last few dishes. 'You look done in,' he said over his shoulder. 'And I'm ready to turn in. I guess we should call it a night.'

So he wasn't going to suggest it. Well, she shouldn't be surprised. She was the one who had insisted on 'slower' the last time things had got out of hand. The ball was really in her court now.

'If you're sure…' Lily said, aiming the lilt in her voice at pure temptation.

But he didn't look as if he was wavering.

'We've an early start tomorrow,' he said, but the tense lines of his forehead told her he was struggling to do the noble thing. 'It's probably best if we call it a night.'

'Of course.' Lily stood up, but the slight shake of her legs revealed her hidden emotions.

Nic stood too, and rested his hands lightly on her waist. 'It's not just that…' he told her.

He surprised her with his sudden honesty. But she supposed they *were* trying to see if they had any hope of a future together. If they couldn't talk to each other, be honest with each other now, at the outset, then what hope did they have?

'Don't think for a second that it's because I don't want to take you to bed—that I haven't been imagining it every day.' He was rewarded with a flash of colour in her cheeks, and he traced the colour with his fingertips and then his lips. 'But once we take that step I'm yours, Lily. Everything I am will belong to you. We both have a lot to think about…a lot to decide… Let's not rush. We have as much time as we want and as we need.'

She nodded, the smile on her lips now genuine, if a little wary.

He walked her to her bedroom door and grabbed her hands as she reached for the handle. 'Still time to say a proper goodnight,' he said, pulling her close and running the backs of his fingers down the soft skin of her arm. From there he rested his hands on her waist, until there was nothing between them but their heavy breaths.

He dipped his head and brushed his lips gently against hers, testing. But she smiled against him, yielding to him for a moment and then drawing back, yielding and drawing back—until one of his hands was at the nape of her neck, the other was clamped at her waist, and he was backing her slowly against the hard wood of the door. He was desperate for more, to feel her giving herself wholly to him. For her to stop her teasing and give him everything she was...to demand all of him in return.

When she opened her mouth to him and touched his tongue with hers he let out a low groan, his hand fisting behind her back. He leaned back and smiled at her flushed face, laughed a little breathily.

'Oh, you're good,' he said. 'Really, *really* good. But I'll see you in the morning.'

She nodded, biting her lip.

'If you're sure...' she said, with a minxy little smile. 'I guess I'll see you then.'

'I've never been less sure about anything in my life,' he said, and his voice had a little gravel in it as he tried to pull her closer again.

But her hands had found his chest and were pushing

gently. 'No, I won't take advantage,' she said. Then, more seriously, 'You're right. I want us to be sure.'

He nodded, reason starting to return to him as the blood returned to his brain. 'So I'll see you in the morning?'

'I'll be waiting.'

CHAPTER TWELVE

LILY LIFTED THE delicate espresso cup to her lips and savoured the full, rich flavour as it touched her lips. Nic hadn't made it up to the hotel suite yet, but the smell had been so tempting she'd not been able to wait. There was a lot of that going on at the moment, she realised, still not sure what to make of Nic's decision last night to go to his own bed—alone.

It was gentlemanly of him, and deep down of course she knew that it had been the right decision. There was too much at stake, too many ways they could get hurt, for them to rush a decision like that. But... But nothing. The fact that she'd been desperate for him since the moment he'd left her last night shouldn't be a part of their decision-making process.

Well, if you were going to try and temper a girl's disappointment a suite in a five-star hotel in the Piazza di Spagna was a good start. She wandered around the living area of the suite now, stopping to admire the artwork adorning the walls and the artfully placed side tables. It was exquisite—unlike anywhere she'd seen before, never mind stayed. Rosie was still fast asleep in her carrycot, as she had been since they had left the airport. True to his word, Nic had arranged everything they needed, and they had been whisked from house to car to airport to hotel with barely a whimper from Rosie and barely any intervention from her.

There were two doors leading off the living area and she crossed to the one on her left, still a little awestruck by her surroundings. She tried the handle to the door and found it unlocked. She nudged the door open, feeling as if she was about to be caught snooping. An enormous bed—king-size? Emperor? Bigger?—dominated the room, draped with rich silky curtains and topped with crisp white sheets. Her room? she wondered. Or Nic's? Then she spotted the cot in the corner and her question was answered. Her room. And Rosie's. For a moment she wished she'd wake, so that she could share her excitement with her, waltz her around the suite and wow her with all the finery she couldn't yet understand.

But she'd woken her early once before, and that hadn't exactly gone well. She took another sip of her coffee, wondering where Nic had got to. He'd wanted a quick word with the concierge—that was all he'd told her as he'd encouraged her to go straight up to the room. The coffee had been awaiting them, along with fruit and pastries. She'd intended to wait for Nic to arrive before she indulged further, but now she questioned that decision. Well, if he was going to leave her here, he had only himself to blame.

She'd just selected the lightest pastry from the platter when the door opened and she was caught redhanded.

'Glad to see you're settling in,' Nic said, tossing his carry-on bag onto the couch and crossing to the table to grab a pastry for himself. 'These are incredible,' he said, devouring the morsel in a few quick bites. 'Worth flying out for these alone.'

'The coffee's not bad,' Lily said, with a smile to show she was joking. 'And the room's just about adequate.'

He surprised her with a quick kiss to the lips.

'I'm glad you like it,' he said. 'I've not stayed here before, but I've heard great things.'

'Not your usual haunt?'

'No, I normally stay somewhere a little more…rustic. But I promised you girls an adventure in Rome, and I don't think that Nonna Lucia's *pensione* really fits the bill.'

'Nonna Lucia?'

'She looks after me when I'm here—seems to rather like having someone to fuss over.'

'Won't she be offended that we're not staying with her?'

'Actually, I already ran it by her. I knew she'd be offended if she found out somehow. I explained that I was bringing a friend with me, and that we'd need some more space, and she nodded in a very knowing way and said, "Of course." I think maybe I've given her the wrong idea…'

Lily laughed, delighted with this description. 'Will I get to meet her?'

'If you'd like to. I know that we'd be welcome any time. I was just speaking to the concierge about dinner, and he was making some enquiries, but if you'd rather—?'

She thought back to how well a fancy meal had gone last time and didn't hesitate. 'I'd love to. I'd like to see what your life is like when you're travelling,' she said. 'If it's not all five-star suites and divine coffee.'

'Oh, Nonna's coffee is second to none,' he reassured her. 'I'll call her to arrange tonight—if you're sure you don't want to go somewhere more…?'

'I'm sure,' she told him.

'Well, that's dinner sorted, then. What do you fancy doing in the meantime? Settle in here a little longer? Or head out for some sightseeing?'

She glanced around the room, caught sight of the bed in the other room, and suddenly lost her nerve. 'Let's go out,' she said. 'I don't want to waste a minute of this trip.'

'Brilliant,' Nic replied. 'What about Rosie? I don't want to wake her if she's not ready, but Rome's not known for being pushchair-friendly. There should be a baby carrier around here somewhere, though.'

Torn, Lily tried to decide what to do. She didn't want to wake the baby, and risk her grumping through the afternoon, but the whole of Rome was waiting for them and she couldn't wait to see it. She glanced at her watch, wondering how much longer she would sleep. Perhaps another half an hour…

'What about this?' Nic said. 'We head up to the roof terrace—I can carry the carrycot. We take in Rome from above, and once she wakes we hit the town.'

'Perfect.'

An hour later Rosie was awake, looking from Nic to Lily, wondering who was most likely to give her attention and a cuddle. Lily got to her first, reaching down to the carrycot, which Nic had tucked into a shady corner, and scooping Lily into her arms.

'What do you think she makes of it so far?' Nic asked.

Lily laughed. 'She's been asleep since we left the airport! But I'm sure she'll love it as much as I will.'

'Shall we dig out that baby carrier and find out?'

They wandered out from the hotel with Rosie strapped to Lily's front, and the heat of the summer afternoon hit them hard. The roof terrace had been shaded, with creeping plants over gazebos, but out on the street there was nothing more than her wide-brimmed hat to protect her and Rosie's pale skin from the burn of the sun.

'You okay?' Nic asked.

'I didn't realise how hot it is,' she told him, fanning her face. 'The terrace was so shady.'

'Let's keep off the main streets, then,' Nic said, taking her hand and leading her down one of the winding side streets that led off the main drag.

She breathed out a sigh of relief as they walked along in the shadow of the buildings, the blare of car horns and buzzing mopeds fading behind them.

'Better?' he asked.

'This is lovely.' She squeezed his hand as they passed a sleepy-looking restaurant, its owners still at their siesta, perhaps.

'So, what do you want to see? The Colosseum? The Vatican? Trevi Fountain? We can start wherever you like.'

'They all sound nice…' Lily started.

'But…?'

'But this is nice too,' she finished, smiling up at him as he pulled her to a stop.

The lane had meandered past delicious-smelling

bakeries and traditional-looking *trattorie* until it had become no more than a sun-dappled alleyway, with apartments on either side, their balconies spilling colour and texture as flowers hung down from the walls.

'Seeing Rome like this…it's something I never really imagined. But what I'm most looking forward to about this trip—' She bit her lip, looking for the confidence she needed to make this confession. Then she remembered his honesty the night before, and knew that she owed him nothing less than the truth. 'I want to spend it with *you*. Whether we do that at the Colosseum or here—and frankly this is the prettiest little street I've ever seen—doesn't seem that important.'

She watched him carefully, wondering what he had made of her words. The expression on his face left her none the wiser. Then, instead of speaking, he dropped his head and his lips landed on hers, soft and gentle. Their warmth, his taste, was becoming deliciously familiar. With each time they kissed she felt more comfortable, and that heat in her belly grew, leaving her wanting more and more. The backs of his fingers brushed the skin of her neck, her collarbone, and it was only as she instinctively moved closer that she remembered that Rosie was there between them—physically as well as emotionally.

With a smile, she pulled away. Nic met her gaze and held it for a few seconds, then, with his eyes on hers until the last minute, he dropped his head slowly and kissed Rosie on the top of her head.

He straightened, meeting Lily's eyes with an intense look. 'I want to make you promises, Lily. I want to tell you that I'll be everything you deserve. But I can't.'

Lily froze, not wanting to break the intensity of the moment, knowing that Nic had more to say.

'I've been here before, Lily. I've tried to be the family man, tried to support a partner and a family, and it didn't end well.'

'Nic, you can't blame yourself for what happened to Max.'

'If that was all I had to feel guilty about…' His voice was filled with anguish and his eyes were faraway, lost in the past. 'It wasn't just Max I let down, Lily. It was Clare. After what happened she needed me. Needed her fiancé to be there for her, to talk to her about what had just happened. To try and find a way to get past it. I couldn't do it.'

'Nic, everyone copes in different ways.'

'That's no excuse. She needed something from me—something very simple—and I couldn't give it to her. It was *my* fault that our relationship broke down after Max died. *My* fault that we fell apart when she thought she was already at rock bottom. You need to know this, Lily, before you decide where you want this to go. You need to know that if—God forbid—it all goes wrong, and you lose Rosie, I can't promise to be there for you. You deserve someone who can.'

Lily stood and stared at him for a moment, and shivered even in the thirty-degree heat. This was what he'd been hiding, then—this was the shadow she'd glimpsed and never understood.

'Nic, I can't believe that it was all your responsibility. I'm sure you tried your hardest.'

'You're right—I did,' he said, his voice steadier now. 'I tried my hardest and it wasn't enough. I like you—a hell of a lot. I don't want to keep fighting it. But if we're doing this you deserve to know what you're getting into.'

Lily placed her hands either side of his face and reached up on tiptoes to press a kiss to his lips. 'Nic, I trust you. You've done more for me these past few weeks than just about anyone else I can think of. You can say what you like, but if there's a crisis heading my way I know I want you there with me. Nothing you tell me about your past is going to change that.'

His face softened slightly, and she let herself hope for a moment that she'd got through to him.

'I want to do this,' she went on. 'I want us to take these feelings seriously. I'm not talking about sitting back and seeing what happens. I'm talking about working hard to make each other happy.'

He closed his eyes for a brief moment, and then leaned forward and kissed her quickly, sweetly.

'Can we walk?' he asked, keeping hold of her hand as he started moving again, towards the arch of sunlight at the end of the lane.

She said nothing, knowing that he was still working through his feelings.

'I don't know how I thought I could stop myself,' he said at last.

Lily bit her lip, wondering whether she was supposed to understand that enigmatic sentence.

'Falling for you, I mean.'

She risked a glance up at him and saw that it wasn't only tears that had made his eyes bright. There was a light there—something bright and shining. A smile that hadn't quite reached his lips yet but was lighting his face in a way that she recognised.

'You're sure that you don't want to get out now? Because I'd understand.'

'I'm going nowhere, Nic. But are *you* sure you're ready for his? Because I come as a package deal, remember?'

'I know that. I don't know how I thought I could fall for you without falling for Rosie as well, but I tried—and I failed. I want you for everything you are. And that includes the way you care for Rosie.'

'And you're okay with that?'

By his own admission he'd been fighting it, and fighting it hard. How could he be so sure now?

'I'm not going to lie and say that it doesn't hurt. Sometimes when I look at Rosie, growing all bonny and fat and healthy, it does make me think of my son and everything that he and I missed. But it's too late, Lily. She's a part of you, and I feel like she's becoming a part of me too.'

She was falling for him too—she knew that. The feelings that had been growing these past few weeks had only one possible end point. She smiled up at him and saw relief wash over his features as she reached up to kiss him, pressing her lips hard against his, trying to show with her body what she couldn't find the words to express.

They wandered the city hand in hand for another hour or two, with Rosie alternately snoozing or cooing from her baby carrier. The Trevi Fountain was magical, even packed with tourists, and the coffee in a little *piazza* café was hot and strong—but it was the light in Nic's eyes that made the afternoon perfect...the way he sneaked touches and kisses when they found themselves alone, the promise in his eyes and his body and the feelings for her that he had already declared.

When Rosie began to grumble, a little tired, they headed back to the hotel. Once she was tucked into her carrycot, all ready to be clipped into her pram when they went out for dinner, Lily headed out into the living room, a little nervous to be alone in a hotel room with Nic after all that had been said, all that had been re-solved between them. She found Nic by the sofa, pour-ing glasses of something deliciously cold and sparkling.

'Something to start our evening off with a bit of a pop,' he said as she approached. 'Nonna's expecting us in about an hour, but if you need a bit more time...?'

Lily glanced at her watch. 'I think Rosie will sleep for another two hours at least, so as long as we don't have to disturb her that should be perfect. Just enough time to shower and change.'

Nic raised an eyebrow. 'You know you look per-fect as you are.'

Lily had to laugh. He must have it bad, she thought, knowing full well that there was formula on her T-shirt and that she'd perspired more than was strictly lady-like during their walk.

'Don't give me that look,' Nic admonished. 'You could go out without doing a thing and be the envy of every woman in Rome.'

'Flattery will get you everywhere.'

She said the words without thinking, with a chuckle and a sip of her wine. But when she lowered her glass and met Nic's eyes it was to find them full of the pas-sion they'd barely been suppressing all afternoon.

'An hour?' she asked, thinking of everything they could do in that time—all the possibilities open to them now they had admitted what they were feeling for one another.

'An hour's not nearly enough time for everything I've been thinking of,' Nic said, his face full of promise. 'And I think I might want a good meal first...'

Now, *that* sounded encouraging: the sort of evening one needed to carbo-load for.

Nic crossed the room until he was by her side and took the glass of Prosecco from her hands, placing it carefully on a side table before taking her in his arms. One hand sneaked up her spine and rested at the nape of her neck, the other settled in the small of her back, pulling her close against his hard body.

She let out a breathless sigh, wondering how they were meant to make it out of this hotel room without things getting out of hand. Reaching up, she cupped Nic's face in her palm, enjoying the rasp of his stubble against the smooth pads of her fingers, the hardness of his jaw and the softness of his cheeks. When her fingertips found his mouth, he kissed first one finger then the next.

With her thumb she explored the fullness of his bottom lip and the cleft of his chin. When she felt she knew every inch of his face she stretched up on tiptoes and traced the path of her fingers with her lips. Butterfly kisses that teased and promised more, but she wanted to savour every moment. They had all night to explore one another. And while there were parts of him she was desperate to know better, she was determined to make the most of every minute with him. Not to rush a single second of the experience.

For so many years she had waited, wondering when it would be her turn to have a family of her own. Now that she had found it she wanted to remember every moment, appreciate every sensation. Finally her lips found his, and she brushed a gentle kiss across his top lip, and then the bottom. Nic's fingers flexed behind her head, twisting strands of hair but not pressing her closer, not taking what she wasn't ready to give.

His body was strung like a bow, and with every caress she felt more tension in his muscles, more possession in his hold at the small of her back. When her thumb brushed the sensitive skin behind his ear his mouth opened in a groan, and she could resist temptation no longer.

She explored the warmth of his mouth, tested the limits of his restraint, measuring the desperation in his hold. The man was determined—she had to give him that. He'd said they should wait, and it seemed that wait they would. But she had only just started exploring, and at a guess they still had a good forty minutes before they had to leave.

When her tongue touched his, the fire she'd banked in his veins burst free. With the passion she'd seen in him earlier he possessed her mouth, his hands roaming now, rather than settling her against him. One dropped to the curve of her buttock, alternately caressing, exploring and pressing her against him. The other moved from nape to collarbone, and then lower. When his thumb brushed against her breast she moaned into his mouth, sure that at last she was going to get everything she had been fantasising about for the past month.

But he broke off their kiss, moved fractionally backwards until there was a good inch of space between them.

'You...are an absolute...siren.'

She gave him her most minxy smile as he struggled to speak, his voice ragged and breathless.

'And I am going to make you pay for that later. But for now a shower—a cold one, I suggest—and then let's go to dinner.'

'Spoilsport.'

But she couldn't be disappointed really—not when she'd seen the effect she'd had on him, and now knew better than ever what she had in store when they got home. Waiting had done nothing to temper their passion before now, and another couple of hours could only make them more ardent.

She hadn't known what to expect of Nonna's *pensione*, and at times when they'd passed by the brightly lit windows of the Trastevere area she'd feared that they would find themselves in either a fine dining restaurant, where she would feel awkward and out of place, or one of the *trattorie* designed to trap tourists—all plastic vegetables and fake bonhomie. But when she walked through the door of Nonna's her fears instantly vanished.

This was neither pretentious nor tacky. It was—almost instantly—*home*. The moment they walked through the door she found herself enfolded in a generous matronly bosom and kissed on both her cheeks. Nic had pushed the pram across the challenging Roman cobbles and was now wrestling it up the front steps, leaving Lily undefended against this friendly onslaught.

'*Bella*, you are the friend of Nico. You are so very welcome tonight,' she said, kissing her again on both cheeks.

'Signora Lucia, it's a pleasure to meet you.'

'*Tsch*, you must call me Nonna—like my Nico.'

At that, Nic finally made it up the steps with the carrycot, and Nonna's attention was lost completely as she peered into the carrycot and spoke in a loud whisper.

'And your *bambina*. She is a beauty. Nico told me this and now I see. *Bella*—like her *mamma*.'

Lily blushed, both from the compliment and the mix-up. But she was distracted from correcting her by the sensation of Nic's arm settling across her shoulders. The gesture was comforting, possessive, natural, and she turned into the warmth of his body.

Nonna bent over the pram again and Lily held her breath, hoping that the baby wouldn't wake up and fret through their dinner, but Nonna only stroked her cheek and muttered a string of Italian babytalk.

'Come—I have lovely table for this lovely family,' she said, and she stood and led them to a table set for two, tucked in a private corner. A candle flickered on the crisply ironed cloth and Nonna pulled up a bench for them to set the carrycot on.

'When she wakes up you call me and I come see her, okay?'

Lily was filled with such a sense of warmth and welcome that she felt tears welling behind her eyes.

'You didn't correct her,' Nic said, his voice carefully casual, and Lily knew he was referring to Nonna's use of the word *'mamma'*.

'I didn't really know what to say…how to explain… Anyway, you distracted me.'

'Me? What did I do?'

'That casual arm around the shoulder. I couldn't think for a minute.'

'An *arm*? After what you tried earlier, you couldn't think because of an arm?'

She laughed. 'Well, maybe the arm brought back a memory or two,' she clarified. 'What must she think of me? A mum with a new baby, out for dinner with a man who's not the father. Wait—she knows you're not Rosie's dad, right?'

Nic took a sip of the Prosecco that Nonna had poured when she'd shown them to their table. 'She knows. And I think it's as clear to you as it is to me that she already adores you both. She doesn't care about the details of how Rosie came into our life any more than I do. She can see that you love her like a mother.'

'But I'm not, am I? Rosie and I have spent all this time getting to know each other, trying to see how our lives can fit together, and it could all have been for nothing. We could get back to London and find that everything's changed. I could lose Rosie—and then what?'

'First,' Nic said, pressing her hand into his, 'I'm sure that whatever happens with Helen you're never going to lose Rosie completely. I think that your sister loves you, and loves Rosie, and she knows that you're both better off with each other in your lives. If Helen was to turn up tomorrow and take Rosie away—we'd try and cope…together.'

She took a deep breath, forcing her body to relax. She wasn't sure where the sudden surge of fear and apprehension had come from. Perhaps it was inevitable, she thought. With things going so well in one part of her life now that she and Nic seemed to be finally finding their way towards happiness, some other aspect of it had to fall apart. Surely this was too good to be true—

a kind, handsome man, a romantic getaway in Rome, a beautiful niece whom she thought of as a daughter...

'Are you okay?' Nic asked, concern creasing his forehead.

Lily nodded, determined to throw off this sense that it was all going too well. It would be unforgivable to ruin this evening just because of some strange sense of foreboding. There was no such thing as karma. The universe wasn't going to punish her for being happy with Nic by taking Rosie away.

'Better than okay,' she said, and after glancing around to check that no one was looking she sneaked a quick kiss. 'Sorry—just a wobble. I guess I'm still not quite sure what I am to Rosie—mum or aunty. It's going to take a little time to get used to what other people might think.'

'It doesn't matter what anyone else thinks. What matters is that you and Rosie are happy.'

'Well, we are. Blissfully,' she replied honestly. 'This has been just a perfect day, Nic. I don't know how to thank you.'

'Oh, well, I can think of an idea or two,' he replied with a cheeky grin. 'But there's no need to thank me. The pleasure of your company for today is thanks enough.'

She smiled back, and then turned her head as Rosie stirred in her cot.

'Will she wake soon?' Nic asked.

'Maybe just for a feed, but she normally goes back to sleep after a bit of a cuddle.'

'She's changing so quickly,' Nic said, watching her as she wriggled awake.

Lily reached out and touched his arm, knowing that

he was thinking of Max. But he wasn't frowning when she looked up at him. Instead he had the same soppy, dopey expression that she normally wore when she was talking about Rosie.

'It's amazing to watch her, you know. I feel very lucky to be a part of it.'

'We feel pretty lucky too,' Lily told him. 'I know how hard you've found it, but having you here for me these past few weeks…I'm not sure what I would have done without you.'

'You'd have done fine,' he told her. 'But you're right. Some things are better when you can share them with someone.'

'I'm glad you said that,' Lily said, trying to lighten the mood. 'Because I have to nip to the bathroom. Are you okay with her for a minute?'

Before today she'd have watched him carefully, trying to judge his reaction to the thought of being left alone with Rosie. But now she trusted him to tell her what he was feeling. To tell her if she was asking too much.

'Of course.'

He pulled her down for a brief kiss as she passed him, and she was filled with a sense of warmth and well-being.

When she returned from the bathroom it was to find Nonna seated at their table with the baby on her lap drinking from her bottle and lapping up the attention. She moved to stand beside Nic, but when she arrived Nonna stood, offering her her seat back.

'I cannot resist such a beautiful baby,' she told Lily. 'Nico tells me she's hungry and I find myself sitting like this. I think I'll never put her down. She is so wonderful I keep her for ever.'

'I hope she wasn't causing trouble?' Lily replied.

'Not at all,' Nic reassured her. 'Nonna just couldn't resist. I hope that's okay?'

She told him that of course it was, and when a shout emerged from the kitchen both Nic and Lily held out their hands to take the baby.

Lily could almost feel the weight of her in her hands, but Nonna passed her to Nic instead, and Lily was left watching as Rosie settled happily into his arms.

'Ah... Daddy's girl, I think you say. I must go back to the kitchen now, but if she cries I will come straight away and take her. You two need a quiet dinner. Lots of talking,' Nonna commented sagely, before bustling in the direction of the kitchen.

Lily watched as Nonna walked away, her mouth slightly open in surprise.

'What can I say?' Nick commented with a laugh. 'She's quite a force. I'm always too terrified to argue with her. I think she's crazy about you, though.'

'Crazy, perhaps,' Lily agreed. 'You didn't even flinch,' she said, 'when she said Daddy.'

He took a deep breath, and Lily knew that he was working up to something.

'You know that I've never thought about having any more children, but when Nonna said that my initial reaction wasn't horror or fear. Instead I thought about how much I liked being a dad. How I might like that again one day.'

Lily couldn't speak. She'd paused with her glass halfway to her lips and now found that she couldn't move. Was he talking about starting a family? With *her*? For a fleeting second she could see it—the three of them, the four of them…God, maybe even more—but then a gentle panic started to nag. Things were moving too quickly, surely, to be talking about this now.

'I didn't mean right away,' he said, interpreting her expression. 'I just meant that one day I think I might want it again. And I've never thought that before.'

Lily finally took the sip of her wine, buying herself a few more moments to calm herself.

'I'm glad if me and Rosie have helped.'

The words sounded trite, even to her, and she wondered how she had wandered into this politeness—wondered at the distance that seemed to have sprung from nowhere.

She *wanted* Nic to want a family. Deep down, she wanted Nic to be part of *her* family. Surely that was what it was all about? Getting to know someone, exploring a relationship. She'd always envisaged marriage, a husband. Equal partners. But now she wondered if she'd really thought about what that would mean. She'd never considered that her family growing meant that she was a smaller constituent part. Since Rosie had landed on her doorstep she'd been everything to her, and it was going to take some getting used to if she wanted Rosie to share her affections with someone else.

She wanted to show that she could do it herself. Wanted to build a family and keep it close. What did it say about her if she couldn't do it? If one day she wasn't the person Rosie turned to?

Their starters arrived and she ate, watching Nic and Rosie, despising the curl of jealousy she couldn't deny, despite the fact that she knew it was ridiculous. She pasted on a smile, not wanting Nic to guess that her thoughts were still dwelling on Rosie's willingness to go to him. It was just one bottle, she reminded herself. Not a competition, or anything.

Rosie finished her bottle with an enthusiastic gurgle, and the familiar sound broke Lily's tense mood.

'Do you want to take her?' Nic asked, looking a little hesitant.

Well, maybe she hadn't hidden her worries as well as she had hoped.

'You cuddle a little longer if you want to,' Lily said—and meant it. How could she begrudge these two some time together? Rosie deserved this full-on attention—deserved the full force of Nic's smile and the warmth and comfort of his arms. There was a connection between the two of them, Lily acknowledged, and she was glad of it.

'So, did you tell your sister about this little excursion?' Lily asked, finding it a little strange that Kate hadn't called for a run-down of the latest developments.

'Well, it all happened so fast...' Nic said with an expression of insincere innocence. 'I only just managed to tell her that I had to go away. There simply wasn't time to tell her that you two were coming as well.'

'By which I take it to mean you were too scared to confess?'

He laughed. 'The woman's capacity for inappropriate questions knows no bounds,' he said, holding up his hands in defeat. 'It takes a stronger man than I am to volunteer for that sort of grilling.'

'Oh, gee, thanks—so you leave me to handle the fall-out when we get back?'

'Is there a chance that she might just conveniently never find out?' Nic asked, looking hopeful.

'Not any chance, I'm afraid. You're right—she sniffs these things out, and if she ever discovered that I'd kept it from her there'd be hell to pay. *So* not worth it. She has to forgive *you*—you're her brother. If I held back on her I'm not sure that she'd ever take me back.'

Nic laughed. 'I'm not so sure about that. Some of the lectures I've endured—I think she's rather more concerned with you than with me.'

Lily could imagine. Kate was protective of her friends at the best of times, but since Rosie had come on the scene, and Lily's life had become at least twenty-seven thousand times more complicated, she'd stepped things up a level. Lily had tried telling her that she didn't need to worry so much, but Kate seemed determined to be the gatekeeper to Lily's life.

Conversation flowed like wine through the rest of their dinner, and by the time Nonna was cooing over Rosie as she brought over their coffees the earlier tension had disappeared completely. Well, not *disappeared*, exactly. It had morphed into a different sort of tension.

The sort that drew her close to Nic's side as he manoeuvred the pram back to the hotel. The sort that had her up on her tiptoes and stealing a quick, hard kiss in the hotel lift. And the sort that made her draw away from him, a little shy, once they'd reached the privacy of their suite.

But her kiss in the lift had clearly fired something in Nic, and the moment they were through the door his arms were around her, lifting her and moulding her, until his lean body was perfectly fitted to her soft curves and his lips had found hers in a kiss that stole her breath.

All thoughts of shyness fled under the onslaught of sensation: hips and lips on hers, his hands in her hair, the cold wood of the door behind her back contrasting with the heat of his body. She tore her lips away and tilted her head, inviting him to kiss the soft skin of her neck. He responded greedily, nuzzling at her collarbone, sipping kisses from behind her ear, biting gently on her shoulder.

She let out a groan as she let her body loosen, her weight held entirely by door and man, and instead focussed her energy on Nic, on kissing and exploring and reaching bare skin.

Until a snuffle from the pram behind him drew her up short.

Her body froze instantly and Nic backed away, a question in his eyes.

'Sorry…' she gasped, fighting for reason as much as she was for breath. 'I nearly forgot…' How could she have forgotten that Rosie was right there? That she was responsible for a little human life before giving in to her own needs and desires?

But Nic didn't look concerned, or even shocked that she had put her own passions above her responsibility to Rosie.

'Don't worry about it,' he said, kissing her again on the lips, but gently this time. 'She was fast asleep and perfectly safe. You didn't do anything wrong.'

She let out a long breath, thankful to have this understanding, intelligent man in her life. Someone who saw her worst fears even more clearly than she saw them herself.

'Why don't you get her settled? Take your time,' he added, with an expression full of dark, seductive promise. 'I'm not going anywhere.'

Take your time. Why had he said that? It seemed as if she'd been in her bedroom for an age, and he paced the living room, waiting for her to return. He could hear Rosie, grizzling slightly—disturbed, he guessed, by the move from warm pram to cold cot. *Settle quickly,* he pleaded with her silently, desperate to pick up where he and Lily had left off.

He poured wine, for the sake of something to do, though he knew that they wouldn't touch it. He'd sipped one glass all night and Lily had barely started hers.

Finally the door to Lily's room opened, and he turned on the spot to see her closing it softly, peeking through at the last minute to make sure that Rosie was okay. With barely a whisper the latch closed, and they were alone at last.

He forced himself to stay where he was—not to rush over and hold her against the wall as he had earlier. He'd moved quickly—too quickly—when they'd first arrived back, and she'd ended up looking uncertain and concerned. He couldn't risk that again. Instead he'd wait for her to come to him, as she had before they'd gone out for dinner, teasing him with her kisses and caresses.

She crossed the room to stand in front of him, but kept her body from him still. He stood firm, determined that she must reach for him and not the other way around. She'd dropped her eyes. He loved to see bashfulness warring with passion in her posture and in her features. Was she having second thoughts? God knew *he'd* had enough over the past few weeks. But none tonight. He wouldn't ever again, he suspected, after his revelation this afternoon of what she'd come to mean to him.

Caving at last, unable to keep himself from touching her, he brushed his lips gently across her cheek. 'Everything okay?' he asked gently.

'Fine,' Lily said, finally looking up.

Her smile was brave, but not entirely genuine. There was still something troubling her, he knew.

'What is it?' he asked, pulling on her hand until she dropped down next to him on the sofa.

'Nothing's wrong,' she said, but then paused. 'It's just hard…trying to do what's right for Rosie and what I want for me.'

'Those two things aren't mutually exclusive, you know,' he told her gently.

'I know. But when we came in just now I just wasn't thinking. I mean *at all*. Anything could have happened and I'd have been completely oblivious.'

The smug smile was halfway to his lips before he got it under control.

'That's not true, Lily,' he reminded her. 'As soon as she made a peep you were right there. You can do a good job of taking care of her *and* have a life of your own as well. Trust me,' he said, wrapping an arm around her shoulder. 'You're doing an amazing job. But if you want to turn in now, cuddle up just the two of you in your room, then I would understand.'

She thought about it for a long minute.

'It's not what I want,' she told him, her voice carrying a slight waver. 'I know what I want—you.'

He breathed a long sigh of relief. He'd meant what

he'd said—he would have kissed her gently goodnight and watched her shut her bedroom door behind her—but, God, was he glad that he didn't have to.

He'd wrapped his arm around her shoulder to comfort her, but as his fingers brushed across the soft skin of her upper arm the caress turned from soothing to sensual, and his fingertips crackled with the electricity that surged between them.

Lily turned to him, but he knew the next move had to come from her. If she'd had doubts—if she *still* had doubts—he'd understand, and he wouldn't rush her.

Slowly, quietly, she moved closer to him, until her lips were just an inch from his, the lower one caught between her teeth. He could bite it for her, he thought, imagining the warmth and moistness of her mouth. She looked from his eyes to his lips and reached out her hand. Her thumb caught his lower lip, as it had earlier, caressing gently. He opened his mouth to her, inviting her in, and finally, excruciatingly, she leaned forward and pressed her lips to his. But it wasn't surrender on her part—it was triumph as she kissed and tasted and explored.

He ran his hands down to her hips, pulling her closer to him, and swallowed the satisfied groan that emerged from her mouth. Now, with no distractions, no limits on their time, no reason not to do everything he had ever imagined…it was intoxicating. He pulled her closer still, until she was nestled onto his lap, her arms around his neck. When he could hold back no longer he stood, lifting her as if she weighed no more than a feather, and started towards his bedroom.

She pulled back for a moment and gazed into his

eyes. 'Yes?' he asked, hoping with every part of his being that he had judged this right.

'Oh, God, yes,' Lily replied, her voice barely more than a husky murmur. *'Yes.'*

CHAPTER THIRTEEN

LILY CRACKED AN eyelid and glanced at the clock on the bedside table—it was nearly six. Rosie would be up again soon, and Lily didn't want her to wake up alone in a strange place. She eased herself out from under Nic's arm, careful not to wake him, and threw on what she could find of her clothes. She sneaked out of the room, closing the door softly behind her.

Rosie was awake when she went into their room, happily gurgling in her cot. 'Morning, sunshine,' she whispered as she got closer. 'Did you remember we're on holiday?'

She picked up the phone and arranged for hot water to be brought up, then started digging in Rosie's bag for formula and a bottle.

Once she'd answered the discreet knock at the door and made up Rosie's breakfast she wasn't sure what to do next. In the night she'd fed Rosie in bed, and then crept back to Nic and initiated round two, and three... What if Nic woke this time and found her gone? It didn't seem like the right way to start their day. But bringing Rosie into their bed—it screamed *family*, and she wasn't sure if they were ready for that.

I'll go back to him, she decided eventually. It might

not be the right thing to do—there was no way to know until she did it—but getting back into her cold bed alone didn't seem like the right thing, either.

She tiptoed back into Nic's room, trying not to wake him as she eased herself under the blankets without dropping either baby or bottle.

She settled into the pillows and looked around her. This was it, she thought. Beautiful baby...beautiful man. This was how she had always imagined Sunday mornings would be. Admittedly, their path to here had been a little unconventional, and, yes, it was a Thursday, but now she was here it seemed pretty perfect to her.

It was almost impossible not to reach out and touch Nic. She wondered whether it was possible to wake him just by staring at him. Apparently not. But Rosie didn't have the same scruples as Lily and was more than happy to wake Nic up, practising a raspberry noise with a mouthful of milk. Lily tried to mop up without waking him, but the stirring hand beneath the sheet gave him away and she knew that Rosie had managed what she hadn't dared.

She watched his face as he swam up from sleep. A lazy smile lifted his lips as he realised she was there: he'd forgotten, perhaps. Though how he couldn't remember last night, when it was seared on her memory, she had no idea. His face fell when he spotted Rosie and he pulled himself up on the pillows, blinking rapidly and wiping sleep from his eyes with the heels of his hands.

'Morning.'

His voice was gruff, and not entirely friendly. She instinctively pulled the blankets a little tighter around them, feeling suddenly vulnerable under his scornful gaze. Was it her presence or Rosie's that was the problem? She knew the answer to that—he'd been more than happy to see *her*, it had only been when he'd spotted the baby that his face had turned to stone. And when his face had dropped, so had Lily's.

'Sorry, we didn't mean to wake you.'

She *was* sorry for waking him, but she didn't see that she really had anything else to apologise for. Nic was the one who had told her he was ready for this. That he'd struggled in the past but wanted her and Rosie to be a part of his life. He couldn't have expected her to sneak back to her own bed this morning as if nothing had happened, could he? Or to leave Rosie where she was and pretend that this wasn't the reality of her life?

Nic tried pasting a smile back on to his face but it was too late: the damage was done. The cracks were showing anyway, and Lily knew that however much he might say otherwise he wasn't as ready for this as he'd said he was. He would have been happier not to find them both there this morning, and that cracked Lily's heart more than just a little.

'No, it's fine—just a surprise, that's all.'

A surprise? It shouldn't have been. If he really understood her life—and how could he decide if he wanted to be a part of it if he didn't understand it?—then surely he should have expected this.

She hadn't known when she'd woken in the dawn light what to expect of this morning—whether they would be awkward, or whether the natural-as-breathing intimacy of last night would carry through to today.

The last thing she'd expected was this: the sight of Nic climbing from the bed and pulling running shorts from a drawer.

'I think I might make the most of the early-morning temperature,' he said, not meeting her eye. 'Fit in a quick jog before it hits thirty degrees. You don't mind, do you?'

Did it matter what she thought? It was pretty obvious that he was going, either way.

As the door to the bathroom shut she looked down at Rosie and breathed out a long sigh. Last night everything had seemed so perfect, so right. She had known even then that it was too good to be true.

Nic counted his breaths in and out as his feet struck the unfamiliar cobbles, trying to pace himself around the irregular maze of streets and alleyways. That was maybe the most cowardly thing he'd ever done, and no number of heel-strikes was going to make him any less ashamed of it. The look on Lily's face had been heartbreaking. A mixture of confusion and sorrow.

He pushed himself harder and checked his watch: he'd been gone forty-five minutes. The guilt was more than a twinge—it was closer to a knife in his gut. He really should go back. But what to say to her?

He'd seen her face. How could he make her see that he'd meant everything he'd said to her yesterday? When he'd told her he was falling for her, that he wanted both her *and* Rosie in his life, he'd meant it—and he'd thought he'd known what he was taking on.

But nothing had quite prepared him for the sight

of them both when he was barely awake, barely conscious. There had been a split second when he'd seen a different baby, when he'd been in a different bed. And the thought of what had happened, of the different reality that he was waking up to, had crushed his heart for a moment.

This was harder than he'd expected, but that didn't mean he was giving up. Anything worth having was worth fighting for. Hard. But how could Lily know that he felt that way? He'd already told her that he didn't know if she could rely on him, and now he'd gone and proved it—he'd bailed at the first opportunity. As far as she was concerned he'd got what he'd been looking for and then left her alone in his bed while he pulled on clothes and headed out through the door.

He turned back to the hotel, wondering what he'd find when he got there. Her bags packed, perhaps. Or the suite empty, her clothes gone from the wardrobe and her lotions missing from the bathroom.

He let himself into the suite and was relieved to hear her singing in her bedroom, Rosie gurgling along. There was clearly something about the combination of nursery rhymes and power ballads that was irresistible to that girl.

Obviously encouraged, Lily turned up the volume and sang even louder. The door was open and he crossed the living room, resting his shoulder against the frame as he watched her dancing around, pulling faces to try and make Rosie smile. Despite his serious mood, he found himself smiling too.

But he knew that he was intruding on something personal, so he cleared his throat, drawing her attention. Colour rose on her cheeks as she turned towards him, and she stopped singing instantly.

'You're back.'

'Yes. And I'm sorry for leaving like that.'

She dropped her gaze, but not before he could see the hurt in her eyes. He had a lot of explaining to do—and a lot of making up. For weeks they'd been moving so slowly, feeling their way towards trusting each other, and then with one rash move—running instead of staying and explaining—he'd destroyed something of the bond they'd built. Had he learnt nothing from the way things had ended with Clare?

'Are you hungry?' he asked. 'I thought we could call down for some breakfast and eat up here. I know that I've upset you, and I think it would be good to talk.'

She didn't answer for a moment; instead she picked up Rosie from the bed and held her against her chest. Her arms were firm around her, and Nic knew that the cuddle was more for Lily's comfort than for Rosie's.

'Sure,' she said eventually. 'I'll order something while you take a shower.'

He washed quickly. Part of him wanted to delay this conversation—delay the moment when he had to look at Lily and know how much his selfishness had hurt her. But it wasn't fair on her to make her wait longer than she already had for his apology and his explanation. So he grabbed a towel and dragged it over his limbs.

The softness of the cotton reminded him of her tender caresses last night—the way that every sensation had been heightened until even the brush of the sheet against his back had driven him to heights he hadn't recognised.

He glanced at the clock as he walked towards his wardrobe. He had meetings today—it was why he was here, after all—but the thought that he'd have to leave in an hour, whether things were settled or not, twisted that knife in his gut.

When he arrived back in the living room a waiter was laying a breakfast of pastries, cold meat and absurdly good-smelling coffee on the table by the window. Lily was standing, looking out over the city, Rosie still in her arms. She had grabbed a handful of Lily's hair, and Lily was gently teasing her as she eased it out of her grasp.

She turned—must have heard his footsteps—and the smile dropped from her face at the sight of him. She looked guarded, wary, as if about to do battle.

'This looks nice,' he told her, and could have kicked himself for hiding behind pleasantries.

She just nodded—didn't even answer as she settled Rosie into the bouncy chair by the table and then sat herself.

'Lily, I'm sorry,' he said as soon as the waiter had left the room. 'I shouldn't have just taken off like that. You have every right to be angry with me.'

She nodded—which didn't do much to help the guilt in his belly.

'I should have stayed to talk to you, to explain what I was feeling.'

She met his gaze head-on and nodded. It was everything he'd feared. Everything he'd warned her of. He'd let her down.

'Right. You should.'

Good. She wasn't going to make this easy on him. He didn't deserve *easy*. He deserved to see how his actions had affected her. This was what he wanted. To be Lily's lover and partner. Maybe—if he could fix this unholy mess he'd made—more. He couldn't expect all that without giving everything of himself in return.

'Why did you go?' she asked.

He tried to find the right words to express what he had felt, to tell her that he'd been hurt but it hadn't been her fault.

'It was seeing you and Rosie like that, when I was barely awake. It just brought back…memories.'

Her face softened and relief swept through him like a wave. She understood. He'd known deep down that she would. She wouldn't be the woman he thought she was if she wasn't able to sympathise with another person's pain. But that didn't make what he'd done right. He should have spoken to her, explained what he was feeling, rather than running from the pain and from her. That was what he'd done at the start, when he'd first met her. If he couldn't show her that things had changed, if he *hadn't* changed, then what chance would he have of showing her that they could be happy together.

She nodded. 'I understand,' she said.

And maybe she did. But that didn't mean she'd forgiven him. She picked at her pastry, and he knew that hurt was still simmering under the surface.

'But you could have asked for my help, my support.' She gave him a long look before she spoke again. 'What are we to each other if we can't do that?'

What are we to each other? Genuinely, he didn't know. Had he been naïve, thinking that they could make a relationship out of good intentions? Maybe there was too much history, too much pain. After all, he'd been tested once and hadn't come out of it well. But the only way to know was by trying, and so far things weren't looking great.

'This is why me and Clare…' he started. 'I couldn't talk. She needed me to. I tried. I couldn't.'

She let out an exasperated sigh. 'I don't want to hear again that you let Clare down because you wouldn't talk to her about how you were feeling. It wasn't fair of her to expect you to grieve the way she wanted you to. I wasn't planning on making you do anything you weren't comfortable with this morning. But instead of finding that out you decided to bail. You don't have to talk to me about your feelings for your son, but if we can't find a way to communicate with each other then we're lost before we've even really started.'

Her words made him stop his pacing. He'd never considered that maybe there was another side to what had happened in his last relationship. That perhaps he wasn't entirely to blame. If only the same could be said about this morning.

From the corner of his eye he caught sight of the clock on the wall and cursed under his breath.

Lily followed his eyeline. 'Your meeting,' she said, remembering.

'I don't have to leave just yet.'

'But you'll be late if you leave it much longer. It wouldn't exactly give the right impression. If you don't get this contract signed then what was the point of us coming here? You should go.'

What was the point of them coming here? Could she not see that the whole thing had been his—clearly misjudged—way of contriving to find some time for them to get to know each other? The whole point of this trip was *them*, not the business.

But she was already heading back to her room, and he didn't have to ask to know that he wasn't invited to follow her.

CHAPTER FOURTEEN

THE HOTEL DOOR closed behind Nic and she breathed out a long sigh—disappointment? Relief? She wasn't sure. Her heart had started hurting the moment he'd left the suite earlier that morning and hadn't stopped since. His brief return and apology hadn't helped. It wasn't that she didn't forgive him—he'd clearly been in pain, and she could understand and sympathise with that. But instead of asking her to face that pain *with* him, trying to find a way to get past those feelings *together*, he had turned from her. Literally run from her.

Twenty-four hours in Rome. Well, their time was nearly up. By the time Nic got back from his meeting she'd need her bags packed and ready to go, and they'd have to go straight to the airport. There was no time to fix this before they had to leave, and her shoulders slumped with sadness that a day as sweet and as perfect as yesterday could be tarnished so soon.

Rosie had gone back to sleep, so she moved around the room quietly, tucking her belongings into bags and cases, checking under the bed and in the bathroom drawers.

Rosie gave a whimpering little cry in her sleep, a sound Lily didn't recognise, and she stopped her packing and crossed to the cot. Whatever had upset her hadn't been enough to wake her properly, and she'd settled herself back to sleep, but Lily watched her a little longer, feeling a swell of trepidation. It was just the remnants of her disagreement with Nic, she reasoned. Making her see trouble where there was none.

Rosie gave another sniffle, and this time Lily reached into her cot to check that she wasn't too hot. The air-con was on, and the thermostat was showing a perfect eighteen degrees, but her skin was just a little clammy and warm. Lily pulled the blanket back, so that Rosie was left under just a sheet, and then dug the thermometer out of the first aid kit she had brought with her.

Rosie's temperature was on the high side of normal. Maybe she'd picked up a cold, Lily thought, trying not to let her mind race ahead. She had some infant paracetamol in her case, and she woke the baby to feed her some. She barely opened her eyes, but swallowed down the medicine, and Lily told herself just to keep an eye on things and not to panic as she rocked her gently.

Nic arrived back from his meeting and she could see from his face that it had gone according to plan. That was something, at least. And the paracetamol had seemed to do the trick with Rosie. Her temperature had returned to normal, and she seemed to be sleeping easier.

A maid had turned up to pack Nic's things, so by the time he was back they were all but ready to go. They stood in the living room, their cases at their feet as they waited for a porter, and Lily wondered if they would ever rediscover the intimacy they had felt yesterday. Perhaps she had overreacted when Nic had left this morning, but it wasn't just her sadness and disappointment that was between them. It was more than that. At the first instance of something hard in their relationship Nic had decided to leave rather than work at it.

Yesterday they had been full of optimism about the future—aware of the challenges they might face, but ready to tackle them together. This morning had shattered that illusion.

Nic wanted to face his demons alone, and so must she.

She'd worked so hard to be a good mother to Rosie that she knew she could do it alone, that she didn't need Nic by her side to be a good parent, to hold her and Rosie together in their little family. She just needed to remember that. Remember that the most important thing in all of this was to be a good mother. Everything else came second. If that meant protecting Rosie from someone who wasn't ready to be in her life then she would have to do that, however much it hurt.

The flight had been short and uneventful, their way smoothed by Nic's charm and first-class tickets. Again his preparations had been thorough, and the onboard staff had responded to everything Rosie had needed, though she had slept for most of the flight. Lily had kept thermometer and paracetamol in her handbag, and kept a careful eye on her, looking out for any signs that this might be more than a cold.

Nic had asked her more than once if she was okay, if Rosie was okay, if there was anything that he could do. She'd smiled and said no thanks, needing to focus on Rosie. With her baby still grizzly and unhappy there was no time or space in her head to tackle this frosty wasteland that was expanding between them.

Now, in the luggage hall, Rosie started crying feebly, and it didn't seem to matter what Lily did—she paced, she rocked, she bounced—she wouldn't stop. She took her temperature again, and as soon as she saw the number on the little digital display—nearly two degrees higher than when she'd last taken it—she was reaching for the phone.

She dialled the NHS urgent helpline and bit her lip with nerves as she waited for her call to be taken. Nic guided her through the airport and out to their car as she answered the operator's questions, telling her what Rosie's temperature was and how sleepy she'd been.

The car pulled away from the airport and she barely even noticed. She had no time or energy to mark the end of their trip. Her ear was glued to her phone, and her eyes flitted between Rosie and the thermometer. She cast Nic the occasional glance and noted that he looked grey, drawn. No wonder, she thought, given everything he had been through.

But she had to focus on Rosie. She had to funnel out Nic's pain and concentrate on her girl.

Finally, after running through a seemingly endless list of questions, the operator spoke in a calming, measured voice that made Lily instantly terrified.

'Now, I know that you're in the car, so what I'm going to suggest is that you go to the nearest hospital with an Accident and Emergency department. If you can give me your location I'll be able to let you know where that is. Or if you want to pull over I'll arrange for an ambulance to come to you.'

Lily had never believed that a person could feel their

own heart stop, but in that moment she could have sworn her every bodily function ceased. She didn't breathe, blood stopped flowing in her veins, she stilled completely.

'Lily, love, are you still there?'

She nodded, before finding her voice and asking the driver for their exact location, then relaying it to the operator on the phone.

Lily thanked her for her help and hung up. She turned back to Rosie, who was sleepy, but still grizzling in her car seat.

'Lily?'

She could barely bring herself to look at Nic, because she needed to focus with everything that she had on Rosie. She had to give her her full attention. She couldn't bear to lose another member of her family—and this time she knew if it happened she would be the only one to blame. She was solely responsible for taking care of Rosie, and she had to make sure that she got better. If she didn't...it wouldn't just be Rosie she was losing. How could she ever face her sister again if she let anything happen to her?

'Lily, what's going on?' Nic asked.

She turned towards him but couldn't meet his eye. Instead she kept her gaze around his jaw, noted the tension there, and the pallor of his skin, but couldn't let herself worry about that now. Couldn't let herself think of anything but Rosie.

'We have to go straight to a hospital,' she told him. 'They didn't say what they thought might be wrong, but they want her checked out asap.'

'Three minutes,' their driver called from the front seat. 'Hospital's just up ahead and there's no traffic.'

Lily couldn't allow herself an ounce of relief. She had to stay alert, stay ready, make sure that she was focussed only on her little girl.

Nic reached for her hand and squeezed it gently. 'Lily, I'm sure they're just being cautious. Rosie's going to be fine.'

She opened her mouth to answer, but her voice wasn't there. Instead tears were welling in her eyes and threatening a flood. She couldn't do this. Not with him here. Not with his fear of the worst-case scenario written so plainly on his features. Her only responsibility was taking care of her family, and Nic had told her and then proved this morning that when things were tough he wasn't going to be there for her.

Lily unbuckled her seatbelt and put her hands on the straps of Rosie's car seat, ready to have her out of there as soon as the car pulled up outside A&E.

The click of Nic's seatbelt being unbuckled drew her attention, and she glanced over at him. 'You don't need to come in.'

'It's okay,' he said, though the dread and fear in his face told a different story.

'No.' Lily took a deep breath, knowing that she had to do this—for her niece, for her family, for herself. 'I can do this on my own,' she said firmly.

Nic stared at her, clearly shocked. Was there relief there too? she wondered. There must be. He'd never wanted to get involved with a family…never wanted to expose himself to the hurt and pain that might be waiting for them around the corner. She couldn't make him do this for her, and she couldn't walk into that hospital with someone who might bail on her at any moment. It was better to do this now, end things here, and know exactly where she stood, exactly who she could rely on as she walked into the hospital.

'I'll come in with you, Lily. You shouldn't have to do this by yourself.'

But she didn't want him there out of duty or obligation—didn't want him there against his better judgement. She wanted him there because he was part of her, part of Rosie. Because they were a family. He was offering half-measures, and that just wasn't good enough. Not for her, and not for Rosie.

'No!' Lily shouted this time, the tears finally spilling onto her cheeks. 'We're better off on our own,' she blurted. 'And not just today. We made a mistake, Nic. This was never going to work. We're better off accepting that now, before it goes any further. You know I'm right. You know that you don't want to be inside that hospital with us. I'm sorry, but it's for the best. It's over, Nic.'

As they came to an abrupt halt Lily grabbed for Rosie, lifting her out of the car seat. The driver opened the door behind her and she ran from the car, focussing on Rosie's face, refusing to look back.

CHAPTER FIFTEEN

LILY UNLOCKED THE door to Kate's flat one-handed while Rosie slept peacefully at last in the crook of her arm. She'd never used her friend's key without asking before, but with her own place still a building site and her relationship with Nic in tatters she had nowhere else to go.

It had been a long couple of days. She wished she could curl up like Rosie, block out the world and sleep through the day. The last seventy-two hours had consisted of nail-biting terror and endless waiting while doctors drew blood, ran tests, muttered together in corners.

Until this morning, when a smiling junior doctor had come to give her the news—all clear. They had been worried about meningitis, they'd told her when she'd arrived at the hospital, and had run a slew of tests. But every one had come back negative. It seemed that Rosie had been battling a nasty case of flu, and after three days of topping her up with fluids and paracetamol they were happy for her to be discharged.

After settling Rosie in her carrycot she plugged in her phone, dreading what might be waiting for her there. Nic had called a couple of times, and then passed the baton on to Kate. But Lily had found that she didn't know what to say. She'd breathed a sigh of relief when the phone's battery had died and she'd not had to think about it any more.

But now that she was back, and Rosie was on the mend, she knew that she had some thinking to do. And—she suspected—some apologising. Kate, for one, would be furious that she'd been incommunicado for more than twenty-four hours. And Nic…?

She had no idea what she could expect from him— if anything. Looking back at that car journey, she was ashamed of the way she had behaved, and saw in her behaviour a reflection of his, of everything she had criticised him for that very morning. She'd not talked about what was scaring her; she'd not tried to explain. Instead she'd decided that she had to do things on her own, in her own way, and left him out in the cold while she got on with it.

But the thing really twisting the knife in her stomach was the fact that she knew he had been hurting already. Seeing Rosie sick, the trip to the hospital, the not knowing what was happening… It must have brought back so many memories. And instead of trying to help, or even to understand, she'd pushed him away.

Just as she was putting on the kettle, hoping that coffee would make this awful day better, a key turned in the front door. Kate, home from work. Or Nic? she thought suddenly, with a stab of guilt in her belly. Did he have a key to his sister's place?

She thought for a moment about trying to sneak out the back way. But her best friend and her brother had stood by her these last few weeks—the most challenging of her life—and it would be cruel of her to push them away now. The thought of facing Nic's hurt and Kate's disapproval was terrifying, but it couldn't be put off for ever, she knew.

She breathed a sigh of relief when Kate's curls appeared around the door.

'Lily!' she exclaimed with a double-take. 'You scared me half to death. What are you doing here?'

The blunt words were muffled as her face was trapped in a cloud of curly hair and she was squeezed in a tight hug.

Pulling back, Kate held her at arm's distance as she gave her an assessing look.

'Of course you're here—stupid of me. How are you doing?' she asked, though Lily knew from her tone that she wasn't expecting an answer. 'Not great, I imagine, from everything that I've heard. Rosie okay?'

Lily nodded, unable to speak after being shown such kindness when she'd been expecting the opposite.

'Now, I need coffee, and I need some sort of baked goods, and then we're going to talk,' Kate carried on, steering Lily back into the kitchen and pulling mugs from the cupboard as the kettle came to the boil. 'That brother of mine has been walking around with a face like a month of wet Sundays, and you're not looking much better yourself. And as it seems like neither of you knows how to operate a telephone or carry out a conversation—despite you having clocked up almost sixty years on this planet between you—an intervention is required.'

Lily dropped onto a stool and opened her mouth to speak.

But Kate stopped her with a pointed finger. 'Uh-uh. I'm talking first. You're sitting like a good girl and listening while I tell you just why *you're* an idiot for pushing my brother away, and *he's* an idiot for letting you and for somehow managing to screw up a romantic whirlwind trip to Rome. And then you're *both* going to apologise and find a way to make this work before your twin glum faces drive me mad. Am I clear?'

Lily didn't know what else to do but nod and accept the coffee that Kate placed in front of her, some of the hot black liquid sloshing over the side of her cup with her enthusiasm.

Despite her rousing sentiments, and her insistence on speaking first, Kate sat and listened quietly as Lily gave her a summed-up version of what had happened in Rome—skirting very quickly round the 'sex with your brother' part and instead focussing on the 'thinking we were falling for each other and then he freaked out and left' part.

Not for the first time she wished she could have fallen for someone else—anyone other than her best friend's brother. Maybe then she could have just spilled out all her worst pain, everything Nic had done wrong, every way he had hurt her and upset her. But knowing how much Kate loved him, how much she knew that he was really a good guy, she couldn't do it.

She couldn't explain what had happened without seeing for herself how much responsibility they both carried for the way things had fallen apart. No, Nic *shouldn't* have left with barely a word the morning after they had made love for the first time. But she should have given him the space he'd needed. Recognised that grieving was a long process, full of setbacks and surprises. That he must have been as taken aback by the turn of events that morning as she had.

And she couldn't deny that pushing him away when he must have been every bit as frightened for Rosie as she had been had been cruel. She just hoped that it wasn't unforgivable.

'So you're both idiots—that's what you're telling me?'

Once again Kate had managed to find a way to compress their entire torturous, complicated lives into one simple sentence.

Lily nodded. 'Though I'm pretty sure I'm the bigger one.'

'You both want to make this up. You're both sitting at home moping rather than doing something about it. Seems pretty equal to me. You know that he wouldn't leave the hospital, right? Slept that first night across a couple of chairs in the A&E waiting room? It wasn't until you texted me that Rosie was fine and I passed it on to him that he would leave. He wanted to be there… just in case.'

Lily dropped her head into her hands, her heart swelling and breaking a little at the same time, ashamed of the way she had behaved, but pleased at this demonstration of Nic's commitment to her—and to Rosie.

'So what do I do about it?'

'Do you want him back? Really?'

She was surprised Kate could ask her that after everything that had just been said—after she'd explained how much she felt for him, how stupid she had been. But in the words she could hear more than a hint of sisterly protection, and Lily knew that she was crossing some sort of rubicon. Say yes now and she wasn't just committing to Nic, she was committing to his family. She was promising not one but two of the people she cared for most in the world that she was committed to them, that she wouldn't hurt them.

'I do,' she said seriously. 'I want us to try again.'

Kate leaned over and gave her a hug with uncharacteristic gentleness, both in her body and her words. 'Glad to hear it. Now, you go borrow my room and get some sleep—you look hideous—and we'll talk again tomorrow.'

Lily felt her body growing heavier. The lack of sleep these past days was catching up with her, and she knew that Kate was right. She needed rest, needed to recharge. And then, when Rosie was better, she'd call Nic, beg his forgiveness, and see if there was any way to rescue what they had so briefly found in Rome.

A few days later Lily reached across to the coffee table, trying to grab her phone without disturbing Rosie, who was asleep on her lap.

It was a message from Kate.

I have a plan. I'll be home in an hour—make sure you're in.

Lily glanced down at the sleeping baby and thought for the millionth time how lucky she was to have her safe and well in her arms—the doctors had given her a clean bill of health, her temperature was gone, and she was feeding and sleeping as normal. The only reason she was being cuddled to sleep instead of drifting off on her own in her cot was because Lily was still nervous of letting her go, still haunted by her worst fears.

It was how Nic must feel every day, she thought, unable to shake the unease of knowing how easily a child could be lost, how impossible it would be to fill the void she would leave.

The doorbell rang, and Lily softly cursed Kate. How could a grown woman, a successful barrister, forget her own house keys on a daily basis?

She set Rosie down, careful not to wake her, and picked her way across the living room. She threw open the door, and had already half turned back when she realised what was wrong with the scene. Kate's slight shoulders wouldn't block the sunshine, wouldn't cast a shadow that was solid and masculine and...

'Nic?'

CHAPTER SIXTEEN

'HI.'

In that moment he knew he'd done the right thing: 'borrowing' his sister's phone, sending that text, coming to see her. Her voice brought memories flooding back...their one night in Rome, their walks around the city, the way she'd heard him confess his darkest fears about his character and told him that she still trusted him. What they'd found together was too important to let it go without a fight.

But maybe Lily was tired of fighting. She looked tired: black bags under her eyes, her shirt unironed, her skin pale. But none of that mattered. Because all he could see was what made her beautiful to him.

How had they managed to get it all so wrong? He thought back to that night in Rome—he couldn't even remember how long ago that was. Four nights? Five? It felt like a lifetime... Everything had seemed right with the world. He'd had the woman he loved, relaxed and happy and contented in his arms. He'd felt peaceful at last, after a decade of running from his memories.

And then in a half waking moment of confusion he'd pushed her away. That one push had spiralled and had a butterfly effect on everything—until he hadn't even recognised who they were to each other any more.

He'd been in so much pain—watching her suffer, watching Rosie suffer—and utterly paralysed with fear that he would lose them both. He should have argued when she'd told him that she wanted to face it alone. Should have told her that he *knew* this pain, *knew* this fear, and that they would be stronger if they faced it together. All he'd been able to do was wait, haunt the hospital waiting room until he'd known that Rosie was going to be okay.

'Come in,' she said, though her voice was hesitant.

He followed her through to the kitchen anyway. He couldn't bear the thought of leaving without things between them being back where they had been. Without her knowing what he'd realised as he'd sat in the hospital, waiting for news, wanting to be nearby just in case she needed him. He loved her. That was why he hadn't been able to go home to his huge, empty apartment. It was why his heart had felt empty for days— why he hadn't been able to sleep or think straight until he'd made the decision to come here and fight for what he wanted. He just hoped it was what she wanted too.

He took a moment to watch her, to refamiliarise himself with her features, with the colour of her hair, the line of her nose and the angle of her smile. Did she know how much he had missed her? How he had missed Rosie as well? Missed the mess and the noise of the two of them at home?

Lily was hovering by the table, and he realised that in his eagerness to look at them both he'd not yet spoken. She looked uncertain, as if she might bolt at any moment, and with that his anger towards her dissipated.

He'd been furious for a while that she wouldn't even answer his texts, that she had left him sitting and wondering whether Rosie was even alive, but seeing her now, seeing the evidence of the emotional toll of the past few days, he found that he couldn't add his anger to her list of troubles.

'The text was from you?' she asked, her voice tremulous.

'I wasn't sure you'd see me. I'm sorry.'

'I would have,' she said. 'I wanted to call…to talk. But after the way I behaved I…I couldn't.'

'You *could*,' he told her. 'That's what you've been trying to show me, isn't it? That we should be finding ways to support each other? I'd have supported you, Lily, if you'd let me. So how is she?' he asked at last, and suddenly his arms felt empty, light, as if they needed the weight of the baby in them to know that she was okay.

Lily wasn't the only one who'd become part of his heart, and he knew that could never be undone.

Never mind his arms, his heart had felt empty these last few days, missing its other half, missing that which made him whole. At first he'd thought it was just the memories making him sad—the thought of another funeral, another tiny white coffin. But when the feeling had persisted long after he'd known that Rosie was in the clear he'd known there was another cause.

Knowing how that felt, knowing what it was to be without her, it suddenly seemed stupid of him to be angry, to hold a grudge. Why jeopardise this? Why risk the chance of being happy?

He met her eyes and tried to show her everything with that look. Everything that he had felt and thought and hoped and feared since he'd last seen her. But it wasn't enough. He had to be sure that she understood.

'I'm sorry,' he said. 'I'm sorry for leaving that morning. I'm sorry that you didn't think you could rely on me when Rosie was sick. I'm sorry it's taken me all week for us to get to this point. I love you, Lily, and I want us to fix this.'

She stared at him for a moment. He wasn't sure what she'd been expecting, but it was clear from her expression that it hadn't been this.

'*I'm* the one who should be apologising,' she said. 'I shouldn't have judged you so harshly when we were in Rome. I shouldn't have pushed you away when Rosie was sick because I was still angry with you.'

'You don't have to apologise,' he said, reaching for her hand and allowing himself a small smile when she didn't pull back. 'You were so worried about her—you had to do what you thought was right at the time.'

'It doesn't make the way I acted any better.'

Nic shrugged. 'We can't change what happened—what we said or did. But if you still want to we can forgive each other. See if we can try harder, do better.'

She smiled, although it still looked tentative. 'I'd like that.'

'I can't promise that I won't have another day like that one in Rome,' he warned. 'There will be times when I feel sad. When I look at Rosie and remember Max. Things might not be smooth sailing just because we want them to be.'

Lily nodded. 'And I can't promise I'm not going to make mistakes, either. It's quite a lot to get used to, this parenting thing. I might need help. Sometimes I might need space.'

'I *can* promise that I will always love you, though. That I will always want you—want you both—in my life.'

'Then I can promise to remember that. Even when I'm upset and angry. I love you, Nic.'

A tear sneaked from the corner of her eye and he reached out with his thumb to wipe it away. The last tear she would shed over him, he hoped.

Rosie started to stir in the bedroom and Nic smiled. 'Can I?' he asked.

Lily nodded and he went to pick the baby up, moved himself beside Lily on the sofa.

'She's really okay?' he asked.

'Right as rain. They were just being cautious. Absolutely the right thing, of course. But it did give me seventy-two hours I'd very much like to wipe from my memory.'

'Just as long as she's okay. And as long as *we* are.'

He placed a tentative arm around her shoulders and his whole body relaxed when she turned into him, burying her face in his neck for a long moment and taking a deep breath. He wished they were at home, that there wasn't a chance his sister might walk through the door at any moment.

Taking advantage of the privacy, temporary as it might be, he dropped a kiss on the top of Lily's head. When she looked up at him he caught her lips with his, holding her there in a long kiss, pouring all the emotion of the last week into it. She moaned as she opened her mouth, and he sensed her longing, her love for him.

As they leaned back in the sofa, nestling together, their little family of three, a thought came to him—and a question…

EPILOGUE

LILY LOOKED IN the mirror. As with pretty much everything else in her life, this wasn't exactly what she'd had in mind. She had always thought she would walk down the aisle on her wedding day looking like something out of one of those bridal magazines. She had never expected to do it eight months pregnant.

The day she'd found out she was expecting their baby had been one of the happiest of their lives. But when they'd sat down and worked out the due date they'd realised that, as always, things were a little complicated. The church and the venue had been booked, and everything had been planned for months. It had seemed silly and vain to change the date of their wedding just so that Lily could buy a gown in the size that she wanted.

After the briefest knock on the door Kate appeared, Rosie propped on one hip and a grin on her face. 'How's the blushing bride getting on?' she asked. 'Better than my brother, I hope. The poor guy's so nervous he can't even eat. Don't know what he's worrying about, personally. Not like you can run very fast in your condition. If you tried to ditch him he'd catch up with you and drag you back.'

'And hi to you too.' Lily laughed, accepting a glass of something sparkling and a kiss on the cheek. 'I'm fine. Better than fine. I'm flippin' brilliant and I cannot wait to be officially your sister. How long have I got?'

Kate checked the time on her phone. 'Three minutes. Right—have we got everything? Old, new, borrowed, blue?'

Lily nodded. Not that she needed any of those things. As long as she had her family she had everything she wanted.

'Let's get you hitched, then.'

She walked into the church and saw Nic waiting for her at the end of the aisle. Any nerves she might have been hiding fell away. She had never felt so happy and in love and safe and secure in her life.

As she turned to look at her guests she saw Helen in the second row, a tissue pressed to her eyes. Her sister looked well, *really* well, better than she'd seen her for a long time. She was making tentative steps to get to know Rosie, and focussing on looking after her own health.

Rosie, still in Kate's arms, went ahead of her up the aisle, so when she reached Nic her little family was all together. Looking around her, Lily felt more lucky than she ever had, and knew as she said 'I do' that nothing could make this moment more perfect.

* * * * *

THE FAMILY THEY'VE LONGED FOR

ROBIN GIANNA

This book is dedicated to awesome cousins

George, Christie, Soula and Django.

Thanks so much for answering all my questions
and giving me great insight into your
Alaskan world.

Prepare to have me come visit soon! xoxo

CHAPTER ONE

"Just follow the standard orders for her release from the hospital as I wrote them," Dr. Aurora Anderson said into her phone. "I know Dr. Jones has her chart, but he doesn't know all the nuances of her problem. Any questions, call me and I'll get back to you as soon as I can."

Overhead, the last call for her flight to Alaska was urgently announced and she huffed out an impatient breath as the intern asked a few more questions.

"Listen, I have to board my plane. I'll call when I get to Fairbanks. You need to follow my instructions. Yeah, I *get* that Dr. Jones is filling in for me while I'm gone, but I already talked to the parents about the plan. I don't want anyone deviating from that and confusing them. They know I'll be seeing their daughter as soon as I get back, and that they only need to contact Dr. Jones if something seems wrong."

Rory shoved her phone into her backpack, grabbed her carry-on bag and ran to hand her boarding pass to the airline attendant, ignoring the disapproving frown the woman gave her. Being late to board wasn't catastrophic, but messing around and changing her orders for a patient post-op absolutely might be, so she couldn't worry about being the last on the plane.

After four years of med school, five years of residency and finally getting the board exam under her belt, she'd damned well earned her title: Doctor of Pediatric Ortho-pedic Medicine. She knew all this second-guessing from the intern was because she wasn't yet an attending physi-cian. But having her orders followed was supremely im-portant—not only for the patient, but for her future on the doctors' roster. If all went well, she'd have a permanent position there in a matter of weeks, and she'd never have to think about uprooting her life again.

She wrestled her bag into the overhead compartment and apologized as she squeezed her way past the two peo-ple in her row before finally plopping into the window seat. She drew a calming breath and pulled out her phone again, calling a nurse to give her instructions about a couple of other patients before they were told to turn off all elec-tronics for takeoff.

Why they insisted on that, she had no clue, since people used computers and phones around all kinds of electronic medical equipment and not once had it interfered with test-ing and diagnostics. Then again, she thought to herself, she wasn't an engineer, so she should stick with what she knew instead of offering opinions—something a few people in her past had frequently pointed out…one of whom she'd be seeing again this week whether she wanted to or not.

That painful realization had her stomach twisting like a terrifying tornado. Seeing him again, being in her home-town at all, was going to be torture; it would bring back all the horrible memories, all the guilt, all the sorrow she'd tried so hard to leave behind.

The plane lifted, propelling her toward the one place she absolutely didn't want to go. She swallowed hard, try-ing to control the sickly feeling in her stomach, and tipped her forehead against the window to stare down at what had been her home for the past nine years.

The dizzying concrete mass of freeways connecting the hulking city of Los Angeles and all its suburbs couldn't be more different from where she'd grown up. Where she was heading now.

With serious effort she managed to move her thoughts to the patients she'd just performed surgery on, and the others she was scheduled to see in her office the rest of the week. It wasn't going to happen now. Because a different kind of patient needed her help. The woman who'd always needed some kind of care or guidance throughout Rory's whole life.

Her sweet, wacky, childlike mother.

The plane rose higher above the clouds, leaving LA far behind. Rory dropped her head against her seatback and closed her eyes.

It would be okay. It *would*. Being with her mother for the next week would be really nice, since she'd spent so little time with her these past nine years.

Her mom loved her life in Eudemonia, Alaska, and hadn't been too interested in visiting Rory in LA. The few times her mom had come to Southern California had been a joy, and a huge source of entertainment to everyone she'd been in med school with, and later her friends in the hospital. There weren't too many people like Wendy Anderson, and her unique way of dressing was startling even in a big city like Los Angeles.

A smile touched her lips at the memories—until reality hit her like a hard fist all over again. Taking care of her mom would be the easy part. The hard part would be being back home. The worst part would be seeing Jacob Hunter again.

Yesterday, the sound of his voice on the other end of the phone had made her heart jolt hard in her chest, then hammer wildly—even after she had found out the reason he'd been calling. He'd been letting Rory know about her mother's emergency surgery for a ruptured appendix, telling her that she was fine, and now just needed some nursing and recovery time.

Unbidden, the face that had fascinated her since the fourth grade appeared in her mind and memories of him spread to her heart, bringing a melancholy pleasure and unrelenting pain. Though their friendship—and more—was long over, she would always cherish the memories of their childhood together, and their years as lovers in college.

But theirs had been a love that had resulted in the worst thing ever to happen to either of them.

She squeezed her eyes more tightly shut, as though she could squish the memories right out of her brain. It hadn't happened in nine years, so clearly there was no point in trying now. Still, she worked to think, instead, about her mother's idiosyncrasies, which made her laugh and sometimes drove her crazy, even though she loved her to bits.

From the time Rory had been barely more than a toddler, she vividly remembered her mother insisting that she call her Twinkle-Toes or Twinkie instead of Mom. Possibly because she adored wearing dance and fairy costumes, but mostly because actually acting like a mom had never been on her radar.

There were memories of the two of them doing all sorts of unorthodox things—like painting every lampshade in the house neon so they'd glow in "pretty colors"; like deciding that creating rock sculpture Voodoo talismans all around the house would keep them safe after Rory's father died. Rory had helped with all that to make her mom feel more comfortable even as she had inwardly rolled her eyes—as she had when her mother danced spontaneously whenever the mood struck, not caring if there were other people around or not.

So many of the things her mother did were adorable and funny. But sometimes embarrassing—especially once Rory had become a teen. She found herself managing to smile in anticipation of what might greet her today at the house she'd grown up in, knowing that spending time with her unique mother was the only thing that would make this trip bearable.

The moment the plane touched down at the Fairbanks Airport, Rory felt like a ten-pound weight had dropped onto her shoulders. Looking out at the snowcapped peaks of the Alaska Range, she felt the memories she'd tried to stuff down flood back. They forced her to think about what had happened the last two times she'd been home.

One thing had turned out to be the biggest mistake of her life, which had left her with a shredded heart she knew would never be repaired. The other had been her father's funeral, two years later. He had bravely suffered through diabetes, then kidney failure, for more years than she could remember. Neither one of those memories were things she wanted to revisit and remember, but being here again thickened her throat even as she promised herself she wouldn't fall apart.

The forty-five miles from Fairbanks passed way too fast, and soon she was driving into the city limits of Eudemonia. The moment she saw the familiar stores and homes, and the trees which were now mostly naked except for a few straggling golden yellow leaves still clinging to the branches, her chest squeezed even tighter.

Finally the tiny house she'd grown up in came into view, surrounded by birch, aspen and spruce trees that were bigger than she remembered. Cozy and charming, in a worn sort of way, the house stood atop the small hill she'd rolled and sledded down as a kid, her mother rolling and laughing along with her while her dad watched and applauded—the hill she'd run down nine years ago, stumbling and falling, somehow getting in her car, tears making it hard to see, grief making it hard to breathe, to leave for LA.

God, she *had* to get these feelings under control before she went in to see her mother.

She hit the brakes and sat there, waiting for the sickly feeling to pass. She gulped in a few breaths, admitted she was as ready as she'd ever be, then turned her rental car off the road to bump across the uneven grass.

She could *do* this. She had to. She had to find a way to get through the next week without becoming a weeping mess all over again.

A single bulb dangled over the crooked wooden front porch, and a giant stuffed rabbit wearing a green army helmet sat on an overturned bucket to greet visitors. Why a rabbit, Rory had no clue—since it was early October, not Easter—but, boy, she couldn't wait to find out. Though it was likely her mom didn't have any reason other than she liked the way it looked.

The whole place appeared even more dilapidated than it had when she'd last been here for her dad's funeral. She'd called regularly, but she knew it had been cowardly of her to avoid this place, and consequently her mother. She felt bad about it—she did—except that being here made her feel even worse. Maybe someday she would be able to face what she'd done and deal with the pain.

Nine years hadn't accomplished that—which meant that "someday" was still a long way off. If it ever came.

She knew she was beyond blessed that her mom had lots of friends to spend time with. Close friends who always looked after one another. People who were a big part of the reason why her mother sounded like her happy self whenever they spoke.

But what her mom had gone through with her surgery wasn't normal, everyday stuff. Rory knew her mother was supposed to be doing all right, but she might still be in a lot of pain. How on earth would her mom have coped if Rory *hadn't* come home?

She had no idea. Which made her realize all over again that, despite everything, she felt glad to finally be here for her mom.

She planned to nurse her mom with lots of TLC. Then, with any luck, she'd be close to her normal self by the time her mom's sister, Rory's Aunt Patty, came to take over. Much as she dreaded spending time at home again, getting her mother healthy enough for Rory to feel okay to leave her had to be the goal.

She stepped up to the front door and paused to pick at the paint flaking from the side, making a mental note to call a painter to get it done next summer. She knew it was too cold to paint now, but getting it on the schedule would be better than nothing.

Her job as a resident pediatric orthopedic surgeon provided her with enough money to live on and pay for this kind of repair stuff. And now that she'd passed her boards she'd be making a lot more. Assuming she got the permanent job—which was another reason to get back to LA as quickly as possible for her interview, before someone else snagged it away from her.

Even though it was barely six thirty, the vibrant golden sun was already setting in Eudemonia, Alaska—long before it would be in LA. She gazed at the fading orb, loving the way fingers of light slipped through the branches and lit the yellow leaves and hills. Up on the mountains the brilliant reds of the moss and lichen in the tundra glowed beneath the setting sun, and Rory was surprised at the warm nostalgia that filled her chest. It was so completely different from the warm temperatures, the concrete roads, the masses of cars and buildings and people that made up LA.

Thinking of the warm temperatures made Rory shiver as the chilly air sneaked down inside her jacket, and she shook her head at herself. Her friends here would laugh at what a wimp she'd become, thinking it was cold now, in early October. They'd probably all still be wearing shorts and T-shirts and thinking it felt downright balmy—but, hey, when she'd left Southern California earlier that day it had been almost eighty degrees. *Anyone* would feel the contrast, right?

She turned the knob and the door squeaked open. No surprise that her mom hadn't locked it, since Rory didn't think it had ever been secured in her whole life. In fact, thinking about it, she wasn't sure it even *did* lock. And wouldn't her California friends be flabbergasted at *that*?

"Hello? Mom? Twinkle-Toes?"

The light in the small living room was so dim it was hard to see, and she peered at the worn chairs, not seeing any sign of her mother's small frame. Sounds of marching band music, of all things, came faintly from the back of the house, and Rory had started to move toward her mother's bedroom when she appeared in the hallway outside the living room, with a small, curly-haired brown dog trotting beside her. Rory hadn't met him yet.

"Aurora! I'm so happy you're here! Come give your mama a big hug."

She hurried toward her mom, partly because she looked a little unsteady, walking with the pink cane she held in her hand. "Mom. Twinkie."

She gently enfolded her in her arms, being careful not to squeeze, and her throat clogged with emotion at how good it felt to hold her. Until this moment she hadn't even realized how much she'd missed seeing her and being with her. The pain of being in Eudemonia was so intense, the pleasure of seeing her mom often just wasn't enough to counteract it.

No doubt about it, she was a coward. A weakling.

"You shouldn't be wandering around with no one here.

You just got out of the hospital this afternoon. What if you fell?"

"I knew you were coming. I knew you'd be here to take care of me, marshmallow girl."

Marshmallow girl. It had become her nickname after they'd filled her hot chocolate cup to overflowing with them one Christmas. It had become a tradition, with the various pups they'd had over the years gobbling up the marshmallows that had scattered on the floor. Why that had stuck in her mother's mind she had no clue, but she'd always kind of liked it when she called her that, remembering all the silliness of her home life.

"Yeah. I'm here to take care of you."

She pressed her cheek to her mother's soft, warm one, thinking of all her years growing up, when she'd played parent to her mom instead of the other way around.

"How are you feeling?"

"Like I had a knife stabbed in my tummy—that's how!" She looked up at Rory with a mix of a grimace and a grin on her face. "Can you believe I had a bad appendix? After all the special herbs I eat and drink to stay healthy!"

"Yeah. Who'd have thought it? Maybe your appendix has had too much fun all these years, just like you, and got plain worn out."

"I'm not even close to worn out." She grinned and playfully swatted Rory's arm. "So I'm just as happy to not have a boring appendix. Good riddance to it, if it couldn't keep up with the fun and appreciate all the special teas and foods I gave it, right?"

"Right. Good riddance, appendix!"

Rory had to chuckle as she led her mom to what she knew was her favorite chair. No point in getting into a discussion on the subject of herbal supplements, and which ones her mother might avoid, since she'd never been interested in her daughter's opinions in the past.

She reached down to scratch the dog's ears as he wagged his tail. "Is this Toby? You described him to me, but he's even cuter than I expected."

"He's the best little doggie. He keeps me company and protects me just like the talismans."

Noting that the dog hadn't even barked when she'd walked in, let alone come out to see who was there, Rory smiled inwardly. Her mother believing the dog protected her was more important than whether or not it actually did.

The fact that she'd only started worrying about that after Rory's father had died had been a surprise, since her sweet dad had been an invalid for so long he'd hardly have been able to deal with an intruder. But in her mother's eyes he'd been a superhero. And she'd been right. The way he'd tried to be there for them even while bravely dealing with his illness had made him one tough, heroic man.

"I'm glad you found such a wonderful dog to be here with you." She tucked her mom into the chair and kissed her forehead. "Are you hungry? I'm going to find you a little something to eat. And later I want to take a look at your incision. But before that I need to see all your hospital dismissal papers and read the instructions. Where are they?"

"In the kitchen somewhere. Linda brought me home and put them on the table, I think."

"I'm sorry I wasn't here in time to get you from the hospital. They told me you were being released tomorrow, and then when I called from the airport they told me you'd already left. That really makes me mad, by the way. I wanted to be there for you."

"I know. I was hoping you'd see the hospital gown they had me in—it was a powdery blue, with these funny little cats on it that were *too* cute. One reminded me of our old Brutus…" Since nothing much ever irritated her mother for long, she gave with a smile and a shrug. "But *you're* here now and *I'm* here now. We'll have lots of big fun once I'm feeling better."

Fun. The name of her mother's game. It was going to be nearly impossible to feel like having fun while she was here, but she'd give it a try for her mom's sake.

"You're going to have to take it easy on the fun while you heal. They told me the rupture was an emergency and they had to use a full traditional incision instead of doing it laparoscopically, so it's going to be a while before the pain is gone."

The thought of how serious that might have been had Rory reaching for another, longer hug.

"I'm going to see if there's food in the kitchen. If not, I brought some stuff in my bag to tide us over until I can get groceries from the store tomorrow. Sit tight for a minute."

The kitchen light was an overly bright fluorescent strip in contrast to the low living room lights, and Rory made another mental note to get more lamps in the other room, so her mother didn't trip over something.

Two gritty, slippery steps into the kitchen brought her to a halt.

From the look of the coffee cans full of colored sand all over the table, her mother's newest creative project was sand art. Glass containers were filled or partially filled in landscape scenes, and Rory recognized one of them as being the Alaska Range they could see from the back of their house—those beautiful mountains she'd always stared at as a child, dreaming about climbing them some-day and crossing over them to somewhere different and big and amazing.

She picked up the jar with the mountain scene and ran her finger across the glass, looking at the brown and green sand topped with fine grains of white. She'd done that, hadn't she? Crossed that mountain. Become the kind of doctor few women were.

She'd thought she'd be looking at those mountain ranges forever, together with Jake. She'd thought they'd make a home and a family in Eudemonia, that they would work as doctors here and in Fairbanks and live happily ever after.

Except their "happy" had died, leaving an "ever after" impossible. She'd run hard and fast away from here— because she hadn't been sure she would survive if she'd stayed. She'd made a new life for herself—going to medical school in LA instead of Anchorage, like she and Jake had planned.

But her life still felt hollow. Full to the brim with work to keep her mind busy and her heart detached from the rest of the world. That detachment had taken a lot of time and effort to achieve. It was exhausting.

She drew in a deep breath and glanced around the kitchen to see that there was as much sand on the floor and the table as there was in the cans. Crunching toward the refrigerator, she peered inside, deciding she'd better get the floor cleaned up as soon as she'd taken some food to the living room and read the discharge papers, so her mom wouldn't slip on all the tiny grains. The last thing her mother needed was to fall and rip open her stitches.

The refrigerator was bare of anything but milk. There was also a little cheese, so Rory sliced it to serve with some crackers she found in the cupboard. She shook sand off the bottom of the hospital papers Linda had put in the middle of the table and went back to the living room.

"Here's a snack for you. I'm going to read through this stuff, then get some more food from my bag."

"This will be plenty. I'm not very hungry."

"Just eat what you can and we'll go from there. I understand if you're not feeling like it, but you do need at least a little so you get your strength back."

Rory straightened from putting the plate on her mother's lap, and was about to sit in the only other chair that had a decent light when she heard the front door open and looked up.

Her heart stuttered, then slammed hard into her ribs.

Jacob Hunter.

She didn't want to look at him for more than a moment, yet she found herself staring, riveted. He looked like he always had—and yet he didn't. A little older but, impossibly, even better. He was still tall and lean, with angled features that were still startlingly beautiful: dark eyes that could see right through a person, and lips that were almost too full and yet perfect for his face. The black silky hair she'd loved to run her hands through long ago, when it had spilled to his shoulders, had been cut short enough to be respectable for the town doctor, but still it brushed his collar, not fully tamed.

He held a bag in one hand and, yeah, just as she would have expected, despite the chill in the air he was wearing a slightly shabby T-shirt that showed his shoulders and biceps were even more muscular than seven years ago, at her father's funeral. No shorts, but the jeans he wore fit his physique perfectly, making him look more like an Alaskan cowboy than a medical professional.

Her heart beat its way up into her throat, making it hard to breathe. She'd thought she was prepared to see him— but not this soon. Not tonight. Not when she was barely ready to deal with being back in town at all.

"Hello, Aurora."

He and her mother were the only two people who called her that. Her mom did because she'd always thought it such a romantic name for a baby born under the Northern Lights. The *aurora borealis*. And Jacob had often called her that because he'd known it annoyed her, and teasing had always been his way of telling someone he cared about them.

Not that he cared about her anymore. Not after all that

had happened between them. Not with all the time that had passed since they'd spoken.

"Hello, Jacob."

"I didn't know when you were getting in, so I thought I'd check on Twinkie."

Twinkie. It also struck Rory that he was the only person who called her mother that other than her. Until that moment she hadn't thought about the familiarity that came with names and nicknames. None of her other friends had ever called her mom Twinkie—why had *he* picked that up?

Probably because he'd been around the house and participating in an awful lot of the crazy over the years. Funny how he had the kind of steady, predictable, wonderful family almost anyone would appreciate, and yet he'd enjoyed being at her zany, very unpredictable and unorthodox house just as much as his own.

"That's nice of you, but you don't need to worry about her now that I'm…here." She'd almost said *home*, but had stopped herself, because this wasn't her home anymore. Never could be.

"Might as well take a look while I'm here." Jake scratched the dog's head and it looked up at him with the same delighted expression as her mother did. "How are you feeling? Have you taken the pain medicine they gave you?"

"Oh, yes. I'm following all the directions they gave me. But I'm still in a lot of pain, so it's not working too well."

"Sorry you're in pain. It's not always easy to control the first couple days out of surgery. Let me take a listen to your heart and lungs."

He reached back to the stethoscope he had looped into the back pocket of his jeans, then pressed his long fingers to her wrist while looking at his watch. Afterward he even pulled a portable blood pressure monitor out of his bag to check that, too.

Meanwhile Rory just stood there, feeling strangely uncomfortable, having no idea what to say or do now that he was here. The awkwardness hanging between them wasn't surprising, even though she'd foolishly hoped that seeing him might leave them both feeling indifferent. That had clearly been a pipedream, considering their parting years ago hadn't exactly been full of rainbows and smiling understanding between the two of them.

Her legs felt a little wobbly, and she briefly considered sitting down, but that would have left her on an uneven footing with him—looking up even more than her five feet four inches required her to.

Jacob's gaze suddenly turned back to Rory, and she swallowed at the mix of emotions in his eyes—the same anger and hurt and confusion that she felt tangling around her own heart…that had seared her to the depths of her soul when she'd left nine years ago.

"Your mom said your Aunt Patty's coming to take care of her after you're gone. She still working at the army base in Anchorage?"

"Yeah. She lives with her son Owen, who's stationed there. She scheduled next week off, so I'll only be here for a short time."

Those dark eyes seemed to bore right into her, and the long pause after she'd answered left her fidgeting—until he finally broke the silence with the question she didn't want asked.

"So, how's your life?"

"Good. Everything is great."

God, when had she become such a liar? If there was one person who had to know that wasn't true, it was Jacob. But there *were* good things about her life, right? Although her job was about the only thing that came to mind.

"I just passed my board exams, so I'm officially a doctor of pediatric orthopedic medicine. I was supposed to be interviewing today, for a permanent position at the hospital, but I had to reschedule it for next week."

Again, he didn't speak, and even as she squirmed under his serious gaze memories of the time they'd been apart got mixed up with all the years they'd been together. It was as if nothing had changed between them.

For a brief moment she had the shocking urge to go up on her tiptoes and give him a kiss hello on that luscious mouth. Which proved that her brain's muscle memory was stronger than her common sense when it came to him. But of course that wasn't surprising, was it? They'd known one another since they were kids in elementary school.

Except kissing those lips hadn't happened until college, so that might not be the best explanation she could have come up with. Besides, all that felt like a lifetime ago.

He didn't respond, instead handing her a business card, his expression unreadable. "I'll be going, since you're here to look after Twinkie. Here's my number if you need to reach me. She's supposed to have a follow-up appointment with her surgeon in a few days. I can take over after that."

That uncomfortable flutter in her chest just wouldn't go away, and she swallowed at the realization that she'd be seeing him way too much during this visit if she had to do as he suggested.

"Maybe you forgot I'm a doctor too," she said, trying to somehow infuse some light humor into the words, even as the air felt like a heavy shroud hanging over her. "And a surgeon. Very used to dealing with post-op issues. After she sees her own surgeon I can take care of any problems she might have."

"Just the same as always." Annoyance and disapproval were clear in the dark eyes that flicked across her. "You can do *everything* better than anyone else. You never *listen* to anyone else."

"That's not what I said. I just meant—"

"I know what you meant. But here's the thing: I have all the equipment to take her vitals and deal with any problems at my office, not to mention pain meds and antibiotic ointment for her incision and replacement bandages. So get over your ultra-independent self and bring her to my office after her appointment so I can take a look."

"Jake, it's just not necessary to—"

"Don't worry," he interrupted with a mocking smile on his face. "Since you have to be in control of everything, I won't shut you out of the process."

"I don't... I don't have to be in control of everything!"

She folded her arms across her chest, which was starting to burn a little. She'd made one horribly bad decision—admittedly a life-changing decision, but still... That didn't make her controlling. It made her foolish. Regretful. Broken.

"What's that supposed to mean?"

He didn't bother to answer that, just picked up the bag he'd brought and moved toward the kitchen.

"I have some food. I figured you wouldn't have had a chance to go to the store. I got it when I was in Fairbanks earlier, since the selection at Green's Market can be slim pickings sometimes. In case you don't remember."

Rory stared after him, trying to figure out how to handle all this as he moved out of sight.

Then her mother spoke. "It's so sweet of that Jacob to bring us food, isn't it?" her mother said, with the adoring smile on her face she always had when Jake was around, clearly oblivious to the tension between the two of them. "He always was something special. I remember—"

"I'll see if he needs help." Rory didn't want to be close to Jake in the small kitchen, but she definitely didn't want to listen to her mother's glowing diatribe about how perfect and wonderful he was.

But the truth…? He really *was* nearly perfect.

Yes, he had that impatience thing that sometimes boiled over into irritation. And he'd always left his socks in the middle of the floor, apparently not considering them to be "real" clothes that had to be put in the laundry bag. And somehow, he'd never seen pot lids as counting toward actual dishes that should be washed. But otherwise…

Perfection in human form. He just was.

She was the one who was totally and horribly flawed.

Just before she got to the doorway, a loud curse and then a series of crashing sounds came from the kitchen, and suddenly she remembered.

The sand. *Crap!*

She sprinted the last few steps, and once she hit the kitchen the toes of her boots slid across the linoleum and nearly jammed into the top of Jake's head, where he lay flat on his back on the floor. Cans and boxes were strewn everywhere, and a split plastic jug glugged a small river of milk onto the ancient blue linoleum.

"Oh, my God, are you all right?"

She knelt down next to him, her hands on his shoulders, his chest, traveling down his arms to see if they felt intact.

His deep brown eyes, surrounded by thick lashes, looked up and met hers, and for a long, arrested moment time felt suspended. Her heart thumped hard in her chest and it took all her willpower not to lean over and kiss him, just as she'd wanted to do earlier. Just as she'd done for so many years.

Her heart squeezed with familiar pain and longing as she forced herself to lean back instead of forward. "What hurts?"

"You're the orthopedic surgeon. Take a guess."

Something about the expression in his eyes told her

that maybe he wasn't talking about physical injuries. That maybe his mind was going back in time too, the same way hers was. To the pain they'd shared and yet experienced in totally different ways.

She choked back all those wonderful and awful feelings that insisted on flooding back. "I'm guessing your tailbone is bruised, and maybe an elbow or two, but otherwise you feel okay."

For a split second his hand lifted toward her, before his fingers curled into his palm and he dropped his arm. He sat up, then shoved to his feet.

"Yeah, a few bruises."

He glanced down at his clothes and brushed off some of the clinging sand, clearly avoiding looking at her, before he began picking up the groceries that had been flung all over the kitchen.

"Don't worry about the milk," she said, hurrying to grab a kitchen towel to mop it up, even though it looked like Toby's happy licking was going to take care of it for her. "Or anything else. I'll put it all away. Thanks for bringing it."

His eyes met hers again, grim now. Probably he could tell she was beyond anxious for him to leave—but wouldn't he want to get away from her just as much?

"No problem. Also, even though neither of us wants to hang around each other, we need to do what's best for your mother." He shoved a few things in the fridge, then set the rest on the counter. "Which means you bringing her in to see me in a few days. Just let me know when."

Unexpected tears clogged her throat as she watched his long legs take him from the kitchen in fast strides, despite the risk of slipping, and she angrily swallowed them down. It shouldn't make her want to cry that he didn't want to spend time with her. Why *would* he? If she were him she'd keep as far away as possible from the woman who'd wrecked their dreams. And hadn't figuring out ways to avoid him been at the top of her mind the minute she'd bought her plane ticket?

But the quiet tears slid down her cheeks anyway.

CHAPTER TWO

"I'M GOING TO up your dose another twenty-five milligrams, Wilma," Jake said as he wrote a prescription for his elderly patient. "Your blood pressure is better, but still a little high."

"Okay, Dr. Hunter. I'll take it every day if you think I should."

He paused and glanced up at her. "You told me you *had* been taking it every day."

She took the paper he handed her and made a sheepish face. "Maybe not *every* day."

"If it's hard for you to remember I can have Ellie get you a pill box that helps you keep track. Are you going to Fairbanks soon, so you can fill this? Or do you need one of us to get it for you?"

"I want to get supplies before the snow comes, so my son's taking me tomorrow."

"Good."

He helped the woman down from the examination table and gave her a few more instructions. After she'd left the small room he wrote a note to himself to talk with her son to make sure she both got and took her medicine, then started typing his exam notes into the computer.

Ellie, who'd been office manager of this place for as long as he could remember, poked her graying head in the door. "Your mom's here with Mika."

"Already?" He glanced at his watch, wondering how it had gotten so late. "Have her come in here while I finish this up."

The gleeful shriek that had been part of his world for the past eight months had him smiling before he even looked up from the computer. "I see he's in a happy mood. Thanks for watching him again, Ma."

"He's such a good boy." His mother beamed down at the baby in her arms. "He was cranky before his nap, but he's been all smiles since."

"I just need to finish up these notes, and then I have one more patient to see. Can you take Mika to my office to play until I'm done? Shouldn't be long."

"You still have things for him in there? Your dad bought him a new toy in Fairbanks today, but it's at our house for when we're babysitting. I told him he was going to spoil the child to death, since he'll be getting all kinds of toys for his birthday. One-year-olds deserve a special party, don't you think?"

"I don't think he cares if he gets a party, but I *do* know he'll love the attention." He glanced up and smiled. "As for the spoiling—you were both good at that with all three of us, growing up, but I think we turned out okay."

"Yes, you sure did. Two doctors and a lawyer? Not bad at all."

"Yeah, except Timothy always said I'd be the doctor, Grace would be the lawyer and *he* wanted to be the Native American chief. I think he still kind of wishes that had happened, instead of planning to come work here next year when he's finished with his residency."

He finished the notes and stood. The serious look his mother sent him was a surprise, considering their light conversation.

"What?"

"Have you invited Rory over for dinner yet?"

"No, and I'm not planning to—which I already told you."

Seeing her in the office when she brought in her mother was going to be difficult enough. The last thing he wanted was hours of small-talk with the woman he'd thought would be with him forever—the woman who'd crushed his heart into tiny pieces, then stomped on them for good measure.

"She's busy with her mother, and I'm busy with work and Mika."

"Then *I'll* invite her. I want to catch up with all she's been doing since she moved to LA."

"Go ahead and invite her, then. Just don't expect me to come, too."

"Jacob," she said in a disapproving voice. "It's been a long time. I know things were…bad for both of you. But can't you two just be friends now, since you went through the same heartache together? You were such good pals for such a long time."

Good pals. That had been true for what seemed like nearly his entire life—until they'd become lovers. And then had come the happy surprise…before the horrible shock and the heartbreak. The fact that his mother wanted him to be friends with Rory now told him she had no clue how bad it had really been.

He wished he didn't still feel the bitter resentment and hurt. But seeing her for even a few minutes last night had proved he still wasn't ready to move on from that.

Maybe he never would be.

The moment he'd walked in through her mother's front door a storm of emotion had swarmed up and strangled him. Far more than he'd expected, considering it had been seven years since he'd last seen her at her dad's funeral, and they'd barely spoken then.

But he hadn't forgotten the amazing deep green of her

eyes—like moss on a hillside in the summer. The honey highlights in her silky brown hair. And when he'd slipped and fallen on that damned floor, and she'd leaned over him, he'd been stunned that she smelled exactly the same as she always had. She obviously still dabbed grapefruit oil on her skin—something her mother had encouraged her to use as a child, claiming it boosted the immune system and made people feel more cheerful.

Rory had always rolled her eyes at her mother's conviction about all the things herbal oils would do for a person, and he'd sometimes wondered why she used it when it she claimed she didn't believe in it. Obviously she liked the stuff, no matter what she said about it.

If he closed his eyes he swore he could still smell her. But he wasn't going to tell his mother about all those memories and the discomfort—damn it, the *anguish* he'd felt when Rory left. Or that it was careening around inside of him all over again.

Before he could come up with some kind of answer that would satisfy her, Ellie poked her head in the door again.

"Rory Anderson is on the line. She says she thinks her mom has a urinary tract infection. She's having trouble passing urine, and it's cloudy. She's wondering if she can get an antibiotic from you."

He hesitated, then opened his mouth to say he'd write it and Ellie could call it into the pharmacy in Fairbanks. He forced himself to close it again. His policy was never to prescribe medicine—especially antibiotics—over the phone. He had to see the patient first, make sure it was really what they needed.

But maybe this time he could make an exception, since Rory was a doctor. He could leave a prescription at the front desk for Rory to pick up, and he wouldn't have to see her—except for the day after her mother went to her surgeon for a follow-up.

No. Much as he didn't want to see Rory, he couldn't let his feelings urge him to violate good medical practice. Rory dealt with bones in her job. Who knew when she'd last had a patient with a UTI? Not to mention that a lot of surgeons called in antibiotic specialists for post-op infections. Truth was, there was no way around it.

He grimaced. "Tell her to bring Wendy in right now. We'll fit her in before the day's over."

"I feel fine, Aurora. I mean, yes, it really hurts to go to the bathroom, but my stitches hurt, too. I don't see any reason we have to go see Jacob. Can't I just take more pain medicine?"

"A urinary tract infection isn't something to mess around with, Twinkie. Not when you were on a catheter post-op and are having fever and chills now. You don't want it to get worse and result in a kidney infection. Plus, you'll be more comfortable when an antibiotic gets rid of it."

"I just hate going to doctors."

"Who doesn't? Except *this* doctor is one of your favorite people, so quit complaining. He already said he'll squeeze you in this evening."

Which had her feeling relieved that her mom would get the meds she needed, but totally dreading having to see Jake again, even though her mother would love it.

"Okay. I guess it's true that seeing Jacob is always fun. But why can't *you* just get me an antibiotic, if that's what you think I need? Isn't that why you went to doctor school?"

"I went to doctor school for a little more than that." Trust her mom to make her laugh, even as Rory was a ball of nerves. "But I can't prescribe medicine here. I don't have a medical license or privileges in Alaska."

"Well, that makes no sense. You were *born* here, for

heaven's sake! Can't you just show them your birth certificate?"

"It doesn't work that way. I'd have to apply and take a test." Which she wasn't going to do, even though there had been a time when she'd thought she'd work here forever. Now the goal was to get that position at the hospital in LA and make her move away from here permanent.

She stroked her mother's wavy blond hair that barely showed any silvery threads. It still hung nearly to her waist, as it always had, and Rory wondered if she could convince her to let her cut it, at least a little, so it would be easier to take care of.

Then again, it was such a part of who her mother was that it was probably worth the extra work, so she gently twisted it and secured it into a semi-tamed ponytail.

"Then just take the test."

"Maybe someday." Meaning *never*. "But until then the only way for you to get an antibiotic is to go to a doctor here, and Jacob is close by."

"Well, if that's what we have to do," her mother said, shaking her head in clear disbelief of the protocols involved in medical care. "When do we leave?"

"Right now." Her stomach squeezed, but she stiffened her shoulders and helped her mom get her coat on. The sooner they got there, the sooner it would be over with. "They're closing his office soon."

It was just a ten-minute drive from her mother's house to downtown Eudemonia—if you could call it downtown.

At the age of eight Rory had been amazed when she'd gone to Fairbanks for the first time, to do some clothes shopping. Before then her mother had sewn or knitted all of it—until her dad had decided they should stop home-schooling her, and send her to the public school instead.

She'd stood out like a sore thumb at that school for a while, until she'd learned how to fit in, and one of those ways had been wearing off-the-rack clothes. She'd met Jacob Hunter at that school, too—the boy who'd become her hero.

She'd had no idea that a real downtown had more than a post office, a few stores, a medical clinic and multiple bars. Bars being the most important things in a town, as far as many residents were concerned. But, hey, *something* had to help everyone get through the nearly twenty-four-hour darkness of winter and the bitter cold and isolation of those months, right?

No doubt the bars were still the places where Eudemonians and others from nearby towns got together to listen to local musicians, play cards, checkers or poker and socialize.

Memories of those days had her smiling for a split second—until she remembered she wasn't a part of this place anymore, and sure wouldn't be doing any of that while she was here.

A couple of cars were parked behind the clinic, and as soon as she spotted a gleaming black pickup truck, with big, knobbly wheels ready to tackle the snow when it came, she knew it was Jake's. He'd always loved black cars and manly trucks, saying how he'd have one someday, when he was a doctor like his dad.

A vision of his first beaten-up car, which he'd bought in high school with the money his dad had paid him to keep the clinic clean and take care of the medical waste, popped into her head. He'd still been driving it when all hell had rained down on their heads, and she was glad it wasn't still around so she didn't have to see it and remember.

Not that she didn't remember it as if it were yesterday anyway.

"No need to hurry in, Twinkie," she said as she helped her mom from the car. "Take your time."

"I know I'm a pain, marshmallow girl. I'm walking

slower than Grandma Lettie did when she was ninety-five. But my belly still hurts a lot, darn it."

She grinned up at Rory, and the tightness of her chest eased at her mother's upbeat attitude toward life. Wendy Anderson had always been an odd little thing, but she was special in so many ways. Rory knew she was blessed to have her as a mother, even though she had often been more like the parent and her mother more like the child.

"You could never be a pain. I love you." She kissed her mother's cheek, then opened the clinic door for her.

Ellie Sanders stood there, ready to take them back to the examination room, and Rory smiled at the woman who'd worked in the clinic for as long as she could remember. "Hi, Ellie. Thanks so much for fitting Mom in."

"No thanks necessary, Rory. Besides, it's thanks to Dr. Hunter, too, not just me. I'm never in a hurry to leave all the excitement of this place and be all alone at home."

The twinkle in her eyes showed she didn't really feel lonely, and Rory nearly asked about her kids and grand-kids but decided not to go there. She didn't want to recon-nect too much to this town she'd be leaving again soon.

"He's waiting for you in Room two."

Rory's heart seemed to skip a beat with every step down the hallway until they finally reached the room. The door was partly open, and inside she could see Jake's mother standing there, talking to someone out of her line of vision.

Her heart gave another unpleasant kick. She didn't re-ally want to make stiff and uncomfortable small talk. But then she started to get annoyed with herself. Was she going to hide away like a child the whole time she was in town?

She pushed the door fully open and there was Jacob. She blinked, and for a second her brain couldn't quite grasp what she was seeing. Then her heart shook hard, before diving straight into her stomach at the realization that he was holding a baby close in his arms...smiling and kissing its cheek.

Had he married and had a child? He might have. Why wouldn't he? Growing up, all he'd wanted was to take his dad's place as Eudemonia's doctor. To marry, have a family and put down even deeper roots than his partly Alaska Native family had generations ago.

She gulped, trying to get air. Maybe the baby was a patient. Except there was no one in the room except him, his mom and the infant. It wasn't likely he'd be taking care of a child without any parent around, cuddling it and kissing it and looking at it adoringly.

"Hello, Rory. I haven't seen you in forever," Beth Hunter said with a tentative smile. "I was worried I wouldn't get to see you while you were in town."

"Hi. I'm... I'm only here for a short time. Until Mom's sister comes to take over."

Jake glanced up from the baby and his smile faltered. The effort he put into shoring it up again was obvious as he moved his gaze to her mother.

"Twinkie, I'm glad you've come in. If you do have a UTI we definitely need to get it taken care of so it doesn't make you sick while your body is already working so hard to recover."

"I hate to bother you, but Aurora insisted."

Her mother walked closer and gave the baby a couple of gentle pokes in its tummy. It grinned.

"He's getting so *big*! My goodness, I can't believe it. Then again, I haven't seen him since the party your mom gave to celebrate his adoption. How old is he now?"

"He's almost a year, Wendy. Can you believe it?" Beth said. "We're having a birthday party for him next week— I'll be sure to send you an invitation, if you're feeling up to coming."

"Oh, I think I will be—with my Aurora here to help

me get well and my sister Patty's coming soon. How are *you* doing, Beth?"

"Doing very well, thanks. My grandson keeps me hopping, that's for sure."

Rory watched everyone beaming at the child and it took her a herculean effort not to pass out, she felt so woozy.

Adopted? The baby was really *his*? Did the baby belong to a lover, too? Someone he was committed to? Had he wanted to adopt for that reason? Had he married the baby's mother and her mom just hadn't thought to tell her?

The baby reached up his little hand to grab a wad of Jake's hair and he turned, chuckling, to extricate it from the chubby fist. "Ouch! I don't tug on *your* hair, now, do I?"

The baby gurgled and laughed in response, and the sound, along with the sweet, loving smile on Jake's face as he looked down at the baby, made Rory feel physically sick.

This was what *they* should have had together. *She* should have had this baby and the life they'd always planned. Instead it had been stolen after one catastrophic decision, changing both their lives forever.

"Twinkie, why don't you take a seat on the exam table?" she somehow managed to croak. "I'll meet you out in the waiting room."

Blindly, she stumbled down the hall and out of the building, gasping in gulps of cold air. Her knees wobbled and she sat on the step, tucking her head between her knees to try to gather herself.

How embarrassing to fall apart this way. What had happened was long ago and far away, and the last thing she would ever want to be was an object of pity. To have Jake's mother, Jake himself, shaking their heads sadly because she hadn't been able to move on the way he obviously had. Because she hadn't even wanted to.

Selfish. She was being horribly selfish—just like the

night she'd made that terrible decision. Going out on that rescue, being all self-righteous, telling herself and everyone else that she was doing it to save someone, when in truth it had been for the adrenaline rush of it. The feeling of self-satisfaction she'd craved. There had been a half-dozen other people who could have taken her place to rescue that man...

She *had* to put aside her feelings. The right thing to do was to try to feel happy for Jake that he had the kind of life he'd always wanted. That he was living in this town, working alongside his dad as a family physician, with the child he'd adopted. Maybe a woman he loved. He deserved that kind of happiness even if she didn't.

She heard the door open behind her and lifted her head. She stared across the parking lot at the ruby and gold sunset and tried to compose herself. A gentle hand landed on her shoulder. It was too small and light to be Jake's.

"Rory, I'm sorry if it was a shock to see Jacob's son. Obviously your mom didn't tell you."

Rory just shook her head, not trusting her voice.

Beth Hunter sat on the cold step beside her and propped the baby on her lap. He had on a little red jacket and knit hat, though Beth wasn't wearing any kind of coat. But then, she was a Native Alaskan through and through, and her children were just like her and their dad. This baby would grow up like all of them, special and wonderful, and Rory swallowed down the tears that suddenly threatened to choke her.

"Do you want to hear the story about Mika? That's what his mother named him—Mika. Do you want to know how it came about that Jake adopted him?"

Did she?

Turning her head so she couldn't see the baby's sweet face as she shook from the inside out, she nearly told Beth that she'd rather not hear it. But not knowing the story wouldn't change a thing, would it? She'd still feel this deep ache that he had this beautiful little child. That they didn't have one together. And if he was in love with someone else—that wouldn't matter, either.

"Sure."

"A single woman came to Eudemonia to take a job with the oil company nearby. She was pregnant, and either didn't know who the father was or didn't want to say. She came to Jake for prenatal care, and he delivered little Mika here at the clinic. When the baby was only about two months old, his mama came in feeling very feverish with a stiff neck. She was confused, and presented with photophobia."

A fear of light, along with the other symptoms Beth mentioned, likely would have meant one thing for the woman, and that one thing would have been very bad. Rory kept quiet, but forced herself to turn and look at Beth and the baby cuddled against her.

"Jake suspected it was bacterial meningitis, and immediately gave her a combination of IV antibiotics while he did a spinal tap to confirm the diagnosis. But she'd waited too long to come in, and while Jake and his dad did everything they could she died within hours. There was this sweet, tiny baby boy in the office, with Ellie watching him and his mother was gone... Jake—well, it was hard on him. He wondered if there was something more he should have done. And little Mika was all alone."

"Jake shouldn't have felt that way. He knows that kind of virulent bacterial infection has to be caught early or it's over. It's not his fault that she died," Rory said dully, knowing that everyone had said nearly the same thing to her, nine years ago.

Not her fault. But it had felt like her fault anyway, and how could she ever know for sure?

Beth nodded. "He knows that—but still... It was hard.

He'd brought little Mika into the world and he felt a connection to him, you know? He was allowed to foster the baby until the adoption went through a couple months later. And now he's a member of the family and my first grandbaby."

"He's a lucky boy."

And Rory meant it. He was. The Hunter family were some of the best people she knew, and he'd be raised in the same awesome way Jake and his brother and sister had been raised. With love and guidance, a strong work ethic and a love for Alaska—especially Eudemonia.

Somehow the news that Jake wasn't married and wasn't in love with the baby's mother had her breathing slightly easier, even as she tried to figure out how to deal with him being a father. Then again, not being in love with Mika's mother didn't mean he wasn't in a serious relationship.

And why was she even wondering about that? It wasn't as though either one of them wanted to get involved with each other again.

"So," Beth said quietly. "How are you? Happy in Los Angeles?"

"I'm good. Fine. I love my job."

What else could she say? That she loved her job and spent all her time doing it so she wouldn't have to think about anything else?

"Tell me again what kind of doctor you are? Jake never said."

Of course he hadn't. Because he didn't want to think about her and what had happened to make her change her plans and go to LA any more than she did.

"I'm a pediatric orthopedic surgeon. I take care of children's broken bones and congenital bone disorders. You might remember I broke my leg falling out of a tree when I was ten? That whole experience amazed me—when I saw the X-rays and how they put it back together. I knew then I wanted to be a bone surgeon."

She wouldn't share the fact that the only reason she'd even thought about becoming a doctor was because of the Hunter family, how Jake and his brother had always known that was what they wanted to be, just like their dad.

"Sounds like you're making a big difference in people's lives. You must be proud."

"Yes, it's a good job."

"And LA is light-years from here. I bet that was a big adjustment."

"Warm and sunny year-round? Yes, very different from here." She forced a smile. "Then again, there's nothing like the clear air, open skies and bright stars of Alaska. I admit there are times when I miss it."

"Well…" Beth hesitated, then seemed to change her mind on whatever she'd been about to say. "We'd love to have you over for dinner some night while you're here. Before you go back. Your mother is more than welcome, too."

"I doubt she'll be feeling up to it."

Beth probably knew it was Rory who wouldn't feel up to it, but she let it pass.

"I'll ask her, though. Thanks. And, Beth…?"

"Yes?"

Rory let herself reach out to stroke the baby's round cheek, and its sweet softness made tears sting the backs of her eyes. "Congratulations on your grandbaby. He's just beautiful."

"Rory—"

The door opened and there was Ellie again, interrupting whatever Beth had been about to say. It was beyond a relief.

"Your mother is all set, Rory."

"Thanks."

She stood and reached down to help Beth to her feet as the woman propped the baby on her hip.

"Thanks for telling me about Mika and his mother. That…helps."

Beth squeezed her hand. "I'm always here if you ever want to talk."

No, she didn't want to talk. She wanted to hide in her mother's house, take care of her, then get out of Eudemonia and bury herself in work again. She wanted to commit to that job in LA, far away from here.

"Thanks, but I'm fine."

That lie stuck in her throat as she met her mother and Jacob walking down the hallway to the front entrance. He was so handsome, so familiar, so…distant. He'd schooled his expression into one of cool professionalism, obviously as intent on keeping an emotional distance from her as she was.

"Definitely a UTI, so it's good you brought her in. I have a couple of sample packets of antibiotic here," he said, handing them to her. "I'll have Ellie send a prescription to a drugstore in Fairbanks, too, because she'll need to be on them for at least five days."

"Thanks. We appreciate you seeing us tonight. Sorry we kept you from… Mika."

Their eyes met, and the pain she felt deep inside was reflected in his eyes as he reached to take the baby from his mother's arms.

"Not a problem. He'll have to get used to having his daddy get home late when there are patients to see. Right, buddy?"

Daddy. Buddy. Her throat tightened all over again, and she knew she needed to get out of there.

Just as she was about to turn to her mother the baby leaned forward, slapped his little hands against Jake's cheeks, and pressed his nose to his. God, it was like something out of a beautiful family movie, and the sweetly intimate picture nearly made the dam burst.

Somehow she gulped back the tears and grabbed her mother's arm to hustle her toward the front door. No way was she going to humiliate herself by crying right there in front of all of them. But if she didn't leave right that second, that was exactly what was going to happen.

She felt like every hour would be a matter of survival.

CHAPTER THREE

WITH THE CLINIC CLOSED, Sunday was the best day for Jake to catch up on life, and he strapped Mika into his car seat so they could head to Fairbanks. His parents had offered to have him and the baby drive with them to get supplies, but he'd rather not be stuck going to some of the stores to do the things his mother considered vital. Like picking out balloons and other stuff for the party she was planning for the boy.

"Your grandma is pretty excited about your birthday, Mika," he said. "Does it hurt your feelings that I don't want to do any of the decorating she thinks is so important? All I want is to show up with you and eat cake—does that make me a bad dad?"

Mika grinned, babbled and kicked his feet, which Jake took as confirmation that the child didn't think he was a bad father at all. He leaned in to kiss the baby's cheek, and as he did so he suddenly remembered Rory's expression when she'd walked into the office and seen him doing exactly that.

It could only be described as *devastated*. Every drop of color had drained from her face, and he'd been about to hand the baby to his mother and reach for Rory because he'd been so worried she might faint. Then she'd turned and practically run from the room, and he'd let her go. He knew the woman inside out, and the last thing she ever wanted from anyone was sympathy.

Even when life had thrown such a cruel blow at them she'd refused to lean on anyone, had cut herself off from her parents and her friends.

And from him. Especially him.

He hadn't known what to do. He'd tried over and over to reach out to her. To hold her. To have them grieve together. To heal together, somehow move on with their lives together after this huge loss.

But what had she done?

She'd upped and left, crushing his dreams. She'd abandoned their plans, their future, the deep love they'd shared. She'd abandoned *him*, leaving him to bleed alone.

His jaw tightened with the memories. Yeah, she'd left without so much as a goodbye, and as far as he was concerned the shorter her stay here in Eudemonia, the better. He wanted to be the bigger person, to forgive and forget and move on. He thought he had. But from the first second he'd seen her in her mother's living room, he'd known he was wrong.

What he'd felt at that moment had forced him to face the fact that he'd never forgotten even one little thing about her: her spunky, take-no-prisoners attitude toward life, softened by her loving and giving nature, her independent-to-a-fault spitfire nature that got her into trouble sometimes, her heart-shaped pixie-like face that always changed expression with the wind. Sweet, amused, angry, contrite… You never knew for sure what you'd see there.

He still remembered the exact moment he'd met her, in the fourth grade at the school outside Fairbanks he'd gone to since kindergarten. Remembered the way her beautiful green eyes had fixed on his when he'd told the kid bullying the new girl with the weird clothes to buzz off.

She had looked at him with admiration and awe, as if

he was Superman, and from that moment on he'd loved spending time with her. Fishing, bicycling, playing ball, riding snow machines. She'd always acted like he was the best person in the whole world to spend time with, and he'd felt exactly the same about her.

Then college had come—and living in the same dorm building had changed things. One night, with a few illegal beers under their belts, talking had turned into kissing, and the electricity had shocked them both. From that moment their relationship had changed, and what he'd seen when he looked into her eyes had been exactly what he'd felt for her. A love so deep and clear it had made him weak, just as it had also made him strong.

He closed his eyes. She'd been a part of him for so long. And then she'd been gone for nearly as long. All through medical school without her, then moving back here with no Rory around anymore, he'd been able to fool himself that she no longer was.

He'd been wrong.

He shoved down the memories and opened his eyes to kiss Mika's soft hair before closing the door, wishing he could kiss Rory, too, and hating himself for that. What they'd had had been special, but she'd destroyed it—and a part of him along with it. He'd better keep remembering that. She couldn't be trusted to be honest, to share what she was feeling, to stick around. No way could he let her sneak back inside his heart for even the few days she would be home.

Not *home.* Not for her—not anymore.

He dragged his thoughts back to the list of things he needed in Fairbanks and got in the driver's seat. The truck started with a roar. He stared up at the heavy gray sky, thinking he should get in more supplies than usual, with the possibility of snow on the way. October didn't usually have precipitation, but you never knew. And any Alaskan had to be well prepared for anything.

He'd barely gone five miles past the fourth and last traffic light in Eudemonia when his phone rang and he saw it was Ellie.

"What's up?"

"I got a frantic phone call from Pooky Green, saying his son got hurt riding his dirt bike. He's sure his arm's broken and wants to bring him to the clinic. I called your dad, but he said they're already in Fairbanks."

"Did you tell him we don't do broken bones? He needs to take him to the ER in Fairbanks."

"Well, actually, I...um..."

Something about her sheepish and apologetic tone had him wondering what was coming next. "What? Spit it out."

"I know Rory is a bone specialist, who works with kids, even. So I told Pooky to bring him into the clinic and see if *she* can look at him. His car isn't running too well, and he's worried about driving it all the way to Fairbanks before he works on it. So I figured why not see if she can do something first?"

"Damn it, Ellie." He didn't want to see Rory, and he sure as hell didn't want to work with her. "I wish you'd stop trying to take care of everyone in town. I'm going to Fairbanks, so I'll take the kid to the ER."

"Um... I already called Rory. She said she'd come to the clinic to look at him, and see what she thinks. She's already on her way. But you don't need to come—I'll let her in and show her where everything is."

Jake swore under his breath, counted to ten, then unlocked his jaw. "No one's going to work at the clinic without either me or Dad around. I'll meet her there. But please don't do this again."

"Oh, I won't! Thanks, Jake! I know Pooky and Eli really appreciate it. You're the best."

Her elated tone had him shaking his head, realizing she considered this a huge victory and hadn't listened to a thing he'd said. "I'm going to talk to Dad about docking your pay for this."

Her peal of laughter in his ear before he hung up tugged a reluctant grin out of him. Yeah, there was nothing like working in a place where you'd known everyone your whole life.

But Rory had chosen to leave it all behind her.

He wasn't going to think about it. Not now, and not ever. It was long ago and didn't matter anymore. He'd gotten pretty good at almost forgetting all about her. He'd moved on with his life, successfully shoving away all the hurt and pain and disbelief that, in the middle of the worst time in both their lives, she'd left without a word. Now here she was again, bringing memories back.

He didn't want to get stirred up about her again. His life here was good, and he had little Mika now, to enrich his life and make him laugh. Yeah, maybe it would be nice to find a woman to share his life with someday, but when he did he'd be sure it was someone who'd stick it out through the tough times. Who'd be truly committed to staying in Eudemonia forever.

He swung his truck into the parking lot and recognized Rory's rental car from when it had been parked in front of her mom's house. It looked like Pooky was already there, too, and he fought down the burn in his gut at the fact that the woman who'd abandoned him had waltzed into his clinic like she had a right to be there.

He drew in a deep, calming breath. It probably wasn't fair of him to feel that way. She'd come because Ellie had asked her to, and she was obviously trying to help. If she could save Pooky and his kid a trip to the ER he should be happy about that.

With Mika in his arms, he went in and found the whole

crew in the first exam room. Rory was taking the boy's pulse, looking down at her wrist. The bright overhead light brought out the highlights of her smooth soft hair that skimmed across her cheek as she studied her watch.

"Your pulse is a little fast, but it's probably because you're in pain," she said, sending a smile to Eli. "Doesn't look like any break has affected your arteries or circulation, but I'm going to examine your hand and wrist now, just to be sure. Does it feel numb or tingly?"

"No. Just my arm hurts super-bad."

She nodded. "From the position of your arm, I'm positive it's a dislocated elbow—and, yeah, that's *really* painful, I know. The good news is I can manipulate it back into position. But we'll get an X-ray to confirm that there's nothing broken before I do that."

Jake could see the kid's arm was misshapen, and twisted right at the elbow, and found he had to agree with her diagnosis. He handed Mika to Ellie, then stepped forward. Rory lifted her head, obviously surprised to see him— which seemed ridiculous, considering he and his father were the only two doctors who worked there.

"I'll get the X-ray taken care of," he said.

"Ellie said she'd get the machine. I know how to operate most all of them."

"Yeah, well, this is *my* family's clinic and it's *my* responsibility to make sure everybody here gets the care they need."

Her lips tightened before she turned back to examine Eli's hand and fingers, moving them up and down and asking the boy questions.

Jake felt slightly annoyed with himself that he'd spoken in such a harsh tone. It wasn't very professional and she didn't deserve it. But somehow he hadn't been able to help the way it came out. Being around her seemed to dredge up all the bad feelings and resentment he'd thought he'd put behind him.

"Thanks again for seeing him, Rory. I can't believe you're a bone doctor these days," Pooky said.

"Neither can my mother." Rory sent him one of her cute grins before her expression turned calm and professional again.

Jake watched Rory work, carefully touching and examining the boy's arm until she finally placed his hand gently on his lap. "Everything seems okay circulation-wise," Rory said. "Let's get that X-ray to confirm nothing's broken before I move your elbow back into place."

"Here's the machine," Ellie said, rolling the portable X-ray into the room with one hand, holding Mika on her hip with the other.

"I was just coming to get it," Jake said, frustrated that he was standing there doing nothing while everyone else was working in his clinic. "Why don't you take Mika to my office now?"

Ellie gave him a look that said he was being rude and, damn it, he knew he deserved it.

He focused on getting pictures of the boy's arm in several positions, with Rory silently assisting beside him. When they were finished her shoulder pressed into his side as they both studied the X-rays, and he edged slightly away to try to escape the warmth of her body.

"Yep—see there?" she said, pointing. "Thankfully nothing's broken. I can reduce the elbow back to its correct alignment, but you probably know it'll hurt like crazy." Her eyes looked up to meet his. "Do you have any twilight sleep or some other conscious sedation he can have while I do it?"

"We do. Hardly ever have a need for it, since we don't do this kind of thing here, but occasionally I have someone in a lot of pain or nearly hysterical, and we need to get them relaxed and out of it."

"Good."

They both showed Eli and his dad the X-rays, explaining what they were looking at and what Rory planned to do.

Considering Rory's take-charge nature, Jake was surprised at how she included him in the conversation—like they were a team instead of her taking over the whole thing. Which made him feel even more ashamed of his attitude about her being here today and taking care of the boy so he didn't have to take a trip to the city and wait hours to be seen in the ER.

To make up for it, he knew it was time to verbally give her credit.

"You're lucky Dr. Anderson is in town for a few days and can take care of you, Eli," he said. "Only a trained orthopedic surgeon should do an elbow reduction on anyone other than a toddler. Otherwise you'd have had to go to Fairbanks."

"But it's good that you have all the other stuff we need here," she said, and the smile in her eyes made him even gladder that he'd made the gesture to applaud her. "I bet you have the right kind of splint, but if you don't I brought a few different kinds of splints and casts, not knowing what we might need."

"You brought splints and casts in your luggage? I guess you don't believe in packing light."

"You never know when a medical emergency is going to arise. I like to be prepared—as you know."

Yeah, he *did* know. He'd often teased her about it, since she'd always made sure she had a more extensive emergency preparedness supply than most. Probably because for a long time her dad hadn't been well enough to take care of such things, and her mom had been very blasé about it, despite living in a place where you needed to be ready for all kinds of weather and storms.

As she had through much of her life, Rory was the one who had taken care of running the house and all that needed to be done. She'd done it without comment or complaint, which was one of the things he'd always admired about her.

Their eyes met again in a long connection that told him they were both remembering all kinds of things her comment had brought to mind.

Such as the time they'd gotten lost together on a hiking trip near Denali and spent the night in a pup tent he'd thought was ridiculous for her to bring along for a day trip. But she'd insisted—just in case. When it had got too dark to find their way until the next morning, that tent had made their night a lot more comfortable than it would have been without.

Memories of being spooned together with her in that small cocoon, her firm rear and soft body pressed against his, made his breath feel short and his heart heavy.

He quickly turned to get the anesthetic that would help the boy to be semi-asleep, so he wouldn't feel the pain of the reduction.

Jake placed an IV in Eli's arm and administered the medication. He gave it the few minutes it needed to kick in, made sure the boy was in twilight sleep, then nodded at Rory. "Good to go. You need help?"

She was still such a small thing, and he couldn't imagine the strength she needed to manipulate bones and do the kinds of surgeries she did. Obviously, though, she wouldn't have passed the five years of residency training it took to be a pediatric orthopedic surgeon if she didn't have the physical ability.

"I'm good. This particular manipulation is more technique than raw strength. Hip surgeries are the toughest, in terms of muscle power, but I manage."

She sent him a half smile, then moved her attention to Pooky. "I'm going to pull down hard on his wrist to fully release the bone from the socket, then lever it back into place. It looks kind of awful, so you might not want to watch."

"I'll be okay," Pooky said. "I've done and seen all kinds of stuff in my years of hunting."

Jake decided he'd better keep an eye on Pooky anyway. Being a hunter who butchered animals didn't have a lot to do with watching your young son's arm being manipulated in a way that looked completely unnatural.

"Ready? Here we go," she said.

He watched Rory pull hard on the boy's wrist, then slowly and gently maneuver it back into the socket in what was clearly a very expert maneuver.

"Looks like…that's it," she said, leaning back with a satisfied nod. "In place and good to go—but let's take one more X-ray to confirm."

Jake moved toward the machine, glancing up at Pooky as he did so. Sure enough, the man looked ashen, and was listing to one side on his chair. Jake switched direction, striding over to grab him before he fell out of the chair and they had another broken bone or a cracked head on their hands.

"Whoa, there. Steady, now."

In seconds Rory was right there with him, obviously seeing Pooky move at about the same time he had. She went to Pooky's right arm, with Jake to his left, tugging him upright, and then they both pressed their hands to his back to tuck his head between his knees.

"Take some deep breaths and keep your head down for a few minutes," Jake said.

"I'm…sorry. Felt a little lightheaded. Can't believe it."

"Trust me when I say it's totally normal. When it comes to your own kid, especially, it's upsetting to see a limb all out of whack like that."

Rory's green gaze met his over the man's head, and for the first time since she'd been back they shared a real smile. It felt better than it should, but the way his chest lifted in response to that smile of hers told him he couldn't deny that he still cared for her. That even after all this time, and all that had happened, the closeness he'd felt with her still wrapped around his heart like a twisted, deeply rooted vine. So deeply rooted he knew he might never be free of it completely.

"You go ahead and get the X-ray," she said. "I'll stand here and make sure he's okay."

Glad that the film showed the elbow right back where it belonged, Jake got busy getting the splint they needed while Rory talked gently and quietly to Pooky. Not all surgeons had good bedside manners, but she did. Not that it came as a surprise. She'd always been one of the most caring and empathetic people he knew.

"It'll feel sore and bruised for quite a while, Pooky, so don't be surprised by that. Over the next few hours I want you to pay attention to how his circulation seems. If his hand or his arm starts to discolor or feel tingly, call me or Jake right away—okay?"

Together, they worked to put an L-shaped splint on the boy's arm, managing to get it fully in place and in a sling before the anesthetic wore off and he slowly became alert.

"Not quite good as new, but you'll be there soon," Rory told the boy, with another one of her warm smiles. "You'll need to keep it in the sling for two or three weeks except when you're resting. Keep your arm elevated as much as you can, ice it when the splint is off and come back to see me in two days. We'll see how it looks then."

A questioning frown dipped between her eyes and she looked up at Jake.

"Is it okay with you if he meets me here? It's not entirely necessary—I could go on a house call to see him instead."

"No, definitely see him here. How about 10:00 a.m. Thursday?"

His selfish feelings about her working here had been childish and stupid. She was obviously a good bone doctor who knew what she was doing, and taking care of patients in and near Eudemonia to the best of their ability was the whole reason the clinic was here.

"And you don't even need to bring your own supply of splints—if he needs a new one we have plenty. In several colors."

"Except I brought the perfect ones for Alaska—camouflage, if you can believe they make them. I guess they're for hunters who want to hide in the trees, even with a broken arm."

Another shared smile, this one bigger and more intimate, and he turned away from the power of it. Tried to move his thoughts from that moss-green gaze and her sweet lips by talking with Pooky and Eli. He was hyperaware of how close she was, and how that damned grapefruit scent kept sneaking into his nose, bringing with it memories better left forgotten.

Both answered a few more questions, and Rory handed Pooky a card with her phone number on it before they left.

With the patient and his father gone, Jake couldn't decide exactly what to do. Probably send Rory back to her mother's house, then he and Ellie could get the place cleaned up with Mika in his playpen for a short time. Except, ridiculously, he found he didn't want to ask her to leave quite yet, in a total reverse of how he'd felt an hour ago.

"It was nice of you to come take care of Eli. Saved them a long trip and an even longer day."

"I was happy to. I'm sure there are plenty of times you have to play doctor here after hours."

"Yeah. But still, it was nice. So, thanks."

"No thanks necessary. So…"

Her voice faded away, as if she didn't know what else to say, and he sure didn't, either. An uncomfortable silence hung between them, until they both spoke at once.

"Listen, I'm sorry I was…unpleasant when I first came in. It's just that—"

"I know this is hard for both of us, but—"

They both stopped and chuckled awkwardly.

Jake figured he'd better spit out his apology so they could get this discomfort over with. "Like I said, I'm sorry. I didn't know how it would feel, seeing you again, and it's been harder than I might have expected. I know it's been a long time, but I'm going to be honest. After everything that happened, being around you churns up too much of the past, you know? I just don't want to hang around you and try to be friends again. It doesn't feel like somewhere we should try to go. But I do want to be civil and respectful while you're here."

"All right." She gave him a slow nod. "I agree that friendship isn't a goal we can have. So, civil and respectful it is."

He reached out to shake on it, enfolding her hand in his, and the feel of it there had him staring at her for several long heartbeats. He wondered how the memory of the way her hand felt in his could be so strong, as if it was yesterday and not years ago that he'd held it every chance he could.

He pulled it loose and dropped his hand to his side. "Deal. You probably want to go on to your mom's now, in case she's needing you. If you need me for anything, you know how to reach me. I'll be here when Pooky and Eli come back for their appointment with you."

Her eyes stared into his and he thought for a second she

had more to say, until she turned, grabbed her coat from the wall hook and left without another word.

A dozen emotions clogged his chest as he watched her go. He didn't like feeling any of them. Didn't like the upheaval currently tipping his world uncomfortably sideways. Yeah, the quicker Rory's aunt came to take care of her mother, the faster his life would go back to normal again.

And it couldn't come too soon.

CHAPTER FOUR

"I'M SO GLAD my surgeon thinks everything's going as it should, aren't you?" Wendy asked as they got into Rory's car, parked outside the hospital and the doctors' offices in Fairbanks. "I mean, I really didn't think so, since it still hurts so much. But he must be right that I'm healing."

"See? I said you were doing well post-op."

Though why she bothered commenting she had no clue, since it was clear her mother didn't believe she knew much of anything when it came to medicine. And she was well aware that it wasn't just Twinkie who couldn't think of her as a surgeon and a doctor who knew what she was talking about. Plenty of her friends in LA lamented the same thing—that their families always thought of them just as a son or daughter or a sibling, and had a hard time truly believing in their professional skills.

Then again, they'd also noted that there were a few friends and relatives who called all the time to talk about their aches and pains, or cornered them at every gathering to show them something on their body that they'd prefer to look at in an office setting instead of at a party.

Since Rory kept pretty much to herself outside the hospital, she didn't have that kind of thing happen to her. Another reason isolating herself in LA wasn't a bad thing, right?

Her mom's lack of confidence in her knowledge didn't

matter. Rory felt blessed to be here, keeping tabs on her recovery and reassuring her until it was time for her to go back to LA—even if her mother respected her surgeon's and Jacob Hunter's opinions a lot more.

"I just don't understand why it still hurts so much, though."

"Your body was sliced open and one of your organs was taken out just a few days ago, Twinkie. Your body needs time to heal, so try to be patient."

Rory wouldn't tell her that she thought the stitching wasn't the *best* job she'd ever seen, and hoped her mother wouldn't care much about what the scar looked like after it was healed.

"Trust me, you're going to feel up to dancing again in no time."

"I hope so! I just wish you'd be here all winter, so we could have our holiday party and hang homemade biscuits and seed sculptures on the trees for the critters. So we could sing our Christmas songs and dance together with some friends."

Rory's throat closed at the sweet smile on her mother's face and the look in her eyes. Never would she criticize Rory for not living in Eudemonia, no matter how much she wanted her there. In fact she couldn't remember a time when her mother had gotten on at her about much of anything, having always believed in live and let live.

But kids needed guidance—though she supposed it had been her mother's attitude, combined with having to help take care of her dad, that had made Rory the strong, go-getting person she was.

Too much go-getting, sometimes—which had proved to be a very bad thing.

For all her faults and quirks, Rory loved her mom. She realized all over again how much she missed spending time with her.

An idea struck her, and while it wasn't even close to the first time, maybe right now she had some real leverage behind her to convince her mom to come to LA with her. She'd wanted to make that happen ever since her dad had died. And now she couldn't deny that the thought of getting away from Eudemonia and Jacob Hunter as soon as possible made her want it even more.

"You know, even though you're recovering well, it's still going to take a while for you to be good as new. How about coming back to Los Angeles with me? Now that you've seen your doctor we could leave pretty much right away. Tell Aunt Patty she doesn't have to worry about taking time off work to help you. I can take care of you until you're feeling like yourself again. It's warm there, and we'd have a great time doing all kinds of fun things."

"I don't know, marshmallow girl..." A frown dipped between her mother's brows before she turned away to look out the side window. "This is where I belong. I grew up here. My friends are all here. All my memories are here. You as a little girl...me and your dad."

"I'm not asking you to move there, Twinkie." Though if it were up to her that would be the perfect scenario. "Just to have an extended vacation. With me. Until you feel better. How bad could it be?"

Her mom finally turned back to look at her. "I just don't think it's for me. I'd miss my house. I'd miss everyone, everything that's here. Though I *do* miss you so much."

Familiar guilt chewed at Rory's gut, since she knew all too well that she should come back to Eudemonia more. Now, with the years of training behind her, she'd have a little more vacation time. But the deep ache from all the reminders of her past mistakes made her hate being here. Not to mention the horrible discomfort of seeing Jake again, which was even worse now that he had his own little one.

His clear statement that he didn't want to try to be friends anymore.

Thinking about all that made her feel like she was suffocating from the pain of it all—which told her loud and clear that she still couldn't handle it.

"Will you at least *think* about coming back with me? Trying it for maybe a month?"

"All right. I'll think about it."

Rory couldn't recall her mother ever agreeing to do even that, so that was a small step forward, right? Now she needed to ponder on what might convince her mom to move past just thinking about it to doing it, because she wanted to be near her so much, but staying in Eudemonia just wasn't an option.

She glanced at her watch, realizing that since her mom's appointment had run long she didn't have much time before she was supposed to be at Eli's house to check on his arm.

When Ellie had called her, confirming their Thursday appointment in the office, her chest had tightened with that suffocating feeling again and she'd offered to go see Eli at his home a day earlier before she'd thought twice about it. Maybe Jake would be mad about her not including him, but that was too bad. She'd see the child, pass her opinion on to Ellie and Jake could follow up if he wanted to.

"I need to check on the boy I saw in the clinic the other day—do you know Pooky's son, Eli? I told him I'd swing by the house to make it easy on him. You want to come along and talk with Pooky? Or would you rather go home first?"

"I think I'll go on home. If that's okay? Walking around more than usual and then the doctor poking and prodding me has tired me out."

"Of course that's okay. Listening to your body and when it's telling you to rest is an important part of getting stronger."

Ten minutes later she had her mom tucked into her chair with an ancient knit throw over her knees and the small dog happily curled on top of it. With a snack on the table by her side and the television on, she should be good until Rory got back.

"I shouldn't be gone long. See you in just a bit, okay?"

"Don't worry about me. Toby and I will probably take a nap."

Her mother's eyelids were already drooping, and Rory smiled as she leaned down to kiss her forehead. "Get some rest."

She crept out through the front door and managed to find Pooky's house about twenty minutes later, despite her GPS getting totally confused. The outskirts of Eudemonia hadn't changed much in the years she'd been gone, and the simple directions and landmarks he'd given her made it pretty easy to remember her way around.

As she approached the hill where the worst decision of her life had begun, her throat thickened with unwanted memories.

"What do you mean, I shouldn't come along? Part of what I do, what we both do, is go on rescue missions, Jake. There's no physiological reason for me not to get on that snow machine and help, and you know it. It'll be fine. We'll be fine. I promise."

She worked to haul in a few deep breaths. Somehow she had to shove down the horrible emotions clogging her chest—because what was the point in reliving the past? Thinking about it, crying about it, reliving it over and over, couldn't change a thing. It hadn't before, and it sure wouldn't now.

In a hurry to put that hill behind her, she pressed the accelerator nearly to the floor. The danger in navigating these curves forced her to focus on the road instead of on all the other things she didn't want to think about.

A wooden board appeared next to a gravel drive, an address written on it in thick black ink, and she nosed the car up the slope, glad to finally be there. She drew a few deep, calming breaths before knocking on the door. In mere seconds it swung open, and a slightly worried-looking Pooky stood in front of her.

"Thanks for coming, Rory. Really appreciate it. Especially since my truck's still not working right and I've got it up on jacks to try and fix it."

"Happy to."

Maybe Jake wouldn't be so annoyed if he knew about Pooky's car problems and how he couldn't have made it to the clinic anyway. As soon as the thought came, she asked herself why she cared if Jake was annoyed or not.

"How's Eli doing?"

"Been hurting a lot, to be honest. Doesn't like me taking the splint off to ice the arm, but I've been doing it anyway."

"That's good. Keeping the swelling down as much as possible will help it heal. It'll also help with his mobility when it's time to start using it again."

"He's back here, feeling a little grumpy," Pooky said with a small smile as he led her to a small living room. "He's not happy having to sit around until it's better."

"Can't blame him. Sitting around is a drag—especially for a kid."

The boy's glum expression showed his dad hadn't been exaggerating about how he was feeling.

"Hi, Eli. How's the pain?"

"Hurts. But not as bad as when I first did it—that was the worst."

"You were really tough and brave, though. A dislocated elbow is no joke, and you did so well through the whole reduction. Let me take a look."

She crouched down, concentrating on getting the splint

off without jarring his arm. The knock on the door didn't get through to her brain until Pooky moved to answer it.

"That's probably Jake."

Her heart gave a quick thud before she lifted her head to stare at him. "Jake?"

"Yeah. I told him you were coming here today, instead of keeping to the first plan we had to meet at the clinic tomorrow, and he said he wanted to be here, too."

She bit back a groan. *Why* couldn't she get away from the man for more than a day?

She heard the murmur of the two men talking, then all too soon Jake was standing right next to her. It wasn't hard to avoid eye contact, since she was concentrating on Eli's arm and asking him questions, but that didn't help her hyperawareness of his closeness, his broad form, the scent she realized she'd never forgotten even after all this time.

"Looks good," she said to both Pooky and Eli, studiously ignoring Jake. She reached to pat the child's shoulder and gave him a reassuring smile. "I know it probably doesn't feel that way to you. Bruising isn't pretty, I know, but your elbow is definitely in the right position. Just keep icing it and elevating it and be patient."

"We need to get another X-ray at the clinic in a few days, when your car's up and running," Jake said. "I wish Dr. Anderson had told me she'd decided to take a look at his arm here today. I would have picked him up and taken him to the clinic myself."

Even if he hadn't called her *Dr. Anderson* she'd have known he was beyond irritated, as the vibration of anger in his voice was more than clear. Without knowing she was going to, she stole a look at him. Yep, those beautiful lips of his were pressed tightly together and the eyes that met hers weren't even close to warm. Instead, they glittered with an edge of anger she'd seen on only rare occasions, and she knew that a blowup just might follow.

It didn't matter, she told herself, even as her heart beat a little faster. He could be upset and disapproving all he wanted, because her coming here today for a follow-up with the boy had made it easier for Eli and Pooky. And for Jake, too, because she knew he felt as uncomfortable around her as she did him. Except here he was anyway.

"Probably in a couple weeks you should find an orthopedic surgeon in Fairbanks, to take one more look before you take the splint off for good," she said.

"*You're* not going to be here then?" Pooky asked in obvious surprise.

"No. I'm leaving in just a few days."

"Which is why it was important for me to be here today—even though you obviously didn't think so," Jake said. "Because *I'm* not going anywhere."

Her fluttering heart kicked hard. His words obviously referred to a lot more than just this moment. They were a statement about nine years ago when, devastated and consumed with guilt, she'd fled this town, refusing to look back.

"So." Somehow she forced herself to sound relaxed and professional as she stood to her full height and managed a smile. "Call me if you have any concerns over the next couple days, and get a referral from Jacob to whatever orthopedic doc he recommends. If I don't see you before I go, best of luck, Eli. I'll see myself out, so Jake can talk with you a little more."

She reached for Pooky's hand, noticing the way he glanced at her and Jake, clearly sensing the strange vibe going on between them. Then she patted Eli's shoulder one more time, slid on her coat and hurried toward the door.

It was ridiculous to feel she needed to escape conversation with Jake, but for some inexplicable reason she did. Finally in her car, she was nearly free and clear when she heard Pooky yelling her name.

She turned to see him running out through the door with a huge shopping bag in his arms, and wondered what in the world was in there.

"Rory! Wait!" He came up next to her car door, a little out of breath.

She wound down the window, and had opened her mouth to ask what he needed when he started talking again.

"All of a sudden I realized I need to pay you something."

"No, you don't. No need at all—I promise. I'm not working. I'm just here to see my mom. I was happy to help."

"I want to. Please." He held out the bag, and the way it listed toward the car told her it weighed a ton. "I'm sorry I don't have cash to give you, but I want you to have this."

"Seriously, Pooky, you don't—"

"I went hunting a week ago and bagged a caribou. It's already butchered. Fresh and good, I promise."

She opened her mouth to protest some more, but by now Jake had come up behind him. The expression on his face reminded her of how things went around here, with everyone helping others and sharing what they had when they could. If she didn't accept Pooky's payment it would probably be upsetting to the man, so it was the only polite thing to do.

"Thank you. It's really unnecessary, but I appreciate it. I haven't had caribou in a long time. Mom will love it."

"Great! Makes me feel good to think I can help your mom get well."

His wide, pleased smile as he opened the back door of the car and set the bag on the seat made her glad she'd accepted the meat, even as she wondered how long it would take her mother to eat it all by herself. It would probably be in the freezer for the next couple years.

"Well, thanks again—and best of luck to you and Eli. Take care."

"Come back and see us soon, Rory. It's been way too long."

She didn't answer because, yeah, it *had* been too long, but seeing Jake standing there with his arms folded across his chest, looking at her with slightly narrowed eyes, didn't exactly make her want to book a flight back next month.

Pooky headed into the house and Jake wrapped his hands over her car door and leaned forward. It probably wouldn't be nice to wind the window up, even though she wanted to, so she sat there trying to look relaxed.

"We need to talk," he said.

"About…?"

"About us."

Her heart lurched. "Us?"

"Yeah. Us. We've agreed we can't be friends anymore, that we'd go for civil and respectful. But what happened today was neither of those."

"I don't know what you mean. When Ellie called me about the appointment I figured it would work better for me to come here to see him, and then you could follow up as you wish. It doesn't seem to me that it was uncivil or disrespectful to have us see him separately. So what's the problem?"

"The problem is that *I'm* the kid's primary doc, and *you'll* be waltzing out of here any minute, without a goodbye to a single soul, just like before."

His voice was filled with that vibration of anger again, and he leaned through the window, practically nose-to-nose with her.

"You can't disappear for years and then, when you show up for a few days, try to take over the place before you take off again. I don't want you seeing anymore patients while you're here. It's not good care for them when I get left out of the loop then have to play catch-up, trying to figure out what you might have said or done when I wasn't around. You understand?"

"Who elected *you* King of Eudemonia?" She planted her palm against his chest and gave it a shove, but he didn't budge. "I was doing Pooky a favor, since his car isn't running right now."

"Which I'll bet you didn't even *know* when you talked to Ellie, because I sure didn't."

She never could put anything past Jacob Hunter.

She sucked in a breath, which unfortunately dragged his scent into her lungs, and she leaned back the few inches she could to get a tiny bit of distance. "I didn't want to see you again, okay? I admit it. I admitted it before. Hopefully there won't be any reason for us to have to talk at all before I leave. But, fine. I see your point about you needing to know about me examining Eli and my recommendations."

"So it won't happen again?"

"No. I'm leaving soon anyway, so I won't be here to make your life miserable anymore."

"Miserable? You don't know the half of it, Rory. And you know what? I've changed my mind. Before you leave, we *do* need to talk about all you did back then."

His temper had spiked further; his eyes were snapping with it as he closed the inches between them. Mixed in with that temper was something else, and shock skidded through her veins when she saw it.

Desire.

Her heart pounding against her ribs, she watched him spin away, clasp the back of his head for ten long seconds, then turn around again.

He leaned in close once more, his hands balled into fists. "Miserable? Yeah. Confused, furious and a whole lot of other things that made me wish I could hate you. Do you have any idea how—?"

Her cell phone shrilled in interruption, and she'd never

been so glad to hear it in her life. No way did she want to have this kind of upsetting conversation with Jake, and she dug into her purse with shaking hands.

"Hello?"

"Rory? It's Linda. I'm at your mom's house, with some cookies I baked, but the door's locked. When I knocked I could hear her calling from inside, but she's not coming to the door. I'm really worried that something's wrong. Are you close by?"

Her heart felt like it had stopped in her chest. "About twenty minutes away. I'll be there as fast as I can." She tossed her phone on the seat and started the car.

"What's wrong?" asked Jake.

"Linda's at Mom's but she can't get in. Says she can hear Twinkie's voice, but apparently she can't get to the door for some reason. God, *why* did I decide I had to lock the door when she never does?" She gulped back the panic rising in her throat. "I gotta go."

"I'll be right behind you."

"No need. I—"

She stopped herself. There was nobody better in an emergency than Jacob Hunter, and she realized that she wanted him there with her, no matter what had been boiling between them seconds ago.

"That would be good. Thanks."

Shoving her car into Reverse, she swung it down the driveway and saw Jake jumping into his truck. Once she hit the paved road she jammed down the accelerator, trying to fight the fear gripping her.

If Linda could hear Twinkie calling out, that was a good thing, right? Maybe it wasn't something terribly bad. Maybe she'd fallen and couldn't get up because she wasn't very strong yet. That seemed unlikely, but still…

She pushed harder on the gas, and this time driving

by the dreaded hill didn't cause even one second of bad thoughts and emotions. All those were concentrated on her sweet mother, and the fear that had her heart beating double-time.

CHAPTER FIVE

JAKE WAS RIGHT behind Rory's car as she tore up the grassy slope toward her mother's house, and he was beyond glad to finally be there. Not only because Wendy might need help, but because Rory had driven like a maniac on the steep curves of the road—to the point when he'd feared she'd lose control and crash.

He didn't want to think about how it would feel to see that happen...to see her get hurt. He pulled up behind her car as she practically leaped out, running up to the uneven front porch, where Linda stood clutching her hands together and looking anxious.

"Can you still hear her?"

"Yes. I yelled to her that you were on your way with the key, but I don't know if she could understand what I was saying. She must be somewhere in the back of the house, because all I could hear was the sound of her voice, but not the words. I walked around back, calling, but still couldn't understand her."

"It was *stupid* of me to lock the door," Rory said. "A habit from living in LA, I guess."

Jake could see her hand shaking as she fumbled to get the key in the door, and gently took it from her to get it unlocked. "You want me to go in first, since we don't know what's going on?"

Her worried gaze met his for a split second before he pushed open the door. "I... Can we go together?"

"Sure." He reached for her hand, because she looked like she needed the support.

There was no sign of Wendy in the main room when they ran inside, with Linda following.

"Mom? Twinkie? Where are you?"

"In the bathroom. Thank God you're here. I'm... Oh, it's a mess."

Mess? Jake steeled himself for what they might find. Maybe she meant a bathroom mess—which might embarrass her, but would be a hell of a lot better than her being hurt.

Since they couldn't both get through the narrow bathroom doorway at the same time, Rory let go of his hand as she went into the small space. With her in front of him he couldn't see her mother well, but what he could see made his pulse quicken.

The good news was that her mother was obviously lucid, even as she lay on her back. The bad news was that blood covered the floor, and Jake could only imagine how Rory was feeling on seeing it.

"Mom!" Rory dropped to her knees and reached for her mother's hands, which were splayed across her stomach. "What happened? Where are you hurt?"

"I woke up and had to go potty pretty bad. So I got up fast and I hurried too much, I think. I felt dizzy while I was on the potty. When I got up again I think I stumbled over Toby and fell. Right on my stomach...across the side of the bathtub. Oh, it hurts so bad! I'm not sure, but I think my stitches have split open. Can you tell if any of my organs fell out?"

Her eyes were wide and scared, and Jake realized he'd rarely seen her look anything but happy and relaxed. Those two times had been when Rory had been in the snow machine accident that had destroyed their future together, and the week they'd buried her husband.

"That's not likely, Twinkie, so try not to worry. We'll... we'll take a look."

To Jake's surprise Rory turned and reached for him, looking panicky.

"Can you help? I feel... I think it would be good if you helped me find out what's going on."

The fact that she was letting herself lean on him during a crisis did something funny to his chest. If she'd let herself lean on him nine years ago maybe things would have turned out a lot different. Maybe she'd never have left Eudemonia at all.

Not that it mattered anymore. Too many bridges had been burned to go back to the way things used to be.

"Let's take a look."

He ran his hand up and down Rory's back, then kneeled next to her and caught his breath. He could see now that Wendy was fully dressed, wearing tie-dyed pants with a loose waistband that she or someone else had cut to make even looser. The blood staining them down to her thighs was bright red, and the volume of it showed him why Rory had reached out to him. Because it was scary as hell.

He carefully tugged the pants down to expose the long, vertical incision from her surgery, and sure enough it was split open a good four inches. It was still bleeding a lot, and he heard Rory gasp. Thank the Lord Linda had come when she had, because even fifteen more minutes of this kind of blood-loss might have been catastrophic.

"Oh, my God, I can't believe it's wound dehiscence! Who *did* this surgery?"

"It isn't necessarily suture error," he reminded her. "But we do need to find out why it opened up like this."

"She's lost a lot of blood," Rory said in a tight whisper,

though her mother could doubtless still hear her. "We need to get this closed as fast as possible."

He nodded, and reached to grab a hand towel from the sink, quickly folded it, then placed it on the open wound to slow the bleeding, flattening his palm on top of it to apply pressure.

"You sure did a whammy on yourself, Twinkie. But we're gonna get you closed back up, and then we'll get you to Fairbanks."

"Fairbanks? Wh…why?"

"You already know you've lost blood. We need to get some tests done that I can't do at the clinic, and there's a chance you could need a transfusion. They might want to keep you overnight for observation. But don't worry. It's gonna be okay."

He glanced at Rory. She had both hands pressed to her mouth as their eyes met, and he wrapped his free arm around her shoulders.

"Hang in there. I can do this—or we can do it together if you're up to it."

"I… I'll do it. I can do these kinds of sutures and close a wound in my sleep."

"It's harder when it's your own mom—and you're shaking like a leaf."

She was. Without thinking, he tugged her closer and kissed her forehead. Now wasn't the time to worry about keeping his distance from her. Not when she needed him like this.

"You have sutures and supplies? If you don't, I have a big first-aid box in the truck."

"I have everything. I'll go get it now."

"Of *course* you do. Always prepared, Aurora." He sent her a smile and resisted the urge to drop another quick kiss to her forehead. "Get something to elevate her feet, too, so she doesn't go into shock."

She nodded, lurched to her feet and disappeared.

Which apparently gave Linda her first clear view of Wendy and the bathroom floor, and the strange low moan that Linda let out had him cursing under his breath. All they needed was her passing out and needing help, with Twinkie already in such bad shape.

"Linda, sit down. Right now—out in the hall. Put your head between your knees and you'll feel better."

Without responding, she did as he asked, and Jake focused on compressing the wound to stop the bleeding.

The pounding of feet told him Rory was on her way back.

"Check on Linda!" he called. "She wasn't feeling well and I told her to sit down."

The murmur of voices told him Linda was doing better, thank heavens, and in just a moment Rory came into the small room.

"You get scrubbed up first, then take over with compression while I do," Jake said. "We won't get anywhere near sterile, but that can't be helped."

"Okay." She shoved an old blanket and some towels under Wendy's feet. "How you feeling, Twinkie?"

"A little funny. Kind of weak and woozy."

"Hang in there. We'll be able to get this done pretty fast, then head for the hospital, okay?"

She pulled out the items that were inside sterilized baggies, ripped them open so they'd be easy to access after she was scrubbed and set everything on the tray she'd brought. She placed it on the floor, next to her mom, then stepped to the sink.

"I have antimicrobial soap and gloves, so after I scrub you can put the gloves on me," she said, while lathering her hands and forearms.

"Of *course* you do."

"What? You don't carry soap in *your* first aid kit?"

"Yeah, but the possibility of me having to stitch up an injury on an ice fisherman or a hunter in the woods is a lot more likely than you needing it in Los Angeles."

"Well, you already know how I feel about being prepared."

The half smile she sent him was strained as she stuck out her hands. But he couldn't help but be impressed that the scared woman who'd been shaking just minutes ago had been replaced by the efficient surgeon standing in front of him.

"Glove me."

"Are you this bossy in the OR in LA?" he asked as he worked to get the gloves on her hands while trying to follow the correct protocol.

"Not bossy—just efficient." She kneeled to press her forearms against the towel on Wendy's belly, keeping her disinfected hands clear. "When you're done scrubbing, glove up and we'll get started."

"Yes, ma'am."

"You two are so funny together," Wendy said, her voice noticeably weak. "Always ribbing and teasing…even when you were kids."

Rory didn't respond, obviously choosing to ignore Wendy's comment about the two of them and how they'd used to be long ago. He glanced at her face in profile as she lifted the towel, and the familiar way she pursed her lips, narrowing her eyes in concentration, took him back in time to all the things they'd done and studied together.

Along with her mother's words, it made him think about how much he'd missed her—missed her beautiful smile, missed touching her soft hair. Missed the way he'd catch her looking at him sometimes, like he meant everything to her.

He suddenly wondered if he'd miss her all over again after she was gone.

The feelings for her that had tried to resurface from the second he'd seen her again told him he would, damn it. But there was no way it could be even one iota as much as the way he'd yearned for her for a long, long time, even as he'd felt abandoned and betrayed.

"Ready, Twinkie?" Rory asked. "I'm putting analgesic cream around the edges of the wound, so you won't feel it when I'm putting in the stitches. I'm going to hold it together with my fingers and keep compressing for a few minutes to slow the bleeding, then I'll get started."

"I can't believe you can do all this, marshmallow girl. I'm so proud of you."

Jake saw her eyes widen in surprise and she turned to look at him for a second, emotion flitting across her face. Rory's mom and dad had always been happy living simple lives here in Eudemonia, and he knew they'd never understood or even cared much about her goal to become a doctor. He also knew it had bothered her sometimes.

"Thanks, Mom. That's… It means a lot to me to hear you say that."

Jake hoped the tears she blinked back as he handed her the needle and sutures wouldn't interfere with her ability to get the wound closed. "You want me to do it?"

"No. I'm good. Really."

And she was. Her technique was flawless—not that he was surprised. The Aurora Anderson he'd known since fourth grade had always excelled at everything she attempted.

"I'm feeling fine now," Linda called from the hall. "Sorry about that…so silly of me. But I wasn't prepared for… Well, you know. What can I do?"

"We're okay right now, but maybe you can find some clean, older towels we can wash her up with when we're done? Ones she wouldn't mind throwing away?" Jake said.

"I know just where she keeps them. Be right back."

He and Rory worked silently together, except for answering the few questions Wendy asked. Very few, because it was obvious the ordeal had left her feeling weak and tired—which was hardly a surprise.

As Rory finished the last few stitches, Jake dug into her bag and found antibiotic cream. "I figured you'd have this in here," he said. "You want to put it on the closed wound while I get the bandages ready?"

"Yes. Good."

After everything was done, and Wendy was bandaged up, Jake glanced at his watch. "Twenty minutes from start to finish. Think you'd get a world record for that?"

"It was just stitches—not surgery." But she sent him a wide, relieved smile before she snapped off her gloves and reached for her mother's bloody hands. "We're going to get you cleaned up and in fresh clothes, Twinkie, then head for Fairbanks."

"Oh, I don't think we need to go there, do we? I'm fine now."

"Just need to check a few things," Jake said.

"Will you come, too?" Wendy asked with a hopeful expression.

"Are you kidding? Would I let my favorite patient go to the hospital without me? No way."

"I have clean clothes here, Rory," Linda said as she appeared in the doorway. "I'll help you get her washed up and dressed, then I'll take care of the bathroom mess after you leave for the hospital. I'll take Toby home with me, too, so you don't have to worry about him if you have to stay in Fairbanks overnight."

"I really appreciate you looking after him. But I hate to ask you to clean the place up, Linda. You—"

"Not another word. You're not asking—I'm offering. It's the least I can do for my best friend and her amazing daughter."

Amazing. That she was—suturing her own mother with remarkably calm efficiency, her surgical skills making her work far superior to any stitching job *he* would have done.

"I'll wait in the living room," Jake said. "I'll carry her to the car when she's ready, so give me a holler."

"Good. Thank you."

Once Wendy was settled in Rory's car, he moved toward his truck, but paused when Rory placed a hand on his arm. "You don't need to come to Fairbanks. Seriously, we'll be fine."

"I told Wendy I would."

"Jake…" She lifted her hand from him and wrapped her arms around herself. "I can't begin to thank you for all you did today. That was…so scary. And you being here to help was huge in so many ways. But I think it's better if we keep the time we're together to a minimum, like we talked about before. All that at Pooky's was… Well, it's clear how you feel about me. And there's nothing to be gained by dredging up the past, you know? Being around each other isn't going to help with that."

He knew she was right. His anger and frustration with her—which was really about what had happened nine years ago and not today—had nearly boiled over at Pooky's, and he still wasn't sure what exactly he might have said if they hadn't been interrupted. What part of his heart he might have let her see. It wasn't a place either of them wanted to go.

"All right. Send me a text and let me know what they say and if they're keeping her at the hospital overnight."

"Will do. And… Well, thanks again."

She turned, and within moments all he could see were the taillights of her car.

CHAPTER SIX

FEELING A LITTLE rough around the edges after spending the night in her mother's hospital room, Rory sat next to the hospital bed and gulped some coffee. It was a huge relief to see the color back in Twinkie's face after the blood transfusion she'd received yesterday, and her usual sweet smile was back, too.

"Since you're stuck here until this afternoon, I'm going to go ahead and get some winter shopping done while we're in town. Will you be okay until I get back? It won't take me too long."

"Of course, Aurora. I'm happy resting in this comfy bed, and the nurses are all so nice. The medicine they gave me really helps with the pain."

"I'm glad."

"Did you look at the supplies I have left from last year? I think there's a lot…"

"I took an inventory of your bottled water and batteries, and your dry and canned goods. I checked your portable camping lamps and flashlights, to make sure they're working if the power goes out, and one needs a new bulb. It's not bad, but you definitely need more stuff."

"Okay. Whatever you think."

Her mother's utter confidence in her—well, except for the doctoring thing, which just might have changed yesterday—tugged at her heart, and she leaned over and kissed her mother's cheek, emotion filling her chest because she could; because her mom was still here, when yesterday might have been catastrophic if she'd been alone for too long.

And didn't that reality force her to rethink her plans a little? Was it really okay for her to pass her mother's care on to Aunt Patty when this had just happened? Maybe now she'd be feeling about the same as she had the first day she'd been released after surgery. Or maybe she'd be weaker and need more care for longer than expected. And if that was the case Rory would have to reconsider her plans.

If that had to happen, seeing Jake more would be inevitable. But she couldn't put her own feelings, the guilt and pain that kept getting stirred up when she was around him, above her mother's health and recovery.

"Get some rest. I'll be back as quickly as possible."

It was just a short drive from the hospital to the big grocery and supply store where they got all the things they needed that they couldn't get at Green's Market in Eudemonia.

She swung the car into the parking lot, grabbed her purse and list, and headed into the store. In no time she had the cart half full, and realized that a second trip before she went home would probably need to happen. Or a third, if she ended up staying longer.

Rounding a corner, she had to pull up short when she nearly banged into a cart coming the other way.

"Sorry—"

Before the word was barely out of her mouth she saw that the person pushing the cart was tall and gorgeous, with black hair skimming his collar. A baby wearing a knit hat sat in the front of the cart, clutching a sippy cup in both hands, and she could see Beth Hunter behind them, farther down the aisle.

"I see you're no better a driver than you used to be. Always in a hurry," Jake said, his eyes showing a hint of the humor she remembered so well, although at the same time he wore a frown, as though he were genuinely irritated.

Her heart clutched in a way that had become uncomfortably familiar these past few days.

"Yeah, well, the visibility in this store isn't the greatest, what with all the end-caps and cardboard displays they have everywhere."

"True. Except even in a grocery store there are rights of way, and tearing around a corner into the wrong lane is a clear violation."

"Are you going to give me a ticket? Oh, wait—you're a doctor, not a cop."

"A doctor who's on the volunteer police and fire rescue squad in Eudemonia. Maybe I can extend my privileges to here in Fairbanks."

"I'll be long gone before you can make *that* happen."

"True." The humor that had expanded into a half smile flattened into cool indifference. "Stocking up for your mom before you leave?"

"She's not being released until this afternoon, so I figured while we were here it made sense. Though I think I'll have to make a second trip before I go back to LA. I don't want her stranded without enough water and food and essentials if a huge storm comes through."

"How's she feeling?"

"Surprisingly, she seems pretty good. But of course that's while she's lying in a hospital bed, getting pain meds. Being home and moving around might be a different story. I… I want to thank you again for being there for both of us. Doing it all alone would have been rough."

"You do realize your thank-you is more of an insult, don't you? As if you wouldn't have done the same for me, or anyone. As if we weren't always there for each other when we needed to be. Until you left."

His words and the intensity in his eyes made her chest squeeze hard. "I...yes, I know. Sorry, it's just that—"

"Hello, Aurora," Beth said, coming to stand next to Jake. "How's your mom? What a scary thing!"

"Yeah, it was scary. Thank heavens Linda called me and we were able to get there fast."

"And that you and Jacob are both doctors who knew how to take care of her right there. Sounds like trying to get her to Fairbanks while she was bleeding like that might have been bad."

"Yeah. It was a huge help that Jake was there with me." He deserved that credit, no matter what he'd said to her seconds ago. Though it was true. They had always been there for each other. He'd always been there for her. Until she hadn't been able to accept that unwavering support from him anymore.

"Does this mean you're going to bring your mom to my office so I can check on her in a couple days? Or stubbornly refuse to, like before?" Jake asked.

"I've come to appreciate your point about having all the equipment for checking her vitals and drawing blood to send to the lab," she said, trying to sound professional and unemotional. "And her surgeon wants to have her follow-up doc be someone he can reach, or who can reach him, if she has some complication up the road. Which makes sense, obviously."

"Glad you agree."

He inclined his head, and she could just see him battling wanting to say something more, but resisting.

"Call the office and get it scheduled with Ellie for before you leave. Or after, if you want, and your aunt can bring her instead."

"No, I'll bring her. One less thing to bother Aunt Patty with."

"Are you leaving soon, Rory? Or staying longer now?" Beth asked.

"I'm not sure. It depends on how Mom's doing after she's been home a few days. I don't want to overburden Aunt Patty if she needs more help getting around, bathed and dressed than she did before."

"What do you think about coming to Mika's first birthday party? Bring your mom, too," she said. "You could see Jake's beautiful house and some of the family again. I don't think Tim's going to be able to make it, and Jake's dad will be at a conference in Anchorage, but Grace will be there. And friends you haven't seen for a long time."

Probably old friends, who knew all about what had happened. Who probably thought it was long ago and far away and that neither she nor Jake thought about it anymore. Except she did, and it was obvious that he did, too.

"When is it?" Hopefully after she was gone, so she'd have a good excuse not to go. Not to see the small but beautiful family being formed around Jake and his son.

"Sunday."

"I'll see how it goes. Twinkie might not be well enough."

Her stomach balled into a knot at the thought of spending the afternoon in the midst of all that family happiness, celebrating beautiful Mika turning one year old. Then she realized that maybe Beth might help convince her mother to leave Eudemonia for a while.

"Although if she's feeling well enough to attend, maybe you could encourage Twinkie to come back to LA with me. She's reluctant, but I think it's the perfect solution. I can make sure she's healing fine, and getting stronger, and she wouldn't be all alone here as winter comes. She could get outside to walk and exercise, since it's warm year-round."

"That's a very good idea, and I'd be happy to do that,"

Beth said. "Though your mother's pretty stubborn, despite being the sweetest person I know."

"Runs in the family," Jake said under his breath.

"Anyway, I hope you can make it to the party. Speaking of which—I have some more things I need to get for it. I'll meet you at the car, Jake. Okay?"

"Sure."

As his grandmother walked away the baby practically turned himself into a pretzel in order to face Rory, his brown eyes studying her. She found herself unable to look away from his sweet face, noticing how thick his dark lashes were. Very like his daddy's, despite their not being biologically related.

He sent her a sudden wide smile that showed four white teeth—two on top and two on the bottom. The tightness in her belly loosened, to be replaced by a warm glow around her heart. How adorable he was. She wanted to reach out and touch his soft cheek, the way she had when Beth had held him on her lap in front of the clinic that first night she'd met him.

"He's so precious," she murmured, giving in to the urge to run her hand down his small back. "Like a little angel."

"Not always an angel," Jake said. "Sometimes he—"

The baby's arm flailed backward, and then in a quick release he flung his plastic cup right at her, hitting her in the sternum. Startled, she let out a cry, somehow managing to grab it and clutch it to her chest before it fell to the floor.

"Mika! No throwing things," Jake said in a firm voice. He looked up at Rory and shook his head. "Sorry. Just proving he's not an angel, I guess. Are you okay?"

"Fine. Though it's surprising that a plastic cup thrown by a little hand can actually hurt some."

She handed Mika his cup and he threw it back, clearly enjoying this game, and his gurgling laugh had Rory smiling, too, even as her heart pinched.

"I recall that your games of choice were football, basketball and soccer," she said, deciding it was safer to hand the cup to Jake than the baby. "But you might have to add baseball to that list—he's got quite an arm."

"He does. But I'm hoping that's going to pass, since flinging projectiles to get attention sometimes results in bruises and broken things. I had no idea how much a house had to be babyproofed."

"Yeah."

She swallowed down the ache that had stuck in her throat. The ache that was there because she'd lost her chance to experience all the things that came with having a baby, and because her desire to even try again to make it happen had been permanently flattened.

"Where do you live these days? I didn't think to ask."

"I have a house up the east hill. You remember Dave and George from back in high school? They do construction now, and they did most of the building, with me helping when I could. Which gave me a whole new appreciation for the skill involved in that."

A vision of Jake hammering and sawing, possibly shirtless and wearing a tool belt on his lean hips, made her feel a little short of breath.

"Do you think they'd prep and paint Mom's house? I think it's probably too late in the season now, but I'd like to get it on the schedule for next summer. I could pay a deposit, if they want."

"I'm sure they would. They usually have to go to Fairbanks or other towns to get jobs, so they're always happy to have work in Eudemonia when they can. I'll get you their number."

"Thanks." She looked down at the baby again, who was reaching up to Jake and starting to complain a little, obviously fidgeting to get out of there. "Well, I'll let you go. See you in the office when I bring Mom in, I guess."

She swung her cart around and past his, anxious to get going. Relieved to finally be done and through the checkout line, she rolled the cart to her rental car and loading up the trunk.

She was startled when a hand wrapped around her arm.

With a gasp and a near shriek, she slapped her palm to her thudding heart and whirled to see who'd grabbed her.

Jake.

"What the heck?" she demanded. "You scared me."

"Sorry. I didn't mean to scare you. But the things I want to say to you keep rolling around and around in my head. I have to get them off my chest, and I might not have another chance."

They stared at one another, and there it was again. That familiar longing, sadness and confusion that kept filling her heart every time she was around the man.

"You wanting to take your mom to LA makes sense right now, while she recovers, I admit it," he said, his voice taking on a hard note. "But you know what? I understand why she wants to stay here, in her hometown, where she's lived her whole life. And I just have to say it. I thought *you'd* always want to stay here, too—no matter what."

"I *had* to leave," she choked out. "You know that."

"I *don't* know that. Why, when I begged you to stay? You left anyway, without even saying goodbye."

So there it was. She'd hoped maybe he'd forgotten that she'd decided to leave without telling him. Or that he didn't care anymore. That the pain she'd seen on his face since she'd come back was all about their baby and not her. Except if she was honest with herself she'd known since she first moment she'd seen him at her mother's house the night she'd arrived that he still felt upset about all of it.

God, she needed to get out of Eudemonia—before she ended up all messed up again.

"I couldn't stay another day. I couldn't face what I'd

done. I couldn't live with it staring at me every day I was in this town. The whispers when I left a store. The sympathetic or disapproving looks wherever I went. Surely you can understand that?"

"No. I didn't understand it then and I still don't. You had *me* here to help you through all that. We'd have gone through it together." His hands balled into fists. "I loved you. I loved our baby…the future we'd planned. We should have grieved together, healed together. But instead all you could think about was yourself."

"I… I was thinking of him. Of you, too."

"No, you weren't. You left me high and dry. You abandoned me when I was hurting from losing our baby, then broke my heart a second time when you left. You smashed it into tiny pieces when you never came back. And you never even tried to get in touch with me."

Her heart shook hard, then fell into her stomach as she stared at the raw judgment in his eyes, at the anger and hurt. "I… I didn't mean to abandon you."

"No? Well, that's sure as hell what you did. I never knew you could be that self-centered. But you were."

"How can you not understand at *all*?" Anger welled up in her chest, matching his. "How dare you judge me that way? I lost our baby because of a stupid decision. How do you think that made me feel? You can't understand the pain I felt."

"You think I don't understand that pain? I *lived* it, Rory. I lived it twice because of your selfishness."

"Selfishness? It seems to me *you're* the self-centered one, thinking only about how *you* felt. I was—"

The rumble of a truck parking two spaces over had Jake pressing his lips together and tugging her to the other side of the car, his other hand pulling the cart holding Mika, still sipping away on his cup.

Rory gulped, her heart pounding. She didn't want to

talk about this. Not now, not ever. But even as part of her wanted to run the other way, jump into the car and take off, she knew she had to endure this conversation.

She'd already run the other way long ago, hadn't she? She hadn't even realized he believed she'd been thinking only of herself when she had.

It was past time for them to have this conversation—horrible or not. To clear the air and put all this behind them once and for all.

She saw Jake glance around to make sure they were more or less alone before he spoke again, his voice tight.

"You were what? Heartbroken? Grieving? Join the club. Yet you didn't care enough to stick it out with me. For us to deal with it together. I lost you both at once. And I have a hard time forgiving you for that."

A lump formed in her throat, so big she couldn't speak. When she'd finally swallowed it down, she managed to croak out just a tiny bit of what she wanted to say.

"I have a hard time forgiving myself for any of it. If I let myself think about it the guilt drags me under. I had to leave to survive. Don't you understand that?"

Before she even knew it was going to happen tears spilled from her eyes and she swiped hard at her cheeks. She hadn't fallen apart in a long time. The last thing she wanted was to break down right in the middle of this stupid parking lot. In front of Jake and this beautiful child he was building a new life with.

"Rory... Don't."

Strong hands closed around her shoulders and pulled her closer to his warm, firm chest. Emotion welled up all over again. It was just like Jake to reach for her, to try to comfort her at the very same time as he'd expressed how angry and upset he'd been with her. How angry and upset he still was.

The sweetness and strength of character that had always been a part of who he was weakened her even more. She knew if she didn't get out of there she might fall apart completely. She put her hands against his chest and could feel the steady beat of his heart. She forced herself to push him away, even though it felt so good to touch him again, to feel his warmth against her palms.

"I'm done talking about this," she said, working to pull herself together. "You've said what you wanted to say and I hear you loud and clear. It sounds like you practically hate me, in fact, so the sooner I get to LA the happier we'll both be."

"Damn it, Rory!" Anger flared in his eyes, showed in the jut of his chin all over again. "Why do you—?"

His sentence unfinished, he cursed and dropped his mouth to hers in a hard kiss that lasted just a split second before a shriek and something whacking into Jake's jaw set them apart.

They stared at one another for long seconds before Jake took a step back and reached to retrieve the plastic cup now rolling on the asphalt of the parking lot.

Dragging in a gulp of air, Rory watched him give the cup to Mika and turn without another word to stride toward his truck, apparently feeling exactly as she did. That there was nothing more to say.

She lifted trembling fingers to her lips, wondering why he'd kissed her. Except she knew. Yes, he'd been angry and frustrated with her. But just before that… He'd always hated to see her cry.

Shaking, she managed to get inside the car and she closed her eyes, remembering what she'd forgotten for so long. How he'd stayed up for who knew how long the night they'd lost their tiny boy, building the box they would bury his small body in. How he'd carved the name they'd chosen—Adam—into a candle, along with the date he'd been stillborn. How Jake had held her close as they'd watched the candle burn in memory of the tiny premature infant, both of them in floods of tears.

The next day she'd been released from the hospital. He'd taken her to her parents' house so she could rest, and she'd stayed in her room until the funeral. After they'd buried their baby boy in the cemetery she'd told Jake she needed to get a little more rest. Back in her old bedroom, she'd packed up her things, left a note to her mom and dad, and another to Jake. Told them she needed time alone to think, and got on a plane to LA.

And she'd never come back.

Everyone had told her the accident wasn't her fault. That it probably *wasn't* why she'd gone into labor so early. That it had nothing to do with why the baby had been stillborn.

She'd been so sure it was a perfectly reasonable decision to go on the snowmobile to search and rescue that day. Now it seemed beyond stupid. But no one knew for sure why her baby had died in utero at seven months along, and doctors had reassured her that probably something had been wrong before she'd even gone out that night.

She'd wanted to believe it. She'd tried so hard to convince herself it wasn't her fault. But in the end she'd had to get out of Eudemonia to try to heal. To move on somehow when her grief, guilt and despair told her that if she'd been smarter, less stubborn, if she'd listened to Jake, who had told her to stay home that night, that they'd have their son, Adam, in their lives today.

The day she'd left, and all the days after, she'd never considered that it had been a selfish decision—probably because she hadn't been thinking straight. She was stunned that Jake saw it that way, and she realized he was probably right.

It *had* been selfish of her to go out on that snowmobile, even convinced she was doing it for the right reasons. It had been selfish of her to leave Jake when times had gotten tough, thinking only of herself when she'd taken off for California.

Was she continuing that trend? Leaving her mom alone so she could get the permanent job in LA? Was selfish the kind of person she wanted to be?

No. But she didn't think she could come back to Eudemonia, to be reminded of her fatal mistake every single day.

This trip home had become an even worse mess than she'd expected, and she'd expected it to be pretty bad. So how, exactly, was she going to fix it? The solution, again, was to somehow convince her mother that Southern California was the perfect place for her to get strong again, so they could leave soon.

Much as she dreaded going to Mika's birthday party, taking her mother there so Beth could help convince her to go to LA for the winter was her best shot at making that happen.

CHAPTER SEVEN

WHY THE HELL had his mother asked Rory to come to Mika's birthday party? He hoped she wouldn't come. Hell, he hoped Wendy would be feeling well enough for her sister to take over and that Rory would be gone by then.

He put a sleeping Mika into his crib, tucked the blanket under his chin and kissed his plump little cheek, smiling even as his heart squeezed with all the feelings he'd buried long ago, which had insisted on floating back to the surface since Rory had come back to town.

At the beginning, he'd planned not to say a word about it to her. About all they'd lost and what she'd done. He'd been sure it was long behind him—until this week. And he couldn't even put the blame on her for stirring all their history up again.

He was the one who'd brought up the past—first at Pooky's, then right there in the store parking lot, like a fool, for some reason unable to control the need to get it off his chest. Then he'd made her cry. God, he hated to see her cry, and even as she'd infuriated him he'd kissed her without thinking, wanting to somehow stop the tears that weren't even flowing anymore.

And then…?

Despite getting beaned by Mika's cup, and the kiss lasting only a nanosecond, he'd wanted more. He'd wanted to pull her warm curves close against his body, to feel how she'd always molded perfectly against him; to mindlessly kiss her for real until neither of them could breathe, right in front of Mika and whoever else might be watching.

Just that tiny taste of her lips had sent bittersweet memories surging through his heart and his body, making him remember how much he'd loved her, how close they'd been, how she'd once been his—making him remember how sure he'd been that she'd be his lover and his soulmate, his life partner forever.

But all that was ancient history, and now that he'd told her how he'd felt when she'd left he had no intention of revisiting it again. Rory had made a new life for herself, and he'd made the life he'd always wanted here in Eudemonia, even though she'd abandoned it. Now, with Mika bringing new joy to his life, he was one step closer to the full dream. His plan of having the lifelong love of a woman and children of their own right here where he'd been born and raised.

Rory was no longer that woman—and the less contact he had with her while she was here, the better for both of them. But fate seemed to keep throwing them together anyway.

He put away the food and supplies he'd bought, and couldn't help but think about Rory doing the same thing at her mother's house—lugging multiple jugs of water and all kinds of things into the cellar. Wendy Anderson was pretty independent, but through all the years Rory's dad had been sick it had been Rory who'd kept the place running, even coming home from college every month to make sure her parents had everything they needed.

After her dad had died, her mother had accepted that there were things she needed help with. Letting some of the teens and the men in town chop firewood and do heavy lifting around her house made it easy for her to live there alone—a good thing, since by then Rory had been long gone.

That kind of community was just one of the reasons to live in Eudemonia. Everyone knew everyone else, and while that was sometimes a bad thing, mostly it was good. The folks in town took care of each other. Anchorage had been plenty big enough when Jake had gone to college and medical school there. He couldn't imagine living in a place like Los Angeles, where you probably didn't even know your next-door neighbor.

Could that be part of why Rory had chosen it? Had she wanted to be anonymous? Able to disappear into a crowd? She'd said people looking at her, talking about her after she'd lost the baby, had been among the reasons she'd felt she had to leave. He'd never thought about that, but she'd always been so strong he was surprised she'd let that bother her.

It didn't matter anymore. She had her life and he had his, and there was nothing else to say. No more conversations about their past and how he'd felt, because it wouldn't accomplish anything other than to upset them both.

"Hi, Jake," Ellie said as he walked into the clinic. "I see you brought your king-size coffee cup with you this morning. Bad night? Did Mika keep you up?"

"No, he slept great." He sure wasn't going to tell her it had been reliving his argument with Rory a couple days ago that had kept him tossing and turning these past two nights. "You have the patient list for the day?"

"Here. Not too many, so hopefully we'll have some emergencies to keep us busy."

"I wonder what the locals would think about their clinic assistant gleefully hoping for illness and injuries to keep her from being bored?"

Ellie laughed and handed him the list before she sat

down behind the front desk. Jake scanned the paper, surprised to see Wendy Anderson's name listed. Probably Rory had scheduled it quickly, so they wouldn't see one another again too many times before she left, and the way his heart bumped told him it was a very good thing to get it over with. Maybe, with any luck, that meant she wouldn't be coming to Mika's party after all.

He'd seen three patients before he moved toward the exam room where Wendy and Rory waited. His heart gave another weird kick, which annoyed the hell out of him. Why did he keep feeling this way when he kept reminding himself how stupid and pointless it was to get all riled up about her?

The moment he opened the door his attention moved involuntarily to the woman sitting in the chair next to the exam table instead of his patient, the way it should. Like before, the overhead light skimmed over her shining hair, and her green eyes lifted to meet his for a split second before she cast them down, then toward her mother.

Her uncomfortable expression told him she was remembering the anger, frustration and resentment that had spilled out at the parking lot. Maybe she was also remembering the electricity that had zinged from the briefest touch of his lips to hers, the way it was coming to *his* mind as he looked at her beautiful mouth.

Damn it.

He moved his attention to Wendy and forced a smile. "How are you feeling?"

"A little better, I think. Aurora keeps telling me that when your body's been cut open it's normal for it to hurt until it heals. And since it split open again something awful I'm having to heal all over again. I'm trying not to complain and to remember that it's slowly getting better."

"She's getting around better than I expected she would," Rory said. "I've been looking at the old sutures, and the new ones we did, and they look good. But of course you should see what you think."

"The type-A surgeon is offering to step back and let the general practitioner give his opinion? Now there's a shock." He couldn't help but raise his eyebrows in utter surprise. "You're evolving."

"And apparently you're not—still wanting to annoy me at any opportunity."

Her small smile took any sting out of the words, and the tightness in his chest loosened as he smiled back. "Never claimed to be. But, since you're setting such a good example, I'll give evolving a try."

A moment of silence followed, and Jake was filled with a confusing mix of feelings. He was glad they could share light banter like this, even while he was still feeling they hadn't truly finished their heavy conversation from a couple days ago. Except he'd decided there was no point, hadn't he?

He turned to Wendy. "It's good to remind yourself that you're getting better all the time. But you know what? It's okay to complain, too. I remember Rory used to complain about all kinds of things—like the kids who teased her at school, or that the bike she had that was pink when she wanted a bike a boy would ride."

"I'd forgotten that," Rory murmured.

Another small smile tugging at her lips made him feel glad he'd said something to take their minds off their last conversation and all the bad stuff from the past, way back to the fun times when they were kids.

"I spray-painted it blue and black and hand-painted a few swords on it. I didn't realize until years later how awful it looked."

"My Aurora usually did want to run with the boys, didn't she? Always a spitfire, my little marshmallow girl."

"Yeah, she was. I had to keep her from punching some

of those boys in the nose when they teased her. Which was mostly self-preservation on my part. I figured if she got into a real fight I'd have to jump in and beat them up, which wasn't something I was particularly keen to do."

Her gaze lifted to his again as a wry smile twisted her lips. "I was a trial to you, wasn't I?"

Not for most of their relationship. Just at the end.

"Not a trial. An amazing mix of tough little girl and sweetness and adventure and generosity, all wrapped up in a beautiful package. You were like nobody else in that whole school. You were special."

The minute the words were out of his mouth he felt a little foolish. Going down memory lane wasn't advisable—particularly when those memories involved the way he'd felt about her back then, and so many of the years that followed.

"Well, thank you. And a belated thank you, too, to the boy who stood up for me in fourth grade, when I was the fish out of water in a public school setting. You were my hero from that moment on."

Their eyes met again and he felt a strange expansion in his chest, as though her words *meant* something, even though she'd told him something similar many times before. Maybe this was the kind of closure they needed. Compliments to one another…an acknowledgment of what they'd meant to one another before life had got in the way and they'd moved on. It would put a positive ending to the chapter that had had such an abrupt, upsetting and unsatisfactory conclusion nine years ago.

He forced himself to go into doctor mode, asking Wendy a few more questions, taking her vital signs, drawing blood, and looking at her incision. When he was finished he gave her directions on what should happen next.

"Want me to write this down for when Rory is gone? Any word on when your sister is coming to take over?"

"I'm not sure. Aurora…?"

"Aunt Patty's taking this Friday off, so I'm planning to—"

A muffled ringing sound came from the purse on the floor next to the exam bed. Wendy tried to reached down for it, and Rory picked it up and gave it to her.

"Here. But you should let it go, Twinkie," Rory said. "We can't keep Jake waiting while you yak. You can see who it is after we're done here and call back."

"It might be Linda, wanting to know what time to come over with supplies to make the gourd birdfeeders. We're going to give them to everyone before winter."

"It's okay—go ahead and answer, then we'll finish up," Jake said, since the elderly woman looked a little distressed about not answering.

With a disapproving frown, Rory fished the phone from her mother's purse—then frowned even more when she looked at the screen. "It's Aunt Patty."

"Helloooo, sis!" Wendy said, taking the phone and smiling broadly. Her smile faded as she listened, morphing into a worried frown deeper than Rory's. "That's terrible! Oh, dear, of course I understand. Don't worry at all. Aurora will be here for a few more days—and I'm doing pretty well, considering. I'm sure Linda and some of the others will check on me and bring food until I'm feeling up to fixing it myself. It's fine. Please give him a huge hug and kiss from me—and Aurora, too. Tell him we're hoping he gets well soon."

"Wait! Let me talk to her." Rory reached to grab the phone, but her mother hung up before she could get it.

"Well, that's just *terrible* news!" Wendy said. "Owen was injured during a training mission at the base. Broke his arm, and his ribs, too. He's in the base hospital, but they're going to release him tomorrow. She's going to have him come to her house to get better and she'll take care of him there."

"So she's not coming here?" Rory said in a grim voice.

"No, but that's okay. I'm sure Owen needs help a lot more than I do. I'll be fine, Aurora. Don't you worry. I'm moving around okay, don't you think? You said so. And you need to get back to LA for that job interview. I know it's important to you."

"Yes, it is…"

Jake saw her chest heave in a big sigh and their eyes met, hers telegraphing the same thing he was thinking. Her mom shouldn't be left alone just yet, and the amount of time Rory would be here had probably gotten a week longer.

"But I can't leave you alone, Twinkie. I was thinking I should stay a little longer anyway, to be honest. I'll call the hospital and hope it won't be a problem to postpone the interview again. Unless you're willing to come to LA with me? Are you still considering it?"

"I don't know. I mean, I *guess* I'm thinking about it. But there are things here I need to do. The gourds and the Halloween decorations. Our Bunco tournament next month."

Another long, audible sigh left Rory's lips in response to her mother's statement, and Jake felt like sighing along with her.

"Are there other people interviewing for the position?" he asked.

"Yeah." Her face twisted in a grimace. "I don't know exactly how many, but quite a few people who trained at other hospitals are trying to get it, since it's a large orthopedic practice. I'd hoped that training there would give me a big advantage, but…"

Her voice faded away. Then the Rory he knew straightened her shoulders and put that determined look he'd seen so many times on her pretty face. This was the woman who'd climbed trees, operated heavy equipment in various search and rescue operations, and trained to be the kind of doctor few women in the country became.

"Anyway, it is what it is. I'll figure out how to beat everyone else. Maybe being the last one to interview will be an advantage, somehow? Will stop them deciding on someone else before I have a chance."

Yeah, that was indomitable Rory in a nutshell. There was only one time he'd seen her utterly defeated. And now that she'd be here longer he was glad they'd finished talking about it. Maybe they could be near one another without dreading it, or even have a conversation that didn't stir bad memories. Maybe they would be reminded of why they'd been friends for so long before it had all gone wrong.

CHAPTER EIGHT

"OH, COME ON—don't look like that," her mother scolded as she slowly tottered toward the front door of Jake's house. "It's a birthday party. Parties are *fun*! You always loved Jake's family, and they love you. And then there's Mika! Is there a cuter baby on earth than him?"

Rory closed her eyes against the sudden and unforgettable memory of holding her tiny, lifeless baby boy. He hadn't had time to grow to be a pretty, plump, full-term baby. Hadn't lived to grow to be an adorable one-year-old. But for her he would always be the most beautiful baby in the world.

She tried to concentrate on the tree line higher up the hill behind the house, shoving down the image and the memory.

"Mika is very cute—no doubt about it. But, like I said before, it would be better for me to just leave you here and come pick you up later. Can't you understand that it's hard for me to spend time with Jake?"

"No, I can't. You two were together for a long time, and I believe with all my heart that you'll be happier if you bury the hatchet and become friends again. I've lived long enough to know that you can't carry bad feelings around in your heart forever without it affecting your whole body. Poor digestion…your liver…high blood pressure and heart problems. Why, Sam Abbott got diabetes just from worrying too much about money and his business."

Rory bit her tongue. Resigned to her fate for the afternoon, she carried the shopping bag of wrapped gifts she'd gotten on her trek to Fairbanks and helped her mother up the stone steps as a few fat snowflakes began to float from the cloudy sky onto their heads.

They crossed a wide wooden porch that bore zero resemblance to her mother's small, creaky and listing front stoop. It gleamed with what looked like a new coat of polyurethane, and four comfortable-looking rocking chairs with plush pillows sat on either side of the front door. She wondered if Jake left them out all winter or took them to a shed somewhere, and then decided that the less she knew about how Jake lived in his new home with his new baby, the better.

She knocked on double doors painted a deep forest green, and Beth Hunter opened them with a smile. "Rory! Wendy. So glad you could make it. I can't believe you knocked on the door, though. You're like family, after all."

Family. It had felt that way, once, hadn't it?

They stepped across an oblong rug woven in the traditional Alaska Native style that graced so many homes in Eudemonia and elsewhere, and into a room with a vaulted ceiling made of pine logs. The space was nearly as big as her mother's entire house, but even with the high ceiling it somehow felt cozy. Possibly because a crackling fire blazed in the large stone fireplace and large, overstuffed sofas and chairs sat on either side of it.

But the biggest reason it felt cozy was because it was full of people. Jake's immediate family, plus cousins and lots of neighbors, sat and stood everywhere, talking and smiling. Balloons bobbed gently around the room, and a table holding platters of all kinds of food sat beneath one of the large windows, perfect for letting in what light was available during gray days and dark winters.

Rory stood there, absorbing the feel of the place. Warmth. Happiness and pleasure. A place you could count on as being a respite—a place you wanted to be, no matter how tough the outside world had become.

Much like Jake himself.

Her gaze roamed the beautiful room until it landed on the man who owned this house, who'd said he'd helped design and build it. He stood in the center, big and handsome, with a relaxed smile on his face. Mika was curled into Jake's muscled arm, one small fist hanging on to the collar of his daddy's yellow polo shirt.

A mix of emotions fluttered in Rory's heart. Sadness, envy and, yes, a warm and real happiness for Jake. He deserved to have everything he wanted in life and it looked like he was nearly there, with his home in Eudemonia, his clinic practice, his beautiful son. At some point he'd be sure to marry, and the hollowness that filled Rory's chest at that thought told her it was a very good thing she'd decided to stay in Los Angeles for good, so she didn't have to see who he chose to be his bride.

"Jake! Look who's here!" Beth called.

He lifted his gaze and she could see his smile falter before he shored it up again. Maybe someday everything that had happened between them, and his anger toward her because of it, would be so far away as not to matter anymore. She hoped so. For her sake, and for his, she hoped with all her heart that there'd come a time when being around each other didn't bring to the surface feelings and memories they both wanted to forget.

He walked toward her with that easy gait of his, and with one hand reached for her mother's coat. "Thanks for coming, Wendy... Rory. My mother tells me a first birthday party is all-important, so I'm glad you're here to help celebrate."

"Oh, they're just so cute as little ones. No need for any other entertainment when there's a toddler around, is there?" her mother said, beaming. "Is he walking yet?"

"A couple teetering steps, then back down. I keep holding my breath, thinking he's going to bang himself hard somewhere when he falls, but he's like a rubber ball. Just rolls with it."

"I'll take Mika so you can get Rory and Wendy something to drink," Beth said, reaching for the child. "Help yourselves to food, then he can open his presents before we have cake. I don't want to rush things along too much, but the forecast is for a storm moving in. Look, it's starting to snow already. We need to give our out-of-town friends plenty of time to drive home before it comes down harder."

"There's barely any right now, Mom. And I doubt the storm's going to bring much snow this time of year," Jake said, handing over the smiling baby. "But I agree that you should grab some of the Sloppy Joes my dad made, Wendy. They're the best. He's in Anchorage for a conference, and not happy he couldn't be here, so he made them for everyone else to enjoy."

"I'll be sure to have some, then. I didn't even know your dad likes to cook."

"Only very selective things, Wendy, believe me," Beth said, chuckling. "Come on over here and sit down."

Rory watched her mother move away to chat with Linda and some other folks, then looked up at Jake. "Your house is beautiful. You must be proud of it. So it's probably wrong of me to tell you I don't want to be here."

"Because my son's turning one and ours would have turned nine this past spring?" he asked in a quiet voice, shocking her. He knew exactly what she'd been thinking.

"Yes," she whispered. "That and other things."

"What other things?"

She wouldn't tell him that she couldn't get that kiss off her mind. It barely even counted as a kiss, really, since he'd been frustrated and angry with her when it had happened and it had lasted all of one second. Shockingly, though, that briefest touch had reminded her of all the kisses they'd shared. And, if she was honest, she'd like another one—or more. But that would be the worst idea ever. What was the point of kisses that would make her feel even more lonely after she was gone?

"Nothing. Never mind. I'm going to get some food for Twinkie."

She could practically feel him watching her as she moved away, and she hoped he wouldn't notice that someone had gotten her mom a plate of food which she was already enjoying as she talked with her friends. Probably she should eat something, too. But her stomach felt a little queasy.

She'd just decided a carbonated soda might do the trick when Beth stepped in front of her, looking a little harried.

"Rory, can you take Mika for a minute? One of the kids spilled red punch on the throw rug in the kitchen. I want to get some water on it before it stains, and I see Jake just went outside to get another load of firewood."

Before she could answer the child was thrust into her arms. She reacted instinctively, reaching out and then pressing his small, warm body close against her. For a second she hesitated, and then, with a sigh, let her cheek rest against his temple. His wonderful scent—all powder and milk and sweet baby—filled her nose, and she closed her eyes and breathed him in.

She'd expected that holding him like this would make her feel emotional. And she did. But they weren't the kinds of emotions that hurt. Yes, her throat closed a little, but what she felt was mostly a strange calm. A quiet joy. The same deep feeling of happiness for Jake that had filled her earlier.

What an amazing blessing a healthy child was. This little boy who'd so tragically lost his mother was beyond fortunate to have become a part of the Hunter family— and they were beyond fortunate to have him.

"Your daddy is a special person—you know that, don't you, Mika?" she whispered, moving her cheek to his soft hair. "You're a lucky boy to get to spend your life with him. *So* lucky."

He must be feeling tired from all the company and activity, because he laid his head against her shoulder, poked his thumb into his little rosebud mouth and closed his eyes. She looked down at the fan of dark lashes against his round cheeks, breathed in the smell of him again and let her heart ache and warm at the same time.

She gave herself up to enjoying the moment as long as she could. As long as it lasted.

"Sleepy, little guy?" she murmured as she swayed back and forth. "I'll hold you while you get some rest. You've got big stuff going on today, with your birthday cake and all those presents waiting for you to open them. I got you some books for your daddy to read to you, and a little drum so you can drive him crazy. I hope you like them."

"Did you say a drum?"

The low, deep voice in her ear had her lifting her head, then turning her face to see Jake's, just inches from hers. He smelled of the outdoors, and ever so slightly of musky woodsmoke, and of *him*.

"Um…yeah. I looked for a horn, or a tambourine, but I had to settle for a drum. It's only plastic, though, so not super-loud. Darn it."

"I don't know what I ever did to you to deserve that kind of punishment."

"Nothing. You know that." She faced him, and the

humor of their conversation fell away as that familiar hollow feeling made her stomach hurt. "I'm the one who deserves the bad stuff. But don't worry—I live with it every day."

"Rory—"

The sleepy baby lifted his head, blinked, looked up into Rory's face and started whimpering. Relieved that she didn't have to listen to whatever empty platitudes Jake had been about to offer, or hear him lambast her like he had before, she handed the child to him and quickly moved away to sit near her mother.

Cake was being served, and everyone was laughing at the way Mika used both fists to pick his piece up from the highchair tray and stuff it into his mouth, enthusiastically licking at his messy lips and fingers.

Grinning, Jake took a video of the moment, and Rory couldn't help but think about Jake and Mika watching it together and laughing when the boy was older, about the bond the two of them were already forging.

After Mika had eaten as much as possible, and gotten bored with smearing icing around his tray, Jake and his mother cleaned the child up, sat him on the floor and let him rip the paper off his gifts. It was clear that some of the presents weren't quite as interesting to him as the paper, and everyone enjoyed the fun of watching him.

Glad she'd been able to melt toward the back of the room, Rory managed to chuckle along with everyone else, even as she kept glancing at her watch, wondering how long they'd have to stay.

It was beyond hard to watch Jake with Mika and see what an absolutely great father he was—to see the light in his eyes when he looked at the baby, to see an indulgent smile of such love on his face. It squeezed her heart so hard she thought it might bleed.

Yes, she'd seen Jake and Mika together since she'd come

back, but not quite like this. Playing and teasing and laughing. Jake picking him up to hug him and kiss him. The baby wrapping his small arms around his dad's neck and hanging on tight.

This was how Jake would have been with Adam. How Adam would have been with Jake. How they'd have all been together, as a family. Staring at Jake now, at his handsome face and beautiful smile, she realized for the first time since she'd come back, really admitted it to herself, that she'd never stopped loving her best friend.

She was about to turn to her mother and suggest they go, so she didn't have to think about all that anymore, when Jake handed the baby the gift she'd brought and sent her a grin.

"I think I already know what's in here, Dr. Anderson. And it scares me."

"Maybe he'll like the paper more than the present."

"Probably no such luck."

Jake helped Mika open the gift, picked up one of the rubbery plastic drumsticks and tapped the drum a few times. Mika's eyes lit, and he immediately grabbed both sticks and starting pounding on it.

Everyone in the room howled.

Beth covered her ears and said, "Rory Anderson! Did *you* give him that?"

"Um…guilty as charged. Sorry. I couldn't decide what to get him, and I thought it would be fun."

"That's a clear fib," Jake said. "You thought it would torment me."

"Maybe."

Their eyes met, and they shared a small smile that banished some of the melancholy she'd been feeling the past half hour. Mika moved on to whacking the sticks as hard as he could on the hardwood floor, then stood to stagger a few steps to the rustic wooden coffee table, wildly swinging the sticks against the side of it.

"Um…maybe I should have thought this through a little more," Rory said, feeling sheepish about possible furniture destruction.

"Maybe you should have," Jake said, but the brown eyes meeting hers still smiled. "Well, he probably can't do a lot of damage with those sticks. And I already told you I've baby-proofed the house pretty well."

Rory let her gaze travel over the planes of his face, memorizing them all over again since this might well be the last time she saw him. Her mother was more functional every day, and even her extended stay wouldn't keep her here more than another week. Getting back to LA as soon as her mom was able to fully take care of herself had to be her priority. Much as she was enjoying talking with Jake and being near him, she knew it would just make it all the harder to leave.

She made herself turn to see how her mom was doing. "You feeling tired, Twinkie? Ready to go home?"

"I guess I am a little tired. Oh, but it's been a fun day, hasn't it? I'm so glad we came."

"It's been good." Which was something she hadn't expected was possible when they'd been getting ready to come today. Maybe, as she'd thought before, this closure on a more positive note between her and Jake would be a good thing for both of them. "I'll go get your coat."

As she walked toward the front closet she could see Jake watching her, and then Beth stopped her progress.

"I have some food on the kitchen counter for you to take home with you. It'll be good for a few meals, and then you can freeze some of the Sloppy Joe meat for Wendy to eat after you're gone."

"Thank you. Everything was so good, and it's always

nice for her to have stuff ready to eat that she can just thaw."

"Also…" Beth lowered her voice. "Do you still want me to talk to your mom about going to LA with you for the next few months? I'd be happy to, since I think it's a very good idea."

"That would be great." More than great, as then they'd be able to leave soon, solving all kinds of problems. "Could you talk to her while I go to the kitchen? I'll hang around in there for a bit, so she doesn't feel like we're ganging up on her and thinks that it's your idea. Then we'll go, because I think she's getting tired."

"I'll talk with her right now."

Rory found her way to the kitchen, curious to see how Jake had designed it. It had an open feel, like the living room, with a large center island with stools, light-colored cabinets, more hardwood flooring and big windows. It was the perfect size and the perfect design for Alaska, with its long winter nights and long summer days.

Several containers sat on the counter with her mother's name on them and she thought about how nice Beth was, always thinking of others. How she always had been. Jake was like that, too. It struck Rory that maybe she wasn't as much like that as she wanted to be, and just as she was pondering that Jake came into the kitchen to stand behind her.

"Find them?"

"Yes." Her throat closed at his nearness as she remembered her revelation a short time ago. That she'd loved him practically her whole life and always would. "I appreciate all your mom does for everyone."

"She does a lot for me, that's for sure. She takes care of Mika quite a bit, and she planned this party."

"That's…good. I'm sure everyone with a baby, especially someone single, needs lots of help."

Which made her think about him not being single in the

future, and how awful that would make her feel. But how could she think like that? She wanted him to be happy, didn't she?

She'd opened her mouth to say goodbye and hightail it out of there when his hands rested on her shoulders and he turned her around to face him.

"I saw how sad you looked when Mika was opening his presents. I wanted to tell you I was thinking about Adam, too."

"You were?" She stared up into his brown eyes and saw he meant it. "I… That surprises me. You looked so happy, having fun with Mika."

"I *was* happy having fun with him. He's changed my life, and I'm beyond thankful for that." He caught her face in his hands. "But that doesn't mean I'm not still sad for the son we lost. It doesn't mean I don't understand how you feel."

"Thank you," she whispered, and her hands lifted to his chest, slid to the sides of his neck, even before she'd known she was going to touch him.

Everything she'd felt during the party—all those thoughts about him and how they'd been when they were together, how she'd loved him and couldn't stop thinking about kissing him—seemed to short-circuit her mind and stop her heart.

"Jake, I…"

"I know. Me, too."

The eyes staring into hers held something different now. Something hot and alive. And she knew she wasn't alone in remembering the way they'd loved one another once. The way it had felt when they'd kissed and made love, which had always been so much more than just sex.

Fixated on his beautiful lips, her heart thudding hard against her ribs, she quivered as she watched his mouth lower to hers.

The kiss was sweet and slow and wonderful. A gentle rub of his lips against hers as his arms slipped around her, holding her close against his warm, firm chest. Memories of all the yesterdays when he'd held her this way, of the hundreds of kisses they'd shared, melted her heart and stole her breath.

Her hands moved to his hair, tunneling into the thick softness as the kiss deepened, no longer sweet and soft. His body trapped hers against the counter as the kiss escalated into a passionate tangle of tongues that weakened her knees and had her desperate for more.

This was what she wanted. She couldn't lie to herself about that. From the first second she'd seen him again she'd wanted to kiss him. Hold him. Have him hold her. Sensations she hadn't experienced in nine long years overwhelmed her, and she found herself arching into him, feeling his hardness, wanting so much more.

He pulled back, his eyes glittering, his jaw tense. "Rory?"

She tried to speak, but found she couldn't think of a single thing to say or do other than tug his head down to kiss him again. His hands roamed her body and sent shivers down her spine as his mouth devoured hers with a single-mindedness that felt so intense, she was dizzy from it.

"Jacob! Where are you?"

The sound of his mother's voice had them stumbling apart. Rory could see his chest heaving as he tried to catch his breath, which was hardly a surprise since she felt like she couldn't breathe at all.

"Uh…" He shoved his hand through his hair and cleared his throat, then took a quick step away from Rory and worked to adjust the front of his pants. "I'm in the kitchen."

Rory could only imagine what her expression might be like. Jake looked stunned and flushed and she felt that way but times ten. She was about to turn to the sink, to splash cold water on her face, when Beth appeared at the kitchen doorway and hurried toward them.

Something about her expression told Rory that this wasn't about the party, or their guests, or either one of them. It was clear that something was definitely wrong.

CHAPTER NINE

"WHAT IS IT, MOM?"

Rory was impressed that Jake had managed to get his voice under control so fast, answering his mother in a tone that said he, too, could tell she was worried about something.

"Jameson Woodrow just called. Natalia's gone into labor a couple weeks early and he said he's afraid there's something wrong. The midwife they've been seeing is away in Anchorage, probably at the same conference as your dad. He was going to ask your father to open the clinic, but she's in so much pain he can't get her up to move her to the car. I told her your dad's in Anchorage, too, but that you're here. I think you should go up there and see what's going on. Is there someone here who can go with you? If she needs to be moved to the clinic, or even if she has the baby, you might need help with that."

Instantly Rory could see his professional doctor mode take over. "There are a few people here who would come with me. I'll ask. I assume you can stay here and watch Mika? You might as well plan to spend the night here, just in case it takes a long time."

"I brought an overnight bag, thinking the weather might get bad."

"Perfect. Thanks."

They moved back to where everyone was gathered and

Rory watched Jake scan the room, presumably looking for a helper. Even though she dreaded the thought of spending more awkward hours with him, she knew what needed to happen and placed her hand on his forearm.

"I'll go with you. I haven't delivered a baby in a long time, but I'm sure I can help."

He looked down at her for a long moment, his expression inscrutable. She knew what he was thinking, because she was, too. Being together after that scorching and ill-advised kiss wasn't the best idea. But this was an emergency, and having two doctors made a lot more sense than him finding a random friend to assist him.

Finally, he nodded. "All right. But what about your mom?"

"I'll see if Linda can drive her home. Stay with her, too, if she can."

"I'll call Jameson to tell him we'll leave soon, then I'll pull together some supplies."

Linda was more than happy to take her mother home and spend the night. "It's looking like we'll get more snow than we thought," Linda said as she peered out the window at the light flakes steadily falling to the ground. "So I'd just as soon stay put once we're at your house. It'll be fun having a slumber party, don't you think, Wendy?"

"A slumber party! I *love* that idea! I probably can't dance around yet, but we can work on those paper pumpkins and ghost strings for Halloween. Rory got me all the supplies we need."

Wendy's eyes shone with pleasure, and Rory had to face what she'd been trying to ignore. Her mom truly loved living here. She loved her friends and her life here. Much as she wanted her mother to come live with her for the winter in Los Angeles, and was convinced she'd enjoy the warmth of Southern California, she couldn't deny the truth. Moving her to LA for the winter would be more for *her* benefit than for Twinkie's.

"That's perfect, Linda," Rory said. "In case we're gone a long time there's leftover stew and noodles in the fridge, to heat up for dinner, or the things Beth is being kind enough to send from the party. Plus Twinkie and I made cookies the other day, so there's plenty to eat. You'll need to help her get into her jammies, though, because she's still having trouble getting undressed by herself."

"I'm happy to do that. Goodness knows I've had plenty to eat here already, but I'm sure we'll want a late-night snack."

Glad to have all that settled, Rory hugged Linda and her mom, and went to grab her coat. There was no sign of Jake yet, and she hovered around the door, nervous and worried about spending this time with him, but at the same time feeling wired about the trek and perhaps helping this woman deliver her baby.

Now that Jake was about to leave a number of guests stood, obviously wanting to say their goodbyes. Beth was holding Mika and talking with them, but she came over when she spotted Rory by the door.

"Thanks for doing this, Rory. I know Jake appreciates it, too."

"Taking care of people, whether it's this kind of situation or something in my own specialty, is why doctors go into medicine. I'm happy to do it."

"I hope Natalia's okay, and that the baby is, too."

Beth's anxious expression made Rory's stomach drop. For some reason when she thought of labor and birth, even a difficult one, she thought of a happy outcome, with a beautiful newborn.

How was it possible that it hadn't even occurred to her that it might be a terrible situation, like her own had been nine years ago?

That tonight a baby might be born, but not healthy. Maybe not even alive.

God, she'd shoved all that down so deeply. How was she going to handle it if this turned out to be the kind of life-altering heartache her own pregnancy and labor had turned into?

She sucked in a steadying breath. She was a doctor. She had to be brave and tough—be there for this woman and her unborn child and stop thinking of herself. It would be okay. She'd get through it no matter what happened. She could do it. *Would* do it.

"I hope so, too, Beth. I'll do the best I can to help the momma and Jake bring a healthy baby into the world."

Beth's brown eyes were filled with worry for Natalia Woodrow, and with a kind of deep sympathy she knew was about her and the baby she and Jake had lost.

"I know you will."

Jake appeared by her side with several bags stuffed to overflowing. "Ready?"

"Ready. What have you got in there?"

"Transport monitor. Exterior monitor to track the baby's vitals. Pain meds. Surgical equipment. Hopefully everything we'll need, no matter what the situation is."

"You keep all that *here*?" she asked, astonished that he'd have medical supplies beyond the simplest things at his own house.

"You've been gone too long. When storms come through, or the power goes out, or we need to go on search and rescue or whatever situation, we've got to be ready. Getting to the clinic might not be an option."

Search and rescue. Another thing she'd apparently shoved down so as not to think about it too hard after what had happened.

"Of course," she muttered. "So, let's go."

Her heart squeezing all over again, she watched the

sweet hug and kiss Jake gave the baby, then another to his mom, before he led the way to his truck, stashing the equipment on the second set of bench seats behind the front set.

She climbed up into the truck and in moments they'd driven the half mile or so of gravel road that led from his house to the main paved road, where they picked up speed. She tried to ignore the fluttering in her heart from being so close to him after what had happened between them, even as she was thankful this wasn't the small car he'd had so long ago, when she would have been mere inches from his big body.

Tension—sexual and otherwise—seemed to vibrate between them, and she didn't think she was the only one feeling it.

"Where do they live? How far is it?"

"Pretty far—which worries me. About thirty-five miles away, in a little town that sprang up near one of the new oil fields that wasn't open when you lived here. Remember the dry cabins up on the ridge? Where lots of hunters go? It's about ten miles from there."

"What's the road like?" She wasn't worried about the road, but avoiding a heavy silence between them by making small talk might calm her nerves.

"Not bad, really. The oil company put a lot of money into it, so it's fairly smooth all the way into the town. I think the Woodrows live off a gravel road, but in the truck it won't be a problem even if it snows more."

She glanced around at the snowflakes, clinging to the car and starting to cover the landscape. "I didn't really look at the forecast, but it seems early for any kind of real snow."

"Yeah, I can't imagine we'll get much. But I guess you never know."

His face was in profile as he watched the road, and the years fell away as she remembered all the times they'd driven together in a car. Sometimes it had been in his small sedan, other times in her own compact little SUV, which she'd bought once they were in college in Anchorage with the money she'd made waiting tables there.

Confusing and contradictory thoughts swirled through her mind as the miles passed. Thoughts of that kiss, and wanting more of them, warred with her self-protective mode that had been telling her from the day she arrived that she needed to get away from him and Eudemonia and the memories as quickly as possible.

But at this moment that attitude was selfish—like he'd said she'd been before, right? Tonight it was a good thing she was here to help this woman with whatever problem she was having. Surely the distraction of that would put everything out of her mind but work?

But then there'd be the torture of driving back with him.

Except, in a strange way, this didn't feel like torture. It felt oddly nice to be sitting close to him in this truck, despite the slightly disturbing tension zinging around the cab. And suddenly, after wanting nothing more than to get back to California as soon as possible, the thought of going back into her hidey-hole and her normal life in LA felt strangely distant.

Which clearly proved that being back home was making her crazy.

Jake seemed to want to fill the silence, too—but not with conversation about what had happened between them in his kitchen. Which she was glad about, since she didn't want to go there, either.

He asked questions about her potential future job in LA, and told her about the general medical practice in Fairbanks, where he and his father took turns working since the clinic in Eudemonia didn't need both of them full-time.

The conversation helped her relax and forget her strange confusion. And when they finally pulled up in front of the Woodrows' house, flooded with outdoor lights presumably to help them find it, her heart had returned to a normal rhythm.

"Why don't you go knock and tell them we're here?" he said, half of his face lit up, the other in shadow as he leaned into the back seat of the truck. "I'll bring the stuff in."

She turned away from the striking angles of the face she'd seen in her dreams for so long and moved toward the front door. She'd barely lifted her arm to knock when it cracked open and an obviously agitated man peered out.

"I'm Dr. Anderson, and Dr. Jacob Hunter is with me."

"Thank God."

He swung the door wide, then turned and moved into the house, leaving Rory to assume he wanted her to follow. She glanced over her shoulder to see Jake's tall, broad form moving out of the shadows toward the house, and decided to go on in.

"Back here. She's in a lot of pain. I don't know what to do."

Moving through a pretty modern foyer into a good-sized living room, Rory was surprised to see the poor woman lying right there on the carpeted floor, writhing and moaning. Her heart beat harder. She hated to see the obvious distress the poor woman was in. Hopefully it was normal labor pain, but if her husband hadn't been able to get her into the car even between contractions there was a good chance it was more than that.

She knelt down and grasped the woman's wrist to take her pulse. It was high, but that wasn't a surprise, considering how much pain she must be in.

"I'm Aurora Anderson, a doctor from LA, and Dr. Hunter is here with me." She sensed Jake coming up behind her. "Tell us what's going on."

"She said she thought she was in labor, so we called the midwife and were upset to find out she's in Anchorage.

She gave us some instructions on the signs to look for—timing how far apart the contractions were and stuff—and said we should go to Fairbanks to the hospital there when they were twenty minutes apart, to give us plenty of time to drive there."

"But she didn't feel able to do that?" Jake asked, also crouching down beside the moaning woman.

"It seemed okay for a while, but then the contractions starting coming closer and I got worried and said we should go. And then she was like this." Worry etched the man's face. "She'd been sitting and walking around, but then she was in so much pain she just lay down on the floor, and she's been like this ever since. The midwife said last week that the baby was breech, but she expected it would turn. But now it's coming early. Is that the problem? I'm scared. Do you think something's wrong?"

"Let's find out."

Rory watched Jake take the woman's pulse, and didn't think it necessary to tell him her own findings.

"Where does it hurt?"

"Oh, God…" The woman shrieked and moaned simultaneously. She clutched her hands to her swollen abdomen, rolling from side to side. "It…it hurts so much. Is… is the baby…?"

"Hang in there."

Jake's lips tightened and his gaze met Rory's for a moment. She knew it was possible the woman was just having normal labor contractions and had a low tolerance for pain, but somehow this seemed like more than that. Obviously Jake thought so, too.

"Let me feel your belly, okay?"

Rory reached for the woman's hands, gently squeezing, both to try to comfort her and to keep them away from her belly so Jake could give her an external examination.

He glanced up at Rory again. "I think she's in the second stage of labor. I need to do an internal exam. The baby might still be breech, which would account for her extreme pain."

Rory nodded, but didn't say what she was thinking, and knew Jake was thinking, too. A breech baby was going to be a lot more difficult to deliver, unless they could turn it, and a C-section would likely be necessary if they couldn't. These were far from ideal conditions for that, and they'd have to get her to the hospital in Fairbanks to recover, but if that was what had to happen, they'd make it happen.

"Natalia, I want to do an internal exam, to see how much you're dilated. I'm willing to bet you're close to delivering, but let's find out."

He turned to Jameson.

"We're going to need some towels and hot water. Can you light that wood-burning stove and put a kettle on it? Or heat some water in the kitchen? And bring a sheet to put on the floor beneath her. But first a glass of water so she can take some pain medication. I assume you want that, Natalia?"

"Ye-e-s..." she gasped. "Hurts...bad."

"I'm on it, honey," Jameson said as he ran from the room.

In moments he was back with a water glass, then he hurried off again.

"Rory? How about you try to help her sit up enough to take the narcotic while I get it?"

She nodded as Jake rifled through one of the bags. "We know your pain is bad, Natalia, but the narcotic should help," she said. "You're going to have to sit up to swallow. Can you do that?"

The woman gave a jerky nod, even as she cried out again, and Rory struggled to help her to a sitting position. The effort was only partially successful, as she slumped sideways against Rory, but it was enough for her to be able to drink without choking.

"Here."

Jake held the glass to Natalia's lips, tipping it up as he held the pills in his other hand. He poked them onto her tongue and Rory stroked her throat, because she knew that sometimes that helped a person in tremendous pain swallow when it was hard for them to focus on anything but how much they hurt.

Water dribbled down her chin, and she choked a little, but finally she got them down.

It struck Rory how odd it was to be working with Jake this way again. As though they knew what the other needed without having to speak. Was it from all the years they'd been so close that they'd practically been able to read one another's minds?

Jameson ran in with a pile of sheets and towels. Rory spread a sheet on the floor, then the two men helped move Natalia on top of it.

"I need to give you the internal exam," Jake said. "We're going to get your clothes off, and then you're going to feel me touch you so I can check dilation. Okay?"

His calm and gentle voice was so different from his everyday speech. Different from the way he'd spoken to Rory since she'd been back. Except that wasn't entirely true. Tonight, when he'd told her he understood what she'd been feeling at Mika's party, his voice had held that same, caring warmth.

There was no doubt the man was good at reassuring patients, even in stressful situations. But even long ago he'd been good at that, hadn't he? If she let herself, she could still remember his sweetness and concern for *her*, even in the darkest times. Even when he had been hurting, too. And she knew it was past time to finally tell him that.

The two of them worked to remove Natalia's pants—

which wasn't easy, considering she was on her side on the floor again, rocking. Rory hated to see her in so much pain, and she had a bad feeling the worst was yet to come.

Even though she was pretty sure the last thing the woman was thinking about was her modesty, Rory placed a towel over her as Jake reached to examine her. After a long moment his gaze lifted to meet Rory's again, before moving back to Natalia, and she could tell it wasn't good news.

"Baby's ready to come. It's still breech, but not engaged in the pelvis yet, so that's good. It's possible to deliver it that way, but not ideal. So we're going to try to turn it. Are you ready?"

"Oh, God. No!"

"I'm here, honey. I'm here for you. It's going to be okay," Jameson said, holding her hand.

The anxiety on the man's face took her back to all those years ago, when she'd been delivering Adam. How Jake had been there, holding her, kissing her head, trying to soothe her even as his own heart had been breaking. She realized now, feeling a little ashamed, that his suffering was something she hadn't thought about enough.

"We need to get the external monitor on her, so we can check the baby's heartbeat and make sure it's normal before we try this."

The baby's heartbeat. Briefly, Rory squeezed her eyes shut, not wanting to remember when they'd done that for hers. *Theirs.* When it had shown there was no heartbeat at all. Was Jake remembering, too? Or had he delivered enough babies over the last nine years that it didn't feel so personal anymore?

She swallowed hard and focused fiercely on Natalia. *Not* the time for memories to keep resurfacing, good or bad.

"How do we do this?" she asked in a near whisper. "I kind of remember from med school, but not really."

"Wait a minute. Let's get this done first."

His brows lowered in concentration as he attached the monitor. Rory held her breath as they waited for the reading, and slumped in relief to see the strong, steady beat of the baby's heart.

"Baby's okay," she said. Her voice was a little thin but she couldn't help it. "Heartbeat's *good*, Natalia."

The woman nodded, huffing breaths in and out, and Jake sent her the kind of smile that would reassure anyone.

"All right. I'm going to give you an injection of a drug that will help your womb relax, making it a little easier for us to turn the baby. What I'm going to do," he continued as he drew the medicine into a syringe and injected it, "is put my hands on your belly. One by the baby's bottom and one on its head, and see if I can turn it. Are you ready?"

"Won't it be hurt? Won't it hurt the baby?"

"No. Baby is protected by all the fluid and tissue around it. And we'll keep a close eye on the baby's heartbeat to make sure it isn't distressed. If it is, I'll stop. Rory, I want you to keep an eye on the monitor."

"Got it."

She watched Jake do as he'd said he would, his big hands pushing and twisting on Natalia's belly. Her throat tight, Rory glanced at Natalia, wondering what she was thinking. Wouldn't it be disturbing for *any* woman to see the mound of the baby in her belly being shoved and turned? But Natalia didn't shriek or moan at his efforts, at least no more than she had before, so the narcotic and the relaxer he'd given her must be working.

"Heart rate looks good," Rory said, staring at the monitor.

"Okay. I think we're getting there. Baby's definitely moving. Hold on a little longer, Natalia." He continued his manipulation as the minutes ticked by. "How's the heart rate now?"

"Still fine."

"Good. Almost...*there*."

He leaned back, and the broad grin on his face had Rory sucking in the first breath she'd taken for a while. She watched Jake pull new surgical gloves from his bag and snap them on.

"It's head-down now. And I have a feeling your little one is ready to rock and roll now that it's not stuck. Give me some good pushes, Natalia."

She pushed, and to Rory's shock the baby actually crowned. "Oh, my gosh—you were right! There it is!"

It was probably not the most professional thing to blurt, but birthing babies wasn't something she'd done much of, and the last time had been years ago.

"See it crowning, Jameson? Your baby is coming!"

"I can't believe it. You're doing so great, honey." He clutched Natalia's hand. "*So* good. I love you. I love you so much."

Jake spoke encouragingly to Natalia as she pushed, his fingers working to free the baby's head, and then with one more big effort the infant's tiny pink body came into the world, held in Jake's strong hands.

"You have a beautiful baby girl! Congratulations," Jake said, that big smile back on his face. "Can you grab the bulb suction, Rory? And a towel?"

"Yes. Of course."

It was hard for her to speak through the thickness in her throat. Tears stung the backs of her eyes as she grabbed what they needed. She handed the bulb to Jake, so he could clear the baby's nose and mouth while she took a towel to begin wiping the tiny feet and hands. The little pink belly and wet brown hair.

What a miracle. What a beautiful thing to witness, to be a part of in even the smallest way.

Of course she'd seen babies born when she was in medical school, but back then her own experience had been too fresh, too raw, for her to be able to enjoy and appreciate seeing the birth of a healthy baby when her own had died, knowing it might have been *her* fault.

She swallowed back the tears and smiled at this sweet new life. Maybe this was exactly what she'd needed to truly heal. Maybe she'd needed to come back home for a little while, back to where the worst day of her life had happened, to see Jake one last time, to talk about it now that there were years between that awful day and now—and to see this beautiful baby born and be able to feel true happiness for the new parents instead of grief and melancholy.

Rory laid a clean towel across the new mother's chest and Jake wrapped the baby in another towel before giving the infant to her mother.

"There she is. Was it worth all that pain now that she's here?"

"Yes. Oh, yes. She's so beautiful. I can't believe it…"

Natalia beamed as she looked up at her husband. He leaned over to give her a kiss so sweet it made Rory's eyes sting all over again.

"Do you have a name picked out for her?" Jake asked.

"I don't know. Do we?" She smiled weakly at Jameson. "We had two girl names and two boy names, figuring we'd decide what it looked like when it came."

"I think she's definitely a Shae. Don't you?" said Jameson.

"Shae…" Natalia whispered, softly stroking the baby's cheek. "Yes, it's perfect. *She's* perfect."

"I like that." Jake touched the baby's temple. "Little Shae has had a bit of a rough time of it, just like her mama, so we need to make sure she's good and warm. After you've held her for a few minutes Rory's going to get her cleaned up and swaddled while I take care of you. Jameson, is the fire hot and the water warm? Do you have baby clothes and baby blankets that Rory can put her in?"

"Fire's lit and the water's close to hot. Um…where are the baby's clothes, honey?"

"In the dresser your mom gave us. Get a snap under-shirt and one of those warm little onesie things with feet. And there are baby blankets in there, too."

"Sounds nerve-racking, but I'll do my best to find what you're talking about." With a wide grin, looking totally different than he had an hour ago, Jameson dropped an-other lingering kiss to his wife's mouth, moved to throw some more logs on the fire, then headed down the hallway.

"Is it okay if I look for a bowl in the kitchen? I need to put the warm water in it so I can get baby Shae cleaned up," Rory asked Natalia.

"Whatever you need." She stared raptly at her new-born, not bothering to look up at Rory—and who could blame her?

As clearly as if it were yesterday, Rory remembered feeling exactly the same way as she'd held her own new-born in her arms. Staring at tiny Adam's small, angelic face. Kissing his still-warm cheeks.

Beautiful and perfect, even in death.

Her heart constricting, she reached for the baby and Jake lifted his gaze to hers. She drew a deep breath, not sure what she saw in the brown depths of his eyes. Con-cern? Contrition? If that was the case, surely he couldn't feel bad about her being here, worrying about her reliving their baby's birth. This new family had needed her, and she was more than glad to have had the privilege to help.

The emotions twisting through her made her wonder what her expression was like, and yet at the same time it felt impossible to school it into something only joyous and happy. Something not shadowed by the regrets and pain and guilt of the past.

"I'll get her cleaned up while Dr. Hunter takes care

of you. Don't worry, I'll be very careful with your new miracle."

She tried to smile at Natalia, hoping the new mother wouldn't notice how strange her voice was, how nervous and uncomfortable she felt. At the same time she wanted nothing more than to hold this baby and bathe her, get her ready for the big, new world she'd just joined.

With the baby pressed close against her breast, she looked down into the small, wide eyes looking up at her, seeming to study her. "Your mommy and daddy are *so* lucky," she whispered. "Welcome to your life, little Shae."

Jake's arm reached out to touch hers as she moved toward the warmth of the fire, his dark gaze pinning hers. "You okay?" he asked, his voice so low Natalia probably wouldn't hear.

Her eyes met his, but she couldn't speak. Even after this beautiful experience she had hoped would help her heal, she wasn't sure she'd *ever* be okay. But she was going to try to be. She was.

And maybe this time she'd let Jake help her through it, when she just hadn't been able to before.

CHAPTER TEN

"LIKE I SAID, if you're feeling like you want me to come see you and the baby tomorrow, I'm happy to do that," Jake said.

"Thank you," said Jameson, pumping his hand for the tenth time. "I hope she'll be comfortable, and that I'll be taking good care of both of them. But I'll call if something seems wrong."

"I'm sure your midwife will want to come check on both of them, so I suggest you give her a call in the morning to let her know the baby's here. But don't hesitate to call me, if you feel you need me."

If the snow kept coming it wouldn't be an easy trek in the morning, but he couldn't leave them stranded up here if Natalia wasn't feeling well or they were worried about the baby. He definitely wouldn't be bringing Rory, though. From her strained and bleak expression, it was clear that helping deliver this baby had been beyond hard for her.

He thrashed himself for letting her come at all. Yeah, she'd been a huge help, and if he hadn't been able to turn the baby he would have had to call on her surgical skills to do an emergency C-section. But her reaction to the baby's birth, the way she'd looked holding the newborn in her arms, had just about destroyed him.

He'd delivered a lot of babies since they'd lost theirs nine years ago. So many that the birth of a healthy child, or even one with problems, didn't feel personal anymore—didn't bring back the sad and horrible memories of that day, and the days after when Rory wouldn't lean on him. When she'd decided to just up and leave, smashing his heart to bits, along with everything he'd thought he'd have with her.

He'd been hurt. Devastated. And, yes, angry. Understanding why she'd taken off had felt impossible, and he'd been left to grieve alone, with bitterness gnawing at his gut over her actions. Her attitude.

But seeing the pain etched on her face tonight, the deep longing as she'd stared down into the baby's small face, had softened the shell he'd closed around his heart, vowing never to let her back in for even a minute. Maybe it was time to try to forgive. Not forget—because there was no way he'd let himself get close to her again—but perhaps move on from his resentment? Try to understand at least a little why she'd left? He could work on that.

He turned to the woman who'd broken his heart and realized it felt achy all over again. "You ready?"

He watched her look back at Natalia and the baby, now resting comfortably on the sofa instead of on the hard floor, and give them a smile. Someone who didn't know her might think it was a regular smile, but *he* knew it was full of all kinds of emotion. The emotions he could see swimming in her green eyes as she turned them back to him.

"Ready."

He led the way out—and stopped short for a second, not believing the winter world in front of them.

"What the…?"

"Oh, no! How could there be this much snow? And it's coming down so hard!" She stared up at him. "Are we going to be able to get back?"

"Good question." He waded through the thick white fluff and stowed the equipment in the back seat again.

"The roads won't be plowed until we get closer to Eude-monia, but my truck can handle deep snow pretty well. I think we'll be okay."

"Should we just stay here?"

"I'd rather not. Unless you want to?"

He didn't particularly want to bunk down there—for a couple reasons. One was interrupting the new little family having quiet time on their own. And the bigger reason was he didn't think it would be good for Rory to have to spend that many hours around the baby—seeing her again in the morning, maybe even helping care for her.

He couldn't bear the anguish in her eyes. He wanted to get her back to town so she could find her equilibrium again, since this experience had obviously cut her off at the knees.

"No. If you think we'll be fine then I'd prefer to go."

He saw her pumping her thighs up high, nearly to her waist, as she trudged through the snow, and realized that, while he'd grabbed boots at his house before they'd come up here, she was wearing flat, slip-on leather shoes.

"Jeez, Rory! You can't walk through a foot of snow in those. Why didn't you say something?"

"Why would I? I doubt if you have boots in my size hanging out in your truck."

He strode around the car and she squeaked when he swung her up into his arms. "No, but I do have a differ-ent solution."

She scowled, and at the same time a breathy laugh slipped across his face.

"Put me down. I'm perfectly fine."

"Yeah?" The feel of her body in his arms, held close against him, felt beyond good—the way it had when he'd been unable to stop the need to kiss her in the kitchen. "The California city girl who's been wearing a heavy winter coat even in early October has no problem walking practically barefoot in cold snow?"

"It's a good thing I am wearing a coat, too, since you're not dressed nearly warmly enough for this kind of weather and I'm perfectly comfy."

Looking down into her eyes, he saw they still held a tinge of sadness, but they were filled with a smile, too. It was the kind of smile that reminded him of the Rory he'd known and loved before it had all got away from them. Unbidden, memories burned through his brain to join the feelings, the tenderness for her that welled in his chest, and he nearly dropped a kiss to her mouth again.

That would be a bad idea, so he drew a deep breath and looked away from that beautiful green gaze, trying to focus on getting to the truck.

He juggled her in his arms and opened the truck door, then placed her in the seat. "I'm glad you're comfy. And I won't say that coats are for sissies, since I admit it's handy to have one when we're in the middle of a snowstorm."

He lifted his finger to swipe thick snowflakes from her lashes and somehow, without his meaning it to, his finger drifted down her cheek and across her lips. All the laughter left her face and her lips parted as she looked up at him. He could tell she was feeling it, too. All the heat that had been there for so long between them, that had flared into fire in the kitchen, now swirled inside the truck and left him breathless.

Damn. He straightened, then shut her door to go around to the driver's seat. He stomped the snow off his boots before sliding into the dark interior next to her. No way was he going to start things up again with Rory. Too much bad stuff had happened between them, and the last thing either of them needed was to stir it up all over again—especially when she'd be leaving again in a matter of days.

"Put on your seat belt. Things might get a little rough."

"How can you even *see*? It's a blizzard out there."

"Definitely not the best conditions for driving, but once we get about twenty miles closer to town the hilly roads give way to the main road, which is pretty flat."

"I assume you have enough gas to keep us warm if we get stranded?"

"I'm not even going to answer that ridiculous question." He shot her a grin, not wanting her to be worried. "You were always a survivor girl when you lived here, having your parents' house stocked up and prepared for Armageddon. I learned from you—so, yeah, I not only have extra gas, I've got water and food. We could stay up here for days if we had to."

She didn't answer. He turned to see her eyes looking at him across the bench seat and his heart quickened. He hadn't been thinking about what he'd said, really, but suddenly images of the two of them stuck inside this truck, holding one another close and making love to stay warm, were suddenly all he could think about.

He was glad that getting the truck out on the road took all his concentration and his mind off sex with Rory. And keeping the vehicle on the road when he could barely see became a bigger challenge with every passing mile.

After traveling for only about twenty minutes, in the worst conditions he'd ever driven in, he knew there needed to be a change of plan.

"Rory?"

"Yeah?"

"It's bad out here."

"Yeah…"

"I know there's a dry cabin nearby, where a lot of hunters go. I'm pretty sure it's off a road I think we'll be coming to soon. What do you say we bunk there for the night and see how it looks in the morning?"

A long silence was followed by a deep sigh. "I don't

think we have a choice. If we keep going there's a good chance we'll end up in a ditch. I'd rather be in a cabin, where we can build a fire, than stuck in the truck in a snowstorm."

"Then that's our plan. Don't worry. We'll be fine, I promise."

"Being fine isn't what I'm worried about," she said, in a soft voice that had him thinking bad thoughts all over again.

"I know."

His hands tightened on the wheel because, yeah, being fine *wasn't* the issue. Being close together for the whole night alone definitely was.

"Help me keep an eye out for the road. It's off to the right, and there's a sign marking it, but it's going to be hard to see until we're practically on it."

They drove in silence, but he could have sworn the car hummed with something. There was an electricity between them, a new awareness now, with their plight of being in close quarters together. Thoughts of making love with her had his heart beating harder and his body stirring. But he wasn't going to go there. *No way.* Neither one of them needed the tangled-up emotions that would follow a night of ill-thought-out intimacy.

Unbidden, memories of all the great sex between them shortened his breath. With her, it had always been more special than with anyone—both physical and emotional. A deep, multi-layered connection that he'd never experienced before or since. But what would being with her in that way again accomplish? All it would do would be to stir up the feelings clearly still between them, and his heart was sure to feel bruised and battered all over again—maybe hers, too.

No, they'd get set up in the cabin, have something to eat, then sleep. Somehow, though, he had a bad feeling that knowing her body was close and warm might make sleeping more than difficult. Even worse, he couldn't deny that some masochistic part of him was excited about it. Anticipating being alone with her for the first time in a long, long time even as he told himself to cool it. He hadn't wanted to admit to himself that he still missed her being part of his life, but the way he felt at that moment proved he did.

"There!" Rory exclaimed into the silence. "Is that the sign for the road?"

Jake peered through the thick flakes, finally seeing the sign, covered with snow and barely visible. "You have cat's eyes. I think I would have passed right by it."

"You're having to concentrate on driving in this mess. I had the advantage of focusing on one thing."

True. He'd been focusing on driving, finding the sign and her nearness—whether he'd wanted to be or not. "Yeah, well, thanks to you we might be able to bunk down in front of a warm fire very soon."

"You think there'll be wood in the cabin? Or are we going to have to scrounge for some underneath the snow?"

As he slowly made the turn onto the road he sensed her looking at him and dared a quick glance across the seat. Her lips were tipped up at the corners, and his own mouth curved in response.

"I'd think most hunters restock the wood, but probably there are some who don't. If we have to dig under the snow, though, I'll get you some thick socks to put on over your shoes."

Her soft chuckle drifted into his chest and widened his smile. "As if. You've always had an 'I'm the man, and I'll do the heavy lifting' mindset. No way would you let me gather firewood outside while you're the one wearing heavy boots."

"Maybe I've changed."

"No," she said softly. "You haven't changed—at least

not in any way that I can see. Mika's lucky to have a man like you adopt him."

"*I'm* the lucky one."

The unspoken hung between them. The fact that neither of them had been lucky when tiny Adam had died inside Rory's womb, shattering their dream of having a family together. Neither of them had found someone to share their lives with. Except he had Mika now, and his son was the best reason of all to keep his relationship with Rory friendly but distant.

She'd already proved she was a flight risk, hadn't she? There one minute and gone the next. The last thing Mika needed was to get close to someone and then have them promptly exit his life.

The road came to an abrupt halt, with a hilly dead end right in front of them, and through the heavy snow the silhouette of a dark cabin appeared as a shadow.

"We made it." He heaved in a breath that was full of relief, trepidation and anticipation as to how this evening was going to shake out. "Sit tight and I'll carry you in."

Rory looked at his dark profile through the blackness of the truck's cab. When he'd picked her up and held her close to his hard body it had felt disconcertingly wonderful—just like when he'd kissed her earlier. How were they going to find a little distance in this small cabin? She didn't know, but somehow that needed to be the plan for the night.

"Honestly, Jake, I can walk—"

"Stop being your usual stubborn self." A disgusted sound left his lips. "The last thing you need is to start out with frozen feet when we're going inside a freezing cold cabin. So just wait 'til I come around."

She picked her purse up from the floor, watched his shadowy figure cross in front of the truck and considered it really bad news that her heart was already beating an odd little timpani rhythm in her chest and he hadn't even touched her. They weren't yet close together in that cabin, and she knew it was going to be both terrible and wonderful at the same time.

The door opened and his wide torso filled the cab as he leaned in, his eyes glittering in the darkness as they met hers.

"Hang tight in here, promise? It's pitch-black, so I'm going to grab supplies from the back of the truck so we'll have light." He pointed his finger at her until it touched the tip of her nose. "Don't move."

She might be a little stubborn—as he'd always told her—but she wasn't stupid. Much as she didn't want him to carry her in—or kind of *did* want that, if she was honest with herself—she knew getting her feet and the bottoms of her pants wet wouldn't be too smart when they didn't even know if there was firewood in the cabin.

Feeling worthless, not helping him carry stuff inside, she fidgeted until she saw the beam from a flashlight dancing through the snowflakes, illuminating a wooden front door.

Jake's dark form shoved it open. She couldn't see what he had in his arms, but she could tell it was a pretty significant pile and she had to smile. He teased her about always being prepared, yet it looked like he had enough stuff to stay here a week.

Short minutes later her door was swinging open again and strong arms were reaching for her. "There's not a lot of firewood, but there's some. With what I brought we'll be able to get a good fire going until I collect more."

"You had firewood in the back of the truck? Why didn't you tell me?"

With her purse strap slung over her shoulder, she snaked her arms around his neck, figuring it would help if she supported some of her weight as he trudged through the snow.

The temptation to press her lips against his cold cheek was almost too much, and she forced herself to turn her face toward the cabin and away from his tempting jaw.

"I didn't want you to think you wouldn't still have to wear thick socks over your shoes to help me gather it up out here."

This buoyant feeling welling in her chest was absurd. They were stranded in a snowstorm, in a cabin with an outhouse and no running water, and she was there with a man she didn't want to be around. Except obviously, deep inside, she did. Their banter together was like old times, happy times, and she hadn't realized until this moment how much she'd missed feeling lighthearted and happy with Jacob Hunter.

"Uh-huh. And how much stuff do you keep in your truck bed anyway? To think you always accused *me* of being hyper-prepared for disasters. Looks like you're every bit as bad."

He shouldered open the door, quickly shoved it closed against the cold wind and set her on her feet. The flashlight sat on a rickety table, aimed right at his hips and the front of his pants, and she jerked her attention away from wrong thoughts.

"Like I said, I learned from you," he said.

"Where's the wood? I'll get started on the fire—I have some papers in my purse I don't need that I can use to help get it started. What else do you have?"

He pounded his gloved hands together, then reached into a box, pulling out a battery-operated lamp and clicking it on.

"See, I'd have a bigger lamp with a bigger bulb. That thing hardly throws any light at all."

"Do we *need* a lot of light?"

One dark eyebrow was raised slowly at her, and her pulse kicked at the gleam in his eyes that said he was

thinking exactly what she was thinking, even though they
shouldn't be. Because she'd just looked around enough
to notice that there was only one bed in the cabin, and if
they were going to stay warm they were going to have to
get in there together.

She swallowed hard. "No. Because we'll have the firelight, too. Looks like the stack of wood here will last
maybe a couple hours, so that's not too bad."

Quickly, she moved away from him toward the wood-
burning stove and flipped open the door, shoving inside
a few pieces of paper and a new notebook that she hadn't
used yet.

"Here's the kindling and the bag of wood I brought. I'm
going outside to see what I can scrounge up, since I'm already dressed."

The words *already dressed* made her think of getting *undressed*, but of course he just meant he had on his
jacket and hat and boots. Her face warmed at the place
her brain kept going—which she supposed she should be
happy about, since it was so cold she could see her breath
in this place.

Time to get the fire built, you idiot.

The wood was nice and dry, and in no time welcome
flames crackled and spat, filling the space with warmth
and light. She stared at the fire, breathed in the smell of it,
and felt her heart warm along with everything else. How
long had it been since she'd built a fire? Sat in front of one?
Must have been when she'd still been in college—long before she'd moved to LA.

She sat on her rear and poked her feet toward the fire,
since they felt half-frozen in the flimsy shoes which she
realized now she shouldn't even have brought to Eudemonia. She looked up as the door opened and found she
couldn't take her eyes off him.

Yes, he was older. They both were. But the way he

looked now, with a knit hat covering his beautiful black hair, his nose and cheeks pink from the cold, his arms filled with snowy sticks, took her back in time to all those years, from boyhood to manhood, that she'd loved him with every ounce of her soul.

"You... Looks like you had some luck," she managed to say. "How did you unearth it? I supposed you carry a shovel in your truck, too?"

"Is that a *real* question?" He stomped the snow off his feet just outside the door, then kneeled next to her to dump the wood onto the floor next to the dry logs. "Looks like you had luck, too. Good fire. You haven't lost your touch."

No doubt he hadn't, either—but the touch she was thinking about had nothing to do with the fire.

"So, now what?" she asked, and then wished she hadn't. Because the way he was looking at her told her he was thinking exactly what she was. Which was to get the fire blazing as hot as possible, cuddle in that bed naked and relive the past.

"Guess we should eat—though all I have to offer is camping food that'll keep forever. Mom had a great spread for Mika's party, but that was hours ago. You hungry?"

She was *not* going to answer that honestly. Because what she was hungry for was what she'd run away from. What she could never have again.

"A little. What's on the menu?"

"Canned beans. And, yes, I have a can opener." He flashed his devastating grin. "Canned corned beef. Beef jerky. Beef stroganoff."

That brought her out of her rapt attention to the way the firelight flickered across the beautiful planes of his face, his unbelievably sexy mouth. "Clearly beef is your pantry staple. But beef stroganoff? Like, freeze-dried? *Yuck.*"

"Yeah. Pretty awful, but it's better than starving."

"Maybe I'll wait 'til I'm starving."

"Suit yourself."

He pulled off his boots, placed them next to the door, and came to sit cross-legged next to her in front of the fire. He pulled a few cans out of the bag he'd carried in, and several bottles of water, handing her one.

"I recommend against drinking too much, or we'll have to shovel a path to the outhouse."

"Sounds like the perfect way to cap off my stay at home. Haven't been in a frozen outhouse in a long time."

"So there you have it. The highlight of your trip back."

His brown eyes were filled with something she couldn't quite read, and they stared at one another without speaking until he looked away to pull a package of jerky from his bag.

"This one is venison," he said, handing her a piece. "A guy who works for the oil company started a side business, buying meat from some of the hunters around here. It's pretty good."

She took a bite and chewed at the dried stuff. "I've got to admit that's delicious. Or maybe I'm hungrier than I thought." She watched him open the beans and eat a spoonful right out of the can, then scoop another bite onto the spoon and hold it to her mouth.

"What happened to warming it up on the fire first?"

"What happened to the girl who used to love cold beans?"

His eyes were dark and alive, lit with humor and a heat that matched exactly what she was feeling as she stared at the way he slowly licked the sauce from his lips. It made her feel so breathless she opened her mouth without thinking, and he poked the spoon into her mouth, then followed it with a brief press of his lips to hers.

He pulled back an inch, and she managed to swallow the beans before he came in for another. The way his mouth moved on hers, soft and unhurried and tasting of sweet beans and hot sex, made her heart beat in slow, heavy thuds. Barely able to breathe, she cupped his warm, stubbly face in her hands and let the feelings wash over her, let herself absorb it and feel all the things she shouldn't be feeling.

Their mouths separated and she looked into his eyes, now deeply serious.

"I shouldn't kiss you. I know that," he said, his breath feathering across her moist lips. "When you first came to take care of your mom I wanted to keep my distance. When that didn't work out I promised myself I'd work on being your friend, putting the bad stuff behind us. Putting aside my anger with you and remembering why we'd liked each other from the time we were kids. But sitting here with you now, I can't do that, either. Stupid or not, I want to be with you one last time."

"Me, too," she whispered. "I didn't know it. I didn't want to see you, either. I know you hate me. But I want to be with you, too, just once. Once more."

"Rory." His hands tightened on her shoulders. "I never hated you. I loved you more than I've ever loved anyone. Was I furious with you? Beyond disappointed? Hurt bad? Yeah, I was all those things. But I never hated you—even when I wanted to."

He kissed her again, and she clutched at him as he lowered her to the hard wooden floor, devouring her mouth until she felt dizzy from it. Flames leaped inside her, hotter than any fire, and she slipped her hands inside his shirt, loving the softness of his skin, the way it shivered at her touch.

Memories of all the kisses they'd shared tangled with the incredible deliciousness of this one. He tasted the same. He tasted like Jacob Hunter—the man she'd loved her whole life. Rory's heart shook and fell, and she wrapped her arms around his warm back and gave in to the sensations she'd missed so much.

Then he sat up abruptly, leaving her confused. She pushed onto her elbows, her heart sinking as he stood and walked away from her across the room. Had he decided this was such a bad idea that he was able to stop? She knew it was beyond a bad idea, but she'd never have been able to stop, to walk away, when all she wanted at that moment was to kiss him and get naked with him and make love with him for the rest of the night.

"You…you changed your mind?"

"Hell, no," he growled as he grabbed the bedframe and started dragging it toward her. "But this floor's too hard to make love with you the way I want to, and it's too damn cold to get naked this far away from the fire. So the bed and all the blankets are coming to the fire."

Relief had her laughing, then getting up to help. "I always said you were a genius."

"Not a genius—just a man who wants to get both of us stripped as fast as possible and under the covers without freezing in the process."

The fire in the stove was the perfect height for the mattress. She and Jake tucked a sheet over it before he threw a few more logs in the stove. Then he reached to undo the big buttons on her coat and slide it off her shoulders. Without moving his gaze from hers, he pulled her sweater up over her head, and the rush of cold air from the back of the cabin skimmed her skin, even as the fire warmed her.

He must have seen her shiver, because he pulled her close and kissed her, at the same time tugging down her pants. With a gentle push he sat her on the bed and pulled off her shoes and socks, breaking their kiss again to wrap his hands around her foot.

"Your feet are like ice! Why didn't you *say* something?"

"Once you started kissing me I didn't notice."

"I can relate…" His eyes gleamed. "And I know just the thing to warm you up."

Like he had when he'd carried her to the truck, he scooped her into his arms and practically dumped her into the middle of the bed. He grabbed the blankets and an old comforter he'd brought and tossed them on top of her.

She watched him do a quick striptease, throwing his clothes far enough from the fire that they wouldn't scorch, until he was standing in front of her breathtakingly naked.

For a long moment she let herself admire the masculine beauty that was Jacob Hunter: the way the firelight flickered on his skin, highlighting the dips and angles and defined muscle, the jut of his erection, the body she'd explored so thoroughly that she'd known every inch of it—every tiny scar, every imperfection.

She lifted her gaze to meet his and her breath caught in her throat at the way he was looking at her. The way he had all those years ago, when their lives had been wrapped together completely. And somehow, here tonight, it felt as if the entire world had shrunk down to just the two of them, emotionally and physically close in this tiny cabin covered with snow.

"There's a problem here," she said. "You're still out there freezing, and I'm under the covers waiting for you."

"Fixing that right now," he said, and he crawled on all fours across the mattress and dropped a kiss to her mouth before joining her under the heavy blankets. He slid off her bra, then his hands roamed her body, making her shiver in a totally different way than she had been moments before.

He kissed her again, deepening it, and all worries that this was a bad idea, that they shouldn't be doing it, fell away and she kissed him back, desperate to feel that connection with him once more.

His arms brought her body tight against his, and the way his skin slid against hers felt so delicious she gasped into his mouth. She stroked her hands up the hard planes of his chest and over his shoulders, remembering every little bump, every crevice, as though it was yesterday they'd been together and not years ago.

He lifted his mouth from hers and stared down at her. "I want to see you. Just for a minute. I want to see your body in the firelight. I promise I'll warm you up."

He tugged the blanket down to expose her breasts, his fingers slowly tracking its downward slide. Across her collarbone, over her breasts, caressing her nipples. She arched up in a silent invitation. His lips tipped at the corners, then he lowered his mouth to suck and lick, and she clutched the back of his head, moaning from the pleasure of it.

God, she'd missed this. Missed feeling this way—missed holding him and touching him and kissing him. She waited for the guilt to wash over her, the awful regret for her actions that terrible day, but it didn't come. All she felt was a deep need to be with him, to enjoy this one time they had together before they went back to their separate lives.

"Frozen yet?" he asked as his mouth and tongue slid leisurely across her skin, his hands following. "I love looking at you. Your body is more beautiful than I remembered. But if you're cold I'll cover you up."

"Cold? Are you kidding? I feel like I'm burning up."

He chuckled against her skin as his hands moved lower to touch between her legs, making her gasp. "Burning up is exactly how I'm feeling, too."

The touching, the way his tongue licked her breasts and her stomach and her hipbones, made her quiver and gasp, and she reached for him, wrapping her hand around his erection to make him feel good, too.

But in moments he pulled himself loose. "God, Rory. I need to be inside you now."

"That sounds good to me."

"Damn it."

He got up from the bed and she felt suddenly cold, had to reach for the covers. "What the heck…? What are you doing?"

He rifled in his jeans pocket and held up a condom. "You're not the only one who's always prepared."

Breathlessly, she laughed as he put it on, but her amusement quickly died in her throat as he slipped between the sheets and covered her body with his. Warm and hard and oh, so wonderful, he grasped her hips and slowly filled her, and it felt like all the times before, but somehow even better. She wrapped her arms around his back and kissed him, everything gone from her mind except the amazing way he made her feel.

They moved together in a devastating rhythm, faster and harder, their kiss broken as he stared down at her, his eyes glittering with the passion she remembered so well.

"Rory…"

Her name fell from his lips in a way that told her he felt the same deep connection that had filled every broken piece in her heart. As their bodies convulsed together in physical pleasure the past was forgotten, and for this short moment, at least, she felt almost whole for the first time in nine years.

CHAPTER ELEVEN

"YOU COLD?" JAKE held Rory's sweet body close to his beneath the covers, her head pillowed on his shoulder.

His heart was all jumbled up at how good it felt to have her in his arms again, even as he reminded himself that she'd be gone again all too soon. And that even if by some miracle she might want to stay, he couldn't trust her not to up and bolt just like last time. He couldn't ever trust her with his heart again.

"Only the top of my head. Your body is like a furnace," she murmured.

"I can get my hat for you."

"No. Stay in here with me."

He looked down at her. At the way her hair swept over his skin. At her beautiful lips, which somehow tasted even better than he remembered. At her pert little nose and heart-shaped face.

Part of him wanted to just lie there peacefully with her, warm and snug together in front of the fire. But another part of him—the part that had never fully gotten an answer on why she'd left the way she had—still wanted an answer to that question.

Maybe it made no sense to care about that after all this time, but he couldn't help it. He'd wondered for the past nine years, and he needed to know why she hadn't let herself lean on anyone—least of all him—when times had got tough.

Yeah, he wanted the answer more than he wanted the peace, he supposed, and there would never be another time like this to ask. Cozy and intimate and all alone, with no interruptions and nowhere to hide.

"Why did you leave, Rory?"

She was silent for a long time, and he thought maybe he wasn't going to get an answer after all when she finally spoke. "You know why. We already talked about this."

"We lost our baby. It was hard and it hurt, but it didn't have to mean the end of our relationship. Of all our plans. You told me you hated hearing the whispers, seeing people talking about the accident. About the way the snow machine flipped with you on it. But was that a good enough reason to leave me without even a goodbye?"

"I didn't say goodbye because I knew you must hate me," she whispered. "God knows, I hated myself."

"I never hated you. How could you think that? I was upset with you, yeah. Even before we lost the baby, I admit I was mad. You ignored me when I told you to stay home. You insisted on going on the snow machine with the rescue crew when you were seven months pregnant and that was stupid. I *get* that you'd done plenty of search and rescues, but that situation was different. And you wouldn't listen."

"I know. And I'll regret that decision for the rest of my life. Which is why I left."

"Regretting, I understand. But running away from everything? Our plans to go to med school in Anchorage together? Dumping me and leaving me high and dry?"

"If I hadn't gone out on the snow machine our baby might not have died inside me. I have to live with that. I couldn't live with everyone else knowing what I'd done. Blaming me like I blamed myself."

"How many times did I say no one blamed you? How

many doctors and nurses told you that Adam being still-born probably had nothing to do with that night?"

"But no one knew for sure."

Warm wetness touched his chest. The fact that she was crying tempered the frustration rolling around in his chest and he pulled her closer against him.

"No one ever knows for sure why a baby is stillborn. Still, you turned away from me, you wouldn't lean on me. Wouldn't grieve with me. Help me understand why."

She tipped her head up to look at him, her teary eyes wide as they met his. "I... I'm not sure I even *know* why, other than the guilt I felt. And I'm sorry," she whispered, lifting her hand to cup his jaw. "I wasn't able to think straight. But see...? You were *lucky* to be rid of me. I'm not the kind of woman you'd want in your life forever."

Lucky to be rid of her? That was the last way he would ever view what had happened back then. Being with her now, holding her like this, made him face the truth. He'd never stopped loving her—even when he'd tried to convince himself he had.

"You're wrong. You were the only woman I wanted in my life." And now that he'd seen her again, he knew she still was. "Even now, there's nothing I wouldn't do for you. Except trust you. I learned the hard way I can't ever let myself trust you again."

"I understand."

When her eyes filled with tears again a part of him felt bad about what he'd said, but it was simply the truth. And maybe more than saying it to *her*, he was reminding himself not to fall in love with her all over again. Not to put himself in a position where she could crush his soul a second time.

"You have a good life here, with your family and little Mika," she said, sniffing. "I get that maybe I was wrong to run away. But that's behind us now. I'll be leaving soon, so you won't have to look at me and feel angry anymore."

"When I look at you now I think you know that angry isn't how I feel." He couldn't regret sharing that truth with her, because he wanted her to know that, no matter what, he'd always care about her. "And, since you're leaving soon, this might be our last chance to be alone together. How do you feel about making the best of it while we can?"

A real smile, like the ones he'd used to love to see all night, touched her lips. "There might be a lot of things I'll never feel good about. But kissing you isn't one of them."

She rose up over him, the firelight flickering over her glorious nakedness, and he looked up at her beautiful face before she kissed him. Heat hummed between them and he held her close, giving himself up to the moment while he could.

No matter that he knew he'd miss her again, far too much, when she left.

"I can't get it loose to fix it, Twinkie," Rory said, lying on her back as she stared up at the stupid pipe connection under the kitchen sink that wouldn't stop dripping. She gave the wrench another mighty twist on the pipe, but it didn't budge. "It's like the elbow is frozen to the other piece. We'll just have to keep this bucket under here until a plumber can come."

"Jacob's always happy to fix stuff around here when he can."

Rory scooted out from under the sink and sat up so fast she nearly cracked her head on the top of the cabinet frame. "What? Don't call Jake. It's not fair to bother him with stuff like this. He's busy at work, and with the baby."

And his busyness wasn't the only reason she didn't want him here. Their night together had been the best thing to happen to her in a long, long time, and she'd keep the memory close to her heart when she went back to LA. But they'd both agreed that spending any more time together while she was still here would just shake up old feelings that were better left alone.

"I already called him. He said he'd come over when he could," Twinkie said as she walked into the kitchen with an armload of stuff and a big smile. "Leave that and come paint with me. We haven't done finger paints since you were a little girl. Won't that be fun?"

"Finger paints?" She stared at her mom. Was she kidding? "Uh… I think I'd rather use a brush. You do have some, don't you?"

"Yes, but don't be a traditionalist. Humans have used their fingers for eating and artwork and all kinds of things forever. I feel like being primal today."

A snorting laugh left Rory's nose at that—until the word brought that night with Jake roaring into her brain again. *Primal* was exactly how it had felt. Making love almost with desperation, like they couldn't get enough of one another. If she closed her eyes she could still picture his spectacular nakedness in the firelight, and she got a little short of breath just thinking about it.

Maybe spreading paint around with her fingers would be a good outlet for the sexual energy surging into her head and body after all.

She took some paper from her mother and unrolled it onto the table as her mother lined up the paint pots next to it.

"I think I'm in the mood to make fairies," Wendy said as she sat down, so excited that she was waving her hands around. "I might even add some glitter—which I have here if you want some. What are *you* in the mood to make?"

Rory couldn't say what she was in the mood to make, as more visions of Jake burned her brain. "I think I'll just go with something abstract."

"I always liked your abstracts. Very creative."

They chatted and painted, and Rory had to admit there was something therapeutic about swirling paint with her fingers. It made her think about how enjoyable it would be to swirl some on Jake's body and then...

Stop it, she scolded herself for the tenth time. *It was one night and one night only, remember?*

She tried to switch her attention to her mother's painting, and it struck her that she was recovering remarkably well—able to get around quite easily on her own, now. She'd even mostly dressed herself this morning, other than Rory putting on her socks and shoes, since it still hurt a little for her to bend over. It was clear her mom would be fine without her, so long as she had Linda and her other friends to check on her each day.

"You seem to be feeling almost yourself now, Twinkie. Maybe all those herbs really do have healing qualities," she said, and then took a breath to talk about heading back to California. For some inexplicable reason she wasn't sure she was ready to go, even if Twinkie was well enough to be on her own. "How do you feel about me getting my job interview rescheduled for pretty soon?"

"Do you have to go?" Her mother's eyes were suddenly sad as she looked up from her art.

"My job is there. Or will be." She leaned across the table. "Please come with me. Just for the winter. Please?"

"Aurora, I just don't know. But I'm thinking about it. We'll see if one of my fairies here gives me a sign about what to do."

"You're going to let a fairy that you made yourself help you decide?" Rory had to smile. And then she wondered what kind of paint she could swirl on her mom's picture that would tell her to come live with Rory for a few months, because the thought of leaving her made her chest ache.

"I hear you, poking fun. But it's like tea leaves or coffee grounds. Patterns come together to tell a story. To see the future."

"I wish—"

"Anybody home?"

Her heart dipped, then jumped. How could Jake be coming in the middle of the afternoon like this? She'd expected he'd be hours, probably showing up just before dinnertime.

He appeared in the kitchen doorway with Mika in his arms. Her heart pitched again as she stared at the man who'd had his hands and mouth all over her body just days ago. Filtered sunlight from the kitchen window lit his features, and he looked beyond handsome in a flannel shirt and jeans that had her attention going straight to his body. Those memories got stirred up all over again, and she yanked her gaze back to the bundle in his arms.

Looking at Mika's adorable little face had her relaxing, and the quickened beat of her heart settled into a warm calm. "What are you doing here?"

"Plumbing, I believe."

"Why aren't you at the clinic?"

"Dad's back, and I have the day off."

"Well, it's nice of you to help us on your day off. We're finger painting, believe it or not," she said, wiggling her painty fingers. "How about joining us?"

Jake grinned as he put Mika down on the floor. The child toddled a few steps before going back to his knees and crawling remarkably fast until he pulled himself back to a standing position at the table.

"Looks like he might have some interest in that."

"I'll get some paper for him," Wendy said, standing to move toward the art closet in the living room. "Smaller pieces that'll be just the right size. I bet he'll like all the colors."

Still clutching the table leg, the child grinned up at Rory and the warmth in her chest grew. She looked at Jake, and the way he was watching the child with love and pride made her heart both pinch and expand.

"He's walking even more than he was at his birthday party, isn't he?"

"He can walk—he just gets impatient with the slow pace and switches to crawling because it's faster."

"You sure he belongs in Eudemonia and not LA? A slow pace is practically the law here."

Jake's smile faded, and she wasn't sure why. Could it be because he wasn't ready for her to go back? Or maybe he knew she wasn't sure she was ready, either.

"No, he's an Alaskan through and through. Maybe he can paint while I look at the pipe. Is it this one here?"

"Yes, but the pipes are stuck together tight. Did you bring some spray oil to loosen it? I couldn't find any, believe it or not. Clearly dropping the ball in my usual preparedness."

He shook his head, and as he headed toward the sink paused beside her chair. His fingertips brushed her neck, making her shiver.

"You saying you think *I'm* a weakling? I'm insulted."

"If you think that's what I'm saying, then since I couldn't do it, I guess you mean I'm a weakling."

"No. It's just that men are physically stronger than women. It's a fact."

"Something I heard endlessly when I was studying orthopedic surgery as a reason why I should choose something else."

Amused brown eyes met hers, and she thought of all the times he'd teased her about so many things. About how even when it had annoyed her she'd loved it at the same time, because it was the way he'd shown her how much he cared about her.

A sudden vision of his big, muscular body, naked and warm and beautiful, made her breath catch. No doubt about it—Jacob Hunter was one physically strong specimen of a man. Emotionally strong, too.

Her chest got a little tight, and she knew she needed to do something to loosen it. She reached up with a paint-covered finger and marked the left side of his jaw with a swirly green X. "Want me to show you how strong I am?"

"What? Is this X marks the spot? You gonna pop me?"

"Brace yourself. Are you ready?" What she really wanted to do was kiss the X and then move on to his mouth, but she waved her fist at him before tapping his chin with it.

He grasped her wrist and lowered his face close to hers. "You've heard about playing with fire and getting burned? You want to go up in flames?"

Oh, yeah, she *did* want to go up in flames, if the burn was from Jake.

When he lowered his mouth to hers, she parted her lips, and when she touched her tongue to his she heard him draw in a breath just before the kiss got deeper and wet-ter. Without thinking, she lifted her hands to his cheeks as she tipped her head, wanting more of the deliciously tempting taste of him.

"You think he'd like colored paper better, or plain white?"

At the sound of her mother's voice they pulled apart, and the heat in the brown eyes inches from hers had her quivering from head to toe. And then she laughed as she looked at the paint all over the poor man's face.

"Why, you two are really getting into the spirit of this, aren't you?" her mother said, beaming. "I never thought to paint myself or you. What a wonderful idea, Aurora!"

"Rory's always been full of good ideas," Jake said, his voice rough. He straightened and turned toward the sink. "But I'd better get these pipes fixed if I don't want to be driving around with paint all over my face."

"Before you do, can you put Mika on my lap?" asked Rory. "I don't want to get paint on his clothes."

"I have a feeling he's going to have paint all over his clothes anyway."

Jake sat the small boy on her lap and she breathed in the baby scent of him, letting herself rub her cheek against his soft hair. She picked up one of the paint pots and had to laugh at the way his pudgy fingers happily dipped inside before rubbing the paint all around the paper.

"Look at him having fun!" her mother exclaimed. "He's like one of the family already."

Her belly tightened at her mother's words. Rory held out a second color to Mika, kissed his round cheek and wished with all her heart that she had a beautiful child like this. But he belonged to Jake, and Jake would never belong to her again. She'd made sure of that, hadn't she?

They played with the paint together and his joy, the delighted baby noises he made, were so adorable she found herself wishing the moment would go on for hours. But his attention on swirling the paint didn't last very long, and in a short time he was wriggling to get off her lap.

Shoving down her disappointment, she tried to secure him with her elbows so he wouldn't fall. "Jake, can you get Mika? My hands are all gooey."

"Yep. Done here anyway."

She watched his long body scooch out from under the sink and unfold into a standing position. Two long strides and he was lifting the boy from her lap, and she couldn't help but feel a little bereft.

"All fixed, thanks to my superior strength. You can wash up now, if you want."

"Thank you for getting us water again. I think I'm done with finger paints for the day." Unless Mika decided he wanted to play with the paints a little longer after all. "But maybe you should wash your face first. You look a little scary."

"Geez, I forgot." He laughed. "Thanks for not letting me walk around town like this."

"Wouldn't want people to think the town doctor had lost his marbles."

"Except there've been a couple times recently when I think maybe I have."

Their eyes met and she found it hard to turn away from that intense brown gaze. Yeah, maybe they'd both lost their marbles, getting involved again even for such a short time. But she'd always been crazy when it came to Jacob Hunter. Probably nothing would ever change that.

As she washed her hands she realized the pleasure of holding the baby and playing with him wasn't over just for today—it would be over permanently very soon. That reality made her feel melancholy enough that she figured she should book her flight home as soon as possible. Staying away from Jake hadn't come close to happening, and while she was glad they'd had this time to clear the air a little and make peace with the past, it was time to get back to her life.

Her life filled with work and not much else.

"You know what I haven't had in front of my house for a long, long time?" her mother said as she washed her hands, too. "A snowman! It's warmed up some today—perfect for snowman building. How about you two take Mika outside for his first snowman?"

"I think he'd like that," Jake said. "Rory?"

She turned, and the entreaty in his eyes made her chest expand all over again. The clear desire she saw there was to spend another hour with her, the same way she wanted to with him, despite them agreeing not to. It was too late to protect her heart from caring about him again, and taking new memories back to LA—memories of her time with both Jake and Mika—seemed like the best idea in the world.

"Not much possibility of making a snowman in Los Angeles. So, yes, I'd love to make a snowman with the two of you. Let's go."

CHAPTER TWELVE

ROLLING THE BALLS of snow to make a snowman was more exciting to Mika than Jake would have thought, and for some reason the baby laughed out loud when Jake stacked the smallest one on top of the other two.

"There's the snowman's head, Mika. Now we need a face."

"Stones for the eyes," Rory said, poking them into the snowball. "More for the mouth. And here's a carrot for the snowman's nose. Can you put it right where its nose should be?"

She handed him the carrot and Mika stabbed it into the side of the snowman's head. It made Jake laugh, but Rory actually doubled over with mirth, tears in her eyes that this time he could tell were happy ones.

The joy he could see on her face, which was glowing with the pleasure of the day, made him wonder about what her life in Los Angeles might be like. She'd always worked hard, from the minute she'd arrived as the odd one out at the public school after being homeschooled for the first eight years of her life. But he wouldn't be surprised if she'd buried herself in work in order to forget about everything else. It was easy to do when you were studying medicine, and probably even easier if you were a woman competing for an orthopedic residency, and then a job, in a field filled mostly with men.

Rory's cheeks were pink from the cold and the exertion of rolling snow and stacking it, and Mika's were, too. Probably time to head back home, though he couldn't help wanting to spend as much time as he could with Rory before she left. Watching her now, though, enjoying the sparkle in her green eyes, loving the sound of her laugh, brought back that uncomfortable feeling he'd had before. The feeling that he could fall hard for her again, and God knew he didn't want his heart to hurt the way it had the last time she'd left.

"All that painting and snowman making means Mika missed his nap," he said. "I should get him home."

The mirth and joy faded from her face before she nodded. "Of course. It's been…so much fun. Oh, Lord, now I sound like my mother. But it has been. Thank you."

"For what? The plumbing repair?"

"For forgiving me enough to hang out with me. For letting me spend time with your son."

"Rory… I thought we'd talked this through." He hated the idea of her going to LA still dragging along the burdens she'd carried with her the last time, and he pulled her close so she could look into his eyes. "I've forgiven you. The past is the past."

"I… Thank you. It means a lot to me to hear you say that."

He dropped a quick kiss to her forehead and then let her go, resisting the urge to kiss her for real. Everything that had needed to happen between them—a new understanding and forgiveness—had been accomplished. Time for both their lives to go back to normal.

"When are you heading back to LA?"

"I'm going to call tomorrow to schedule my interview, then book a flight, so probably in just a day or two."

"Well, I probably won't see you before you go, then. Good luck with getting the job."

"Wait—we have one more thing to do." She pulled off her hat and handed it to Mika before picking him up in her arms. "Let's put this on the snowman's head so he stays nice and warm, okay?"

Jake watched her lift up his son, so he could try to put the hat on the top snowball, and the picture of the two of them made his heart physically hurt. She looked so vulnerable, and a mix of joy and deep sadness flitted across her beautiful features. She was obviously loving the time with Mika that they'd never gotten to have with Adam.

It was good she was leaving in just a day or two. His emotions—and hers, too, he thought—were getting tangled up together again, and that was the last thing either of them needed. Probably he should have resisted kissing her and making love with her, but he couldn't deny that being with her that way again had been incredible. The best he'd felt in a long, long time.

But sex between them, however good, was fleeting and dangerous. Even when he didn't plan to, he found himself kissing and touching her anyway. What could he do now, though? Say goodbye this minute, before things got any stickier between them? Before something else happened that would make it harder for both of them when she was gone.

He stepped over to take Mika from her arms, but the baby fussed and resisted. He'd thrown Rory's hat on the ground and pulled off his own, determined to flatten it onto the snowman's head. Finally, he wriggled so much she had to put him on his feet.

"I guess the snowman *does* look better in your hat, Mika," she said.

She turned to Jake, and the look of longing in her eyes made his heart beat harder at the same time as he took a backward step. Self-preservation was kicking in, big-time, and he feared if he didn't get away from Rory right now his heart would get pummeled in a way he never wanted to experience again.

Mika might not be happy about it, but he moved to take the boy's hat off the snowman anyway.

"How about dinner tonight?" she asked as their eyes met. "I'll bring stuff from here…cook dinner for the two of you."

"Rory, I don't think—"

"Just dinner. That's all. Then I'll be leaving for good."

Dinner, and then after Mika was in bed hot sex between the two of them, which would make it harder for both of them when she left? God knows, he wanted it again more than anything…

Except that wasn't quite true. He wanted it more than anything except another aching heart.

Somehow he made himself reach around to pull her arms from him, and his chest constricted at the confusion and hurt in her eyes as he did so.

"I'd like that, but I can't. I have plans I can't break. Sorry. Best of luck in LA, okay?"

He grabbed Mika and strode to his car, afraid that if he slowed down he'd cave. He'd turn back and reach for her and kiss her breathless and invite her to his house. And where would that leave them? One step closer to falling in love again, and he just didn't want to go there.

Yeah, his gut told him, spending the evening with her would be a very bad idea, and he got Mika into his car seat as quickly as possible.

Then he made a mistake. He let himself look back at Rory, to see her with her arms wrapped around her body and her beautiful face looking as wistful and forlorn as he'd ever seen it. And he could swear he felt her eyes on him even as he hit the gas and drove down her mother's snowy hill to the road.

* * *

Rory finished cleaning the dishes that had been waiting for the sink pipes to be fixed, staring out the window at the snowy scene that earlier had delighted her.

Now it just made her feel sad. Empty. Embarrassed.

And utterly confused.

In the kitchen earlier, Jake had teased and touched her. Flirted with her. Even surprised her with a delicious kiss that had curled her toes and made her forget that her mother was close by in the other room. Then he had seemed to be having the same wonderful time she'd been having with Mika. Snowman building and laughing at the baby when, awed by the cold white flakes, he had started stuffing them in his mouth.

Jake had tossed a few snowballs at her that had scored direct hits and had had both of them chuckling and remembering all those years they'd played and rolled in the snow together, from the time they were kids and all the way through college.

But then the thought of never seeing him again, or at least not for a long time, had made her chest hurt and her throat close. She'd impulsively asked to have dinner with him and Mika. Be with them one last time. Enjoy more of Jake's heart-stopping kisses and maybe make love the way only they could.

How that felt was something she'd nearly forgotten, and she wanted one more close moment with him to cherish. Wanted to take those memories back to LA with her, to keep her company during all the lonely days.

And what had happened?

He'd basically told her to take a hike and head on back to LA, then practically left skid marks on her mother's snowy yard as he'd driven away.

She tossed down the dishtowel and shook her head. The only explanation was that after the flirting and fun he'd gotten cold feet about seeing her anymore, knowing she was about to leave. Which she just didn't understand—because they'd already kissed and made love and talked things through, hadn't they?

"Aurora?"

She turned to see her mother walking toward her, remarkably steadier with her pink cane than she'd been the day Rory had first arrived, despite the scare of her sutures opening.

"Can I get something for you, Twinkie?"

"No, I want to talk to you."

She came close and wrapped her arms around her, much the way Rory had wrapped her arms around Jake not long ago.

"I've been thinking a lot. I just can't come to California with you. To live with you. But I will come for Christmas. If that's okay?"

Rory folded her slim body close, looked down into her mother's eyes, and suddenly found it hard to speak. Her quirky little mother, like no one else in the whole world, was willing to visit her at Christmas, even though it was one of her favorite times of year here. She didn't particularly like LA, and she missed her friends and her home when she came, but she loved and wanted to be with Rory enough to visit anyway.

It struck her like a sledgehammer between the eyes that Jake had been right. Escaping to California, leaving her parents and Jake behind, had been selfish. She hadn't seen it that way, but it was the painful truth.

The sledgehammer hit a second time. How she felt right now—missing her mother and Jake and the place where she'd grown up before she'd even left town—told her that all the emotions, all the reasons she'd left didn't exist anymore.

Living in LA wouldn't bring Adam back. It wouldn't

let her spend time with her mother, either, and after being with her these past two weeks she knew she didn't want the long miles between them anymore. And it wouldn't let her and Jake explore the fire, the love, that had started burning between them again, and she knew right then that she wanted that more than she'd ever wanted anything in her life. Wanted to see if the two of them could continue to talk and work through their past. To be together and to love one another on their way to a new future. To create a family of three, with Mika.

Would Jake want that, too? Did he feel the same way about her that she did him? God, she didn't know—which terrified her. But what she did know was that she had to find out.

"I love that idea, Twinkie." She swallowed hard before she tried to talk again. "But you know what? I might not even get that job. And if I don't I might even come back here to live. I… I might try to date Jake again. What would you think about that?"

Since she had no idea how Jake would react to her telling him she wanted to stay in Eudemonia and be with him, she couldn't make any promises to her mom. If he rejected her it would crush her heart too much for her to stay here full-time. But the days of her not seeing her mother for months on end were over—even if that meant steeling herself to endure seeing Jake with someone else.

"Oh, my goodness, Aurora, I can't think of anything I'd like better than for you to move back home and to be with Jacob again. That would be a dream come true."

For her, too. Her new dream.

"I'm not promising. I have to see how it goes."

She had to see what the man who held her heart and future in his hands had to say when she told him she still loved him. As scary as that felt, she'd do it.

Hadn't she always gone for what she wanted?

And she wanted Jacob Hunter back.

They clutched one another and Rory kissed Twinkie's cheek, then let her go. "I have something I need to do. Will you be okay for a while? I'll make a plate for you to warm up, in case I'm not back for dinner."

And if things went the way she hoped, she definitely wouldn't be.

"I'm just fine, marshmallow girl. I'm going to rest for a bit anyway."

With her mom settled in her favorite chair, Rory felt her stomach churn with nervous energy. How was she going to approach this? Just knock on the door and have him wonder why she'd come chasing after him when he'd told her he had plans?

That thought made her heart stop. What if he really did have plans? What if he had a date?

She wrung her cold hands and paced the kitchen. Maybe she should wait until tomorrow, just in case… But as soon as the thought came she knew that now she'd had this earth-shattering revelation she'd never sleep tonight if she didn't go over there and get this done.

The snowman caught her eye. "That's it! The perfect excuse," she murmured to herself.

Mika's hat was still perched on the snowman's head. She'd take it over to the house, say she'd thought he might need it. Yeah, it was probably a weak and transparent excuse, but it was better than nothing, right?

She shoved on her coat and boots, ran out to grab the hat and jumped in her car as butterflies flapped in her belly.

Getting to Jake's house and getting this over with as quickly as possible was the plan. She could only hope the evening would turn out the way she wanted. If it didn't she knew it would end up being the second-worst day of her life.

CHAPTER THIRTEEN

JAKE SAT BACK and took a swig of beer, thinking about all that had happened between him and Rory and wishing she hadn't come back at all. He'd thought that other than wanting answers from her about why she'd left without a word, any feelings for her were long gone.

But here he was, sitting here and wanting her beside him. Wanting to kiss her again, to get her naked again, to laugh and joke with her again. It was stupid when she lived thousands of miles away and had already proved she wouldn't hesitate to abandon him if life got tough.

Having her back in town was messing with his mind—no doubt about that. And the truth was he wasn't sure it wouldn't still be messed up long after she'd gone again.

Mika crawled across to the sofa and pulled himself to his feet, trying to get a toy that he couldn't quite reach from the cushion. He started to wail way more than usual for something like that, and Jake wished they'd foregone the snowman making and come home for his nap. Both because his baby would now be happier and because he might not have these uncomfortable feelings rolling around in his chest.

He picked the child up and poked a pacifier into his mouth, gently rocking him back and forth. Then the doorbell chimed. He frowned, wondering who could be at his door. He hoped it wasn't a medical emergency, because he felt pretty worn out and he had a feeling that it was due more to emotional stress than lack of sleep.

When he opened the door his heart kicked in surprise. Rory stood there, wearing her puffy down coat and holding Mika's hat.

"Hi," she said, sounding a little breathless. "You...we forgot about Mika's hat. I thought he might need it."

She held it out and he took it, trying to decide if he should just thank her, say goodbye and shut the door, or if that would be too rude.

"Thanks to Mom and her knitting he has more hats than one baby could ever need. But I appreciate it."

"Can I...can I come in?"

He wanted to say no, but even as he was thinking that was the best response for both of them he found himself swinging the door open wider.

"Sure. Your California blood is probably too thin for this weather."

"I think my blood is thickening a little, and I'm finally remembering what it's like here in October. I wasn't even tempted to put on long underwear today."

Lord. He was not...*not*...going to ask her what kind of underwear she did have on. Even though suddenly he desperately wanted to know.

Time to cut to the chase—and if he had to be abrupt, like he'd been earlier, to protect himself, then so be it. "What can I do for you? Mika's pretty cranky from all the outdoor activity and missing his nap. I need to get him down for the night."

"You can go ahead and do that. I'll just...you know... wait down here in a chair."

"Rory. What's this about?"

"I realized there's something I need to say to you. Something I need to ask you. If you'll just give me five minutes of your time, I'd appreciate it."

He drew a deep breath, wondering what she could want to talk about. Hadn't they covered all the bases in their prior conversations? Still, he'd needed to talk to *her* when she'd first shown up, to get some things off his chest even when she hadn't wanted to go there. He owed her the same courtesy, whatever this was about.

"All right. Take a seat and I'll be back shortly."

The baby was nodding off as he carried him upstairs, and barely stirred when Jake slipped on his footie pajamas and held up some picture books.

"What do you want to read?"

Mika's response was to droop his head against Jake's shoulder and close his eyes, and he knew a book wasn't happening tonight. Which was just as well, since Rory was waiting downstairs. He hoped whatever she wanted to talk about wouldn't end in something uncomfortable or unpleasant. But he had a bad feeling that was exactly what it was going to do.

Gently laying Mika in his crib, he tucked in his blanket and kissed his soft cheek. "Sweet dreams."

The words had him thinking of his own dreams. They had altered some when Rory had left, but the fundamentals of what he wanted were the same: to live and work and grow old in Eudemonia, and raise a family here with the woman he loved. He knew that wasn't asking too much.

But Rory wasn't that woman, and he found himself dreading whatever she'd come here to say to him tonight.

Rory watched Jake come down the stairs and her heart jerked hard in her chest. Now that she was here, all her carefully rehearsed words seemed to dry up and choke her. But it was too late to run, and she had to tell him how she felt.

He came to within a couple yards of her, which made her feel even more nervous. Gone was the Jake who'd been angry, talking with her in that store parking lot, crowding her and grasping her arms as he spoke. Gone was the Jake who'd kissed her in his kitchen and made love with her in the cabin. Gone was the Jake who'd teased her at her mother's house, who'd touched her and kissed her.

No, this was the Jake who'd told her earlier that he had plans, then walked away. His expression was cool and unreadable and she stood up—because she couldn't keep sitting in that chair for another second, trying to act like this was some normal, relaxed conversation between the two of them.

Too much of her future happiness was riding on this.

"Jake?"

"Yes?"

"I…um…"

He took a few steps closer and a sigh left his chest. "What is it, Rory? What is it you need to talk with me about? I'm listening."

She stared into the familiar face she'd loved for so long and gulped, before blurting out the first thing she needed an answer to. "How would you feel about me living here again? Permanently? In Eudemonia?"

He went still and stared at her. "What do you mean?"

"I've been thinking a lot." She nervously licked her lips but forged on because his reaction, his words, were so important she could barely breathe. "I miss my mother, and the older she gets the more she's going to need me. I… I didn't admit to myself that I missed this town until I came back. And I definitely didn't admit to myself how much I missed *you*, until this time we've spent together forced me to see it. But I did, Jake. I missed you so much. Every day of these past nine years I've missed the man I fell in love with in the fourth grade."

He didn't respond, and her knees began to shake.

"I love you," she whispered, laying her heart on the

line. "I've realized I never stopped loving you. And already I love little Mika. The more time I spend here, the more distant LA feels. The more I ask myself if I really want that job, want to live alone like I have for nine years. I've wondered if it would make me happier to come back here to work instead. To be with you and Mika instead. And now I know the answer. *You're* my happiness, Jake. You and Mika."

He stared for a long moment, shock etched on his face. When he still didn't speak, she forged on with the biggest question of all.

"I love you. And I'm ready to lean on you, now, in a way I wouldn't let myself before. For us to lean on each other, like you talked about." She drew a shaky breath and finally asked the question. "So I want to know... Do you still love me, too?"

He stood still as a stone for ten long seconds before he spun around, his back to her, his hands locked behind his head. Her heart beat so hard against her ribs she thought they might break, because while she hadn't known what to expect, his reaction—this silence—couldn't possibly be good.

Finally he turned, and she clutched her throat at the sight of his grim expression. This was *not* the look of a man about to declare that he loved her in return, and she started to shake from the inside out.

"I will always care about you," he said, obviously choosing his words carefully.

Oh, God. The brush-off. The *I like you as a friend* speech. His kisses, his touch, the sex—none of it had been about love. Obviously for him they'd been about the past and lust and long-lost memories. Not even close to what she'd been feeling.

"But I can't risk loving you again, Rory. You have to understand that. I can't trust you to stay, because I know how bad it felt when you betrayed that trust before. And I have Mika now. My son is a huge part of my world, and I can't risk having you become a big part of my life again—a big part of *his* life—knowing all that could blow up in our faces. Do you understand?"

"I wouldn't leave again. I've grown. Learned. Put the past behind me. Surely you see that?"

He slowly shook his head, and as he did so she could practically feel her heart breaking into a million tiny pieces.

"I'm sorry, Rory. I just can't. It was too hard the first time. It's better for both of us not to go there again."

She wanted to argue. Wanted to convince him she meant every word. Wanted to hang on to him, beg and plead with him to love her and be with her.

Somehow she managed to cling to the thin, frayed edges of what pride she had left, and stayed silent. She nodded, turned and walked out the door.

Somehow she made it home, with tears coursing down her cheeks and dripping onto her coat.

Home. No, it wasn't home. Eudemonia wouldn't ever be her home again.

Jake had thought that once Rory had left for LA, life would smooth out and become normal again. That her being back was what had tipped his world sideways and messed with his equilibrium. The past showing up in the form of Aurora Anderson had left him frustrated and confused, his feelings for her something he just couldn't figure out.

But she'd been gone for almost a month and everything still felt off-kilter. Her shocking declaration of love and her insistence that she wanted to move back here, try to find again what they'd lost, had knocked him utterly sideways.

He'd made the right decision, telling her it couldn't work. That he couldn't risk it. There was no way he could be sure she wouldn't take off a second time, crushing him all over again—and maybe Mika, too.

But that conviction—his certainty about that—hadn't kept her from his dreams. Every night in his sleep he was thinking of her, laughing with her, making love with her. Tasting her mouth, feeling her soft skin against his. Then he'd wake with a smile, and the feeling that he was holding her sweet body in his arms, except when he'd look they were empty.

He shook his head, irritated with himself. It hadn't been that long since she'd been gone. Lord knew it had taken years for him to get over her before. He just needed a little more time to forget her—which would be a whole lot easier than letting her back into his life only to have her take off again, leaving him even more devastated than last time.

He moved from the exam room to ask Ellie about his next patient—then stopped dead when he saw that both his mother and Wendy Anderson were standing in the clinic foyer, staring at him with very strange expressions on their faces.

Something about the way they were looking at him made him oddly uncomfortable, and he frowned. "Is something wrong?"

"Yes. Can we talk to you privately?" his mother said.

His mother and Wendy wanted to talk to him privately? What the hell could *this* be about?

"Uh…sure. Come to my office."

The two women sat in the chairs in front of his desk and for some reason he went to sit behind it, instead of in a chair next to them. He felt the need for an inanimate object to be between him and the stern disapproval he could clearly see on their faces.

"What's going on?"

"Wendy recently heard from Rory that she was offered the job she wanted in LA," his mother said.

He had no idea why his stomach pitched and tightened at that news, because it was hardly a surprise. "That's what she'd worked for—what she wanted—so good for her."

"Wendy has also learned that it's actually *not* what she wanted. That she'd decided to move back home, work here or in Fairbanks, and try to have the kind of relationship with you that you had before. Except you told her you had no interest in that."

Well, hell. The fact that Rory had told her mother surprised him, but it didn't change anything. Didn't change that her thinking she wanted to move back might last all of a nanosecond. Didn't change that she could crush him to pieces all over again. "I will always care about Rory. But I'm sure you can both understand why I didn't think that was a good idea."

"Why not?" his mother demanded. "She's had a long time to grapple with the past. With the decisions she made. You've had time, too. And I know you still love her."

He leaned back in his chair and looked up at the ceiling, trying not to let them see what he was feeling. What he'd felt since the second Rory had come back.

Did he still love her? The way his heart still ached and his stomach churned proved that was a no-brainer. If there was one thing he'd learned for certain during those few weeks she'd come back was that he'd always loved her. That he'd never stopped loving her.

Never would.

But that had nothing to do with reality. With trusting her to be there for him and for Mika no matter what.

Missing her might pass. His heart being broken a second time never would.

He decided not to go into that whole conversation and cut straight to the point. "Why are you two here?"

"Jacob." Wendy leaned forward, and the sweet smile she always had on her face had flattened into an expression of such seriousness he couldn't quite believe it was her. "My Aurora loves you—has always loved you. I know this. When the bad things happened it messed everything up, which broke her heart and your heart and my heart. And Beth's, and your dad's, and my Walter's heart, too. So many broken hearts... But now she wants to fix things. Don't *you* want to fix things? Don't you want both your hearts...all of our hearts...to be whole again?"

"It's too late." Apparently, not sharing his feelings wasn't an option, and he drew a deep breath before he forced himself to go on. "When I thought about her coming back home, making a life here, it also made me think about how bad it would feel for her to leave again, and I knew I couldn't go through that one more time. It was..." He had to stop and swallow down the surprising emotion that thickened his throat. "I just don't want to do it. She could be here for a few months, or a few years, then change her mind. What would that do to me and Mika?"

"Jake." His mother's voice was soft now, caring. "I know how bad it was for you. I also know how bad it was for her. But don't you think it says something that even after all these years she still loves you and you still love her?"

"Love isn't everything. Her leaving nine years ago proved that, didn't it? I loved her more than anything, and she supposedly loved me. But she left anyway. Surely you know that trust is just as important as love. Maybe more important."

"Jake. You know as well as anyone that there are no guarantees in life. People get sick, people die, people hurt one another." His mother pressed her hand to the top of his. "If you live your life looking for a guarantee that nothing will ever happen to hurt you, if you won't let yourself be vulnerable to that hurt, you'll end up missing out on the best things in life. Don't you see that Rory coming to you and letting herself be vulnerable that way proves she's learned that hard lesson? You need to trust that she has."

He rubbed his hand over his face. It sounded so logical, so easy to do—just trust her again, let himself be vulnerable to the kind of pain that had twisted him in knots for years. But the way the knots had tightened all over again told him it sure as hell wasn't something he could risk.

"If she comes back to Eudemonia and then leaves again the place I belong…the place I've made my life…will never feel the same. I'd finally gotten past thinking of her during everything I did here. Missing her everywhere I went. Missing her every damn day. I don't want to be messed up like that again. I don't want *Mika* messed up like that."

There. He'd laid his bashed and bloodied heart on the table for both women to see. Surely they understood what he was talking about? They loved this place as much as he did, and had painful memories of their own. No guarantees—he understood that. But to *ask* for that pain by letting Rory back into his heart and his life…?

"Well, I have a solution that will give you a chance to be with Rory again, see how it would be for the two of you, without the risk to your life in Eudemonia that you're so worried about," Wendy said.

"What?"

"You and Mika move to LA. Simple. You take on one of those temporary doctor jobs, live with Aurora and see what happens. If in six months or a year you still don't trust her, believe in her, love her enough, you come back home and your life here will be waiting for you. Just like you'd never left. And Mika will still be little enough that he'll soon settle right back in to his life here, with you and everyone who loves him."

He stared at her, absolutely incredulous. "Twinkie. You love Eudemonia as much as anyone I know. You hardly even wanted to visit Rory in LA—you didn't even want to go for the winter. You of all people should understand why that's a terrible suggestion. All I've ever wanted was to live and work *here*."

She stood and leaned across the desk in a distinctly un-Wendy-like move that surprised him all over again.

"I loved my Walter. If he hadn't been by my side all those years my life would never have been as happy, even after he got sick. Did I always love Eudemonia, too? Yes. But if my husband—the only man I ever loved—had wanted to move somewhere else, and wanted me to go with him, I would have. Because a place is just a place. But the person you love is everything."

Wendy's words seemed to echo in his chest, demanding that he listen. He absorbed them, let himself really feel what she was saying, finally realizing she was one hundred percent right. He still loved Rory, had never stopped loving her, and since she'd been gone he'd missed her all over again anyway—just like before.

Could going to LA be the perfect solution to his fears and doubts? Give him the possibility of finding the kind of life with Rory he'd always wanted, always thought they'd have? If it didn't work out, the bad memories would be in LA, not here. Being in Eudemonia without her wouldn't feel as bad as if she came back for a while, then left. And it wasn't as though he wasn't missing her here anyway.

But, God, he couldn't deny that the thought of putting his heart and body and soul in her hands again scared him to death.

His gaze moved to his mother, who sat there nodding in firm agreement.

"You've got nothing to lose, Jake, except a little time. But what might you have to gain? I don't think I have to tell you that being with Rory the way you used to be just might be the key to real happiness for you. Happiness to last the rest of your life. Living with less risk might be safer. But also sadder and more lonely. Isn't the kind of love and happiness you used to have with Rory worth a little risk?"

He stared at both women, his chest expanding with emotion. Adrenaline surged through his veins, because they were both right. What he and Rory had before Adam died, before it all got away from them, was worth the risk to his heart.

It was worth everything.

CHAPTER FOURTEEN

BEYOND GLAD TO have finally finished packing the last of her things, Rory kneeled to tape shut a box of books. Was she nervous about the decision she'd made? That was an understatement. But she was done hiding. Done running. She had hidden and run for so long she hadn't even realized she was still doing it until she'd gone back home.

Until she'd fallen in love with Jake all over again.

Not exactly accurate. That love had always been there. She'd just refused to let herself feel it anymore, and staying away from him had let her stuff it so far down it had lain dormant until being with him again had brought it all to the surface.

Maybe he'd never trust her…maybe he'd never let her be in his life again the way she wanted. Maybe the love he'd had for her was gone in a way hers never would be. But hiding in LA wasn't going to help her have the life she wanted.

It had taken nine long years of hiding, but she finally felt like herself again. The woman who went for what she wanted.

Jake would shake his head if he heard her say that, but once in a while her stubbornness just might be her best asset. Because she'd decided she wasn't taking Jake's rejection lying down. Until she'd done everything she possibly could to convince him she loved him, that they belonged together and that she'd never, ever leave him and Mika and Eudemonia, she wouldn't accept that it was over for good.

The doorbell rang and she figured it was the moving guys, ready to get all her things on the truck to take to Alaska. She squared her shoulders. This was it. The first step toward her new life. A better life. A life where she could see her mom whenever she wanted. A life in the town she loved.

A life with Jake and Mika, if all went as she planned.

And if it didn't she'd accept that pain. Because even trying to have a life with the two of them would be worth every second of the heartache that would follow Jake's rejection of her love, if that's how it turned out.

She wiped her sweaty hands down her jeans and went to answer the door.

When she opened it her mouth fell open and her heart dove straight to her stomach.

"Jake. What…? Why…? How…?"

"Lots of questions there, Rory." He gave her a crooked smile, but she could see the tension in his eyes. "Can I come in?"

She swung open the door, unable to find her voice. They stood in the small foyer of her apartment—the place she was leaving behind for good—and stared at one another for long seconds before Jake finally spoke.

"It's been a month since you showed up at my door to tell me you love me." He reached for her hands, tightened his fingers on hers. "Every day and every night of that month I've thought of you. Missed you. Wished things could be different between us. But I was too scared to let myself be with you again. Too cowardly to risk my heart again."

"I know," she whispered, hardly believing that he was here, that he was talking about what had happened the last time she'd seen him. That he'd missed her and thought of her. "I understand. I was cowardly, too."

"I planned to stay being that coward, wrapping myself in a self-protective blanket of mistrust, convinced it was what I wanted and needed to do. Until two women named Beth and Wendy came to my office."

He drew her closer, and her heart pounded so hard in her ears she feared she wouldn't be able to hear what was coming next. "And what did those two women say to you?"

"They pointed out that hiding away in Eudemonia, refusing to see what could be between us again, was no way to find my future happiness. I'd convinced myself I was plenty happy until you came back. But that was when I knew there was a big piece of happiness missing from my life, and that piece is you."

"Oh, Jake." She swallowed down the emotion filling her chest and stepped toward him. "All I want is a chance. A chance to prove to you how much I love you and that I'll never, ever leave you again. That's all I want."

"Me, too."

He cupped her face in his hands and her heart shook hard at the sweetness, the love she saw so clearly in his eyes.

"Which is why I'm moving to LA to be with you. Me and Mika. I'm going to take a job here, and we'll see where being together again takes us. We'll be away from the bad and the good memories of Eudemonia that might cloud things up and confuse the issue. It'll just be you and me, finding out what's still between us. A new beginning. What do you say?"

She sniffed back the tears that threatened and flung her arms around him. "I'd say I love that idea almost as much as I love you. Except there's one thing—I didn't take the job. I packed all my stuff and it's going to be trucked to Eudemonia today."

"What?" He stared down at her. "You didn't take the job? You're planning to move back to Eudemonia?"

"Yep. When I came back here I wallowed in misery because you didn't trust me and didn't want to be with me—didn't want to love me, and let me love you and Mika. But then I realized I'd wallowed for nine long years and I was done with it. I decided to be the stubborn Aurora Anderson you teased me for being over more years than I can remember. I decided to come back to Eudemonia and pound on that heart of yours until you let me inside again. I love you too much to quit now. And if you never love me back, I will know that at least I tried."

He pulled her close and buried his face in her hair. They stood for long minutes, just soaking one another in, until he finally lifted his head.

"I do love you, Rory Anderson. I love your stubbornness and preparedness and adorableness. I love your adventurous spirit and toughness and sweetness. I love everything about you. Even when you hurt me I loved you. And what I've accepted this past month, let myself appreciate and be happy about, is that I will always love you, no matter what."

His mouth lowered to hers in the most beautiful kiss of her life, which slowly moved from tender to hot until they finally broke apart.

She looked up into the brown eyes she loved so much and tightened her hold on him. "If you want to move to LA I'll stay. But what I really want is to move back to the place I belong. The place we both belong. With you."

"Other than hearing that you still love me, those words are the best thing I've ever heard in my life."

He kissed her again, and when they came up for air his

smile was so dazzling her heart squeezed tight with the overwhelming love she'd felt for him forever.

"Come on. Eudemonia and Mika are waiting for us to come home."

EPILOGUE

Three years later...

WENDY ANDERSON'S SMALL house was filled to overflowing for her annual Christmas party. She and Rory and the others had spent weeks making biscuits and seed sculptures for the animals, and everyone had enjoyed hanging the treats on the trees outside.

"Time for our own goodies now!" Twinkie called to everyone, clapping her hands and grinning. "Come on inside."

Chatter and laughter moved from outside to inside as the guests took off their coats and hats and headed to the kitchen to grab food from the table.

Rory looked at Mika's adorable face, pink from the cold, and reached for his hat—because otherwise it would probably end up on the floor for Toby to chew on.

"You hungry?" she asked the four-year-old.

"Starving!"

"I have something just for you," Twinkie said. "Come with me to the kitchen."

Jake came in the front door, carrying Audrey, their Christmas baby. Their miracle baby, who'd be celebrating her first birthday in one week.

"We need to get some food in this child because she

keeps trying to eat the animals' biscuits," Jake said. "I know it won't hurt her, but—*yuck!*"

"Yuck!" Audrey repeated as she beamed and waved her hat around.

Rory wrapped her arms around her husband and their baby and laughed. "Don't let Twinkle-Toes hear you say her biscuits are 'yuck,' Audrey," she teased, kissing her daughter's soft round cheek. "She's said she has a special treat for your brother, so I'm betting she has something for you, too. Come on."

Jake reached for Rory's hand and the three of them squeezed their way through the crowd and into the kitchen. Rory stopped next to Mika and laughed at what her mother had given their son.

"You think there are enough marshmallows in that hot chocolate, Mika?" Jake asked. "Did you leave any for me?"

"No. They're all in here."

Mika pointed at his cup, which was overflowing with a teetering mound of small marshmallows. The top ones were tumbling onto the counter and the floor, where Toby was munching them down.

"Our little marshmallow boy," Twinkie said, an indulgent smile on her face. "I have another whole bag, so don't worry. There's plenty for Audrey. And for you, too, Aurora."

"Good thing. I'd hate to be left out of the marshmallow fun."

She looked up at Jake and their eyes met over their baby's head. Her heart gave that familiar squeeze that happened every time she saw her husband. Her children. The beautiful family she'd been blessed with. The family she and Jake had come so close to never having together.

She picked up a few marshmallows, poked one into Audrey's mouth and another into Jake's, then lifted onto her toes to press her lips to her handsome husband's.

"Now you taste sweet, like a marshmallow."

"And you taste sweet like Aurora Hunter."

He lowered his mouth to hers again and her heart expanded with an overwhelming joy at how incredibly lucky they all were.

He moved his mouth to her ear. "You about ready to go home? Because I am. These two are going to be tired from all the excitement, which means…"

"Which means you'll want to go to bed early, too?" Rory asked in faux innocence.

"Funny how you've been reading my mind for about twenty-five years now." He grinned. "Not sure I can read yours, though. What are you thinking?"

"That I'm the luckiest woman in the world to have the world's most wonderful husband. And the *other* thing I'm thinking is for me to know and for you to find out."

He laughed. "You know I love a challenge, Dr. Hunter. Is it that you're thinking about how much I love you?"

"And how much I love *you*. And something else."

His eyes gleamed and he tugged her close to whisper in her ear. "Then hurry up and eat your marshmallows, so we can go home and I can get started on finding out what that something else is."

* * * * *

RETURN TO ME

JACQUELIN THOMAS

Prologue

"*I* wish I'd never met you," she muttered as she ripped clothes from hangers, tossing them into a tattered suitcase.

"Jasmine, I'm sorry you feel that way," Austin Du-Grandpre responded. "The truth is that we're toxic together, so it's best to end things now."

A cold, congested expression settled on her face as she hurled a string of profanity back at him.

Jasmine was leaving town with her best friend, and Austin thought it was a good idea. They needed some separation. They had dated for two years and the relationship was tumultuous at best. For the past month, Jasmine had been pressuring Austin for a marriage proposal. When nothing came of it, she decided to give him an ultimatum—marry her or she would leave town and find a new man.

Austin chose the latter. Jasmine was free to start over with someone new. Perhaps she'd be much happier.

Her mouth took on an unpleasant twist as she shot daggers toward him with her eyes. "I can't believe I wasted all this time with you. I should've known better than to get involved with someone like you..."

Austin opened his mouth to utter a retort, but remained

silent. He would not allow himself to be baited into another argument with Jasmine.

"Did you ever love me?"

"That wasn't the problem."

She frowned with cold fury. "Then what is it? I'm not good enough to be your wife—the wife of a lawyer?" Jasmine folded her arms across her chest. "What? You wanna be with some snobby ivy league graduate...huh?"

"Jasmine, the problem is that you and I are not a good fit," Austin stated. "You can't go around starting fights with every woman who looks my way. I come home to you every night, but you still accuse me of cheating...we're just not good together. You like to party and you get angry when I tell you I'm tired."

Her face was marked by loathing. "Why shouldn't I have a good time? When you're home, all you do is work. It's always about your clients."

"You knew I was an attorney when we met." He paused a moment before asking, "If you find me so boring, why have you been pushing so hard for marriage?"

"All of my friends are getting married and it's not like I'm getting any younger, Austin. Any man would want me for a wife...anyone but you." Jasmine met his gaze. "But it's cool. You see, I know what you really want and it's the one thing you won't get. I'm gonna make sure of it."

He frowned. "What are you talking about?"

Jasmine shrugged, then closed her suitcase. "Doesn't matter."

Coming out of the musing, Austin looked down at the birth certificate in his hand as if seeing it for the first time.

He wasn't.

He had stared at it many times since procuring the copy from Jasmine's former best friend, Cheryl. They left Dallas, Texas, with Las Vegas in their sights.

Then one day Cheryl was back home. She requested a meeting with Austin, shocking him with the news that Jasmine was pregnant when they left town.

Austin could not believe she would just put the child up for adoption. He eyed the birth certificate once more. He was never listed as the father. In fact, the space was blank.

She had taken his son from him—the one thing that would hurt him most.

Chapter 1

"Aren't you going to dance with the bride?"

Austin's sister, Jadin, was standing before him.

His gaze slid to find her identical twin dancing with her new husband. Austin's mouth turned upward into a smile. "Maybe later. I don't think I've ever seen Jordin look so happy."

"She's just married the man of her dreams, big brother. She's completely over the moon."

A sea of people dressed in tuxes and bright dresses in summer colors roamed through the elegant space, admiring the paintings and photographs dotting the cream-colored walls. Surrounded by fourteen acres of live oak groves with serene views of the Ashley River, Austin's mind was elsewhere.

"You look distracted. Everything okay?"

"I'm fine," he responded. "Uh… Aunt Rochelle is trying to get your attention."

Jadin grimaced. "I guess I'd better see what she wants. That woman is getting on my last nerve today. Ever since she broke her ankle, she acts like I'm her personal maid."

"You volunteered your services, remember?"

"Do me a favor. Next time I open my mouth, punch me in it."

Austin bit back his amusement as he watched his sister make her way across the room. He hadn't known their aunt long, given his mother's determination to keep him from that side of his family, but it was enough to know she could be very demanding.

His eyes traveled to the table where the wedding party was seated. There were a couple of bridesmaids engaged in conversation. One of the ladies was Dr. Sabrina Collins, whom everyone affectionately called Bree—the woman who had adopted his son when Jasmine had placed him up for adoption.

Austin's gaze locked on her. She looked up, meeting his gaze. When she smiled, he felt the weirdest sensation—a strange mixture of both calm and excitement churning through his bloodstream like a virus, quickly spreading until he could hardly breathe.

Austin gave himself a mental shake. He wasn't looking for a romantic liaison. He sought to get back what had been taken from him. He never had the luxury of a relationship with his father, due in part to his mother's bitterness over losing the only man she ever loved to another woman. Her actions forced him to watch on the sidelines as his father doted on his twin sisters, Jordin and Jadin. Austin vowed his child would not tread down that same painful path.

With the help of a private investigator, Austin had succeeded in locating the child in Charleston, South Carolina. He thought it a blessing and fate that his son lived in the same city as his father and siblings. Austin had been taking steps to build a relationship with his family. Locating his son here, too, was perfect.

However, he was not prepared to discover that the woman raising his son was also the best friend of his sister, Jordin. This could be a potential complication, but he was not going to let this stop him from petitioning the courts to reverse the adoption.

Austin walked out on the balcony to enjoy the June weather. It was bright and sunny, but the temperature was just right. He agreed with guests who'd commented that the day was perfect for the wedding celebration.

He stood out there enjoying the picturesque grounds before navigating back through the doors and sea of wedding guests toward the nearest drink station, where he ordered a rum and cola.

At the sound of laughter, Austin turned in time to watch as Jordin and Ethan cut slices of their wedding cake. His sister looked happy and very much in love.

He smiled.

"What are you doing over here by yourself?"

Austin glanced over at his father. "Getting one last drink."

Etienne surveyed his face. "You okay, son?"

His gaze traveled back to Bree. "I am." The truth was that he had missed the first two years of his son's life and it filled his heart with an unrelenting ache. His pain was a shadow that resided in the corners of his heart but never failed to appear morning, noon or night.

"How are you dealing with the idea of Jordin being married?"

Etienne shrugged. "Ethan's a good man and he'll make her happy—of that, I have no doubt…but I have to confess, I'm feeling a mite old right now. All of my children grown…" He turned to face Austin, giving him a faint smile that held a touch of sadness. "I hate missing out on so much of your life."

"It wasn't your fault."

"It doesn't lessen the pain."

Austin believed his father because he felt the same way where Emery was concerned.

The office was empty when Austin arrived Monday morning around seven. He'd been working at his family's Charleston firm for a year but wasn't normally the first to arrive. Today he wanted to get an early start. It helped him to keep busy.

Austin entered the break room and made a cup of coffee.

The office manager, a woman in her early forties, walked in and gasped. "Oh, goodness... I'm sorry, Austin. I didn't expect anyone to be here. I'm usually the first to arrive."

"I woke up at five and couldn't go back to sleep, so I decided to come in a little earlier," he explained. "No point in wasting the time doing nothing."

She nodded in agreement. "I have to tell you...your sister's wedding was beautiful. Oh, my goodness... Your family really knows how to throw a wedding."

"It was nice," he told the office manager. "I enjoyed meeting your husband, Gwen. It turns out that I went to high school with the son of one of his frat brothers."

She smiled. "He told me. This world isn't as big as we think."

Austin couldn't agree more.

They talked a few minutes more while she waited for her tea to brew.

"I'd never been to Lowndes Grove Plantation before Jordin's wedding," Gwen stated. "And that house...it was stunning."

Austin agreed. "Jordin told me that it was built around 1786. The owners did a great job with the restorations."

"I almost want to have another wedding. Just to hold it there."

He smiled, then checked his watch. "Time to start my workday. I'm covering for Jordin while she's on her honeymoon."

"You've been pulling a lot of long hours, Austin." Gwen picked up her cup of tea. "Work-life balance, okay?"

"I'll keep that in mind." Austin took his coffee and headed to his office.

As soon as he sat down, his focus shifted to the stack of documents on his desk.

It was almost eleven when he called one of the paralegals and asked, "Were you able to get the information we needed from the mother?"

"Yes, I emailed it to you a few minutes ago."

"Thanks," he said before hanging up the phone.

Right after lunch Austin reviewed a couple of Jordin's cases. He appreciated the fact that she was so organized with everything he needed right where he could find it.

The sound of a baby crying in the hallway caught his attention, and he felt a wretchedness he'd never known before.

A stab of guilt lay buried in his chest. Maybe if he'd handled things with Jasmine differently, he might have had a chance to be with his son.

From everything he'd been told about Dr. Bree, Austin believed her to be a good woman. According to Jordin, she was also a very good mother to Emery. He wanted what was best for his child. It was this desire that conflicted him.

Austin intended to be a part of his son's life, but he worried about the effect it would have on Emery. He was safe and secure with Bree. The little boy didn't know he had a father. How would he respond when Austin made his presence known?

Austin walked back to his desk and picked up a file. He had just returned to the office from the courthouse. It was after five, but he wasn't quite ready to call it quits for the day. He'd always driven himself hard, putting work ahead of pleasure.

He also wanted to make his father proud. Austin had a lot of respect for both his father and uncle. Etienne and Jacques DuGrandpre had the same passion for law as their father, and his father before him. It was no wonder he, Jordin and Jadin all became attorneys.

It was in their blood.

He worked another two hours before shutting down his computer.

Tonight, he was leaving work earlier than usual. It was 7:30 p.m. Austin wanted to spend some time at the gym before he went home.

Just as he did every time he was on his way out, Austin paused in front of the large, looming portrait of Marcelle DuGrandpre, his grandfather. Austin's heart swelled with pride. Despite all odds during a time of racial tension, his grandfather opened the doors of the DuGrandpre Law Firm in 1960. When he died, Austin's uncle and father took over, the legacy continuing with their children.

"I miss him."

He hadn't heard anyone enter the room. Austin glanced over his shoulder. "Jadin, I didn't know you were still here. I thought I was the only one working late."

"Unfortunately, I will be putting in some long hours all week," she responded.

Austin had grown close to his twin sisters, Jadin and

Jordin, since moving to Charleston a little over a year ago from Dallas.

"I met him once," Austin told his sister. "Granddad was in town for a conference or something. He came to the house."

Jadin smiled. "I'm not surprised. He was all about family."

"I remember thinking that I was in trouble." Pointing to the portrait, he added, "He had that same stern expression on his face. But then he smiled at me."

"People used to think he was mean, but he wasn't. He would do anything he could to help others. He even offered his services pro bono to those who couldn't afford to pay."

"He was a good man. I'm glad I had the chance to meet him." Austin escorted Jadin to her car, then strolled down the next row to where his SUV was parked.

He drove the short distance to Holbrooke Boot Camp Gym, which was owned by his brother-in-law, Ethan.

He needed a strenuous workout to expend some of his pent-up energy. He'd been on edge ever since locating his son. Austin gathered his bag and navigated inside.

After a two-hour intense training, Austin still found himself wound tight, his frustration banked, but not eliminated.

When he arrived home, he pulled up his contact list on his phone. He stared at the names for a solid ten minutes before shutting it down. Austin considered calling a young woman he'd spent time with in the past, but changed his mind. She'd made it clear on several occasions that she wanted more than he was willing to offer.

Austin liked her, but she reminded him of Jasmine and that was a path he wasn't willing to travel down again.

He wasn't looking for a serious relationship now—his

thoughts were consumed with his son. Austin's heart ached with the knowledge that he had a child who was just beyond his reach.

Chapter 2

Bree Collins exited through the doors of New Beginnings Preschool, heading to her car. She checked her watch. She had taken Monday off to wind down after Jordin's wedding. Since Jadin was currently working on a high-profile case, Bree volunteered to run the necessary errands for the wedding, returning rental items and finalizing payment.

Today she wanted to get to the office early enough to have her first two cups of coffee while reviewing notes before the arrival of her clients.

Her receptionist was on the phone when she arrived.

"Good morning, Casey," Bree greeted.

"Hey, beautiful."

She loved the woman's bubbly personality and genuine demeanor. Her patients adored Casey.

"How was the wedding?" the receptionist asked.

"It was very romantic and beautiful," Bree responded. "I don't think it could've been more perfect."

Casey's infectious grin always set the tone for the day. "I know Jordin looked stunning."

"She did," Bree confirmed with a smile. "Speaking of weddings, have you and Eric set a date yet?"

Casey nodded. "We're getting married in October. On the tenth."

"That's wonderful."

"Now that we've picked our wedding day, the engagement feels more real to me." Casey handed her a stack of files. "You're booked all morning and two appointments after lunch."

"Light day…"

"Don't worry, you have a full day tomorrow."

Bree strolled into her office. Her eyes landed on the photograph of her son that sat on her desk. Her heart sang with delight whenever she thought about Emery.

When she lost her husband, Caleb, just before their second wedding anniversary, Bree wasn't sure she would ever recover. As a psychologist, she worked with others who were dealing with grief, but when it came to her own… Bree found herself in a bad state of mind.

It wasn't until she decided to adopt that she found hope again. When she met Emery, it was love at first sight. The moment she laid eyes on him—Bree knew he was the child for her.

Bree picked up Emery and headed home. She was thrilled to see her little boy and looked forward to spending some quality time with him after dinner. He was a very happy and secure soon-to-be three-year-old.

"Mommy, I wanna 'nana."

"Don't you want to eat dinner, sweetie?" she asked. "Mommy's making fried chicken and macaroni."

"Shick'en…mac'roni…yummy."

Bree laughed. "That's what I say. *Yummy.*"

As soon as they arrived home, she turned on the television for Emery, then went straight into the kitchen, where Bree washed her hands, then poured oil into a fryer. While it heated, she seasoned four chicken drumsticks and boiled water for the macaroni.

She placed the chicken in the fryer and the cheese and macaroni in the oven, put a load of Emery's clothes in the laundry and then returned to the kitchen. She washed her hands and checked on the food. Bree enjoyed being a mother. She considered it her one true purpose in life.

For a moment, she allowed herself to think about her late husband. He had been her best friend and she missed him. Enough time had passed since Caleb's death for Bree to consider dating.

Although she had gone on a few dates, she had not met a man who could hold her interest for one reason or another.

After dinner Bree cleared the table and filled the sink with hot water.

She was down to washing the skillet when the telephone rang.

A telemarketer.

Her mouth thinned with displeasure.

Bree put another load of clothes in the washing machine before giving Emery a bath.

She was glad that he went down easily. She hadn't finished the story before the little boy was sound asleep.

"My little man...you're so tired." Bree kissed his cheek. "Sleep well."

She tiptoed out the room.

Bree folded the rest of the laundry and carried it to her bedroom. She watched television as she put the clothing away.

After a quick shower, she got into bed with her laptop.

A friend of her emailed copies of the photographs she'd taken at Jordin's wedding. An easy smile curved her mouth as she scanned through them. She was truly happy for her friend. Ethan seemed to be a wonderful person and it was obvious that they were very much in love. Bree prayed they would have a long life together.

Her eyes landed on a photograph of Jordin's brother.

"You're a cutie, Austin DuGrandpre," she whispered. They hadn't been formally introduced, but she knew who he was—Jordin and Jadin spoke of him often.

Bree continued to stare at the photograph.

He looked so handsome in the light gray suit he wore. Tall, lean and muscular, Austin wore a smile that lit his chestnut-colored eyes and accented the tiny scar over his left eyebrow.

I wonder if he's dating anyone?

She chuckled to herself. She couldn't seriously be thinking about Jordin's brother in this manner.

Bree turned off the computer. If she hadn't, she'd be staring at Austin for the rest of the evening.

"*Mrs. Holbrooke*, it's nice to have you back," Austin greeted when Jordin strolled into his office a week later.

Her smile broadened. "I hear you've been holding down my clients for me. Thanks."

"I didn't have to do much."

Jordin sat down in one of the chairs facing him. "How are things with you?"

"I'm fine. Why?"

"We didn't get to finish our conversation about Bree and Emery."

"It was your wedding day—not the right time or place but nothing's changed," Austin responded, girding himself with resolve. "I want my son."

"I understand completely," Jordin said. "I would feel the same way if I were in your shoes. This is just such a complicated situation. I had no idea that Emery was your child. I celebrated with Bree when the adoption was finalized."

"I didn't know I was a father." He paused a moment before asking, "But you still think that I should wait?"

"For now," she responded. "I know Bree and you have nothing to worry about, Austin. She's a wonderful mother to Emery. She adores that little boy."

"He's *my* son. I never gave permission for him to be adopted."

"Unfortunately, courts have held that fathers unaware of their children may not later object to the children's adoption, particularly when the father's lack of knowledge was his own fault."

"I will argue that my lack of knowledge was due to dishonesty. Jasmine deliberately kept me in the dark about her pregnancy. She wanted to hurt me—I'm sure that's why she never told me that she was pregnant. Jasmine put Emery up for adoption because her boyfriend didn't want to raise another man's child."

"Don't take this the wrong way, but what did you do to her?" Jordin asked. "Why would she be so cruel?"

"She's always been vindictive. It's one of the reasons why we didn't work out as a couple. She wasn't happy when I broke up with her."

"But not telling you about the baby—it's malicious."

Austin nodded.

"I know how badly you want to unite with your son, but I suggest that you take some time and get to know Bree first before you say anything."

"Why should I do that?"

"Bree is also an innocent party in all of this, Austin. She doesn't deserve to be punished for loving your son. There has to be a way for you two to work this out."

He hadn't once considered Bree's feelings in this situation. Austin was simply focused on bringing his son home where he belonged, but his sister was right. Bree hadn't done anything wrong.

"Austin, I watched more than once as Bree suffered through bouts of endometriosis. She was in agony to the point it was crippling. I've never felt so helpless as to witness her pain and be unable to help her in some way. Finding out that she wouldn't be able to have children only made that pain worse. She once told me that she was born to be a mother and I believe her. If it's not handled carefully, losing Emery might just take all of the life out of her."

"Jordin, can you introduce us?" he asked. "Getting to know her might make this a little easier for everybody concerned."

She nodded. "Sure. Ethan and I were thinking about hosting a dinner party on Saturday. I'll invite her."

"Thanks so much, sis."

"I know you can't really see it right now, but I know that there's a way for you and Bree to come up with the perfect solution—one that will work for both of you."

"I don't intend to snatch Emery out of her arms, Jordin. I just want to be in his life. He's mine and I want to raise him. I'll be fair to Bree. I promise."

"He means the world to her."

"I haven't met him yet, but he already owns my heart, sis."

She nodded in understanding.

"How did she come to adopt him in Las Vegas?"

"Bree lived there for three years. Her husband was a musician and played for a couple of performers at Bally's. He died a year later…killed in a car accident. I think adopting Emery helped Bree heal through that horrible period in her life. When the adoption was final, she moved here to Charleston."

"Is she from this area?"

Jordin shook her head. "No, she's actually from Georgia. She was my college roommate and we clicked right from the beginning. She's been my best friend ever since."

She rose to her feet. "I'd better get to my office and return phone calls. I'm sure I have a stack of messages."

"You shouldn't," Austin said. "I talked to everybody who had called you up until yesterday."

"Thanks again, big brother." She paused in the doorway and said, "Oh, Austin... *I's married now.*"

He laughed. "That you are. One day I'll take that leap—don't know when, though."

"As soon as you find the right woman."

Austin thought about his sister's words. He'd once thought Jasmine was the right woman for him. She was anything but the right one. There was a time when he was crazy in love with her, but then Jasmine began taking him for granted. She used his love to manipulate him into doing whatever she wanted. When he finally came to his senses, the arguments started.

They tried to make it work for three years. Austin had no regrets when he broke up with Jasmine. He had thought long and hard and decided to do what was best for him.

But Jasmine had gotten back at him in the most hurtful way possible.

Austin didn't know if he would ever be able to forgive Jasmine for keeping his child away from him.

Nausea rolled through Bree, tightening her stomach and making her mouth water. She gripped the door frame. Any second now she was going to either throw up or wind up on the floor, doubled up in pain.

She hated being in such pain from her endometriosis, but was thankful that it wasn't as bad as it had been in the past. Bree sank down to the floor of the bathroom, the coolness of the ceramic tile against her skin bringing a measure of relief to her.

Her stomach rolled again as the spasms weakened her. One hand pressed to her mouth, Bree crawled over to the toilet.

Bracing her hands on her knees, her stomach released its contents.

For a long moment Bree remained where she was, weak and trembling, a sour taste in her mouth.

Finally, she pulled herself up, washed her face and brushed her teeth.

An hour later, Bree felt much better and was on her way to the office. It was Friday and she was looking forward to a weekend of fun and relaxation.

Jordin and Ethan were hosting their first dinner party tomorrow night. Bree wondered briefly who else would be in attendance. It didn't matter really. She was grateful to sit and have some adult interaction for an evening. It would be the perfect ending to a busy week.

Chapter 3

Austin arrived at Ethan and Jordin's home fifteen minutes early. He was surprised to find that Bree had already arrived. She was standing at the wrought iron railing on the second-floor balcony, facing Jordin as they talked.

He stared at Bree, looking her over. The deepening sunlight framed her figure, outlining her curves. She was beautiful in a simple, natural way. Austin was shocked to feel desire streaking through him like a current.

Jordin saw him and waved. "C'mon in. The front door is open."

Austin entered the house and was met by Ethan. "Hey…" he greeted. "Your wife told me to just walk in."

"No problem. Good to see you, man."

He heard footsteps behind him and turned to see Jordin descend the stairs followed by Bree.

"Austin, I want you to meet my best friend," she said. "Actually, she's more like a sister to me. Bree, this is my brother, Austin."

He was rendered speechless for a moment by her beauty. Austin swallowed hard, struggling to recover his voice. "It's a pleasure to meet you," he said finally.

His eyes darted to hers and locked.

He cleared his throat softly.

She met the smile and the hand that was offered. "It's a pleasure meeting you, as well. I've heard a lot about you."

Austin lost himself momentarily in their chocolate depths. His gaze fell to the creamy expanse of her neck. She was dressed to perfection in a teal-colored, sleeveless silk dress. Bree was tall and slender, but with an athletic build. She wore her shoulder-length hair in soft curls around her heart-shaped face. Her flawless skin was the color of a new penny.

"Dinner will be ready in a couple of minutes," Jordin announced. "We're still waiting on a few people to arrive."

"Would either of you like a glass of wine?" Ethan offered.

"I'm fine," Bree responded.

"Austin?"

"I'll take a glass."

Austin could feel Bree's eyes studying him. He met her gaze, forcing her to look away. He smiled to himself.

The front door opened.

"Hey, family," Ryker said with a grin. "Look at this… the newlyweds are hosting their first dinner party."

His wife, Garland, gave him a playful pinch. "Leave them alone."

There was something in the wistful turn of Bree's lips that made Austin sense the pain beneath the surface, and he longed to make it better. She had lost her husband in a tragic way and he could only imagine that while she was truly happy for Jordin—grief still resided in her heart.

Jadin arrived with a date a few minutes later, whom she introduced as Michael.

Austin leaned over and said to Bree in a low voice, "I guess we should've brought a plus one."

"I think you're right."

"Well, will you be my plus one for the evening?"

She turned, easing into a smile. "Sure."

Austin glanced up and saw Jordin standing in the doorway. She gave him a quick thumbs-up, then announced, "Dinner is ready."

He and Bree were seated beside one another.

"How do you like living in Charleston?" Bree inquired as she used her fork to slide the fettuccine noodles around her plate.

Austin smiled faintly, laid his napkin across his lap and, picking up his knife and fork, sliced into a strip of grilled chicken. "I'm enjoying it. I've always liked this area."

He took a bite of his food. The delicate Alfredo sauce and chicken were cooked to perfection.

"Jordin, did you cook this?"

Ethan chuckled and was awarded a sharp glance from her. "Just so you know, I *can* cook. I will confess that I called Aubrie for help with ingredients and such."

"It's delicious," Ethan said.

Everyone agreed.

"Does Aubrie ever hang out with the family?" Austin asked. "I think I've seen her maybe three times since I moved here. I'd like to get to know her better, especially since she's my first cousin."

"My sister spends a lot of her time in New Orleans," Ryker announced. "She goes there to spend time with the chef who mentored her in culinary school. Each time she comes back with new entrées for her restaurant."

Bree took a sip of her iced tea. "She must really enjoy her work."

"I'm not so sure this is just about her work," Jordin stated. "I think there's another reason why she spends so much time there."

Jadin agreed. "Aubrie isn't talking, but I suspect she's seeing someone."

"She was always one to keep secrets," Ryker said. "My parents keep hoping she'll come to her senses and join the firm, but it's not going to happen."

"How's Aunt Rochelle doing?" Jordin inquired.

"She hates being on crutches, having a cast on and not being able to drive. Mom's driving my dad crazy. He threatened to come stay with us until she's back on her feet." Ryker wiped his mouth on his napkin. "I love my mom, but when she doesn't get her way…"

"When Aunt Rochelle isn't happy—nobody's happy," Jadin said.

They all agreed.

When they finished their meal, they gathered in the family room.

Austin couldn't tear his gaze away from Bree.

Members of his family wandered in and out of his line of vision, locking Bree and him together, but nothing could shatter the connection alive and sizzling between them.

She felt it, too.

He could see it in her eyes, in the firming of her luscious lips. Just as he could see that she was trying to make sense of what she was feeling.

Their gazes connected and held.

Bree was an incredibly beautiful woman. Ravishing didn't even come close to describing her.

Austin broke eye contact with her and stared down into his glass of wine. He bit back a satisfied smile. Good to know he wasn't the only one being twisted into knots. However, he couldn't help but wonder if this attraction he felt would complicate his plan to get his son.

Bree was powerless to stop staring into the most beautiful set of eyes she'd ever seen. They were a stunning chestnut brown with golden flecks throughout, large and thickly lashed. Austin DuGrandpre bore a strong resemblance to his father. They had the same honey-colored skin, a muscular build and both stood about six feet three inches.

Men shouldn't have eyes this pretty, she thought.

He wore a light blue dress shirt that fit snugly over wide shoulders, then tapered, tucked into slim-waist navy trousers.

Austin smiled, revealing two small dimples Bree hadn't noticed before. She tried to throttle the dizzying current racing through her. He radiated a vitality that drew Bree like a magnet. Whenever he laughed, his full-throated masculine sound sent strange waves through her stomach.

Girl, you need to focus.

It wasn't easy, though. Austin made Bree feel things she hadn't experienced in a long time. Not since Caleb.

At least I still have those feelings, she reasoned silently. For a while she worried that they had died with her husband.

"Jordin told me that you're a psychologist."

"I am," Bree confirmed.

"I think it's cool. I've always been fascinated with human behavior, especially when it comes to the criminal mind."

"Okay, you know I'm going to ask the *question.* Why do you defend criminals?"

He chuckled. "I've come to expect it. All criminal defense lawyers are asked this question. It's part of the criminal defense experience."

"I'd like to hear your response, as well," Garland said. "I don't think it's something I could ever do, especially if I knew my client was guilty."

"Innocence is not the chief driver for me," Austin stated. "You all may find this strange but I enjoy working with guilty people. I have an interest in the causes of human conduct. I search to find the humanity in the people I represent, no matter what they may have done. I started out practicing family law, but I didn't find it as fulfilling," Austin said. "Nobody knows this, but I once considered studying forensic psychology. I have a bachelor's degree in psychology."

Bree reached for her glass. "Really?"

He nodded. "I love law and psychology—pursuing law just seemed the natural way to go for me."

There was something in his manner that she found soothing. It was easy to talk to him. "That's because you're a DuGrandpre," Bree responded. "It's in your blood."

"I suppose so," Austin said with a smile.

She felt a lurch of excitement within her. "It seems we have something in common," Bree told him. "I briefly considered going into law, but decided that I loved psychology more."

"Do you have any regrets?"

She shook her head. "I know that I'm exactly where I should be."

"I feel the same way."

Bree felt there was some type of deeper significance to the visual interchange between them.

The thought struck a vibrant chord in her.

She contributed to the conversation going on among everyone, but found herself studying his profile.

Bree had to deliberately shut out any awareness of Austin just to focus on Jordin's words.

"What do you think about a girls' night next weekend?"

"That's fine," she responded.

Jadin agreed, then asked, "What about you, Garland? Can you join us?"

"She can," Ryker answered for her. "It'll do her some good to get away from the children."

Garland pointed to him and replied, "What my husband said…"

At the end of the evening, she bid everyone a good night. As she gathered her purse, Austin volunteered to walk her down to her car.

"Bree, travel safe," he told her.

She tingled as he said her name and a quiver surged through her veins. "You do the same."

Bree unlocked the door and got into her car. She was soon pulling out of the driveway and traveling toward the freeway.

It had been a long time since a man had struck her interest, filling Bree with a strange inner delight.

Two days later Bree walked out of Marbelle's Children's Boutique, juggling her tote and a couple of shopping bags in her hands as she neared her car.

"Hey, are you following me?"

She glanced over her shoulder, her steps slowing. "Austin…what are you doing on my side of town?" Her heart danced with eagerness over seeing him again.

"I have a client who lives over here. Hey, thank you for being my plus one the other night. Everyone was coupled up…it could've been a little awkward if you hadn't been so gracious."

"I didn't mind. I enjoyed talking to you," she responded. "You're a very interesting man."

He grinned. "Do you have some time for lunch?"

"Sure." Bree looped her purse over her shoulder while her insides jangled with eagerness. She felt the blood surge from her fingertips to her toes. "So, where are we off to,

Austin DuGrandpre?" She was thrilled that he wanted to continue their conversation.

"There's a little place around the corner."

She chuckled a little. "You use that line often?" she asked playfully, glancing at him.

Austin laughed, full-throated and sexy. "I don't believe I've ever used it before, as a matter of fact." He adjusted his long stride to her much shorter one.

"I wouldn't recommend using it again," she remarked with a chuckle. "The only thing around the corner is a bank."

He laughed. "I'm still learning my way around."

"There's a sandwich shop that's two blocks away. It's walkable."

"Perfect. Let me help you with your bags," he offered.

They walked past a pizza place in full lunch swing, the scents of robust sauce and spicy sausage filling the air.

Bree's stomach rumbled. If he heard, there were no outward signs of it.

"You in the mood for pizza?" Austin inquired.

"Not really." Although the pizza smelled great, at noon the place was usually overrun by high school kids, and Bree didn't want to get caught in the wave of teens.

In the middle of the next block, the sandwich shop was trendy and casual.

"Have you been here before?" she asked.

"No. How's the food?"

"Very good. I highly recommend the club sandwich. It's roasted turkey breast, smoked ham with bacon and avocado. The roasted garlic mayonnaise is made in-house and is delicious."

"You find a table and I'll order our food," Austin suggested.

Bree found one near a large window facing the street. She hadn't expected to see him quite so soon. They would've run into each other at some point, she knew. This was perfect as she had been thinking of him earlier.

Austin walked up with two trays laden with sandwiches, potato chips, pickles and drinks.

Bree blessed the food.

"Jordin tells me that you have a little boy." He bit into his sandwich.

"I do," she exclaimed with intense pleasure. "He's my whole world." If Austin hadn't mentioned it, she would've told him about Emery. It's one of the first things she usually told men who seemed interested in her. It helped to eliminate the ones who were simply looking for a good time.

"That's cool."

"Do you have any children?" Bree inquired as she studied his profile.

It took a moment for him to respond. She wasn't sure he'd heard her. Bree opened her mouth to repeat the question.

"No," Austin interjected. "But I'm looking forward to having a child one day." He wanted to bring up the subject of Emery, but didn't want to make her suspicious as to why he'd be so interested in her son, especially since they'd just met.

"I think being a parent is probably my best achievement. My late husband and I really wanted children." She took a sip of her drink. "He would've loved Emery."

"I'm sorry for your loss."

Bree smiled. "Thank you, Austin. There was a time when it was hard for me to think about Caleb, but it's gotten easier. We had a lot of good times together."

"I can't imagine going through something like that."

Austin took another sip of his water when she moistened the top of her lip with the tip of her tongue. "I know my family would rally around me," he said, shifting slightly in his chair.

"You're lucky in that respect. I have no family," Bree stated flatly. "I've had to deal with everything alone." Austin had no idea just how lucky he was to have supportive family members. Anyone she'd truly cared about in the world was gone except for Emery.

"You're not close to them?"

"I grew up in a drug-infested apartment in Atlanta for the first six years of my life. My mom died of a drug overdose, and I lived with my paternal grandmother. When she died a couple of years later, I was placed with a foster family. I don't have any other relatives—at least any that I know about."

"I had no idea," he uttered.

Bree gave a slight shrug. "There's no way you could've known. Besides, it wasn't that bad. I had good foster parents. We lived in a nice neighborhood in Atlanta, with a great school. I was on the basketball team and even earned several college scholarships." She wiped her mouth with a paper napkin, then said, "I think I turned out okay."

"I agree," Austin said with a smile.

Bree settled back in her chair. "So, tell me about you."

"Well, I grew up believing that my dad cared more for his twin daughters than he did me. Moving here and spending time with him, I found out that it wasn't the case and that I'd wasted a lot of time being angry with my father."

"Jordin adores you," she said. "Jadin, too."

"I have two incredible sisters."

"What made you choose law, Austin?" Bree asked. "Especially since you were angry with your father during that time?"

"I think it was a way for me to feel close to him. Maybe I wanted to make him proud."

"What's the story behind that scar above your eye?" she questioned.

"You noticed?" He grinned. She smiled back.

"When I was in the ninth grade, I got into a fight with a bully at school. He picked up a stick and hit me with it."

"Wow... I hope he got the worst of it."

"Oh, I left some scars," Austin stated. "When I saw that I was bleeding, I lost it. I was told that it took three people to get me off him."

"I had a fight in high school," Bree said. "It was with a jealous teammate. She got into some trouble in one of her classes, so she had to sit out a game. It was my chance to finally show the coach what I could do, so I took it and I got her spot." She sipped her tea. "The thing is I really needed to be noticed—it was the only way I could go to college. My foster parents were good to me, but they'd made it clear that with four kids—we needed to try to get as many scholarships as possible."

Austin took a sip of his drink. "My dad paid for my college education and trust me, I'm grateful. I've already started an education fund for my children."

"I thought you didn't have any," Bree interjected.

"It's never too early to start planning," he responded.

She smiled. "You're a very smart man, Austin. I have a college fund for my son, as well."

It pleased Austin to hear this. At least Emery had been placed with a responsible woman. "How did you end up in Vegas? Was it because of your husband?"

"After I graduated, I landed a great job there with a mental health center. My husband was a musician and found work right away—it just worked out. But when he died, I didn't want to stay in Nevada. Jordin had been urging me to move closer to her for years, and since she was the closest thing I had to family, I moved to Charleston and decided to open my own practice."

"When I was growing up, people didn't openly admit to seeing a psychologist. They didn't even talk about mental illness," Austin countered.

"In the African American community, there are still some people who consider mental illness to be a white person's disease," Bree stated. "It's terrible because statistics tell a different story. Twenty percent of blacks are more likely to experience some form of mental illness than Caucasians."

"I think it has to do with socioeconomic disparities from slavery to race-based exclusions when it comes to health care."

"It's true," Bree said. "People who live in poverty or have substance abuse problems are at higher risk for poor mental health."

Austin couldn't help admiring her intelligence and compassion.

They finished off their meal.

"I'm glad I ran into you," Austin told her. "I hate eating alone."

"Same here." She wrenched herself away from her ridiculous preoccupation with his arresting face.

"Bree, that's not exactly true," Austin confessed. "The truth is that I'd like to get to know you better. I enjoy your company."

His words pleased her. "I'd like to know more about you, as well."

They exchanged phone numbers.

Bree checked her watch. "I need to get back to my office. I have several appointments this afternoon."

He took her hand in his and kissed her on the cheek. "Until next time."

"Goodbye," she whispered, pulling her hand away from his grasp, his touch sending shivers through her.

Their steps were hurried once they exited the shop. She needed to get to her office and Bree was sure that Austin had to return to work, as well.

Many hours later she still couldn't escape the gentle look he'd given her as they parted ways.

That evening the phone rang as Bree came out of the bathroom, clad in flannel pajama bottoms and a T-shirt. She padded barefoot around the king-size bed to answer it.

"Hey, it's Austin."

She hadn't expected to hear from him so soon, but his call thrilled her. "What's up?"

"I wanted to tell you again that I had a great time with you. I'm glad we ran into each other."

Bree's heart was hammering foolishly. "Same here."

"Do you have some time to talk?"

"Yes," she responded. "Emery's sleeping, so we're good."

They made small talk for a few minutes before Austin said, "Bree, I have a confession to make. I'm very attracted to you and I'd like to take you out. That is if you're not involved with anyone." He gave a short laugh. "I guess I should've asked this first."

She couldn't deny the spark of excitement she felt at the prospect of dating him. "I'm single, Austin. As for spending time with you—I don't have a problem with it. You're not exactly what I'd call boring."

"I guess the next step is when and where. How about tomorrow night?"

"I need to check my calendar really quick," she said. "I have to attend a fund-raiser at my son's preschool. I'm not sure if its tomorrow or the next day." Bree quickly checked the calendar on her cell phone. "Okay, tomorrow I'm free."

"Can you get a babysitter lined up for your son or is this late notice?" Austin inquired.

"It's not a problem. I have someone who can pick him up from school. She watches him for me whenever I need her. She lives next door."

"That's great to hear." Austin didn't have a problem with her bringing Emery, but Jordin had forewarned him that he couldn't rush Bree where the child was concerned. She didn't bring her dates around Emery until she felt the time was right.

They spent the next sixty minutes on the phone talking. Bree hung up to call her neighbor. "Hey, Miss Sara. How are you?"

"I'm fine, sugar. How's my li'l sweetie?"

"He's doing fine," she responded with a smile. "I'm calling to see if you can watch Emery for me tomorrow evening. I'm going on a date."

"It's about time you got out and found yourself a nice man. I been praying for you."

Bree laughed. "He seems pretty nice." Just thinking about Austin sent shivers of delight down her spine.

"Now, don't you worry about Emery. I'll pick him up from school and make him some spaghetti. We'll have ourselves a good time."

"Save me a plate of spaghetti, Miss Sara." She and Emery both loved pasta. "And thank you."

"It's my pleasure, Bree. You know it's no trouble at all."

She checked on Emery, then made her way to the master bedroom.

Inside she crossed the room toward the walk-in closet. Bree pulled out a black pantsuit to wear to work the next day. She didn't like waiting until the last minute to decide on an outfit. Her eyes landed on vibrant blue maxi dress hanging in the closet.

Bree took it and hung it on the door. *I'll wear this tomorrow night.* It was the perfect "first date" dress. Not too sexy, but showed enough skin to hold Austin's attention.

She was excited. This was the first date she'd had in probably six months. Bree hadn't been sitting down twiddling her thumbs, though. Emery and her work kept her very busy. However, if things went well with Austin; her schedule might open a bit more.

Bree had a good feeling about him. Jordin had always spoken highly of Austin and she could see why. He was charismatic, bringing an air of sincerity with it. It was refreshing to be able to talk to someone who understood her field of work and showed a genuine interest in it. Bree hadn't really put too much thought into it before, but some of the guys she'd dated in the past weren't comfortable with her because they felt that she was analyzing them.

A smile lingered on her lips. There was something different about Austin. If she wasn't careful, this man would own her heart.

Bree stifled a yawn. She was exhausted, but it was still too early for her to go to bed.

She thought she heard a sound and quickly made her way to her son's room.

He had changed positions, but was sound asleep.

She stood there, watching him, her heart swelling with pride. Bree sent up a silent prayer of thanks to God for sending her this beautiful little angel.

She padded barefoot to the bookcase in the family room where the photo albums were kept on the bottom shelf. She ignored the dust gathering. There hadn't been time for dusting because of her busy schedule. Bree pulled out a small blue album—Emery's baby book, taking it with her to the couch.

You were such a tiny little thing. Fragile and amazing. From the moment Emery was placed in her arms, a fountain of love rose within her, stronger than any force she'd known. Bree traced her fingertip along the button shape of his cute little face, and gazed at those beautiful brown eyes staring up at the camera.

She drank in a last long look at Emery's innocent, sweet face, and the love within her strengthened, just as it did every time she saw her son.

The slam of the neighbors' car door cut through Bree's thoughts. She closed the album and slipped it back onto the shelf as the muted sound of voices outside shattered the peaceful silence of her home.

Chapter 4

Austin's hour-long phone conversation with Bree confirmed that he wasn't mistaken in the connection they'd made the moment they met. He had felt an immediate and total attraction. Austin looked forward to seeing her tomorrow evening and beyond.

He settled down in his favorite chair, his fingers dancing to the jazz melody playing on the iPad nearby. His heart beat with the pulse of the music.

The one good thing to come out of this situation with Jasmine was the little boy he had yet to meet. He believed that Bree was a good mother, which put him at ease. Just the short time they'd spent together, he could sense that she had a warm, loving spirit; she was intelligent and caring. There was also an undeniable magnetism building between them.

She's the type of woman I could see myself spending the rest of my life with.

The silent declaration surprised him, but it was the truth. He wasn't just attracted to her physically, he was also attracted to her mind.

A cloud of apprehension settled over him.

How would she react when he announced that he was Emery's biological father? Would it change anything between them?

Austin knew the day would come when he would have to tell Bree of his intentions. As much as he looked forward to building a relationship with Emery, he dreaded the thought that his love for his son might cause her some pain. He hoped that his relationship with Bree would be solid enough to handle the truth.

Notepad and pen in hand, Austin strode into the conference room ten minutes before the meeting was supposed to start and took a seat beside Jordin.

"I'm seeing Bree tonight," he announced in a low voice.

She stared, complete surprise on her face. "To do *what*?"

"Jordin, relax. We're having dinner together. You told me that I should get to know her—well, that's what I'm doing."

"I think it's the best approach," she responded. "But I don't want you leading her on, Austin. She doesn't deserve to be hurt."

"I have no intentions of misleading her, sis. Bree seems like a nice person and I can tell by the way she talks about Emery that she's a devoted mother."

"I can assure you that she loves that little boy with her entire being, Austin. He's happy and secure."

"I can't wait to meet him."

"You can't rush this," Jordin warned. "The goal is to get to know Bree and give her a chance to know you before you drop the baby bomb. I'm sure she's considered the possibility of Emery's biological parents looking for him one day, but I'm also sure that's not a scenario she thought could happen anytime soon. You're going to have to tell her the truth when you feel the time is right, but you need to give her a chance to see the type of man you are. The last thing you, Bree or Emery needs is an unnecessary court battle. I don't think that would be very good for any of you."

"Or you?" Austin challenged.

"Or me," Jordin conceded. "I pray she'll forgive me for keeping this from her. My only hope is that everything will work out for the best this way and she'll understand why I kept silent." She wiped her hands over her eyes. "Not to mention how the rest of the family is going to act when they learn the truth."

Their conversation came to a pause when Jadin entered the room. Austin had chosen to keep his secret just between him and Jordin.

Austin smiled at her. "Congratulations on your win in court yesterday."

"Thanks," Jadin responded. "I'm *so* glad that case is over. I'm thinking about taking next week off just to relax." She leaned back in her seat. "Lord knows I need it."

"You should do it," Jordin said. "I know how hard you've worked for the last six months preparing for trial."

Austin agreed.

"Sooo," Jadin began. "Did you make a little love connection the other night? I noticed you and Bree seemed to be in your own little world. You two talked the whole night."

He chuckled. "We had a nice conversation."

Amused, Jadin met his gaze. "I'd say it was a lot more than that, big brother."

"I'm not denying it. *I like her.*"

"That much is obvious," Jadin interjected. "So, when are you seeing her again?"

"I'm having dinner with her this evening."

Jadin clapped her hands. "Well done."

Austin turned in his chair to face her. "Your date... that's the Michael I've heard so much about? I didn't get a chance to talk to him much at Jordin's."

"That's because you were so into Bree," Jadin responded. "But yes, that's him. I intended to come alone, but he called to let me know he was in town, so I invited him to join me."

"How are things between you two?" Jordin inquired. She pushed away from the table, got up and strolled over to the coffee station.

"Good. He keeps telling me that he's committed to making our relationship work."

Etienne strolled into the room, followed by his brother Jacques.

Other members of the legal team arrived minutes later.

Austin picked up his pen as one of the secretaries passed out copies of the agenda. He hoped this meeting was not one that lasted more than a couple of hours. He wanted to leave the office no later than five o'clock. They had dinner reservations at High Cotton for six thirty, then would return to his place for coffee and dessert.

A smile formed on his lips as an image of Bree entered his mind. Austin made a mental note to ask Jordin about her favorite dessert—he figured it would be a nice way to end the evening.

Austin left the office fifteen minutes later than he'd planned.

He drove out of the Ashley Bakery parking lot, merging into the traffic. Austin pulled up to a stop light, bobbing his head to the song playing as he waited patiently for the light to change.

Austin felt the tiny hairs on the back of his neck stand up.

He glanced out the window, his eyes landing on a gorgeous woman in the car beside him. Austin gave a slight nod in greeting.

She flashed him a sexy grin and winked.

The light changed and Austin was on his way, harboring no regret for not getting her name and number. He didn't care for women who were so flirtatious. He'd had enough of that with Jasmine.

Austin pulled into an underground parking garage ten minutes later.

He got out of the car, grabbed the cake and his briefcase. He walked with purpose through the lobby and into a waiting elevator.

Austin prepped his condo, making sure it was guest ready, then hopped into the shower.

He was dressed and ready by six just in case Bree arrived earlier than expected. She struck him as a woman who was always early to avoid being late. The thought prompted a self-conscious smile.

Austin was about to retrieve a bottle of water from the refrigerator when the doorbell rang. He'd called down to the doorman and told him to send Bree up when she arrived. He stole a quick peek to his watch.

Ten after six.

Smiling, he opened the door.

The vision standing before him left him momentarily speechless.

Bree wore her hair in a mass of loose curls that fell to her shoulders. The wrap dress reached to the floor, giving him a peek of her shapely legs as she walked. He couldn't resist admiring her slender frame and soft curves. She made his temperature rise more than a little.

He wondered if she knew just how sexy she looked.

"I'm early, I know," she said. "I don't like being late anywhere."

Austin bit back his smile. "It's fine. I'm the same way." They had more in common than he would've imagined. Add this to his attraction to her…his feelings for Bree were confused and confusing. He didn't know how to describe them and was too afraid to analyze them.

Bree had opted to meet him at his place since he lived in the downtown area on Concord Street. She surveyed the contemporarily furnished condo Austin called home. She loved the acacia hardwood floors, the double balconies and the gorgeous view of the city. "You have a very nice place."

"Thank you." Austin's eyes bounced around the room. "It needs a woman's touch, though, and probably more furniture."

"I think the way it is actually fits your personality. You don't strike me as a man who likes a lot of stuff in your space. I would say that you're a minimalist. You look put together always, but you're not one to fuss over your looks. You're probably more comfortable in what you have on right now than in a suit and tie or a tuxedo."

Austin had dressed down for the evening. Long, muscled legs filled out faded jeans, and he wore a plain black T-shirt that accentuated the broadness of his torso.

"You're right," he said. "I'm impressed."

Austin grabbed his keys and they headed down to his SUV.

Ten minutes later, they were seated at a table with a scenic view of the street.

Austin had suggested High Cotton Restaurant. She had eaten there a few times, and the food was always excellent. It was her absolute favorite eatery. Bree found the atmosphere at High Cotton relaxing and the food tantalizing. Their first date was off to a great start.

"Why did you choose this place for dinner?" she asked, her gaze fixed on his handsome face.

"It's a favorite of mine," he responded. "Have you been here before?"

She grinned. "Another thing we have in common. I *love* this restaurant."

"I'm glad. I was a little reluctant to try someplace new since this is our first date. I knew what to expect here."

He ordered wine.

All around them, couples sat at tables, leaning toward each other, smiling, laughing, talking. Waitresses moved through the room serving up orders of bar food and drinks. The clink of glassware and the ripples of conversation became a white noise that hummed in the background.

Bree stared into Austin's chestnut-brown eyes and fought to hold on to the control and willpower she had developed over the past few years.

It wasn't easy.

When the waitress returned, she took their food order. Bree ordered the jumbo crab cakes while Austin chose shrimp and grits.

"Tell me more about this wonderful son of yours."

Bree was touched that Austin seemed interested in Emery. "Well, he's almost three and keeps me very busy. I'm not complaining, though. My son brings me so much joy. It's hard to put into words what it means to be a mother."

"It's clear to me that you really enjoy it."

"I've always wanted to be a mother. A short time after

Caleb and I married, I found out that my chances of having a child naturally were very slim. We decided to adopt, but then he passed away. When I felt ready emotionally, that's when I moved forward and Emery came into my life." She looked away. "That's probably more than you wanted to know on a first date."

"No, I admire you for being so transparent."

"I love my son so much—it doesn't matter that he didn't come from my body."

"He's a very lucky little boy."

Bree's eyes grew bright with unshed tears. "I'm the lucky one, Austin. I'm sure every mother says this, but I know this to be true—Emery is a very special child. He loves in such a pure way. When he smiles at me or gives me a kiss… I can't describe the feeling I get." She took a sip of her wine. "I'm sorry for going on like that."

"No need to apologize, Bree. I asked about Emery." He paused a moment before saying, "I'm sure you're just dying to show me a picture of him."

"I have many," she responded. "Would you like to see them?"

Austin nodded.

Bree pulled up some photos on her cell phone and handed it to him.

"He's a handsome little boy."

"Thank you."

She watched as Austin stared at the photos. Bree had never met a man who was so taken with Emery, especially since they hadn't even met.

Their food arrived.

"How's the crab cakes?" Austin asked.

"Delicious as always." She leaned forward and said in a low voice, "I'm trying not to devour them. Don't want to ruin your impression of me after one date."

He chuckled. "I don't think that's possible."

Bree regarded him with amusement. "I don't know if Jordin told you anything about me, but what you see is what you get."

"I like that," he responded. "I prefer to be around some-one who isn't afraid to be herself."

She wiped her mouth on her napkin. "It's the only way I know how to be."

He broke into a grin. "It's nice to meet another well-rounded individual."

Laughter rang out between them.

After dinner, they returned to his condo.

Austin had teased over dinner that he had a surprise for her. Bree couldn't imagine what it could be, and could hardly contain her excitement.

Before taking a seat in the living room, she caught glimpses into other rooms. A formal dining room and an office with floor-to-ceiling bookshelves.

In the room where she sat, a wall beyond the fireplace was covered with bookshelves filled with books. Bree settled back in the chair. It was a very nice house, shabby and comfortable, clean but not too neat. All it lacked was the warmth of a woman's touch…

"I'll be right back," Austin said before disappearing into the kitchen.

Moments later he returned with two slices of banana chocolate chip cake on plates. "Is this from Ashley Bak-ery?"

Nodding, he smiled. "Now, I have to confess that I asked Jordin about your favorite dessert, but the restau-rant was my idea."

"This is the perfect way to end the night," she mur-mured. "Thank you, Austin."

He seemed to be peering at her intently.

"What is it?"

"You are so beautiful."

Austin looked at her as if he were trying to photograph her with his eyes.

"You should try the cake," Bree said. "It's really delicious. It's also Emery's favorite."

She shifted her focus from his face to her plate. Her body ached for his touch and she didn't want to get too caught up in her own emotions. What she felt—her feelings for him had nothing to do with reason.

This is a first date. Slow down, girl.

Austin sampled the dessert. "This is really good. I've always been a carrot cake lover, but this is *good.*"

"A new convert…yeah!"

They laughed.

"I've already packaged up half of the cake for you to take home with you."

"You've just made my baby a very happy little boy. He was asking for some earlier. I'd promised him that we'd pick up a cake this weekend."

Bree was impressed with Austin's unselfish actions. He hadn't known her long, but he was interested in her likes and dislikes. He was considerate in including her son, which scored him major points with her.

Austin brought the half of the cake he'd packaged up for her. "Here you go."

Bree didn't want to keep her babysitter up too late as it was a weeknight and she usually went to bed early. She rose to her feet. "Tonight was amazing," she said. "Thank you for everything."

He moved closer, challenging Bree to deliberately shut out any awareness of him.

"I have another confession to make."

Looking up at him, she asked, "What is it?"

Bree was lifted in the cradle of Austin's arms. "There's something I've wanted to do all evening," he said, his voice just above a husky whisper.

Her body tingled when he touched her.

His lips were warm and soft, and she let go of any misgivings and kissed him back, her heart leaping. Austin was gentle and devastating as his mouth slid from hers and dropped fleeting kisses on her cheeks and her eyes.

When they parted, Bree's lips still burned from the delicious sensation of his kiss.

He walked her down to her car.

"Call or text me when you get home," Austin told her. "I want to know that you made it home safely."

"I will."

He planted another kiss on her lips.

Bree sang along with the radio all the way home.

When she arrived, a full-figured woman wearing a T-shirt and jeans came down the stairs.

"I can tell you had a good time. You practically floating right now."

Bree smiled despite herself. "Miss Sara, what are you talking about?"

"What's that in your hand?"

"He surprised me with a banana chocolate chip cake for dessert," Bree announced. "He gave me half to bring home."

"High Cotton for dinner and then your favorite cake… now that's my kinda man. I'm liking this boy already."

Bree held up her phone. "I need to text him to let him know I'm home safe."

"I made some tea," Sara announced. "Want a cup?"

She handed her neighbor the cake. "Sure. Feel free to have some cake. It's from Ashley Bakery."

"Girl, you talking my language. I'ma have a tiny slice of that cake with my tea and then I'ma go home and get in the bed."

Bree sent a quick text to Austin, then sat and talked with her neighbor while they drank tea.

When Sara left for her place, she made sure all the doors were locked, turned on the security alarm and checked on Emery. He was sound asleep, clutching a Spider-Man toy. He always took a superhero to bed with him.

She ran her fingers softly through his curls, then kissed him on the cheek.

Bree stifled a yawn as she navigated to her bedroom, where she turned on the TV and prepared a bath.

Stepping out of the bubbles fifteen minutes later, she wrapped a thick blue towel around herself and stared in the mirror. Austin's kiss still lingered on her lips. Bree closed her eyes, reliving the way he smelled and the feel of his muscles. His touch was imprinted in the places he'd touched her. It amazed her that a good-night kiss could awaken her in areas that had lain dormant since Caleb's death.

She'd gone on dates in the past, but none lasted more than a couple of months at best. Bree's focus stayed on her son and building her client base. She wanted to remarry, and had no doubt that she would when the right man came along. After an entertaining evening with Austin, she felt that he had a lot of potential in terms of a relationship.

The sound of the television in the bedroom infiltrated her musings. One of those reality shows was on. *Give me a good book any day*, she thought.

Stifling a yawn, she slipped on a nightgown, then padded into a bedroom decorated with a soothing color scheme of purple and silver-gray with black accents.

Bree was more than ready to dive into the four-poster

bed. Her day had been a long one, but so worth it, she decided.

Her summer was off to a great start.

Chapter 5

He tossed an ink pen on his desk before leaning back in his chair. For the umpteenth time that day Austin was reminded of the kiss he'd shared with Bree the previous night. A kiss he had taken before she'd been aware he was about to do so. He sucked in a sharp breath as more memories swept through his mind. Never had a woman's mouth tasted so delectable, so irresistibly sweet. He'd also learned more about his little boy. Unshed tears pricked Austin's eyes when Bree had shown him the photographs of Emery.

His arms held the memory of how she felt in them. She was warm, comforting and solid. This was the type of woman he wanted in his life. Someone he could lean on and not fall. And there would come a time when he would need her strength—Austin couldn't explain how, but he knew it to be true.

The more Austin pondered the thought, he realized that it most likely came from a conversation with his mother. Irene used to always tell him that he needed a life partner who would stand strong when he couldn't. One who would not see it as weakness.

Jasmine had called him weak once. She didn't think he

could stand up to his mother. Austin could never get her to understand that he alone made the decision to break up with her—it had nothing to do with Irene. Truth was that he never would've been with Jasmine had he listened to his mother.

Austin knew that Irene would approve of Bree. She was the type of woman his mother always said he deserved.

He felt a thread of guilt snake down his spine. Irene didn't know she was a grandmother. For that matter, Etienne knew nothing about Emery, either. Everyone was in the dark and this secret was beginning to weigh heavily on him.

An hour later Austin had finished an important document his cousin Ryker needed. He had one more file to read, which wouldn't take long. Then, before leaving for the day, he would call Bree to check in. She would be spending the evening with Jordin, Jadin and Garland—it was their girls' night out.

Bree plopped down on the sofa in her living room after a long day at work. She needed to take some downtime before heading over to Jordin's house. She was really looking forward to a night of food, drinks and merriment.

She had already stopped in at Sara's house to check on Emery. He was too busy with his new picture book to pay much attention to her.

An hour later Bree changed into a pair of jeans and a tank top. She grabbed her keys and drove to Jordin's house. She pulled in behind Garland's car and parked.

"Where's Ethan?" Bree asked. "You didn't kick him out of the house for us, did you?"

"He's spending time with his mother," Jordin responded. "They went to dinner and then they're going to see a movie. They do this twice a month."

Bree smiled. "That's really sweet. He's come a long way."

"I have you to thank for your part in this. Talking to you helped Ethan tremendously." Jordin gestured for Bree to join her. "Here…try this. It's a new recipe."

"This chocolate sauce is delicious," she said. "Are you going to put this on top of the bread pudding?"

"Yes, that was the idea. What do you think?"

"I think it's yummy as Emery would say."

Jordin chuckled.

"Where's Jadin?" Bree asked as she poured three glasses of wine. "I thought she was coming by." She handed one to Garland and one to Jordin.

"Michael's in town. He surprised her earlier today at the office."

Shaking her head, Garland uttered, "I don't know why she won't marry that man. It's obvious that she loves him."

Jordin sipped her wine. "She's sold on our grandfather's legacy of lawyers. Michael's uncle holds a chain of luxury hotels and he was thrilled for the opportunity to be the general manager for the newest one."

Bree sat her glass down on the counter. "Are you talking about the Alexander-DePaul hotels?"

"Yes." Jordin peeked into the oven to check on the bread pudding. "Malcolm Alexander is his uncle."

Arms folded across her chest, Bree leaned back against the granite countertop. "I read the story of how Robert DePaul left everything to the son nobody knew he had. I assumed he was the only child."

"Malcolm's stepbrother is Michael's father."

"How do you think he feels about the long-distance relationship?" Garland questioned.

"Jadin's the one struggling with it," Jordin stated. "She's

tried to end it a couple of times, but Michael's not going to give up on them."

"She'd better hold on to that man," Bree said. "Trust me, being single is not always fun."

"I agree," Jordin responded. "I'm really loving marriage."

"I want someone to knock me off my feet like Caleb did. I'm so ready to be married, pampered and placed on a pedestal by a man who adores me."

"Are you saying that Austin hasn't done that for you?"

She met Jordin's smile with one of her own. "He and I have a good time together. He's a lot more settled, which works for me as the older I become. But I have to admit that I'm kind of falling for him."

Bree stirred the chocolate sauce while Jordin took the bread pudding out of the oven and set it on top of a cooling rack.

"I'm pretty sure my brother feels the same way about you, too."

"I haven't introduced him to Emery yet," Bree announced.

"What are you waiting on?"

"I just feel that it's still a bit too soon," she explained. "I want to wait a bit more to see where the relationship is heading before I bring my son into it."

Bree stirred the sauce once more. "Girl, just smelling this chocolate, I can already feel myself putting on pounds. You know that's the last thing I need right now."

Garland nodded in agreement. "It does smell good."

"Bree, you look great," Jordin told her. "The last thing you need to worry about is weight gain."

"Don't get me wrong, I'm happy with the way I look," she quickly explained. "I just don't want to have to buy new clothes."

Jordin chuckled. "Girl, all I need is an excuse to shop."

"I know. I used to hate going to the mall with you—we'd be there all day long."

"That's why I always treat you to a power breakfast so that we could build up your strength."

Laughing, Bree shook her head. "Since we're on the topic of shopping, what did you buy yesterday? You were leaving some store when I called you."

"That's right," Jordin murmured. "Let's go to my bedroom and get them."

She returned moments later with a shopping bag.

"Aren't these adorable?" Jordin asked, holding up two pink and lavender dresses with matching hats.

"Precious..." Bree murmured.

"Did you get those for the girls?" Garland asked, referring to her young daughters.

Jordin nodded. "When I saw them, I just couldn't resist."

"Kai and Amya are going to love them." Garland fingered one of the dresses. "They're gorgeous."

"And I got this for little R.J. I bought this outfit because the cap looks like the one Ryker wears."

Garland grinned. "He's going to look just like his daddy."

Jordin pulled another outfit out of the bag. "I didn't forget my sweet Emery."

Bree took the gray linen suit from her. "This is so cute. It's adorable." She looked at her friend. "You're spoiling these kids."

"Yes, you are," Garland said. "The girls already know that they can get whatever they want from you."

"They're worth it," Jordin responded. "They're my babies."

She pulled a plate of sandwiches out of the refrigerator, placing them on the counter.

"Ethan and I are planning a cruise," Jordin announced, lounging against the door frame. "Do y'all think you'd be interested in coming with us?"

"I've never been on one," Bree said. "I don't know…"

"Please come on the cruise so that I'll have somebody to hang out with when Ethan's playing basketball or golf or whatever guy stuff he can get into."

"What about Austin? Have you invited him?" Bree asked. "I don't want to be a third wheel if I decide to come."

"I plan on asking him, but wanted to ask you first before I said anything to him."

"I have to think about this for a moment," Bree said.

"Is this going to be a couple's vacation or a family one?" Garland inquired, wedging herself into the seat next to her.

"It's up to you all," Jordin responded. "It'll work either way for me and Ethan."

"Give me all the information and I'll let you know for sure."

Jordin opened the refrigerator and pulled out a couple of steaks. "We're planning for next summer, so we have some time."

Garland munched on some chips. "What are you doing?"

"Taking the steaks out for dinner tomorrow."

Bree broke into a grin. "Aren't you quite the home-maker."

Jordin nodded. "Hey, I need to feed my husband or some other woman will be more than happy to do it for me."

She nodded in agreement. "I love seeing you so happy."

Jordin met her gaze. "I'm over the moon, Bree. I love

being married and I can't wait to be a mother. I'm so ready for a family."

"You're going to be a great mother."

Jordin's expression grew somber. "How have you been feeling lately?"

"Some months are much better than others," Bree said.

Garland inquired, "Are the treatments helping?"

"Not as much as I'd like. The pain can be overbearing at times."

"Bree, I'm so sorry you have to suffer like that," Jordin stated. "Endometriosis is nothing to play with."

"It's a horrible disease," she responded. "But I've learned to live with it."

Bree sampled the white chocolate bread pudding. *"You did that..."*

Jordin beamed with pride. "You really think so?"

"Yes. This is *soo* good."

Garland agreed.

Bree rose in one fluid motion. "I'm just going to have a tiny bit more."

"Girl, dig in," Jordin told her. "You're in the gym three days a week. You can afford to treat yourself."

"Chocolate *is* a girl's best friend," Garland interjected. "Bree, how do you like dating a DuGrandpre?"

"It's not something I ever thought I'd be doing," she said. "But that's because Ryker was the only male I knew and he was married."

"Did you ever meet Angela?" Garland asked, referring to Ryker's first wife, who died in childbirth.

"I did," Bree replied. "Shortly after she and Ryker got married. She was really nice to me."

"Sometimes I wonder if he's thinking of her when he looks at Amya," Garland confessed. "She looks more and more like Angela the older she gets. It's fine if he does...

I just want Ryker to feel comfortable talking about her. I won't feel threatened in any way. Besides, Amya will have questions one day."

"Maybe you should bring her up," Bree suggested. "This will open up an opportunity for Ryker to talk about Angela. Let him know that it doesn't bother you if he wants to talk about their life together."

Jordin agreed. "I love a good love story. The one you're writing with Ryker is inspiring."

"Yes, it is," Bree murmured. "The two of you give me hope."

Garland took a sip of her wine. "From where I'm sitting, it looks like you're writing your own love story with Austin."

She broke into a grin. "Well, I have to admit that we have a lot of sexual tension but we haven't gotten to the chapter where we fall into bed and make wild, passionate love."

"Do you think it's heading in that direction?" Jordin asked. "It's still pretty early in your relationship."

"I don't know, but it's not something I'm dwelling on. You know me...my focus is on being a mother to Emery. I'm not thirsty for a man. It's just nice to have someone like Austin to spend time with. *He is sexy, though.*"

Jordin screwed up her face. "Okay, don't need to hear that..."

They laughed.

"Seriously, though, take your time with Austin," Jordin said. "I don't want to see either of you hurt."

Bree eyed her friend and wondered why Jordin seemed worried about her relationship with Austin. Especially since she initially seemed to be pushing her toward him. Bree had no doubt that Jordin's dinner party had been engineered to introduce them.

After Garland left, she stayed behind to talk to Jordin.

"Hey, something's bothering me," Bree said. "Do you think I'm making a mistake by spending time with your brother?"

"No, of course not. Why would you ask me that?"

Bree shrugged. "I don't know…it was something in your eyes, and then you suggested that we take things slow."

"I only meant that you've both gone through a lot. I *want* you two to be together, Bree. I think you're perfect for each other."

Bree picked up her purse. "I just wanted to be sure because I really like him." Breaking into a smile, she added, "The truth is that I'm crazy about Austin."

The weekend had come and gone. She'd gone to the movies Saturday night with Austin and they'd had a great time together. She really enjoyed his company.

Bree had ended her call with a colleague and was about to head to the kitchen to make blackened salmon for dinner when her cell phone rang again. Her heartbeat quickened when she saw it was Austin.

What was that shivering about? she wondered. Why was she reacting this way to his phone call?

She clicked on her phone. "Hello?"

"Hey, how was your day?"

Bree wished that he didn't sound as good as he looked. Or that when he had arrived to pick her up for dinner last night, he'd not been dressed as though he'd jumped off the page of a men's fashion magazine. Austin always showed impeccable manners by escorting her to his car and opening the door for her. However, it wasn't his manners she appreciated the most.

It was those sexy eyes and handsome face that had

taken her breath away. Bree sighed softly now as the memory rushed through her mind. Only then did she recall the question he had just asked her. "It was fine." Bree nibbled on her bottom lip. "How was yours?"

"My day was good," he responded. "I'm glad it's over, though. Right now, I just want to relax."

"You sound tired. We can cancel tonight if you want."

"No, I want to see you," Austin said. "But if you don't mind, I'd like to just stay in. You can come over here or I'll come to your place—it's up to you. It won't be a late night."

"Just come over here," she responded. "Emery is with Miss Sara. Would you like me to cook something?"

"No, I'll pick up dinner for us."

"Great… I guess I'll see you later, then."

Two hours later Bree opened the door to let Austin inside.

They stood staring at one another with longing. There was no denying that they shared an intense physical awareness of each other.

Without warning, he swung her into the circle of his arms, holding her snugly. He kissed her, sending her stomach into a wild swirl.

Austin's kiss was surprisingly gentle, yet it sent a brief shiver rippling through Bree. She buried her face against the corded muscles of his chest. She had no desire to back out of his embrace.

"I'm so glad you're here."

He gazed down at her with tenderness. "I will be here for as long as you need me."

Parting her lips, Bree raised herself on tiptoe, touching her lips to his.

His lips pressed against hers, then gently covered her

mouth. The kiss sent the pit of Bree's stomach into a wild swirl.

Austin showered her with kisses around her lips and along her jaw. As he roused her passion, his own grew stronger.

This time it was Bree who slowly pulled away. She took him by the hand and led him over to the sofa. She settled back, enjoying the feel of his arms around her.

They sat like this for a while before Bree rose to her feet, saying, "We'd better eat before the food gets cold."

Austin stood up and followed her to the dining room table.

She pulled the containers out of a plastic bag.

They made small talk while they ate.

"Watching Jordin get married—it reminded me of how much I miss being a wife."

Austin wiped at a fleck of food on her cheek. "Do you ever think about getting married again?"

"You want the truth?" she asked.

Austin nodded.

"I definitely want to get married again. To be honest… since I met you, I've been thinking about how long it's been since I've been this close to a man. How long it's been since I've kissed a man or made love." She raised her eyes to meet his. "It's been a while."

"Same here," Austin murmured.

"Just so you know… I'm not trying to seduce you," Bree interjected quickly. "I'm just being honest."

"I appreciate that."

She chuckled. "You look a little disappointed." Deep down, Bree had to fight her own overwhelming need to be close to him.

"Just a little," Austin murmured.

They found a movie on television to distract them from what they were feeling.

Bree made popcorn during a commercial break.

She didn't miss the way his gaze was riveted on her face, then moved over her body slowly. It was a definite turn-on.

Bree handed him the bowl, then reclaimed her seat beside him.

His arms encircled her, one hand in the small of her back. She relaxed, sinking into his cushioning embrace.

When the movie ended, Austin checked his watch and rose to his feet. "I'd better get going. It's getting late. I want you to know that I heard what you said and I respect that."

He brushed a gentle kiss across her forehead. "Good night, sweetheart."

She felt a certain sadness that their day was ending.

When he left, Bree jumped into the shower, hoping the stream of water would cool down the desire she felt deep within.

It was to no avail.

The fire Austin ignited in her refused to be extinguished.

Chapter 6

"I'm taking Emery to see the Fourth of July fireworks tonight," Bree announced over the phone. "I would invite you to join us, but…"

"I understand, sweetheart," Austin said. Deep down he felt a wave of disappointment. This was going to be his son's first time seeing the fireworks display and Austin wouldn't be there to share it with him.

"So, what are you doing today?"

"Uncle Jacques is hosting a cookout. I'm going to go there for a bit."

"I'm going to miss seeing you."

"Same here," he responded. "But we're still on for Saturday, right?"

"Actually, I promised Emery that we'd have pizza and go see a movie. I'm sorry."

"You have nothing to apologize for," Austin said. "A friend of mine is getting married at the end of the month. I'd like for you to be my plus one. The wedding's in Phoenix, Arizona, though. I know you have Emery… Are you able to get away?"

The thought of going away with him was tantalizing, the anticipation almost unbearable. "I'd love to go."

"Great. I'll book a two-bedroom suite for us."

"I'd appreciate that." Bree tried to ignore the smoldering flame burning through her. Austin was a temptation that she found hard to resist, but she wasn't about to turn down a chance to spend the weekend with him.

The following week, Austin worked until late in the evening, preparing for a case. He missed spending time with Bree, but spoke with her almost daily.

Her schedule was also hectic, but he loved that she made sure to leave her office early enough to have dinner with her son most nights. He knew she had an evening group therapy session once a week.

Austin stared at the stack of documents on his desk and sighed. He was in for another late night at the office.

"Knock knock…"

He glanced up at the entrance and smiled. "What are you doing here?"

"I thought I'd bring you something to eat," Bree responded.

He rose to his feet and crossed the floor in quick strides. Austin kissed her. "Thank you."

"I also wanted to see you, if only for a few minutes. I need to get home to Emery."

Austin smiled. "I'm glad you came by."

"I wish I could stay longer, but I really have to go."

He nodded in understanding, while hiding his disappointment.

Bree planted a kiss on his cheek. "Call me later."

"I won't be leaving here until after eleven or so. I'll call you tomorrow."

She glanced over at his desk. "Have fun."

"Yeah," Austin muttered.

Austin and Bree checked into the Alexander-DePaul Hotel in Phoenix. He was relieved when the plane finally landed in Arizona.

Austin sat down in one of the overstuffed chairs. "This is a nice suite."

Staring out a window, Bree agreed. "I just saw the shower in my bathroom and it can fit at least three people in it."

"What are you suggesting, sweetheart?" Austin asked. His gaze was riveted on her face, then moved over her body slowly.

"*Mr. DuGrandpre*, get your mind out of the gutter." Bree found herself extremely conscious of his virile appeal.

Rising to his feet, Austin chuckled. "You were the one who painted this picture in my head." Joining her at the window, he swung her into the circle of his arms. "Not to mention, I'm in this luxury suite with a very beautiful and sexy woman."

He kissed Bree, sending the pit of her stomach into a wild swirl. His lips seared a path down her neck, her shoulders, with tantalizing persuasion.

There was a knock on the door.

She glanced over at him. "Are you expecting someone?"

Nodding, Austin got up and crossed the room in quick strides. "I ordered some lunch for us."

He opened the door to allow the waiter to enter, pushing a cart.

She rose to her feet, moving to stand beside him.

Bree smiled. "Wow. You are full of surprises."

"I heard your stomach growling when we got off the plane," Austin teased.

She elbowed him in the arm as they silently observed the waiter as he placed their dinner on the table.

"So, what are we having?" Bree whispered.

"For starters, we're having seared scallops with bacon, Mediterranean salad and garlic brick chicken."

She rubbed her hands together. "Sounds delicious."

He loved that she was so easy to please.

Austin signed the check and gave the waiter a twenty-dollar tip.

They sat down at the dining table to eat.

He quickly blessed the food before they dived in.

Bree could feel him watching her. "Shouldn't you be concentrating on your food?" she asked.

"I can't believe we're here like this," he confessed. Austin's eyes traveled over her face and then slid downward. "I'm glad we are, though."

"I'm glad, too." Bree wiped her mouth with the edge of her napkin. "It's nice to get away every now and then. I had a crazy week, so this is perfect timing for me."

He stuck a forkful of food into his mouth and chewed slowly. Austin swallowed, then said, "I agree. I enjoy mini vacations."

She took a sip of her ice water. "Another thing we have in common."

"I guess there's nothing left for us to do except get married."

Bree laughed. "Definitely."

The air around them suddenly seemed electrified.

After they finished eating, she pushed away from the table and stood up. "Lunch was amazing," she murmured. "Now I'm going to have to spend the rest of the afternoon in the gym."

"Why don't you get a massage instead?" Austin suggested. "I've scheduled one for you later this afternoon."

"You're too good to me," she murmured.

"This view is incredible," Bree told Austin as they sat out on the balcony, watching the moon and stars. "I could sit here for hours just looking at the stars in the sky and at the city below."

He took a sip of his hot tea. "I could sit here all night watching you."

She stretched and yawned.

"Uh-huh…"

She glanced over at Austin. "Uh-huh *what*?"

"It's past midnight," he announced. "We should probably go to bed." Although he wasn't ready for the evening to end, Austin could tell that Bree was tired.

"But we're having such a good time together." She yawned a second time.

"And you can barely keep your eyes open. Let me walk you to your room." A shiver of wanting ran down Austin's spine. He moved toward her, impelled involuntarily by his own passion.

Bree shook her head. "I can make it across the hall by myself," she told him. "If you walk me over there—I know that I won't be strong enough to let you come back to your own room. I'll see you in the morning."

When she left, Austin headed to the bathroom. He was in desperate need of a cold shower.

Bree took an instant dislike to everything she had packed for the trip and now wished that she had gone shopping earlier.

After her shower, Bree changed into an emerald-green Tadashi dress.

"This is so not me," she mumbled as she stared at her reflection in the floor-length mirror.

Next, she slipped on another dress that she'd snagged on sale at a boutique the day before they left Charleston.

"Not bad," she whispered.

Bree changed again, this time into a Vera Wang silk halter dress in a vivid purple color. She slipped on a pair of silver-and-amethyst jeweled sandals with straps that wrapped around her ankles. Bree added an amethyst ring, white gold and amethyst bangles with matching earrings to complete her look.

She placed makeup on her face with a light touch.

Bree smiled as she looked at herself in the mirror, satisfied with what she saw.

She glanced at her watch.

She had twenty minutes, and the last thing she had to do was her hair. She undid her twists and fingered through her hair, combing through the waves.

Bree could hear Austin moving about in the living room and wondered how he would respond when she stepped outside the bedroom.

His gaze gave her body a timeless sweep and she felt her heartbeat quicken.

"You look stunning," he said.

"Thanks. You look nice yourself."

They were soon on their way to the wedding location.

He backed out of the driveway. "I have to warn you that Will and Jade are a unique couple."

"I don't think I'm going to be too surprised. In my line of work, I've come to meet some *different* people," she said, noticing the smooth sound of the SUV's engine as he drove down the street.

Austin brought the car to a stop at a traffic light.

"How long have you known Will?" Bree questioned.

"Since high school. I've known Jade since law school. I introduced them when he came for my graduation."

They pulled up for valet parking.

Bree noted the immaculate building with a backdrop of mountains that housed the hotel. The architecture probably dated back to the eighteen hundreds, she decided. "Nice."

"It's an old hotel. The owners renovated it a few years ago—Will was one of the interior designers."

Austin offered her his arm, which she took. He had brought her here with him tonight and she intended to enjoy herself.

Austin escorted Bree into the hotel. As they neared the ballroom, she slowed her steps, surveying poster-size drawings of the bride and groom.

"Will drew them," he said.

"He did a great job."

Two tall statues of women stood on either side of the door.

"Oh, my goodness," she whispered. "Austin, they're real people. She blinked."

At the sound of a harpist playing, he said, "We'd better take our seats."

They were seated three rows from the front.

Bree glanced down at the wedding program and chuckled. The front read: *So, You're Going to Sit Through a Wedding: A Practical Guide to Not Falling Asleep.*

"I have to warn you that Will and Jade are very unconventional," Austin whispered. "So, expect just about anything with this wedding."

"Okay," she said.

Bree glanced around, noting that several people seated on the end of the row had flowers in hand. It was not something she was used to seeing at weddings. *This is going to be interesting.*

The bridesmaids, dressed in a vivid rainbow of colors, made their entrance.

Jade made her grand entrance on the arm of her father. She stopped to collect the flowers, building her bouquet along the way to the altar.

When it was time for the bride and groom to say their vows, they played rock, paper and scissors to determine who would go first in saying their vows.

Bree chuckled.

"I told you," Austin whispered. "You never know what to expect with these two."

Jade won and spoke first. "Long ago you were just a dream for me. Thank you for being what you are to me. I love, honor and protect you. Will, I give you my heart for eternity, my friend and my love."

Bree's eyes grew wet. She blinked rapidly to keep her tears from falling.

It was Will's turn to speak. "Jade, I love you, baby. Through all the uncertainties and trials of the present and future, I promise to be faithful to you and love you as long as we both shall live."

Austin reached over and took her hand in his.

The bride and groom exchanged rings and before the pastor could get the words out of his mouth, Will captured Jade's lips with his own.

Laughter and applause erupted around the room.

"I present to you all, Mr. and Mrs. William Manning."

More applause followed.

Wedding guests were led to another room across the hall for the reception. The soft glow of the candles highlighted the hues of purple, teal, orange and traces of gold in the tablecloths. Each table featured edible centerpieces on marble slabs of cascading cheese, cracker and fruit. Marinated olives were placed in stoneware on each table for guests to savor.

"The ceremony was unique but beautiful," Bree said.

Austin wrapped an arm around her. "I like the idea of the human statues."

She flashed him a grin. "It was definitely a nice touch. People can't stop talking about them."

He pulled a chair out for her at their designated table. Bree sat down.

Austin sat down next to her. "Thanks for coming with me."

"It's been a nice little getaway." She ran her fingers through her hair. "I needed a break."

"I know you miss Emery."

She nodded. "I do. I called to check on him earlier and he hurt my feelings a little. He was watching *The LEGO Movie* and didn't have time to talk to me."

"I'm sure when you call back, he will be more than ready to have a conversation with you."

Bree placed her hand in his. "Thank you for saying that."

"Would you like to dance?" Austin asked her.

"I love dancing. I just haven't done it in a long time," she said, taking him by the hand.

Bree walked slowly, her body swaying to the music. "I *love* this song."

Austin escorted her to the middle of the dance floor and began dancing to the music.

One song ended and another began while they were still on the dance floor.

They left the reception right after the bride and groom departed.

Back at the hotel, Bree made a cup of green tea with co-

conut and enjoyed the beautiful view of downtown Phoenix out the hotel window. She took a deep breath, then sipped her tea, hoping it would stop her heart from hammering.

The erratic pounding in her chest had started when Austin had removed his shirt as he strolled across the carpet to the other bedroom. It was as if knowing they were under the same roof and breathing the same air was getting to her.

Separating the two bedrooms was a spacious living room, workspace and dining area, but being in the same suite with such a handsome man… Bree took another deep breath and exhaled slowly.

Trying to put thoughts of Austin out of her mind, she turned back to the view.

There's a full moon tonight. It's so beautiful… I could stand here all night looking at it.

The hotel was in the thick of downtown and the surrounding buildings were massive and numerous, but she still had a beautiful view of the mountains.

"Bree?"

She gasped at the sound of her name and turned from the window.

Austin stood naked except for his pajama pants, which rode low on his hips, looking sexier than he had earlier that night.

"Yes?"

"Why aren't you in bed?"

His masculine scent reached out to Bree, sending her entire body into a heated tailspin.

"I thought you were sleeping," she said, trying to stay in control.

A slow smile touched his lips and her body tingled in response.

The erratic pounding in her chest returned.

Had it truly ever left?

"I couldn't sleep." He rubbed a hand over his face. "You should probably try to get some rest. We have an early flight in the morning."

Bree glanced down at her empty cup and came up with the perfect excuse to leave the living room. "I've finished my tea. Maybe sleep will come now."

When she walked past him, Austin reached out, taking the cup from her hand and placing it on the end table before wrapping a strong arm around her waist and pulling her to him.

His head lowered to hers.

Soon she was kissing him as hungrily as he was kissing her. Bree molded her body to his as if it was the most natural thing, and instinctively wrapped her arms around his neck. Desire felt like talons sinking into her skin, spreading through her body in a heated rush, making her moan deep in her throat.

Bree reluctantly broke off the kiss and unwrapped her arms from his neck before taking in a deep breath. "Self-control, girl," she whispered.

"What did you say, sweetheart?" he asked, dipping his head low to hers.

She stared up into his penetrating, chestnut-brown eyes and wondered if Austin had any idea that they were an aphrodisiac. Just staring into their depths caused crazy things to happen to her.

"Bree?" he prompted.

She recalled he had asked her a question and decided to be honest. "I'm trying to talk myself out of taking something that I want."

He lifted a brow. "Really?"

"Yes."

He placed his hand on her shoulder. "Keep talking. Maybe you can convince us both."

Bree kissed him on the cheek. "Good night, Austin."

His lips curved into a smile. "I'll see you in the morning, sweetheart."

Chapter 7

The August weather was nice and warm, perfect for a day on the golf course. Austin spent the morning with his father at the country club in Charleston trying to learn the game.

He was a novice and found the game was not as easy as he first imagined. "I hope I'm not embarrassing you too much," he said.

Etienne laughed. "You need to learn how to hold the golf club the proper way. That's part of the problem. Keep your grip light."

Austin did as his father instructed, but his heart wasn't in it. He wanted to shout for joy when the lesson came to an end.

On the way to the car, Etienne said, "I want you to know that I'm very proud of the man you've become, Austin."

"You're not just saying that because I became a lawyer, are you?"

He chuckled. "You've heard the whole DuGrandpre legacy story."

Austin nodded. "From Grandfather when he came to visit. He sent me brochures from the top law schools."

"My father had a grand vision of building a family of lawyers. He never seemed to understand that not everyone in the family shared that vision."

"Was there something else you wanted to do?"

"When I was younger, I wanted to be in law enforcement. I pictured myself an FBI man, but my father—he was against the very idea. I didn't want to disappoint him, so I studied law. It wasn't until I started law school that I developed a passion for it. I think my father knew all along that this is where I belonged."

Etienne looked at Austin. "How about you?"

"I wanted to be a forensic psychologist or a profiler." He chuckled. "I guess I thought of myself as an FBI man, as well."

"Like father like son…"

Austin nodded. "I guess so."

"How's your love life?"

"It's funny you bring this up," Austin responded. "I've met someone I really like."

"Good. When do we get to meet her?"

"You already have, Dad. It's Jordin's friend Bree."

"Ah…the beautiful Dr. Collins. She has a little boy, you know? You have to want the whole package if you expect to have a relationship with her."

Austin nodded. "I'm looking forward to meeting her son."

"How long have you two been dating?"

"A couple of months now, which is why I haven't met Emery, but I really like her."

"Are you ready to settle down?"

"I am," Austin responded. "If I wait too much longer, I'll be too old to teach my children how to play anything other than golf."

Etienne laughed. "I guess that'll fall on me."

"Dad, I hate this game."

"Tell me this. How do you feel about bowling?"

"Now you're speaking my language," Austin said. "I know how to bowl and I'm pretty good at it."

"Let's get out of here," Etienne suggested. "They have a fantastic buffet at the country club."

Minutes later they were seated at a table dining on garlic lime chicken, grilled asparagus with lime dressing, four-cheese mashed potatoes with wild mushrooms and onion bread.

"The chef outdid herself," Etienne whispered to him.

Austin agreed. He sliced off a piece of the tender chicken and stuck it into his mouth, savoring the flavor. "Everything is delicious."

After lunch, he drove home to shower and change. He was meeting up with Bree in a couple of hours. Although he was trying to be patient, Austin wanted to meet Emery. He appreciated the information from Jordin and the tidbits shared by Bree, but he desired to meet the little boy.

Austin hummed softly as he pulled into the parking garage connected to the building where he lived.

Inside the condo, Austin walked straight to the bathroom. He showered, slipped into a robe and settled down in the sitting room to watch television. He had enough time to relax before his date.

He lay back with his eyes closed, dreaming of the day when he and Emery could hang out as father and son.

Bree spent the day with Emery, painting in the park.

"Lookit, Mommy. Look at my picture."

"Honey, it's beautiful. Is that the house over there?"

He nodded. "I made it for you."

Her cell phone rang.

"Hey, girl," Jordin greeted. "Emery's still staying with us tonight, right?"

"Yes. Thanks for this. I'm not ready for him to meet Austin yet. I need to see where this relationship is going."

There was a slight pause, then Jordin responded, "Not a problem. Ethan and I love having him with us. We're practicing for our own child."

"Really? You guys are trying to get pregnant?"

"Yeah. I'm looking forward to starting a family."

"I think it's wonderful, Jordin."

"You're cooking a romantic dinner tonight at your house…hmmm… Are you planning for this to turn into a sleepover?"

Bree chuckled. "It's just dinner. We're not at the point for sleepovers."

They talked a few minutes more before ending the call.

She and Emery stayed another half hour at the park.

"We need to pack your bag," Bree said when they arrived home. "Auntie Jordin is coming to pick you up soon."

"Yeah…"

"Which pajamas do you want to sleep in? Batman or Spider-Man?"

"Ninja Tuttles," he uttered.

Emery put his hands to his face and cracked up with laughter.

"You're so silly." Her heart was so full of love for the little boy crawling around on the floor. "My silly little man."

"Mommy, I love you."

"I love you more, baby."

Once his bag was packed, Bree gave him a bath.

He was dressed and impatient by the time Jordin arrived.

"Girl, he thought you weren't coming," Bree said. "He

asked me at least twenty times when you were going to get here."

"Oh, honey, Auntie's sorry for running late. My dad came over and we were talking. I'm sorry."

"I okay now." Emery reached for her hand. "Can we go?"

"You're ready to leave Mommy?"

He nodded. "I be back."

Bree kissed him. "Have fun with Auntie Jordin and Uncle Ethan."

Jordin glanced over at her. "*You* have fun tonight."

Austin knocked on Bree's front door shortly after eight. He had stopped to pick up Thai food for them.

"You look beautiful," he whispered, making Bree's heart swell.

"How did your golf lesson go?" She walked into the kitchen and took a couple of plates from the cabinet.

"We're going to go bowling next time. I had to break down and tell my dad that I have no interest whatsoever in golf. It's just not for me."

"How did he take it?"

"Very well," Austin stated. "I got the impression that he isn't that crazy about the sport, either."

They dined on a spicy shrimp soup, red chicken curry and fried rice.

"You look beautiful," Austin murmured in her ear. "In case I haven't told you already."

"You mentioned it."

Their feet moved to the slow rhythm of "If I Was Your Man," while Austin pulled her firmly against him. The heat of his skin radiated through his white shirt, warming her in the evening cool. Her eyes closed as his fingers tightened around hers, and Bree rested her head against his shoulder.

The song ended and they pulled apart.

As if going with instinct, Austin refused to relinquish her hand as she started to step away. Instead he gave it a gentle tug, pulling her back into his arms. He smiled, his teeth flashing in the candlelight.

He kissed her.

They smiled at each other a long time, until Austin quietly commented, "This feels nice...being here with you like this."

"I agree," she murmured.

"I want more nights like this."

Bree's eyes widened in surprise. "I'm not quite sure what you mean by that."

"I'm not one for partying and hanging at the club. I like what we did tonight—a quiet dinner and dancing." Austin looked at her. "I hope it didn't just get weird between us."

"It didn't." She picked another chocolate-covered strawberry off the platter. "I asked because I don't like to assume."

Austin poured white wine into the glasses, then handed one to her.

"Thank you." Bree took a sip. "I was never much into clubbing. I know it sounds strange since Caleb was a musician. The only time I ever went to a club was when he performed."

He was staring at one of the photos of Emery, prompting a smile on her lips. "I would introduce you, but I don't want to rush it. I hope you understand. Maybe I'm overprotective, but I want his life to have the consistency that mine didn't. Having him get attached to someone and then lose him..."

"You're doing the right thing. He doesn't need to meet every man you date."

"I'm glad we're on the same page, Austin."

"I will meet him one day," he responded. "I don't plan on going anywhere."

"I must admit that I like the sound of that, because I'm not looking for a casual relationship. I'm more of the marrying type."

"Once again, we're on the same page."

Instead of going home, Austin drove to the neighborhood where Jordin and Ethan lived.

He wanted a glimpse of his son.

"Austin, is something wrong?"

"I'm sorry for coming by so late, but I wanted to see Emery. I know he's sleeping and I promise I won't wake him. I just need to see him for myself."

He followed her upstairs to the room where Emery lay sleeping.

His heart filled and overflowed with love as his gaze soaked up the sight of his son for the first time. Austin wanted a closer look, but dared not take the chance of disturbing him. He remained in the doorway for a few minutes before returning downstairs.

He found Jordin in the kitchen, making a cup of tea.

"It's hard to believe that my little boy is in there sleeping. I still can't tell who he resembles most."

"He's a cutie." Jordin gestured toward the Keurig. "Would you like some tea or coffee?"

"I'm fine."

They heard the garage door going up.

"Ethan's home," Jordan announced. "I know you don't want too many people knowing, but I think it's time we told him about Emery. I don't like keeping secrets from him. You don't have to worry. He's very discreet."

"That's fine."

Ethan entered the house through the garage. "Hey…

Austin, I didn't know you were here. I thought you were seeing Bree tonight."

Jordin planted a quick kiss on Ethan's lips. "We need to tell you something, honey."

He looked from his wife to Austin. "What's going on?"

"Emery's my biological son."

"Excuse me?"

"My ex-girlfriend never told me about the baby. She left town when we broke up, then had the baby and gave him up for adoption. After a long search, I've learned that Bree was the adopter."

Ethan's shock was written all over his face. "Does Bree know?"

"Not yet." Austin glanced over at his sister, then said, "I plan to tell her."

"You should've told her before you two got involved."

"I told him to wait," Jordin confessed. "I know Bree and this is not something she's going to handle well. It's better that she gets to know Austin first."

"Okay, I get that," Ethan said, "but your brother's dating her. If you prolong this, I don't think it's going to end well."

"I intend to tell Bree when the time is right."

"Honey, no one else knows about this," Jordin interjected. "Just the three of us."

"I won't say a word, but I think you both need to talk to Bree before she finds out another way."

When Ethan went upstairs, Austin glanced at his sister. "Your husband's not happy about this."

"He doesn't like secrets," Jordin stated.

"I don't, either. I hate keeping Bree in the dark like this, but I need to gain her trust. I need her as an advocate and not an enemy when I go back to court. Although Emery is my son, the courts can decide not to reverse the adoption."

"Would that be so bad?"

"Jordin, if that happens, I won't have any say in my son's life. If things with Bree go sour—I could lose him and I'm not going to let that happen. I intend to make sure no one will be able to just take Emery from me again."

"I understand what you're saying, Austin." Jordin paused a moment before asking, "I need to know something. Do you really care for Bree?"

"Of course I do."

"She doesn't deserve to be played."

"My feelings for her are genuine, Jordin. You don't have anything to worry about, sis." Austin rose to his feet. "Thanks for the coffee and for letting me see Emery. I'm going to leave so you and your hubby can talk."

"You and Bree are good for each other. I want this to work out for all of you."

"So do I," he muttered.

Jordin walked him to the door. "I'll see you tomorrow."

Back at his condo, Austin paced the living room floor. He wasn't so sure that he'd handled this situation with Bree the right way. Maybe it was better to put some distance between them.

He put his hands to his face. *Did I handle this all wrong?*

Maybe it would be better to end things with her now, Austin thought sadly. He had fallen in love with her and the idea of walking away pained him.

Chapter 8

He'd made his decision.

Austin was on his way to see Bree. He was going to tell her everything before they went to dinner. He didn't think it wise to discuss such a sensitive topic in a public place.

She was at her office and requested that he pick her up from there. Her neighbor's car was disabled, so she'd let Sara use her vehicle.

"Sweetheart, can we talk?" Austin asked when he arrived. Her staff had already left for the day, so they were alone in the office.

"Sure," she responded while peering into her computer. "There's something I need to discuss with you. I just need to make a quick note in this file and then I'm done."

Moments later she turned off her computer screen and joined him on the sofa.

Austin reached over and took her hand in his. "Bree, we've been together for a few months now, but I feel like I've known you forever."

She smiled. "I feel the same way about you. That's why I wanted to talk to you. You've become very important to me, Austin. Because of that, I think it's time you met my son."

He was surprised by her words. "Are you sure?"

Bree gave a slight nod. "I'm positive. Instead of going out, why don't we eat in…the three of us. Emery doesn't have a father figure in his life. As much as I love him, I can't teach Emery how to be a man. He needs a positive role model. It should be you, Austin."

He kissed her.

"I promise I will be here for you and Emery. Nothing will ever change that. I can't put into words how much I care about you." Austin held her close. He was finally going to meet his son. To tell her now would likely change that—it wasn't a risk he was willing to take.

"Thanks for watching Emery, Miss Sara."

"It's my pleasure. You know how much I love that li'l boy. He's just so precious." Her gaze traveled to Austin. "Now, who is this handsome man?"

"This is Austin DuGrandpre."

"Whose son are you?"

"Etienne," he responded.

She seemed pleased with his response. "He represented my father several years ago. Your daddy is a good man."

The moment had finally arrived for father to finally come face-to-face with his son.

A little curly-haired boy burst into the room. "Mommy…" He peered at Austin and slowed his steps.

"Sweetie, I want you to meet someone," Bree said. "This is Austin. He's your aunt Jordin's brother and he's having dinner with us tonight. Can you say hello?"

"Hel-lo…" He clung to her like a lifeline.

Austin felt an instant's squeezing hurt. He reminded himself that this was their first meeting. Bree had mentioned in conversation that Emery was shy when it came to meeting new people.

He kneeled so that he was eye level with his son. "I hear that you like Batman. Superman, the Hulk and Ninja Turtles."

Emery smiled. "Spider-Man."

"I like him, too."

The little boy looked up at Bree in expectation.

"Austin," she said.

"Au'tin."

He blinked rapidly to keep his tears from falling. Austin spied a Spider-Man toy on the floor in the family room. "Hey, why don't you show me your superheroes?"

"'Kay…" Smiling, Emery went off to his room.

"You know he's going to bring out every toy he has," Bree said with a soft chuckle.

"I'll help clean up."

She seemed surprised by his words.

"I'm serious," Austin stated. "I love playing superheroes. When I was a little boy, I wanted to be Superman."

"C'mon Au'tin."

"I'm coming, buddy." He winked at Bree before walking briskly to join Emery in his bedroom. This was the moment Austin had been dreaming of since he first found out about the little boy.

Joy, like a sunburst, went off inside Bree as she watched the man who had come to mean so much to her spending time with her son.

She could hear them laughing and talking while she prepared dinner. Bree counted herself fortunate to have Austin in her life. Her feelings for him grew stronger each day. There was a time when she refused to even consider the idea of marrying again, but now, she found herself looking forward to the future—hopefully one that included Austin.

The trio enjoyed dinner together. Afterward, Austin and Emery settled into the family room while Bree cleaned the kitchen.

Fifteen minutes later, Bree entered the room, pausing to watch Emery pushing a car toward Austin. She was amazed at how good he was with children. She felt a moment's sadness that she couldn't have a child with him. He would be a great father.

Slow down, girl.

Austin looked up at her and smiled.

She returned it with one of her own. "Looks like you two really hit it off. Whatever you were doing really cracked Emery up."

"He was Thor and I was the Hulk. I'm afraid he knocked me out with his hammer. More than once."

Emery played with Austin for another hour before Bree put him to bed.

Austin watched them from the doorway. It was obvious how much she loved Emery.

They returned to the kitchen for dessert.

Seated at the table with Austin, Bree pushed her plate away and asked, "So, what do you think of my little boy?"

"I'm in love." The words were out of his mouth before Austin realized that he'd said them. "He's such a good kid. I love his personality."

She wiped her mouth on the edge of her napkin before saying, "I noticed that it was like you couldn't take your eyes off him. I've seen you with Ryker's children, but the way you look at Emery…it's just different."

"Maybe it's because I'm crazy about his mother." His gaze was riveted on her face. "I love you, Bree."

She opened her mouth to speak, but no words came out.

Did he just say the L word?

"Please tell me that I didn't hear you wrong. Can you say it again please?"

Austin smiled. "I love you."

Impelled by her own emotions, Bree got up and walked around the table to where he was sitting.

He pushed his chair away from the table.

She sat down on his lap.

Gathering her into his arms, Austin held her snugly. "This feels so right to me," he whispered.

"I love you, too."

After putting the dishes in the dishwasher, they left the kitchen and settled down in her family room.

Austin kissed her, his tongue sending shivers of desire racing through her.

Bree matched him kiss for kiss.

He slowly pulled away, saying, "It's getting late and I have to be in court first thing in the morning."

She groaned in protest.

"I'll see you tomorrow," he whispered in her ear.

Bree wrapped her arms around him. "I don't want you to leave."

"I don't want to leave," Austin responded honestly. "But it's best that I do. I don't think you're ready to take our relationship to the next level."

"I haven't been with anyone since Caleb. My body tells me to keep you here by any means necessary, but I appreciate you for not pressing the matter."

He tightened his embrace, drawing her as close.

"When we make love, I want you to have no shadows across your heart." Austin lowered his lips to hers and kissed her. "Until you're ready… I'll wait."

"You're too good to be true, Austin DuGrandpre."

* * *

The world was suddenly a much brighter place as far as Austin was concerned. He was in love with a wonderful woman and getting to know his son was an amazing experience.

Briefcase in hand, he made his way toward the elevators.

He was soon joined by a colleague. "Graham, I heard you and Judge Walsh had words yesterday."

Patting his blazer pocket, he said, "My checkbook's a little lighter as a result. It's gonna probably cost me money every time I walk into that man's courtroom."

"You might want to set aside some cash, then," Austin responded with a grin. "I hear that he's not the one to mess with."

Graham shrugged. "Walsh needs to retire. He's been around since I was a little boy. And he was old then."

Laughing, the two men stepped off the elevator when the doors opened.

Austin waved at the receptionist as he walked passed her desk. He continued through the doors, which led to the office area.

Rochelle DuGrandpre walked out of her office, heading straight for him. He groaned inwardly.

"Good morning, Aunt Rochelle."

"You know, I didn't think you'd still be here, Austin, but I was wrong."

"Why did you think that?"

"I figured your mama would've convinced you to go back to Dallas. Irene never liked you spending too much time with us."

Austin kept his temper in check. "I'm a grown man capable of making my own decisions."

She smiled. "You sound just like Ryker. I hope you

boys understand that mothers do whatever we have to do to protect our children."

"It doesn't go unnoticed, Aunt Rochelle."

She leaned and whispered, "You have no idea how much it pleases your father to have you here in this firm. It is a dream come true for him."

"It means a lot to me, as well."

Rochelle nodded in approval. "You have a nice day, Austin."

"You, too."

He poked his head into Jadin's office. "Good morning…"

"Morning," she responded, her eyes glued to the computer monitor, engrossed in her work.

The next office was his.

Austin sat at his desk and opened his calendar, reviewing his appointments for the day.

His eyes traveled the room, imagining photographs of Emery scattered around. His first-grade picture…first football team photo and a host of others. They would share many firsts together—something he never had with his father.

The way he and Bree connected brought everything together perfectly. Austin knew she was a devoted mom—he wanted her to see him as the perfect father for Emery. This way, when everything came out, she would not feel threatened.

Austin entered Bree's house, grinning from ear to ear.

"You're up to something. What is it?"

He held up three tickets.

"What are those?" Bree inquired.

"Tickets to the Children's Museum of the Low Country on Saturday. Have you been there?"

"No, we haven't. I'd planned to take Emery before the summer ended, so this is perfect."

She was beyond touched by his gesture.

"Make yourself comfortable," Bree told him. "I need to wake up Emery from his nap."

Austin ventured into the kitchen.

The radio was playing softly and the table was set for three. On the counter was a slow cooker. He lifted the lid and the appetizing smell of chili wafted out.

His stomach rumbled in appreciation.

"What are you doing?"

Turning around to face her, Austin responded, "I was drawn here by a tantalizing aroma. I wanted to see what it was."

"Or you're just hungry."

He laughed. "That, too."

Emery ran into the kitchen.

"Hey, buddy," Austin greeted. "What are you up to?"

"I was sleepin'."

"Little boys need a lot of rest."

"So I can be strong?"

He nodded.

"Au'tin, I happy at you here."

Bree felt a catch beneath her ribs at the pleasure Austin and Emery found in one another. Tears pricked at her eyelids. A deep, tearing need took her breath, and she turned back toward the slow cooker.

Austin was almost too good to be true. She could not imagine anything more perfect than the way things were going with him. This was the first time there were no warning bells going off in her head.

Emery picked up the television remote in the family room.

She soon heard the familiar Spider-Man movie. Her son watched it almost daily.

She heard footsteps in the kitchen, but didn't turn around.

Bree felt his arms around her and leaned into him. Austin's nearness had an arousing effect on her. "Dinner's ready," she murmured, struggling to keep her focus on what she was doing.

Chapter 9

Austin invited Bree to join him for a charity event chaired by Eleanor DuGrandpre. When they entered the ballroom, the crowd seemed to part for her as if in a series of orchestrated moves. He had to admit that she was electrifying. Her hair, her eyes and the way her hips swayed when she walked. The hard tap of her heels against the marble floor sounded like tiny gunshots, even over the noise of the surrounding crush of people.

They found their table and sat down.

Eleanor walked over, plastering her best professional smile on her face. "I'm glad you two could make it. Have some champagne, look around at what our artists have to offer and enjoy yourself."

Austin watched his stepmother navigate through the crowd, charming men and women alike. It was obvious she loved this kind of stuff.

"What are you doing next Saturday?" Bree inquired. "Emery's birthday is Thursday, but we're celebrating over the weekend. We'd love for you to join us for the party at my house."

"I'd love to come." He was aware of his son's birthday and had already purchased a gift for him.

They moved about the room, eyeing the artwork.

"I love this one," Bree said. "It's perfect for my office."

"I notice you seem to love landscapes."

She nodded. "I do. I find that they promote calmness within my clients."

Austin pointed to a painting hanging nearby. "This one's nice."

"I like that one, too."

Jordin walked up to them. "Hey, you two. Found something you like?"

"I think I'm going to bid on this one," Bree stated. "It matches the other paintings in my office."

"Are you just getting here?" Austin asked his sister.

"Yeah. Ethan's flight was late."

"I'm having Emery's party on Saturday," Bree announced.

Jordin exchanged a quick look with her brother. "You know I'll be there for my sweetie."

"Can you believe he's already turning three? My baby is growing up so fast."

Austin embraced her. "He's still got a long way to go, babe. There may come a time when you can't wait for him to grow up."

Bree shook her head. "I don't think so. I dread the thought of him leaving me. I'm already praying he'll choose to stay close to home when it comes to college."

"She's serious," Jordin interjected. "Bree's been saying this since we were in school. She wants to keep her children close to her."

Austin took her hand. "It's a good thing for them to leave the nest, sweetheart."

"I know," she murmured. "I'm fine with them leaving—I just don't want my children spread out all over the country. I want to host family dinners like the ones your family has."

He understood why Bree felt this way. She didn't have family and while she didn't say much about it—he knew it bothered her.

She walked over to a painting a few feet away.

"I need to find my husband," Jordin said, looking around. "I see some pieces that would look great in our living room."

"Talk to you later, sis."

Austin joined Bree. "This is very nice."

"I love this one, too."

At the end of the evening, Austin handed his credit card to the cashier. "I'm paying for all three."

"You don't have to pay for mine," Bree said.

"I want to do this," he said. "I insist that you take the money and put it in Emery's education fund."

"Austin DuGrandpre, you never cease to amaze me."

"Au'tin, it my burtday."

"Happy birthday, buddy. Now, how old are you?"

"I tree."

"Three years old…wow. You are such a big boy."

"Hey, cousin," Ryker greeted. He gave Austin a knowing smile. "Looks like you and Bree are getting along well."

"We are."

"Emery obviously likes you."

"I like him, too."

Ryker asked in a low voice, "So, you thinking of settling down anytime soon?"

Austin simply smiled.

"Look at that…"

"What are you two up to?" Jordin inquired.

"We're not doing anything," Ryker answered, *"Little Miss Matchmaker."*

She broke into a grin. "Maybe I should open a dating service."

"Or you could come help your husband," Ethan suggested. He was standing in the doorway. "Kai and Amya just challenged us to a dance off."

Austin laughed. "You might as well give up now. Have you seen them dance lately?"

Ryker agreed. "Garland has them taking lessons and I have to admit—they're pretty good."

"Honey, c'mon. Let's go get our tails whipped. We're a team so we have to take this hit together."

Jordin chuckled. "I can't believe you're falling for this. I know I can dance. Let's go show these little girls how it's done."

Austin looked over at Bree. "I don't know about you, but I want to see this."

"Right behind you," she murmured. "I want to check on Emery first. They're a little too quiet in his room. Three boys…"

Bree walked in one direction and he in the other.

Austin watched in amusement as Ryker's daughters took to the floor, their moves flawless for a set of five-year-olds. He was loving this, being around family like this. He wanted Emery to experience this, as well—to be surrounded by love.

He leaned over and whispered, "Jordin, I think you and Ethan should give up now. These girls have a whole dance routine."

"I got this."

When Kai and Amya were done, Jordin looked at her husband and said, "You ready?"

"No, I think we should just declare them winners."

She broke into a grin. "I agree."

Austin heard Emery's laughter coming right at him. He pressed himself against the wall and waited until the sound was upon him. He reached out and grabbed the little boy. "You having a good time, buddy?"

"Yes. I have fun."

"Me, too, buddy. I'm having the time of my life."

The following weekend, Jordin had Emery spend Saturday night with her and Ethan because Austin had planned a special surprise for Bree.

"Where are we going?" she inquired.

"To the waterfront park."

She smiled. "For a moonlight walk?"

"That and more," he responded. "We're going to have a picnic near the Pineapple Fountain."

"How romantic."

The park faced the Charleston Harbor and Revenal Bridge and was one of their favorite places to visit.

Austin laid a blanket down on the grass for them to sit on.

They sat facing each other.

Bree accepted the plate from Austin. "This is a beautiful night."

He agreed.

"Did you make all this?" she asked.

Austin shook his head. "Aubrie actually put together the basket for me. I simply picked it up and put it in the car."

Bree laughed. "You're not even going to take credit... not even a little bit. I love your honesty."

Guilt filtered through him at her words. He still hadn't summoned up the courage to tell her the truth about Emery. Mostly because he feared losing Bree.

"What time should I be ready for the barbecue on Monday?" she asked.

"One o'clock."

"I missed the DuGrandpre Labor Day Barbecue last year," Bree stated. "Emery was sick, so we stayed home."

"I wasn't there, either. I went to Dallas to spend some time with my mom. This will be my first one."

"They do it up big, Austin."

"I'm looking forward to spending this one with you and Emery."

"This is nice," she said, her eyes traveling the park. "It's beautiful out here."

"I'm glad you like it," he responded. "I wasn't sure how this was going to turn out. They said it was going to rain."

"I'm glad it didn't," Bree stated. "I would've hated missing out on this. It's very romantic."

Austin wrapped an arm around her. "My life would be empty if it wasn't for you and Emery. I want you to know that."

"You don't ever have to worry about losing me. Whatever this is that's going on between us—I'm in a hundred percent."

Chapter 10

"Come in, Austin," Eleanor greeted warmly as she stepped aside to let him enter the house. "Everybody is outside on the patio."

"I can walk around to the back," he said.

"You'll do no such thing. Get on in here."

He embraced his stepmother. "You look beautiful as always."

"Boy, please… I haven't even combed my hair today."

Austin chuckled. "You can't tell."

After they settled at one of the picnic tables, Bree said, "I'll get your chicken off the grill. I know you're hungry."

"Thanks, babe."

She returned minutes later and placed the plate before him, heaped with mixed greens, chicken and macaroni salad.

"It was the last one ready. Ryker's putting more chicken on the grill, but since you talked about it on the way here, I figured I'd better grab a piece for you while some was still available."

Her cell phone rang.

"I need to take this call."

Bree returned, saying, "Honey, I have to go. One of my patients just tried to commit suicide and I need to see her."

"Do you want me to go with you?" Austin asked.

She shook her head. "No, you stay here with Emery. Fix me a plate, please."

He kissed her.

Austin walked her out to the car.

His father came from the back and said, "Take a walk with me, son."

"Sure."

"I'd like to talk to your mother," Etienne announced as they strolled toward the front of the house.

"Why?" Austin asked, stopping in his tracks. "The two of you haven't spoken in almost twenty-seven years."

"I wasn't a good husband, son. I'm sure she's told you this much."

He nodded. "I don't know the specifics and I don't need to know. It's not my business."

"I owe Irene an apology. As I'm getting on in years, I'm beginning to see things differently. I made some terrible choices in the past. One of those was hurting your mother."

"Dad, I don't think she's ready to have a conversation with you, but I'll pass on the message that you'd like to speak with her."

"Thank you, son. I'd really appreciate it."

"Did you ever love her?" Austin inquired. "Mom never believed you cared as much for her as she did for you."

"I loved your mother more than I can say, but we were young and we both let pride get in the way of trying to work things out. Then I met Eleanor."

"You don't owe me any explanations," Austin interjected. He didn't want to be in the middle of his parents' situation and he wasn't going to take sides again. He'd chosen his mother based on what she'd told him, then found out that it wasn't the complete truth.

Their conversation turned to sports.

"I'm looking forward to football season," said Etienne. "I think the Saints are going to have a good year."

Austin grinned. "I feel the same way about the Cowboys."

His father roared with laughter. "Son, you're dreaming. Besides, where is your loyalty? The DuGrandpres come from strong New Orleans roots."

"I like the Saints, but I grew up in Dallas. I love my Cowboys."

His stepmother approached them. "I've been looking for you," she told Etienne. "You're needed in the kitchen. You promised to make the chocolate bread pudding."

"Yeah, Dad. My mouth's ready for it, too."

Eleanor winked at Austin, then escorted her husband back to the house.

He paused in his tracks when he spotted his sister sitting on a bench alone near the gazebo.

"Jadin, you okay?"

She looked up at Austin and gave a tiny smile. "I'm fine. Just sitting here and reflecting over my life."

"I think Dad's been doing the same thing." He sat down beside her.

"From the time I was old enough to understand," Jordin began, "I knew what it meant to be a DuGrandpre. I knew about the things our grandfather went through to build this legacy he left us." Jadin looked over at him. "I have a man who loves me and I love him…only he's in Los Angeles now. His uncle owns a chain of hotels and offered him the general manager position of the one that just opened."

She glanced at Austin. "He says that he wants to marry me."

"And he wants you to move to LA."

Jadin nodded. "I love my job and I love the firm."

"More than you love this guy?"

"I don't know the answer to that question right now," she confessed.

"I know that you'll make the right decision for your life, Jadin."

"You make it sound so simple. Dad expects us to one day lead this firm. Our grandfather expected this, as well. When Aubrie announced that she wasn't going into law but becoming a chef… Austin, Aunt Rochelle and Uncle Jacques thought she'd lost her mind. Granddad almost had a stroke. He said the DuGrandpre name stood for justice. That the threats, the blood from the beating he endured, the fire and every ounce of sweat oozing from the pores of his body was for the firm. When nobody would hire him after he finished law school—he didn't quit. Granddad started his own firm. When those racists beat him, and burned down the first office, he didn't give up." Jadin paused a moment before adding, "He did all this for us so that we would have something."

"Maybe you don't have to walk out on the firm or Granddad's legacy," Austin stated. "Maybe you can have both the firm and the man you love."

"How?"

"Maybe you should do some research. Visit LA and look for office space. Put together a proposal for expanding the DuGrandpre Law Firm. Talk to Dad and Uncle Jacques about it."

"I hadn't thought of that," Jadin murmured. "Austin, this is a great idea."

"This means that you need to put together a proposal so tight it'll be difficult for them to turn down."

"I may need your help."

"I'll do what I can," he said.

* * *

"I hate that Bree had to leave so soon," Jordin said. "Did she even have a chance to sit down and eat?"

"One of her clients had some kind of setback, so she went to meet them at the hospital. We ate shortly after we got here." Austin looked around. "I haven't seen your husband. Is he here?"

She shook her head. "Ethan left this morning for business. He's going to be gone for a week. I'm trying to find ways to occupy the time while he's away." Jordin frowned. "I miss my husband already."

Austin broke into laughter. "How about Bree and I take you to dinner tomorrow after work?"

"Really?"

"Sure. I'll have her meet us at the restaurant. We can leave from here."

"You don't mind, Austin?"

"You're my sister. If you'd like, you can even stay with me while Ethan's away. Unless you like being in that huge house alone."

"His mother lives in the guesthouse, so I'll probably stay with her. I don't want to put a cramp in your routine."

"If you change your mind, just let me know."

Jordin hugged him. "I'm so glad to have you in my life, Austin. It used to hurt my feelings when I'd write to you and you never wrote me back."

"I'm sorry. I thought Dad was making you and Jadin write those letters."

"We wrote them on our own. We wanted you in our lives."

"Well, now that I'm here—I'm never going away."

Jordin smiled. "This makes me very happy."

"I'm in love with Bree," Austin announced.

His sister smiled. "Does she feel the same way about you?"

"I think so, but it's not like we've talked about it. I don't want to spook her. Besides I'm still getting used to the idea myself."

"Don't wait too long to tell Bree," Jordin advised.

Bree arrived home shortly after eight.

"Thanks for babysitting Emery. How was he?" she inquired.

"He and I had a great time. We watched a movie and he fell asleep near the end so I put him to bed in his room. That was about ten minutes ago." He sat the iPad on the coffee table.

She sat down beside him. "What are you doing?"

"Playing a video game," he responded. "Want to play?"

She dropped down beside him. "Sure."

"You are so cheating!" Bree accused when it was her turn, her laughter doing little to back up the finger she jabbed at Austin's chest.

He gently grabbed her arms. And suddenly she was tucked in the small crease between his half-sprawled form and the back of the couch.

Bree planted her palm on the center of his chest, refusing to admit how tempting it was to simply stay there, and pushed herself up.

Austin shook his head, all *who, me?* "Cheating? We're talking."

She shot him a skeptical look, not buying his wide-eyed innocent routine for one minute. That he would even try it with a mouth like his was almost too much to bear.

Reaching for her, Austin let the iPad fall to the floor.

His mouth kicked up another degree, his eyes heating in the way she'd found so startling at first, but was now beginning to look for. "Have I mentioned how sexy I find you?"

An unbidden belly flip had her glancing away before he could see how his words affected her. "I bust you for trying to cheat, and this is your response?"

"Yes."

The crook of his finger found her chin, and he pulled her back to his gaze.

"But that doesn't make what we've talked about any less true. I'm a motivated guy, set on making sure I don't let something important slip through my fingers. I want you to know what I know."

She let out an even breath, hating the way everything Austin said made sense.

Clicked, as if it was locking into some waiting place within her.

Bree was getting lost in his eyes, feeling herself drawn closer. "What I know is that you want me."

"I've got you." His voice was a low rumble against her ear. "What I want is to keep you. We're good together, Bree. It's not about glass slippers or fairy tales or love at any sight. It's about you and me fitting together. It's about this feeling of rightness. The one I've had since I met you. Tell me that you feel it, too."

"I feel it."

The connection was there. Undeniable between them. Bree didn't want to worry about good judgment or long-term consequences. She simply wanted this man, whose promises sounded too good to be true, to deliver on the one in his eyes. "Austin," she whispered, drawing her leg slowly in, and the man with it. "You make me want…" She couldn't say it. Couldn't even think it. All her rational thought was tangled up in the rising awareness between them, the slow glide of his touch over her skin, the need simmering between them.

"I know..." he whispered. "It's the very same for me. Like I said...we fit."

"This just seems almost too good to be true," Bree said. Deep down, she was waiting for the bottom to drop out of this perfect piece of heaven she had with Austin. She wasn't a negative person—she was realistic.

Chapter 11

The following weekend Austin decided it was time to tell his mother about Emery. He was glad that Bree hadn't pressed him about coming along. He flew to Dallas that Friday after work.

"Mom…" Austin called out when he arrived.

"In here."

He followed the sound of his mother's voice to the kitchen.

Irene looked coolly over the rims of her glasses, her shrewd eyes assessing. Not a single salt-and-peppered strand of hair was out of place, curled back from her temples stylishly and stopping just below her collar. "Nice of you to come visit."

"Mom, I would've come a lot sooner, but I've had a lot going on. Besides, the last time I came home, you were still upset with me for leaving." No one could hold a grudge better than Irene DuGrandpre, Austin thought to himself.

She didn't respond.

"I guess you're still mad."

"I'm not mad. Just *hurt*." She paused a moment before

asking, "How could you choose that *man* over me? I was the one who sacrificed everything for you."

"I didn't *choose* him, Mom. He's my father and I wanted to get to know him for myself. All my life I've heard your version of what happened—I wanted to hear his side, too."

"Oh, so you think I've been lying to you. The man cheated on me throughout our marriage."

"I never said you lied about anything."

"Then what does it matter—he's only gonna tell you something to try and make me look bad."

"He didn't do that, Mom. He accepted his part in what happened. He owned up to being unfaithful."

She rolled her eyes. "How cavalier..."

"When are you going to stop being so angry with him? I'm a grown man."

"Maybe a few years after I'm dead... I might be able to forgive him then." She gave Austin a tiny smile.

He embraced her. "I love you, Mom. Nothing or no one can ever change that."

"So how is Etienne?"

"He's doing well," Austin responded. "Jordin recently got married. She wanted to invite you to the wedding, but I told her that it wasn't a good idea."

"You right about that," Irene uttered. "I'm happy for her, though. I'll send a gift back with you."

"Mom, she and Jadin really want to meet you."

"Why?"

"Because you're my mother and they consider you an extended member of the family. Regardless of how you may feel—you are still a DuGrandpre."

Irene made a face. "Humph. My mama and my daddy's girlfriend used to cook together whenever they came to visit, but I'ma tell you now. I'm not the one for that kinda mess."

Austin laughed. "No one expects you and Eleanor to be anything other than cordial, I'm sure."

"I'm just saying…"

"Dad wants to reach out to you. He wants to apologize."

Irene shook her head. "Tell him to save it for the Lord. I don't want to hear anything that man has to say. The time for it was a long time ago."

"You still love him," Austin said.

"Boy, you've lost your last mind," she declared.

"You divorced my father twenty-seven years ago. If there weren't feelings involved—it wouldn't bother you so much after all that time. Then the fact that you've never remarried, although three different men proposed to you over the years…you still love my dad."

"I never remarried because those guys were fine to date, but they…" Her voice died and Irene released a long sigh. "Son, the truth is that I just couldn't bear getting my heart broke a second time."

She walked over to the breakfast table and sat down. Austin joined her.

"I met your father when I was in the ninth grade. I thought he and Jacques were the cutest boys in school, but Etienne, there was something special about him. He could just smile and I would melt. He was my first love."

His mother had never discussed her relationship with his father before. The only thing Austin knew about his parents was that his mother had gotten pregnant in college and they married. That child died and a few months later, she was pregnant again with him.

"When we lost that first baby," Irene was saying, "Etienne changed. He was happy when we found out that we were having you, but things between us was different. He had just gotten accepted into law school and I graduated from nursing school…" She shook her head. "Things just changed. At first, I thought it was because we were both in school and spent most of our time focused on finishing college. A lot of people thought we wouldn't graduate because we were going to have a child. Your grandfather, especially. I don't think that man ever liked me. He didn't think I was good enough to wear the DuGrandpre name. That's why I never went back to my maiden name. To spite him."

"When did you find out Dad was cheating on you?" Austin inquired.

"The day you were born," Irene responded. "He was nowhere to be found when I went into labor. And when he finally showed up, I could smell liquor and the woman's perfume on him."

"Yet you stayed."

"I didn't leave your father, but I never let him touch me after that. After I had saved up some money and had worked at the hospital for a year, then I decided it was time for me to go. I wanted to make sure I had some security."

"Dad said when he found out that you were in labor, it scared him. He remembered all you'd gone through with my brother, only for him to be stillborn. He went to a bar and got drunk. A woman came on to him and…"

"I know what happened after that."

"He said nothing happened, but that you would never believe him," Austin stated. "The affairs started after that and I believe him. He felt he'd already lost you and he didn't want to be alone."

"Etienne wasn't there when I needed him the most. I was scared, too." A tear slid down Irene's cheek. "We'd both lost a child. He should've been there for me."

Austin reached over and covered his mother's hand with his own. "He realizes this now. Mom, he truly regrets what happened and this is why he wants to talk to you."

Irene removed her glasses and wiped her eyes. "What's done can't be undone. Regardless of any apology, Etienne can't unbreak my heart."

"I'm sorry he hurt you."

She touched his cheek. "You have nothing to be sorry about, Austin. I know that a boy needs his father and I kept you away from Etienne. It was wrong, but I wanted to hurt him for the pain and humiliation he caused me. I'm the one who owes you an apology. Baby, I'm so sorry."

Austin smiled. "I don't think I turned out so bad. You did a good job."

"I'm so proud of you, son."

Irene pushed away from the table and rose to her feet. "I need to get started on dinner."

"Why don't we go out?" he suggested. "My treat."

She shook her head. "There's no way my son is gonna eat somebody else's cooking on his first night home. I'm making your favorite. Barbecue chicken."

After dinner Austin helped his mother clean the kitchen. They settled in the family room to watch television thirty minutes later.

"Mom, I need to tell you something."

"What is it, son?"

"Getting to know my dad wasn't the only reason I moved to Charleston. To be honest, I didn't go there to seek him out at all."

"Then why?" Displeasure was written all over her face. "Please tell me that you didn't go chasing after that Jasmine. Boy, I told you that girl isn't the right woman for you."

"When Jasmine left town, she was pregnant."

Irene gave Austin a sidelong glance. "What's that got to do with you?"

"She was carrying my child, Mom."

"You sure about that?"

Austin nodded. "I found out the woman who adopted him lived in Charleston—that's why I moved there."

"Does Etienne know about this?"

"No, I wanted to tell you first."

"I never liked Jasmine and before you do anything—you need to have a paternity test. I wouldn't trust anything that girl says."

"She didn't tell me. I spoke with Cheryl."

"I'm not so sure you can trust her, either. Why did she wait so long to share this information with you?"

"She was pregnant and said she couldn't face me without telling me the truth of what happened."

"I heard she and Jasmine fell out. That's why Cheryl came back to Dallas. As far as I'm concerned, this is all suspect."

"I believe her, Mom."

"Well, what are you gonna do?"

"I intend to get my son. I never agreed to an adoption and I didn't terminate my parental rights."

"Then just have the adoption nullified."

"It's not that simple, Mom."

She looked at him. "Why not? You're a lawyer."

The woman who adopted Emery is actually a friend of Jordin's. I've been getting to know her."

Irene frowned. "Know her how?"

"I'm dating her, Mom."

"Do you think this is a good idea, son? What happens if you two don't work out? What then?"

"Emery will be my son regardless of my relationship with Bree."

Irene shook her head. "I hope you know what you're doing."

"Emery loves Bree," he responded. "She's a good

mother and I really care for her. If you want to know the truth, I think it's the perfect solution for us."

"Then why haven't you told her the truth?"

While his mother was at work, Austin decided to have lunch at one of his favorite Dallas restaurants.

While he waited for his food to arrive, he made a call. "Hey, sweetheart."

"How are things going with you and your mom?" Bree asked.

"Great. She was a little stiff when I first arrived, but she's fine now. We sat down and had a really good talk yesterday."

"I'm sorry I missed your call last night. After I got Emery settled in bed, I took a shower and fell out."

"I called you because I was missing that sweet voice of yours."

"I miss you. It's a bit strange to not see you every day. I think I've gotten a bit spoiled."

Austin chuckled. "Don't worry, I'll be back in a couple of days."

He paid the check and left.

"Austin…"

He turned around to the sound of a familiar voice. *Jasmine Reynolds.*

"I heard that you left town." She looked around as if suddenly anxious to escape his presence.

"Is that why you're here?" he asked. "Because you didn't think you'd run into me."

Awkwardly, she cleared her throat, arms folded across her chest. "Why would I worry about *that*?"

"Because I know about Emery."

Her smile disappeared. "Cheryl told you. I wish that witch would mind her own business."

"*You* should've told me that you were pregnant."

"Why? Nothing would've changed between us, Austin. You didn't want to marry me."

"So, you leave town with my child to punish me?"

"I left to raise my son alone. I needed to start over someplace fresh."

"*Raise him,*" he uttered. "You gave him up for adoption."

Jasmine looked as if she was searching for a plausible answer. "Once I had the baby, I realized that I couldn't handle being a mother. I tried reaching out to you, but you'd changed your number and I didn't know where you were," she responded. "I placed an ad in the newspaper."

He knew she was lying. "*You expect me to believe that?* This was all intentional. I'm not even named on the birth certificate as his father."

"How do you know that?"

"I have a copy." Austin glanced down at the wedding ring on her finger. "You finally got the husband you wanted—at Cheryl's expense."

"I knew she was in her feelings, but I can't believe Cheryl would betray me like this."

"Are you really going to pull the betrayal card? You married the man she was dating."

Jasmine shrugged. "It's not my fault she couldn't keep him."

Shaking his head, he stated, "You're something else."

"Austin, I don't know what you're planning, but listen to me…you really don't want to pursue this. Cheryl never should've gotten you involved."

"This is my son. Do you really think I'm going to just sit back and do nothing?"

Jasmine looked him straight in the eye. "I don't see where you have much choice, Austin. I hate that things went bad between us because I really loved you. If you want to know the truth… I still love you."

He shook his head. "You don't do what you did and claim to love someone."

"Sometimes you have to make hard choices—this was probably the hardest one I've ever had to make, but I felt it was for the best. I hope that one day you'll be able to forgive me."

"Hardly," he uttered. "Do you ever think about him?"

She glanced down at her watch. "I have to pick up my mother, but I'd like to finish this conversation, Austin. Can you meet me for dinner tonight?"

"How will your husband feel about it?"

"He's in Los Angeles in the studio all week. I married a record producer."

"Sounds like your type."

Jasmine's jaw tightened. "I guess I deserve that. Austin, I know that you think I'm a terrible person, but I did what was best for Emery. Please, Austin…have dinner with me. We need to talk and I promise I'll tell you everything. I owe you the truth."

"What time?"

"Six o'clock. Meet me at Copeland's. It used to be our favorite spot." Jasmine pulled out a piece of paper and wrote on it. "Here's my number. In case you change your mind."

"What's wrong, son?"

"I just ran into Jasmine."

"*What?* Has she moved back to Dallas? If so, I'm so glad that you live in Charleston now."

"I didn't ask, but I guess she's here visiting family. I never expected to see her again, especially not so soon."

"What happened?"

"She said that she didn't tell me about the pregnancy because it wouldn't have changed my mind about marriage. She wants to have dinner with me tonight to discuss everything."

"I heard she got married, but I don't know if it's true."

"She had on a wedding ring," Austin responded. "She told she married a record producer."

"Is her husband here with her?"

"No, ma'am."

"Then you better stay home with me. That girl just trying to get you someplace and seduce you. Boy, you don't need that kind of trouble."

Austin wasn't sure what Jasmine was plotting, but he thought it better to listen to his mother and stay as far away from the woman as possible.

He picked up his cell phone to call her, then changed his mind. He didn't want her to have his number, so he called from the landline.

When she answered, Austin went straight to the purpose of his call. "Jasmine, I don't think it's a good idea for us to have dinner."

"Is this how you really feel or how your mother feels?"

"Why do you always have to go there?" he asked. "Leave my mom out of this."

"Miss Irene never liked me. I believe that's why you didn't want to marry me."

"You're wrong," Austin stated. "We weren't getting along, Jasmine, and things were not getting any better. That's why I didn't want to get married. I didn't want to end up in divorce court."

"Austin, I really want to sit down and talk to you face-to-face. I know Cheryl's probably told you a bunch of mess. She—"

He cut her off by interjecting, "She only told me about Emery. I didn't want to know or hear about anything else."

"How can you be so cold to me? Austin, we were together for over three years."

"I know that."

"So, you have no feelings for me whatsoever? They just vanished with the wind?"

"Jasmine, you're married or so you say. You've moved on and I wish you all the happiness you can muster. What I feel or don't feel shouldn't matter."

"It does to me," she insisted.

"The only thing we have to discuss is Emery."

"Austin, I wasn't ready to be a mother. I thought I could do it, but after he was born—I realized that I wasn't Mommy material."

"So why didn't you just bring him to me? You have to know that I would've taken my son."

"I was still angry with you. I was hurt and I acted out of that hurt. If I could do things differently, I would, Austin."

He didn't respond.

"He is with a good family and he's happy."

"How do you know?" Austin asked. "Do you even know where he is?"

"He's in Vegas."

He didn't bother to tell her otherwise. From the sound of it, Jasmine wasn't interested in her son. As much as it grieved him, she had done the right thing by terminating her parental rights. Emery was with a mother who adored him. He deserved someone like Bree.

"I hope you don't hate me."

"I don't," he responded.

"Austin…"

"I have to go," he stated. "Goodbye, Jasmine."

Chapter 12

"How was your trip?" Jordin asked. "And your mother? I'm sure she was thrilled to see you."

"It was interesting," Austin responded. "My mom and I had a good time together. I have a wedding gift in my car for you—it's from her."

"Oh, that's so sweet." Jordin sat down in one of the visitor chairs. "What made your trip interesting? I got the feeling that it didn't have to do with your mother."

"Jasmine was in town. She's Emery's biological mother."

"And your ex-girlfriend."

Austin nodded. "I was not prepared to see her."

"How did it go?"

"She claims that she didn't tell me about the pregnancy because she knew I didn't want to marry her. Jasmine invited me to have dinner with her that evening to discuss it further. She said she owed me the truth."

"Did you have dinner with her?"

Austin shook his head. "There wasn't much else she could tell me. Nothing she would've said could change this mess she caused. She lied to the courts and gave up her son for marriage to some record producer. I guess it was a pretty good trade-off."

Jordin shook her head. "How did you ever get involved with someone so heartless?"

"I didn't see her true colors until much later."

"You didn't tell her that you found Emery?"

"No, there's no way I would do that—I don't trust Jasmine at all."

"Do you still love her?"

"No. Those feelings went away long before I knew about Emery. She and I were toxic. That's why I ended the relationship."

"If you'd known about the baby, do you think you would've made the same decision? To break up with her?"

"I honestly don't know. I never would've abandoned my son. I do know that Jasmine and I never would've gotten married, but I would be in Emery's life."

"So, what happens now between you and Bree?"

"I don't want to hurt her, Jordin. Like you said, she's an innocent party to this drama. Things are good between us. I won't just snatch Emery from her. She's his mother. I want what's best for him, and right now that's Bree."

"He loves her."

"I know," Austin said. "I see the way his eyes light up whenever he looks at her. It's the same for Bree and she's good to him."

"I can see how much this hurts you," Jordin said. "I can see how much you love your son. Trust me when I tell you that this will work itself out. Look at Ryker and Garland. Their daughters were switched at birth and now they are one happy family."

"I like Bree, but I can't say we're heading toward marriage. Not yet."

"I hear the two of you are spending a lot of time together. I'd say it's a little more than just *like*."

Austin broke into a grin. "I enjoy her company and I admit, I'm very attracted to her."

"Don't play with her heart."

"I wouldn't do that," he assured Jordin.

"I'm holding you to that. Bree is my best friend and I don't want to see her hurt. When she finds out that you're Emery's birth father—I'm not sure what it will do to her, but knowing that you don't intend to rip him out of her arms will help."

Austin enjoyed spending time with Bree and Emery. Some evenings they would order out for dinner or settle in with grilled cheese sandwiches. A few times he'd brought work from the office and while she stretched out on the sofa reading some psychological journal, he would stretch out on the floor with his laptop.

Regardless of what they were doing, Austin was acutely aware of her every movement. Bree felt comfortable around him and he felt comfortable around her. She had allowed him into her space and he had allowed her into his. He'd never shared this kind of closeness with any woman—not even Jasmine. At one point Austin figured he never would, but Bree had proved him wrong.

Just as he rang the doorbell, he heard Emery crying.

Bree opened the door.

Austin halted abruptly at the sight of her holding a sobbing Emery in her arms. His throat constricted at the picture they made. The sight of Bree and his son together did something to his heart he knew he'd never get back.

He instinctively reached for Emery. "What's wrong, buddy?"

"I got a boo-boo…"

"He fell halfway down the stairs," Bree explained. "He has a little bruise, but he's okay." She touched his arm. "I'm glad you're back. We missed you."

Austin broke into a grin. "Really? Can't live without me, huh."

"Naw…" she uttered. "I just said that to make you feel good. I didn't think about you at all."

He laughed. "Good, 'cause I didn't miss you, either." Austin felt his pulse take off at just the sight of her. She was wearing jeans and a pale pink sleeveless top. Her dark brown hair was pulled back in a ponytail.

He calmed Emery enough to put him down, then followed Bree into the kitchen. "What are you making?" he asked, watching her drop a stick of butter into a skillet on the stove, Next, she begin chopping cloves of garlic.

"Shrimp scampi."

Bree swept the chopped garlic into the melted butter, the scent wafting through the kitchen and making his stomach growl. She turned back to the stove, slid several dozen fresh deveined shrimp into the skillet with the butter and garlic, then began to chop some scallions with a cleaver.

It wasn't long before they sat down to eat.

As the hour drew later, Austin offered to give Emery his bath.

"Thanks, I appreciate it," Bree said. "I could use a few minutes to make a couple of phone calls."

After he climbed into bed, Emery handed Austin a book that was already well-read, the pages opening easily to the beginning. "I want to hear this one."

He was curled beside him, holding tight to a blanket and his Thor figurine.

"Yes, if you do not know my face, you will know me by my deeds. I am Loki…" Austin read.

"He Thor's brotha," Emery uttered. "Bad man."

Smiling, he read on, loving the sound of his giggles.

Austin finished one book and was handed another by Emery. *"Goodnight Moon,"* he muttered.

"This is the last one for tonight, okay?"

The little boy yawned.

Austin's eyelids grew heavy as a yawn overtook him. Emery cuddled against him. "I happy you here."

"Me, too." He stifled another yawn. "I don't want to be anyplace else."

Bree hovered in the doorway, her gaze on Austin and Emery as they slept. She wavered with indecision on waking him. She pulled out her phone and snapped a photo of the two, then eased out of the room.

She went to her office and uploaded the photo to her computer.

He looks so handsome, she thought. *They look like they are truly father and son.* No man had ever shown this much interest in her child, but then she hadn't given any a real chance to do so. Austin was different, this much she did know. He was unlike any man she'd ever met, and this list included her late husband, Caleb.

Things were great between her and Austin. The more time she spent with him, the more her body yearned for him. Bree was ready to take their relationship to the next level. Austin had been wonderful by waiting until she was ready.

Her eyes traveled to the picture on the screen. *Austin, I'm ready.*

She heard a sound and looked up.

"Hey, sorry about that," Austin said as he entered her office. "I didn't mean to fall asleep like that. I guess I'm more exhausted than I thought."

Bree turned off the monitor, got up from the desk and walked toward him. "It's no problem."

"It's late, so I'll get out of here."

She stood as close to him as she could get. "You don't have to leave, Austin."

He met her gaze. "What are you saying?"

"I *want* you to stay," Bree responded. "You can sleep in my room."

"Are you sure about this?"

"Yes." His steady gaze bored in her in silent expectation.

In response, she led him by the hand to her bedroom.

He took her mouth as if it was his to do with as he pleased.

Bree's fingers curled into his shirt; her moan sliding free of her mouth and into his, awakening feelings that had lain dormant for a while.

Hot desire.

Explosive.

Consuming and intense.

Standing in the middle of the floor, they undressed each other in silence.

His arms slid around her waist, pulling her in tight. "I knew you were special from the first time I ever saw you. The reason I'm telling you this is because I want you to know where you stand with me before we become intimate. I'm not looking for casual sex. I want something more."

Bree was moved by his words. "I feel the same way."

She watched the play of emotions on his face. Bree lifted her arms, linking them around his neck, holding Austin to her.

His arms tightened until she could hardly draw breath.

"I need you," he whispered, dropping his mouth to the line of her jaw, nibbling at her throat.

Austin swept her, weightless, into his arms and carried her to the bed. After placing her in the middle of the bed, he crawled in behind her.

Bree could feel his uneven breathing on her cheek as he held her close. The touch of his hand was almost unbearable in its tenderness. His mouth covered hers hungrily, leaving her mouth burning with fire.

The touch of her lips on his sent a shock wave through Austin's entire body with a savage intensity. As he roused her passion, his own need grew stronger.

Passion pounded the blood through her heart, chest and head, causing Bree to breathe in deep, soul-drenching drafts.

Holding her close, Austin rolled her across the bed and she went with him willingly, eagerly, entangling her legs with his.

Heartbeats thundered and each breath was a sigh sifting into the quiet. All that existed was the slide of skin on skin, the soft sighs of their heightened breathing, the crashing beats of their hearts.

Later, Bree watched the rise and fall of Austin's chest as he slept, thinking about what had transpired earlier. He made her feel loved in the way that he touched her, kissed her and held her in his arms.

Austin placed a protective arm around her, pulling her closer to him. He never opened his eyes.

When he was sleeping soundly, Bree eased out of bed and padded barefoot to the bathroom to shower.

Afterward, she slipped on her robe and went to check on Emery.

The little boy was asleep, his Iron Man toy in his hands.

A smile trembled on Bree's lips as she watched him,

her heart full of love. The hair on the back of her neck stood up.

She glanced over her shoulder to find Austin standing in the doorway. He must have awakened and found her gone.

He didn't enter, but his gaze was trained on Emery.

No words passed between them as they lovingly watched over the little boy.

Together, they returned to her bedroom.

The next morning Austin slid out of the bed, careful not to make a sound. He tucked the blanket higher around Bree's sleeping form. It was nearly dawn, and the temperature was cool in the bedroom.

He couldn't sleep.

There was too much on his mind. He felt a thread of guilt at the thought of keeping secrets from the woman he was in love with. *There shouldn't be any secrets between us.*

He stretched and yawned.

She mumbled something in her sleep, but didn't open her eyes.

He pulled her closer to him.

Austin never considered that he would fall in love with Bree. His focus had been to right the wrong that had been done to him. But getting to know her changed everything. He found in her a kinship. Before long she had stolen his heart and now here they were—it was time for him to come forward.

No more secrets.

Chapter 13

Bree came downstairs dressed in a pair of denim shorts and a tank top. When she reached the kitchen, Austin already had a skillet on the burner and was half-buried in the refrigerator, pulling out ingredients.

"I wondered where you were," she said.

He closed the door, put a carton of eggs on the counter and turned to face her. "Good morning, gorgeous." Austin kissed her. "Any regrets?"

She lifted her chin, squared her shoulders and looked him dead in the eye. "None." Her body was still humming, buzzing with sensation. "What are you making?" she asked.

"Spinach and mushroom omelets, bacon and toast."

"Can I help?"

He cracked eggs into a bowl and handed her a whisk while he put butter in the pan. "Here you go."

Minutes later Emery ran into the kitchen. "Hey, Mommy...hey, Au'tin."

"Good morning, sweetie," she responded before bending down to plant a kiss on his forehead.

He climbed onto a chair at the counter. Propped on his knees, he asked, "What you makin'?"

"Austin's making us a special breakfast. Isn't that nice?"

Emery nodded. "I happy."

"Me, too, buddy," Austin murmured. "I'm happy, too."

Bree took a seat at the counter while Austin moved around her kitchen as though he'd spent time in it before. Humming softly, Austin opened cabinets, pulling out the ingredients he needed for his meal.

After breakfast, they took Emery to the park.

Austin wanted to talk to Bree, but didn't want to distract her from keeping an eye on Emery. Maybe it was too soon to tell her, especially after making love to her the night before. She looked so happy and he didn't want to ruin that happiness.

"You look like you're in deep thought," Bree said.

"I was thinking about you."

She inclined her head. "What about me?"

"Just in the short time I've known you… Bree, you make me feel in a way no other woman has made me feel. You're incredible."

She smiled.

"The last thing I've ever wanted to do is hurt you."

Bree's eyes traveled to where Emery was playing and stayed. "I'm not worried about you hurting me, Austin. It's strange because I don't trust easy, but with you—I don't have any doubts in my heart."

Her words should've touched him, but instead he was filled with guilt.

She reached over, placing her hand in his. "The way you treat Emery—it's as if he were your own flesh and blood. My son adores you, Austin. He's never taken to anyone the way he took to you. I pride myself on being a good judge of character, so I know that you're a good man."

"I hope you'll always feel this way," he uttered.

Bree gave his hand a gentle squeeze. "I'm sure I will."

A couple of days later, Bree met Jordin at Indulgence, their favorite locale for spa dates.

"I'm so glad you booked this appointment because I really need a massage." Jordin sank down in one of the chairs in the reception area. "This was a crazy week for me. I'm so glad it's the weekend."

Bree pulled the folds of her plush robe together. "I needed a girls' day."

"You're tired of my brother already?"

She laughed. "No, not at all. I just miss hanging out with you and Jadin. I didn't know she was going to Los Angeles or I would've picked another date."

"She and Michael are trying to sort out their relationship."

"Long-distance relationships are a challenge," Bree stated. "It could work if they both put in the effort, which it looks like they're doing."

Jordin took a long sip of her mimosa. "My brother is in love with that little boy of yours."

"I know. You should see them together. Austin gets down on the floor with him, and it's like he and Emery are the only two people in the world. He is going to be a great father."

"Are you thinking about him as Emery's dad?"

Bree smiled. "I'd like that. Austin and I are in a really good space. We love each other, and we're both looking to settle down. I think there's a possibility that we might seriously consider marriage."

"I think it's more than a possibility," Jordin said. "You both want the same thing and that is a family."

It was past one o'clock when Austin knocked on Jordin's door. "Busy?"

She shook her head. "Come in."

He swung the door closed and took a seat on the chair in her office. "I'm going to ask Bree to marry me."

"Wow…that's great," she murmured. "When?"

"I was thinking about tonight, but before that I'm going to tell her everything."

"I'm glad."

"She's a good mother to Emery."

"I told you that there wasn't anything to worry about with Bree."

"You were right. She's the kind of mother I would want for my son. As much as I hate what Jasmine did, I'm glad Emery has Bree. I can tell he adores her."

"How do you think she's going to react to finding out that you're Emery's father?"

"I wish I knew," Austin muttered. "I hope she'll understand the toll this has taken on me. My child was stolen away from me before I ever knew he existed. I intend on being in his life and I was willing to do whatever I had to do to make that happen."

"But then you met Bree…"

He smiled. "I love her. The three of us belong together. The first time we went out with Emery—it felt so right. This is the way it's supposed to be. We are a family. I want to make it official by marrying her—we will raise Emery together."

"I would still advise that you petition the court for paternity and have his birth certificate amended with your name as his father."

"I intend to do that. I want his last name changed to DuGrandpre."

"As it should be."

Chapter 14

"Is Austin in his office?" Bree inquired.

"I think so, Dr. Collins. Do you want me to call him or do you want to just go back there?"

"I need to see Jordin, too, so I can just walk to the back."

Bree decided to go by Jordin's office first. As she neared, she could hear Austin talking and smiled.

What are those two up to?

Just as she was about to open the door, Jordin's words stopped her.

"How do you think she's going to react to finding out that you're Emery's father?"

"I wish I knew," she heard Austin say. "I hope she'll understand the toll this has taken on me. My child was stolen away from me before I ever knew he existed. I intend on being in his life and I was willing to do whatever I had to do to make that happen."

Bree shuddered as shock penetrated her core.

Austin... Emery's father?

She glanced around, hoping no one was paying attention to her. Bree backed away from the door, turned and walked briskly toward the elevator. She couldn't see Jordin or Austin right now.

His words, "I intend on being in his life and I was willing to do whatever I had to do to make that happen," played over and over in her mind.

He had been using her to get to Emery.

Tears filled her eyes and spilled down her cheeks.

Bree wiped her face with the backs of her hands as she made her way to her car.

I can't break down now. I need to think.

Austin wanted to take her child from her and she wasn't about to let that happen.

I can't lose my baby.

Bree drove straight to the preschool to pick up Emery.

Once home, she immediately started packing. "I'm not going to let him take you from me," she whispered as she packed a suitcase.

"Where we going?" Emery asked. "Au'tin coming with us?"

"No, baby, he's not going to be able to come. It's just going to be you and Mommy."

"Why you cryin'? You got a ouchy?"

Bree thought of her broken heart. "Mommy has a big ouchy."

Emery gave her a hug. "You feel better now?"

She nodded. "Thank you, baby."

An hour later Bree stopped by her neighbor's house to let her know that she and Emery would be away for about a week. In truth, she wasn't sure how long they would be gone, but she didn't want to worry her friend.

In the car, she tried to put the pieces together. Now she could understand why Austin was so enamored with Emery. Jordin knew this and aided her brother in getting to know Bree. She had never felt so betrayed in her life.

Bree prided herself on being a good judge of character, but she had been completely off the mark where Jordin and Austin were concerned. It would be a while before they realized that she and Emery were gone. By the time they found out—they would be long gone.

Austin picked up the phone to call Bree. He'd made reservations for them at High Cotton. When she didn't answer, he left her a message with the time he would be picking her up.

He pulled a box out of the small shopping bag. He'd spent his lunch hour looking for the perfect engagement ring and he'd found it. Austin couldn't wait for Bree to see it.

An hour passed.

Austin checked his phone. It wasn't like Bree to not return his call. If she was busy, she normally sent a text letting him know when she would be able to talk. He assumed it must be a busy day for her.

He didn't call her again until right before he left the office for the day. Austin hadn't heard from her, so he decided to go by her office.

When he arrived, it was completely dark.

Austin called her.

No answer.

His gut instincts told him something wasn't quite right, but he couldn't figure out what had gone wrong.

Austin drove over to her house.

When he knocked, there was no answer.

Sara opened her door. "Hey, Austin," she greeted. "Sugar, they're not there. She and Emery are on vacation. I'm surprised she didn't mention it. They left today."

"No, she didn't tell me," he muttered. "Are you sure?"

"That's what she told me. She said they would be gone for a week."

"Did she tell you where they were going?"

Sara shook her head. "Naw, she didn't, which is kinda odd. She usually good about letting me know where she's going. Bree was in a hurry and she looked upset. I called her about an hour ago to check on her, but she didn't answer."

Austin spent the next hour pacing the floor, trying to understand what had happened with Bree. They got along well and thus far, their relationship was amazing. With every minute they spent together, Austin fell more in love with her. And she loved him. He was certain of that.

Why didn't she tell me she was leaving town?

A sick churning started in the pit of his stomach. Spinning around, Austin went to the living room and picked up the phone.

He tried calling Bree once again.

No answer.

Maybe she was on a plane. This would explain why she hadn't returned his or Sara's phone calls. Still, they had prearranged plans to have dinner this evening. Bree never once mentioned that she would be going away. This was something that had come about quickly.

Austin sat in the darkened living room staring out the window and watching the occasional sweep of car lights beam in from the street.

The refrigerator kicked on. The ice maker dumped.

He rubbed a hand over his chest.

It hurt.

Bree's thoughts were jagged and painful as she turned on the dusty road that led to her grandmother's house in

Roseville, Georgia. A heaviness centered in her chest as she felt an inexplicable feeling of heartbreak.

Emery was in the backseat sleeping. He had been no trouble during the four-hour drive from Charleston. She was so proud of him.

Tears filled Bree's eyes at the idea of losing her son. *I love him so much. I can't lose my baby.* Worse, she couldn't believe that Jordin had participated in something like this—they had been close friends since college.

How could she do this to me?

She refused to spend any time thinking about Austin. He could've been honest with her—he didn't have to try to manipulate her. Bree was hurt and furious with him.

The first thing she had to do in the morning after she got Emery settled was to call her attorney. She needed to make sure the adoption was legal. After all, Austin wasn't listed on the birth certificate. She didn't want to lose her son. He was her everything.

Bree looked at her phone.

She had messages from both Sara and Austin. She wasn't in the mood to talk to anyone tonight. All Bree wanted to do was take a bath and go to bed, but she didn't want to worry her neighbor, so she sent her a text.

Hey, I'm okay. Just needed some time to think. Will explain everything when I return.
Bree

After her bath, she saw a text from Sara.

Austin came by. He didn't know you were leaving. Everything OK with you two?

Bree decided to be honest.

No. He is part of the reason I left. We'll talk when I get back.

There was another call from Austin.

Emery was still sleeping, so she joined him in the bed. Bree didn't want to spend a moment away from him.

Chapter 15

Coming to Roseville had always given Bree a sense of peace. It had come as a surprise when her foster parents received a letter from a pastor, informing them that her grandmother has left the house to Bree.

She was in college at the time and traveled to Georgia to meet with the Reverend Moore. He had been using the house for visiting pastors to stay. The church had been paying the expenses of the taxes and utilities for the place since the death of her grandmother.

Bree allowed the church to continue using the house. When the Reverend Moore passed away, the congregation dwindled down until the doors closed for good. She decided to renovate the house and keep it as a place for her and Emery to come and relax.

She loved the way the flowers bloomed all around the porch in summer and how the trees shifted from green to a golden spectrum of orange and red in the fall. It rained around midnight, the raindrops falling in a monotonous drone that lulled her to sleep.

Today, though, she felt restless.

Even the November air seemed to be holding its breath,

waiting for something. She felt that same sense of anticipation inside her like the flutter of butterfly wings. Something was about to happen.

Bree tried to go back to her book, but her mind kept
wandering. She found herself looking down the long dirt
road. If anyone had been coming, she would have been
able to see the dust cloud miles away.

Nothing moved.

The weather was still warm, despite the cloud casting
a dark, cool shadow.

Bree shivered, sensing a change in the air.

Austin burst into his sister's office without knocking.
"Have you talked to Bree?"

Jordin shook her head. "I left her a message earlier, but
she hasn't called me back. Did you try her office?"

"She's not there," Austin responded. "Her neighbor said
that Bree told her that she and Emery were going to be
gone for a week. On vacation. The thing is that she never
mentioned going anywhere to me and she's not returning
my calls or texts. I think she's run away for some reason."

Frowning, Jordin asked, "Why would she do that?"

He shrugged. "Something's up with Bree. I just don't
know what it is."

Jordin picked up the phone. "This isn't making any
sense. Let me try again to see if I can reach her."

Austin sank down in one of the chairs facing her.

"Hey, it's me. Austin and I are getting worried about
you. Can you give us a call or send a text just to let us
know you're okay? *Please* let us hear from you."

"I don't have a good feeling about this," Austin said.
"Do you think she found out that I was Emery's father
somehow?"

"I don't see how she could, but it's the only thing that

makes sense. I know Bree and she wouldn't just take off like this. She certainly wouldn't just avoid phone calls. It's not like her."

"Any idea where she might go?"

"Not really."

"Do you think she'd go back to Vegas?"

Jordin shook her head. "No, she didn't really like living out there."

Her cell phone vibrated.

She picked it up. "Bree just sent a text."

Jordin read it aloud.

"I am fine. I know about Emery and I'm not going to lose my son. I will do whatever I have to do to keep him. Bree."

She looked up at Austin. "I don't know how she found out."

"It doesn't matter now. The only thing I care about is finding Emery and Bree. I can't lose either of them."

"Now that I think about it," Jordin said, "her grandmother left her house to Bree. She used to let a church use it, and she fixed it up. I know it's in Georgia, but I don't remember the name of the town. It's near Atlanta, though."

Austin rose to his feet. "We can search for a deed or tax record."

"She didn't call because she knows that I kept the truth from her, as well," Jordin stated. "Bree's angry with me."

"Once I get a chance to talk to her, I'll fix all of this, sis," he assured her. "I'm not going to let you take the fall for my actions."

"I was the one who told you to wait before telling her the truth."

"Neither of us had any idea that Bree and I would get involved. I should've told her the truth."

"What are you going to do now?"

Austin headed to the door. "I'm going to find out where they are and bring them home. I love Bree and I'm going to tell her that I want a life with her and Emery."

"I hope that we haven't lost all of Bree's trust."

"I'll do whatever I have to do to get it back," he vowed. If he'd listened to his common sense, none of this would have happened. Austin drew in a deep breath and let it out slowly. All the common sense in the world wouldn't change how he'd handled this situation.

He loved Bree. Being with her energized him and gave him hope for a better future. She was the other half of his heart. Giving her up without a fight was out of the question.

Bree stared at the text she'd sent Jordin and silently debated if she'd done the right thing. She had grown tired of all the phone calls and the messages. Despite her anger with Jordin, she didn't want her to worry.

Turning the phone off, she slid it back into the pocket of her jeans.

Her heart broke all over again each time she thought of the man she had come to love. When she lost Caleb, Bree never considered she would ever fall in love again.

But Austin was only using her to get to Emery.

She tried to swallow the lump that lingered in her throat. Bree wasn't sure she could ever forgive him.

If he is truly Emery's father—he deserves to be a part of the boy's life.

She thought back to what she'd overheard of Austin's conversation with Jordin. He hadn't known about the child until after the adoption. If this was true, then why didn't he just tell her the truth? Why all the secrecy?

Bree had a lot of questions, but she wasn't ready to talk to Austin. Her attorney hadn't called her back. She needed to be prepared legally before she sat down to discuss anything with him, so until then—Bree intended to avoid Austin.

She went to check on Emery.

He lay on top of the covers fast asleep.

She left the door open a crack.

Two steps down the hall, Bree turned back for another look. Emery hadn't stirred. Fingers crossed that he stayed that way, she went into his room and sat cross-legged on the floor, putting a puzzle back together.

The truth was that she couldn't stay in Georgia forever. She still had a practice and clients who depended on her. She would have to go back to Charleston.

Or did she?

Bree glanced around the house. With more renovations, she could make it a perfect home for her and Emery.

But what if I lose him?

Emotionally drained and her eyes heavy with fatigue, she made her way to her bedroom.

Completely dressed, Bree lay down on top of the comforter, turning on her side. She was too confused and exhausted to think about the possibility.

Her heart couldn't handle the pain.

Chapter 16

Austin turned up the radio to drown out the thunder exploding around him. It had been nice weather when he left Charleston; once he crossed the Georgia line, it was pouring down rain. He had never enjoyed driving in bad weather conditions and was anxious to get to his destination.

Bakeries, a couple of inns, restaurants and shops lined the main street of Roseville, Georgia. He had never heard of the small town located thirty miles outside Atlanta. According to the welcome sign at the entrance of Roseville, there were about ten thousand residents.

His windshield wipers fought valiantly in a losing battle to maintain visibility. It was almost 9:30 p.m. The streetlights did very little to help. Austin continued driving, heading toward a rural section of town. The lane was long and straight, and unpaved. His tires would be covered in mud, he knew. He had never been a fan of rain.

Following the directions on his GPS, Austin ended up at an ordinary-looking two-story house with white siding and green shutters, sheltered by rows of trees that looked to be over fifteen or sixteen feet tall. The yard looked to be well-maintained.

She'd told him that she didn't have any family, so Austin assumed she was the one taking care of her grandmother's home.

He wasn't going to disturb her this late. He wanted to make sure Bree and Emery were here.

Her car was in the driveway.

Austin released a sigh of relief. *They're here.*

He didn't park in front of the house because he didn't want to scare Bree.

Tonight, he would stay at a hotel and return tomorrow, just before noon.

Austin hoped she was willing to hear him out. He didn't know how she'd found out, but he vowed to make things right between them. He didn't want to lose her or Emery. He wanted them both.

Jordin called shortly after he checked in to the hotel.

"Please tell me that you found her."

"She's here in Roseville," he said. "I'm going to go see her tomorrow afternoon. I don't want to go to the house too early. I know Emery usually takes a nap after his lunch. I figure that's the best time to try and talk to her."

"I feel awful. I should've let you tell her when you'd planned."

"We were right to wait. She didn't know me then. If she's running now—there's no telling what she would've done back then."

"I'm so glad you found her, Austin."

"Me, too."

When their conversation ended a few minutes later, he took a shower.

Austin tried not to think of what lay ahead.

* * *

Leaving the hotel, Austin turned down a side street. Then right one block.

On the corner was an antiques store, the windows filled with colorful bottles, vases and other items. Next door a small café filled up as people poured in to escape the rain and in search of coffee.

Austin found his way back to the house without turning on the GPS. He saw the white picket fence the moment he turned the corner; he hadn't really noticed it the night before. It was a nice touch, he thought.

As he neared the house, Austin eyed the tall oak trees guarding the house.

Her car was still there.

He'd come by earlier than planned because he wanted to make sure she wasn't planning to run again.

Austin parked away from the house. He wasn't ready to face her just yet.

Coward.

He felt terrible over the way Bree found out about Emery. This was not the way Austin wanted it to happen.

Dreams were often hard to separate from reality, Austin discovered as he was slowly awakened by the alarm clock five hours later.

Before Austin opened her eyes to the new day, he stretched on the firm mattress, remembering the way Bree's arms felt around him. He missed her laughter. He missed everything about her.

"Bree." Her name escaped his lips before he could stop it.

The full impact of his situation hit him.

He and Bree might never have a future together. What would this mean for Emery?

* * *

Bree brushed her teeth and ran a brush through her hair before braiding it into a single thick rope that lay against her back. She navigated through the bathroom door, making her way to the dresser underneath a television bolted high on the wall.

She grabbed a pair of jeans, tugged them on and then tucked the ends of her yellow shirt into the waistband. Bree stepped into a pair of flats, intent on getting on with her day.

I need coffee.

In the kitchen Bree set her coffee cup down on the glass-topped table and turned her face to the window. It was still raining.

The dark, gloomy weather echoed her mood.

She closed her eyes as vivid mental images churned through her mind—nights with Austin, dancing, laughing and loving. She remembered the late-night picnic near the moonlit waterfront. Lying in bed, wrapped in his arms, his whispers promising love and other tantalizing delights.

Bree curled in a fetal position, sobbing until no more tears would come. Then she got up and made her way downstairs where she sat down in the den and watched television.

Opening her eyes, Bree steeled herself for what was to come the next day. Her tear-filled gaze returned to the window, watching as raindrops streamed down the pane.

Her life was different now.

Bree wiped her face with the back of her hand. She didn't want Emery to come in and see her crying.

After two cups of coffee, she managed breakfast for them.

She woke him up fifteen minutes later.

After they ate, Bree and Emery spent the morning with her reading to him; watching a movie and painting pictures.

When the clock struck twelve, Bree took meat, cheese and condiments out of the fridge and grabbed a loaf of bread from a wooden breadbox on the countertop. "How about a sandwich?"

Emery nodded. "Ham san'wish?"

She smiled. "I think we can do that."

Bree began stacking meat and slices of cheese on a piece of bread. For a moment she paused, watching as lightning forked across the sky.

She reached for a bottle of mustard, looked up again and saw a black SUV slowly approaching the house.

Her stomach churned with nervousness.

How could Austin have found them so quickly? She hadn't even told Jordin where she was going.

Bree picked up the plate sitting on the counter and brought it over to the table. "Here you are, sweetie. When you finish, I want you to go back to your room. Okay? You can watch the Smurfs movie. I've already put it in."

"'Kay…"

She took a deep breath and headed to the front door. Bree wanted to avoid a confrontation, especially in front of Emery.

Austin got out of his SUV when she stepped outside on the porch.

Tension radiated between them like heat from a fire.

Bree felt an instant's squeezing hurt when her eyes met his. "What are you doing here? How did you find me?"

"Sweetheart, why did you leave town without a word to anyone? We were all worried about you." His words contained a strong suggestion of censure.

"I guess we both know the answers to these questions,"

Bree stated, staring at him with burning, reproachful eyes. "You're Emery's biological father and you want to take him away from me."

"I don't deny that I want to be a part of my son's life, but you have it all wrong. Just let me explain…"

"Why not be honest from the beginning?" Her tone had become chilly.

"I should've been straight with you, but Bree, I was afraid you would panic." He paused a moment before adding, "As it turns out, I had every reason to be worried."

"Are you really trying to turn this on me?" Bree showed her disbelief in the tone of her voice.

"And for your information, I didn't run away. I came here because I needed some time to think."

"That's not what I was saying."

Arms folded across her chest, she asked, "Then *what* are you saying to me, Austin?" Bree threw the words at him like stones.

"I was going to tell you the truth, but that's when I couldn't reach you."

"Aren't you just a little bit curious as to how I found out?"

He nodded. "How?"

"I came to the law firm to see if you wanted to have lunch with me. I'd stopped by Jordin's office just to say hello and I heard you talking with her. How could you two betray me like this?"

"Don't blame Jordin," Austin responded. "She's not the one at fault. *I am.*"

"She knew about this, but she never said anything to me. I guess blood is thicker than water. You're her brother and I'm just a friend."

"Bree, can we just sit and talk? I'll tell you everything."

"We're talking now."

Austin let out a long, audible breath. "Please…"

She sat down in one of the rocking chairs. "I'm listening." Her anger abated somewhat under his expression.

He sat down in the chair beside her. "Jasmine Reynolds and I had been together for almost three years. Our relationship was tumultuous at best, but I thought I was in love, and so I stayed with her until I couldn't take any more. When we broke up, she left town and never told me about the baby."

"How did you find out about Emery?"

"She moved to Vegas with a friend. They had a falling out and Cheryl moved back home. I guess she had an attack of conscience or she wanted to hurt Jasmine—I'm not sure which, but she told me everything."

"How do you know she was telling the truth?"

"When I went home to visit my mother, I ran into Jasmine and she confirmed Cheryl's story."

"Why wouldn't she just contact you?"

"I've asked that same question repeatedly," Austin stated. "The only answer I can come up with is that she wanted to hurt me. We had a bad breakup."

"I was told that the father died before the child was born," Bree said.

"That's obviously not true. I'm willing to take a paternity test to prove it."

She bit her lip until it throbbed like her pulse. "I love Emery."

"I know that, Bree. I love him, too, and I want to be a part of my son's life. I've already missed out on so much."

Her spirits sank even lower. "Tell me the truth. Were you planning to have the adoption reversed?"

"I did," he confessed. "Bree, you are his mother. I want you in his life…please believe me."

"What I believe is that your interest in me was only

because you wanted Emery. And like you said, you were willing to do whatever you had to do to make that happen." Bree shook her head. "I just wish you'd been honest with me from the beginning."

"I admit Emery was the reason I wanted to meet you, but the time we spent together…"

She rose to her feet. "No, don't…"

"What I feel for you is real, Bree."

"I don't believe you."

"You know in your heart that I'm in love with you. I came all the way here to prove it, sweetheart."

Bree peered into his eyes and felt her knees wobble a little at the intensity of Austin's stare.

He cupped her cheek in one hand, and the heat of his skin seeped into hers, causing a flush of warmth that slid through her like syrup.

She ducked her head and slapped his hand away. "Austin, I'm going to be honest with you. There's no way I'm just going to hand over my son to you without a fight. Now, I need you to leave."

"Au'tin," Emery said from the doorway.

Bree had no idea how long he had been standing there. She'd left him in the kitchen eating before coming out to the porch to talk to Austin.

"Hey, buddy," he murmured.

Bree held back her anger, her throat raw with unuttered shouts and protests. The last thing she wanted was Austin hanging around longer, but he had a right to see Emery. She would give him a few minutes with the little boy.

She felt guilty and selfish.

Austin picked up his son. "What are you up to?"

"Playin'…"

Bree didn't say anything, just sat back down while Austin talked with his son. She closed her eyes, her heart aching with pain.

He'd shaken her more than she'd thought he would. Just being near him again had awakened feelings and emotions she was trying to ignore. She had walked into it with her heart wide open.

"I need you to leave, Austin."

"We need to talk this through."

"I can't right now. This is why I left town. I needed some space to think about everything."

"I'm not giving up on us," he said. "I know that you're angry right now, but we have to have a conversation."

"I know," she responded. "I just can't do it today."

"I'd like to spend some time with Emery."

Bree shook her head.

"I'm not going to snatch him up and run away. I'm not that kind of man. Besides, you don't need the distraction of Emery while you're trying to make sense of what's going on." He looked her in the eye. "You can trust me, Bree. He's my son and I will always put his needs first."

"Please have him back by five for dinner."

A lone tear slipped from her eye.

"Sweetheart... I'll bring him back to you. *I promise.*" Austin wiped away the tear. "I'm sorry for the way I handled this."

"Just bring him back."

Chapter 17

Bree stepped aside to let Austin through the front door. She was weak with relief that her son was back. "Mommy missed you so much," she murmured, pulling him into her embrace. "I'm so glad you're back."

"I had fun with Au'tin."

She pasted on a smile. "I'm glad. Little boys are supposed to have lots of fun."

"I want to go watch TV."

"Go ahead, sweetie."

"Thank you for letting me spend time with him," Austin said when they were alone in the living room.

Her gaze became troubled, but she said nothing more, although the small creases stayed between her brows.

"I hate all this tension between us."

No response.

Austin reached for her, but she stepped away. "I can't do this with you."

"Despite what you may think about me, I want you to know that my feelings for you are real."

"The only thing we need to discuss is Emery," Bree said in a choked voice. "Nothing else matters."

"Babe, you know that's not true."

Biting her lip, Bree looked away. She refused to get swept up in the tenderness of his gaze.

The pain of Austin's betrayal still stung. "I need to cook. I wanted to have everything ready, but I couldn't…" She'd spent the time pacing and fearful that Emery might not return.

"Why don't you and Emery have dinner with me tonight?"

"I don't think it's a good idea," Bree responded. "We're not some big happy family."

"You have to eat."

"I don't have to eat with you, Austin."

"I understand why you're upset with me and you have every right to be, but I'm trying to work things out between us."

"I'm just not sure that's possible."

"Bree, what do you want me to do? You know I'm not just going to walk away from my son. We can't just ignore this situation."

"I can't do this right now. I'm sorry, Austin." Her eyes filled with tears. "You can't possibly understand what this is doing to me."

"You're wrong, Bree," he interjected. "I understand more than you know. I was never told about my own child and when I am—I find that he's been adopted."

She silently considered his words and the anguish in his voice. After a brief pause, Bree stated, "I've been selfish. I've been only thinking of myself. I'm sorry that this happened to you, Austin, but I don't regret adopting Emery."

"We both want what's best for him."

"And what is that?" she asked. "To be ripped from my arms?"

He shook his head. "I love you, Bree. I want a life with you and Emery."

"I wish I could believe you, but I'm sorry. *I don't.*"

Deep down she wanted to believe that Austin was being sincere about his love for her, but it was difficult. Difficult because she knew he would do and say just about anything to be in his son's life. She loved him, but without trust…a relationship between them would not work.

"Please don't shut me out, Bree."

"I do understand how you're feeling. What happened wasn't fair to you," she stated. "What I can't understand is why you kept this from me all this time. You had to know how this would play out. Austin, you knew what this would do to me."

"Why can't you see this as a good thing? We love each other."

"That's why you should have come to me, Austin."

"I had planned to tell you…it was the same day that you let me meet Emery. I was afraid if I'd told you then—you would've changed your mind."

"I honestly don't know what I would've done," she confessed.

"Bree, please understand. I wanted so badly to see him."

"Austin, I really need some time to deal with this. Can you please give me that?"

"Are you okay?" he asked without preamble.

Her hand pressed to her stomach, Bree eyed him. "Yes, I'm fine."

"You don't look fine."

"It's a monthly problem."

"Is there anything I can do?"

He wanted to reach across and pull her into his arms and just hold her.

Bree shook her head. "It's something I've had to deal with for a long time."

"Is it like this every month?"

"No, but I've had a couple of severe bouts of endometriosis over the last few months."

She suddenly bent over, groaning in agony.

Austin was instantly by her side, holding her close as she trembled from the pain. "Baby, I'm so sorry you have to suffer like this."

Bree continued to moan.

"Lie down, sweetheart," Austin told her as he escorted her to her bedroom. "Is there something you can take for the pain?"

She gave a slight nod.

He helped her get settled in bed. "I'll get you something to drink."

Austin left and returned with a glass of water.

"Thank you," she murmured weakly.

"Let me make dinner for you and Emery before I go," Austin offered. "I promise I'll leave right after."

"That's fine," she said after a moment. "I don't have the strength to argue."

Austin hated seeing the intense pain etched in her expression. He hated more that he was the one responsible for hurting her, which no doubt factored in the agony she was now experiencing.

As much as he wanted to try and repair the damage, Austin knew he had to give her the space she needed right now. However, he wasn't going to give up on them.

His mother was arriving in the morning. Hopefully, she would be able to get through to Bree. Maybe she could make her understand what he could not.

He retrieved a package of chicken out of the refrigerator. Emery loved fried chicken. It was also something he was skilled in cooking.

When dinner was ready, Austin walked down the hall and knocked on Bree's bedroom door.

"Come in," she murmured.

"Dinner's ready," he said. "How are you feeling?"

"My body hurts, but it's not as bad as before." She eased out of bed. "I really appreciate you going out of your way like this."

"It's the least I can do."

Bree stood up. A wave of dizziness overtook her.

"Sweetheart…"

She swayed.

Strong arms swept her up and laid her back in bed.

Bree doubled over in pain.

"I think we need to get you to the hospital," Austin said.

"Emery…"

"He'll be with me."

She was in too much pain to contest. "I feel like my pelvis is full of razor blades. It hasn't been this bad in a long time."

Tears filled her eyes.

He hugged her. "It's going to be okay, babe."

She leaned into him as another wave of pain ripped through her, causing her to cry out.

After a moment Bree uttered, "I'm ready to go. This doesn't feel right."

Austin pulled into Roseville Memorial Hospital parking lot fifteen minutes later. He signaled for someone to bring a wheelchair to the car.

"Mommy okay?" Emery asked.

"She's going to be just fine, but she needs to see the doctor."

"Mommy tummy hurt."

"Yes, sweetie. My tummy hurts, but I'll be okay."

* * *

After the doctor informed them that Bree would need to have surgery, Austin made a phone call.

"Mom, I really need your help," he stated as soon as Irene answered the phone. "I need you to come to Georgia instead of Charleston."

"Georgia? Why?"

"Bree's in the hospital and has to have surgery. I'll explain when you get here. I'm going to book a ticket for you. I'll pick you up in Atlanta and bring you to Roseville."

"I'll start packing, then. I'll see you soon, son."

Chapter 18

"Who's that?" Emery asked when they stopped in front of baggage claim at the airport in Atlanta.

"That's my mom."

"You have a mommy?"

Austin chuckled. "Yes, I do."

"You don't look like you slept well," Irene said when she entered the vehicle.

"I didn't."

"How is Bree?"

"She's still in surgery," he said in a low voice. "They found a melon-size cyst on her ovary. I asked you to come because I don't want to leave her side and I need someone to watch Emery. I thought it would be a good way for you to get to know him." He would have called Jordin, but with everything coming out about Emery being Austin's biological son, he was worried that would make things worse.

Irene nodded in understanding. This thing with Bree is really bothering you."

He glanced over at his mother. "I love her."

"I can see that."

Austin took her luggage to his car and drove back to

the hospital. The three of them sat in the waiting room for news on Bree, with Irene trying to keep Emery occupied with a coloring book.

Thirty or so minutes passed before he was called to meet with the doctor.

"The surgery went fine," he told Austin. "She's in recovery now. You'll be able to see her as soon as she's awake."

"Thank you."

"Praise the good Lord," Irene murmured when Austin relayed the news from the doctor.

"Mom, the way she suffered... I've never seen anything like it. She was in so much pain."

"That disease is a terrible one."

"I hope that this surgery helps her."

Irene covered his hand with her own. "She'll be fine."

"When Bree's feeling better, I'd like for you to talk to her. Maybe you can reach her mother to mother."

"I don't know what I can tell this woman, Austin. You have a legal right to your son. I'm sure she knows this."

"Bree feels like I manipulated her."

"Well, you did make a mess of this whole thing," Irene uttered. "You didn't do this the right way, Austin."

He stole a peek at her but did not respond.

"Son, I know what you're thinking. I didn't handle the situation with your father right. I admit it."

"But you did what you thought was best at the time," he responded.

"I did what I felt I could live with."

"I did the same thing, Mom. I did what I thought was best. My timing was off, but I intended to tell her everything."

"Your intentions came a little too late."

"I'm aware of that, Mom." Austin didn't need to be reminded of the grave mistake he'd made. He also couldn't feel any worse.

Bree opened her eyes, her vision clearing as the fog lifted. She was in the hospital.

The dull ache in her stomach reminded her why she was here. They'd removed a cyst through laparoscopic surgery.

Austin knocked on the door. "Can I come in?"

"Of course," she responded.

When he walked in alone, she asked, "Where's Emery?"

"He's with my mother."

Panic set in. "What do you mean by that, Austin?"

"Calm down, babe. My mother is in town. I had her come to help with Emery while I was here with you. They're in the waiting room. He's been really worried about you, but I've assured him that you're fine."

She relaxed. "I'd like to meet her and I need to see my son."

"I'll get them."

He left and returned with Irene and Emery in tow.

"This is my mother," Austin said. "Irene DuGrandpre."

Emery was delighted to see Bree. "Mommy, you got a ouchy?"

She painted on a smile. "I'm feeling much better now, sweetie."

"The doctor fixed you?"

Bree nodded. She glanced over at Irene and said, "It's very nice to finally meet you. Thank you so much for coming all the way here."

Not one to beat around the bush, Irene said, "I told Austin that he handled this situation all wrong."

Bree shifted in the hospital bed. "I definitely agree."

"I'm still in the room," he interjected.

"Why don't you go spend some time with this little sweetie?" Irene suggested. "I'm sure he's hungry. I'll stay here with Bree. I'd like to get to know this young lady."

"Despite what's going on between us, I'm glad Austin was here because I never thought I'd end up in the hospital."

"He's a good man, Bree," Irene stated. "Although Austin's approach was not the right way to do this—my son wasn't being malicious."

"Deep down I know he wasn't," she responded. "He was acting out of love for his son."

"He waited to tell you because Austin wanted to see if the child was happy and if you were a good mother. Surely you can understand why he'd want to know this."

"I suppose so," Bree murmured. "I have to confess that I probably would've done the same thing. Only I wouldn't have waited so long to tell him who I was."

"My son really cares for you."

"Trust is a big deal for me," she stated. "And I don't like being manipulated. Jordin and I have been friends since college. Knowing she had a part in this really hurts."

"They were only trying to protect you."

"I didn't need protection. I needed the truth."

Irene nodded in understanding. "I kept Austin away from his father because I needed to get away from him— at least that's what I told myself. There was a part of me that wanted to hurt Etienne. I never considered that I was hurting my son."

"You think I should just hand over Emery to Austin without a fight."

"I'm not saying that at all. I think you two must find a way to work out a compromise because that child will need both of you."

"If Austin gets the adoption reversed, I'll have no legal

right to Emery. I didn't give birth to him, but I've had him since he was two days old. I can't bear the thought of losing my child."

"You love my son, don't you?"

"I do," Bree acknowledged.

"Then talk to him and work this out," Irene suggested. "Austin is not an unreasonable man."

"I know that you're right, but I'm having a hard time with the fact that he manipulated me."

"That wasn't the case," Austin said from the doorway.

"I'm going to spend some time with my grandson," Irene said as she rose to her feet. "And leave you two to talk."

When she left the room, Austin took a seat in the chair facing Bree. "I wasn't manipulating you."

"You deliberately kept the truth from me. You dated me under this cloud of secrecy—what do you call it, if not manipulation?"

"I sought to protect you."

"Unfortunately, it had the opposite effect." Bree paused a moment before continuing. "Austin, I get it. I understand your reasons for doing this, but it doesn't lessen the heartache."

"I'm so sorry."

"I blame myself," she blurted. "Your attachment to Emery…it should've been a red flag of some sort. I should have questioned it."

"You know in your heart that I would never do anything to hurt that little boy. Despite my actions, you have to know that I love you."

Chapter 19

Bree was discharged home later that day.

Irene helped her get comfortable in bed while Austin played with Emery.

She was still a little groggy from the effects of the anesthesia. "I'm going to take a nap," she said.

"You rest, dear. Don't you worry about a thing. We will make sure that little boy of yours is fed."

"Thank you for all you've done, Miss Irene."

When she woke up, three hours had passed.

Bree sat up and swung her legs out of bed. She sat on the edge for a moment, trying to summon the strength to stand. Her fingers curled into fists and she closed her eyes to shut out the pain ripping through the area where she'd had surgery.

Normally, she tried to get by without medication, but not this time. Bree picked up the prescription bottle, opening it.

She swallowed two painkillers.

Bree sat there for a moment, waiting for some of the pain to subside. Using the nightstand for support, she rose to her feet.

"Sweetheart, what are you doing?" Austin asked from the doorway.

"I need to go to the bathroom."

"Let me help you." He was instantly by her side.

She held on to his arm, allowing him to escort her to the toilet.

Austin gave her some privacy.

When she opened the door, he was waiting in the bedroom. "I'm going to sit up for a little bit," Bree announced.

Austin helped her into her robe.

"What's Emery been doing?" she asked. "I hope he hasn't been giving y'all a fit."

"He's hasn't been a problem at all. Right now, he's watching a movie on TV with my mom. They took a walk earlier."

"Has he been asking for me?"

"Yes," Austin stated. "I told him you were not feeling well. He wanted to give you a kiss, so I brought him in here while you were sleeping."

"Thank you for that. Emery believes his kisses make me better." Bree smiled. "I think he might be right."

The pain began to dissipate as she gingerly made her way to the family room and sat down on the sofa.

"Why don't you put your feet up?" he suggested. "You may be more comfortable."

Bree agreed as she changed her position.

Austin covered her with a throw. "Are you okay?"

She gave a slight nod. "I'm fine."

"Mommy…" Emery rushed over to her. "You no feel good still?"

"I'm feeling much better, sweetie."

He was about to climb into her lap, but Austin stopped him by saying, "My mom made some peanut butter cookies. Why don't you go into the kitchen and get some for Mommy?"

Emery half walked and half skipped out of the room.

"You're very good with him."

He looked at Bree. "I think it must come naturally or something. When I look at him, all I want to do is to love and protect him. I would do anything for that little boy."

"That's exactly how I feel."

"It's not hard to see that we both want the same thing for him," Austin said with a subtle lifting of his brows. "We're on the same side, babe."

Bree shrugged her shoulders in resignation, then leaned back and closed her eyes.

The next day Austin arrived to find Bree up and moving about. She had insisted that he go back to the hotel with his mother instead of staying at the house with them. There were times when that independent streak in her could be both endearing and frustrating.

Bree found that the sight of him still managed to take her breath away. She stepped aside to let him enter through the front door.

He handed her a dozen red, long-stemmed roses. "Hi, beautiful. This is for you."

She accepted the gift, asking, "What's this for?"

"Just because," he said, smiling. "You look gorgeous."

An electrifying shudder reverberated through Bree as she sniffed the fragrant scent. "Thanks, and thank you for the roses. This is very sweet of you to do this."

He sat down, leaned back and fit his fingers together. "Looks like you're on the mend."

She smiled. "I feel much better."

Austin spread his hands regretfully. "I hated seeing you in pain like that."

"Hopefully the surgery will help."

"Why don't I put those in a vase for you?"

"There's one in the top left cabinet," she told him.

"Did you know about the cyst?" Austin inquired when he returned to the living room.

"No, I didn't."

He took her hand in his. "I'm glad you're okay. The thought of losing you...it was unbearable."

"Thankfully, we don't have to worry about that."

"I know things have been tense between us. Bree, the bottom line is that I love you." He pulled out a ring box. "You're already the mother of my son. I want you to be my wife. Will you marry me?"

Will you marry me? There was a time when Bree would've been excited about the idea of marrying Austin. Her gaze drifted over to the engagement ring he offered to her, each flawless stone throwing off light in all directions. Her eyebrows shot up in surprise.

It was exquisite.

Nothing could compete with this ring.

"Sweetheart," Austin prompted. "Did you hear me?"

Swallowing once, she peered up at Austin, who waited above her, the possessive intent in his eyes making her ache to give in.

But she couldn't do it. "I'm sorry, I can't."

Austin looked stunned. "Why?"

"I'm looking at this practically," Bree said smoothly, with no expression on her face. "We are both in this predicament and I get it. We get married—it's a way for us to both get what we want. But the problem is that I don't want a marriage of convenience. The way I see it—marriage isn't supposed to be a business arrangement."

"I know," he responded. "It's supposed to be love and commitment forever. Bree, I want that, too." Austin's cheekbones softened as he looked away. "I want a wife who loves me as I love her. I want a life partner to share the ups and downs with, knowing that we're stronger together than apart. You are that person for me."

"As much as I care about you, the truth is that I no longer trust you, Austin."

"What can I do to prove my love to you?"

"I don't know," she responded quietly. "I've been in contact with my attorney and he advised that the first thing we need to do is to have a paternity test done. Your claim to Emery has to be established before anything else."

"I'm fine with this," Austin stated. "Afterward, I want my name placed on his birth certificate."

"I propose that we table this discussion until we get the results back on the paternity test," Bree said.

He frowned in confusion. "Why? We both know that he's my son. Babe, I'm not planning to snatch him out of your arms. I simply want my paternal rights restored."

"If the adoption is voided—I lose any rights to Emery."

"That's why we should get married," Austin responded.

"We should marry for love—not to co-parent a child. It may have been the solution for Ryker and Garland, but that's not what I want for me."

"So, you would prefer that we raise Emery together, but not as man and wife?"

"It's the way it has to be."

"Right now, I know you're upset with me, but you're not thinking clearly. Take some more time to think about this. Bree, we belong together. Our son deserves to grow up in a two-parent home." Austin's heart thudded with hope as he watched her struggle against doubt and move toward trusting him. "We love each other. Before you found out that I was Emery's father—we spoke of taking our relationship to the next level. Please give me a chance to prove that I want to be with you and not just because you are the mother of my son."

"Okay," she whispered. "I'll try."

Austin kissed her on the cheek. "Thank you."

He left to go back to the hotel to pick up his mother.

Bree had insisted on making lunch for them. "I'm not an invalid. Besides, I did all of the prep work earlier."

Although she was still upset with him, Bree still enjoyed spending time with Austin. It meant something that he'd come all the way to Georgia after them. Despite everything, her heart still belonged to him, and for a very brief moment, Bree allowed herself to consider that they might have a future together.

Seated around the dining room table, they enjoyed chicken salad sandwiches, fresh fruit and freshly baked cookies.

"Everything is delicious," Irene murmured. "You must give me your recipe for the chicken salad."

"I'd be happy to," Bree responded.

She warmed beneath the heat of Austin's gaze and her body ached for his touch, but Bree knew that she couldn't allow herself to go there.

"Mom's right. You put your foot in that chicken salad."

She chuckled. "It's my foster mother's recipe. She's won awards for it."

After lunch, they settled on the front porch to soak in the autumn weather.

"This is a lovely little town," Irene told her. "I'd never heard of Roseville until Austin mentioned it."

"That's what most people say," Bree responded. "We call it Georgia's little hidden treasure. We do get our share of tourists here. That's why you see all the boutiques downtown. We have a lake that's a very popular attraction for visitors."

"Would you like to take a walk?" Austin asked.

"Go ahead," Irene encouraged. "I'll watch Emery."

The idea sent her spirits soaring. Bree was feeling a little restless. The walk would do her good.

"Your mother is a very sweet lady. I like her," she told Austin as they walked along the dusty road.

"She said the same thing about you, too."

Austin took Bree by the hand. "I feel like I'm in a Norman Rockwell painting."

Bree laughed. "You're silly."

"I've missed this…hearing you laugh like that."

"So have I."

"Sweetheart, everything is going to be okay. I promise."

She looked up at him. "You really believe this, don't you?"

He nodded. "I do because I have faith in *us*."

Bree couldn't deny the spark of excitement at the prospect of his words, but her faith was not as strong as his. She feared his interest in her was only a result of his desire to be with his son. She wanted him to love her because he simply could not do anything else.

They walked a couple of blocks before returning to the house. Bree was beginning to feel tired. "I think I need to lie down for a bit."

When they returned to the house, his mother and Emery were outside playing with his ball.

"I'm glad you came down, Miss Irene," she stated.

She smiled. "Me, too."

"I hope you'll come over tomorrow. We can continue getting to know one another." She didn't want to be rude—she just wanted some time alone. She just wanted it to be her and Emery for the evening.

Bree walked them out to the car.

He kissed her cheek. "You need to sit down and get

some rest. You've been moving around a lot today. Call me if you need anything."

"I'll be fine," she reassured him.

"I'll see you tomorrow."

Her gaze slowly lifted to his eyes. The moment they made eye contact she was snatched into a web of heated desire.

What in the world is wrong with me?

"Son, everything is going to work out."

"You really think so?"

Irene nodded. "Bree still loves you and I know she'll do what's best for Emery."

"You're right about that. She really loves him," Austin said. "I'm not sure Jasmine could have ever loved Emery like that. She's very selfish."

"I'm glad you asked me to come," Irene stated. "I need to apologize to you for what I did. I was wrong to keep you away from Etienne."

Austin reached over and took her hand in his. "Mom, we're past all that now."

Irene was one of those people who had perfected the art of giving nothing away—expressionless face, emotionless eyes. She had her arms wrapped around herself as she talked.

"I fell in love with your dad the first time I laid eyes on him." Irene smiled. "When he spoke to me, I thought I'd melt right on the spot. It wasn't long before we were spending all our free time together. Six months into the relationship, I got pregnant."

"How did he react?"

"He was happy about the baby and insisted we get married right away. Etienne was there when we told my parents. My father was furious, but your dad stood up to him.

Things were good until we lost little Jon. That's when things changed for us. When I couldn't take the hurt anymore, I left. Deep down I thought he would come after me, but he didn't."

"Why didn't you go back?"

"My pride wouldn't let me," Irene admitted. "Before the ink was dry on our divorce papers, Etienne started parading Eleanor around town. That was the last straw for me. I couldn't stay in Charleston, so I left."

"Any regrets?"

"I shouldn't have put a wedge between you and your father." Irene wiped her mouth on a napkin. "I owe Etienne an apology."

"Maybe you should reconsider talking to Dad."

"I'm considering it."

Austin picked up two paper cups. "Coffee or tea?"

"Coffee, thanks."

He poured a generous amount into each mug, then handed one to Irene.

Despair gripped Austin. He could live with the fact that Bree was disappointed in him, but he could not live with losing her love. He could live with co-parenting Emery with her, but Austin could not live with the idea of her not trusting him. Her love and respect meant a lot to him.

But he was not going to give in to his desolation. Austin was going to win back Bree's love, respect and trust.

Austin and his mother did some sightseeing the next morning. Irene wanted to visit the lake Bree talked about.

"It's beautiful out here," she said.

Austin agreed.

The sprawling grounds of Lake Roseville beckoned to

families and featured an assortment of rustic campsites and impressive villas. They glimpsed a couple of people riding through the wooded area by horseback.

"It says that the water in Lake Roseville comes from Georgia's Blue Ridge Mountains."

"This is where Bree grew up?" Irene asked.

"She lived here with her grandmother for a short time," Austin said. "Bree ended up in the system after the woman passed away."

Irene snapped a few photographs before they left.

Next, he took her to a boutique so that she could purchase a few souvenirs for friends back home.

They drove the short distance to the house.

"You go on inside," he told his mother. "I need to make a couple of phone calls."

He called Jordin and filled her in on everything that had been going on.

"Hey, I need you to do me a favor," he said.

"What do you need?"

"I need to have a document drawn up regarding Emery."

"What do you want it to say?"

After the call, Austin stepped out of the SUV and made his way to the porch. He heard laughter coming from the back of the house and followed the sound.

He found them, together, on the ground with heads bent, pulling out weeds and depositing them in a basket while Emery played with a ball. Austin indulged himself and watched.

They were laughing and chatting. His mother said something under her breath, and Bree's laughter floated across the air to him.

He smiled in response to the happy sound. He loved the sound of her laughter. Humor chased the shadows from her eyes, reminding him of the way they used to be with one another. Austin had missed hearing her laugh.

When she spotted him, Bree gestured for him to join them.

"I didn't mean to interrupt," he said.

"You're not," she responded, a glint of humor finally returning to her gaze. "You're more than welcome to help us with the yard. Make yourself useful."

Austin turned up his smile a notch. "I was just looking at that rake and thinking that I should probably put it to use."

"I'm sure," Bree murmured.

Amusement flickered in the eyes that met his. "Emery, come help me get up the leaves."

"'Kay…" The little boy ran over to Austin. "I help."

He could feel Bree's eyes on him as he raked the yard. She still loved him; Austin was sure of it.

She handed Austin a large plastic bag. "You can put them in here."

"Thank you."

He began raking, gathering up the leaves that had fallen. When Austin neared Bree, she glanced over her shoulder and said to him, "I don't know if Emery's helping or playing."

"I think it's a combination of both."

They laughed.

"Do you have a printer here?" Austin inquired after checking his text messages.

"Yes."

"Jordin just sent you some documents in an email. I need you to print them out."

She swallowed hard, then as casually as she could manage, she said, "I'll check to see if I have them."

"What's this?" Bree asked when she returned minutes later.

"Proof of everything I've been telling you."

She read over the legal document, then looked up at him. "Am I understanding this correctly? You're not going to contest the adoption?"

"No. I just want my name on the birth certificate and shared legal custody." Austin paused a moment before saying, "I told you that I wouldn't take Emery from you, Bree."

"Austin, I wanted you to be in Emery's life," she said, "but I was afraid of losing him if things didn't work out between us."

"Regardless of what happens, we will always be his parents."

Her luminous eyes widened in astonishment. "Thank you for this."

"It was the right thing to do."

Bree wrapped her arms around him. "I can't put into words what this means to me, Austin. I was so afraid of losing my son. I should've trusted you."

"It's in the past," he responded. "Let's just move forward."

She and Austin took an afternoon stroll after lunch. This time Bree took him in another direction.

"I want to show you something." They crossed the street and stood in front of the steps of a church, staring up at the arched doorways and boarded-up windows. "St. Matthew's…this is where my grandmother used to go to church. This building closed down a few years ago. They used to rent the house for guest pastors."

"Why did they close?"

"The pastor died and I guess they just couldn't get

it together after his death." After a moment, she said, "Austin…"

He looked at Bree. "Yes."

"You look like you have something on your mind. Is everything okay?"

"Everything's fine," Austin responded. "I just want this tension between us gone for good."

She took his hand in her own. "I told you that I would try and I meant it. What you did for me today…this helps a lot."

"I miss the way we used to be."

"So do I," Bree confessed.

Austin checked his watch. "We should head back. It's almost time to take Mom to the airport."

That evening they made the trip to Atlanta.

He glanced into the rearview mirror and smiled. His mother and Emery were both napping.

"I think they were asleep before we left Roseville." Bree reached over and gave his hand a light squeeze. "I really enjoyed spending time with your mother."

At the airport Irene gave Austin a hug and whispered, "You need to marry this girl. She's the one for you."

Emery and Bree said their farewells.

On the way back to Roseville, Austin thought about his mother's words. For the past couple of days, he had been thinking more and more about marriage. There was no doubt in his mind.

Austin wanted to marry Bree. Not because she was the mother of his son, but because he loved her more than life itself.

But how could he convince Bree of this?

Chapter 20

The next morning Bree and Emery met Austin at the hotel for breakfast.

"Something's come up with one of my clients," he announced. "I'd planned to stay until the weekend, but I have to leave after we eat."

"Then Emery and I are leaving, as well," she responded. "It's time for us to go home. If you give me an hour, I can pack and be ready to go."

"I can do that."

They finished eating and went to their cars.

Austin followed Bree to the house.

He packed up Emery's things while she emptied out the refrigerator.

Bree moved quickly through the house.

An hour later they were ready to leave.

"So, what happens now?" Austin asked as he carried a sleeping Emery into Bree's house in Charleston. They had been on the road for several hours. He was glad to be back.

"We have the paternity test done and make it official," Bree stated.

"I still want us to be a family."

"I promise I'll think about everything you've said."

"Yes." He touched her cheek. "Our son deserves to have both parents in the home."

"*Our* son..." she repeated. "It's going to take some time for me to get used to the idea of Emery as our child."

"I understand how you feel."

Bree glanced up at him. "I suppose you do in some way."

He looked at Emery. "When do we tell him?"

"Once we're back on solid ground."

Austin wrapped his arms around her midriff. "I have one favor to ask of you. Please don't let this come between you and Jordin."

Bree smiled. "I'm not. I plan to give her a call later today. We'll talk it out."

"I really do love you."

She put her arms around his neck. "I believe you, Austin."

He kissed her to satisfy his burning desire and aching need to feel her lips against his own. Austin drank in the sweetness of her kiss.

Although it was Thursday, it felt more like a Monday, Austin thought as he entered his office. Most likely because he'd been in Georgia for a little over a week and this was his first day back. He shifted his position in his chair, hoping to ease the ache between his shoulder blades.

He'd spent the morning answering constant phone calls, new emergencies cropping up, and now that everything had been taken care of, he dropped into his chair.

Austin breathed in the calm, hoping it wasn't the lull before another storm.

He was tired and his nerves throbbed.

Pam, his legal assistant, knocked on his door and opened it.

"I'm sorry. I know you didn't want to be interrupted."

"It was inevitable," he responded. "What's up?"

"The files just arrived from the district attorney's office. You said you wanted them as soon as they arrived."

"That I did."

He stood, meeting Pam halfway across the spacious room, saving her a few steps.

Austin knew that she'd had the same kind of day as his, so he suggested, "Why don't you take off early? It's almost four and you worked through lunch, too."

"I nibbled on something at my desk."

"Not good enough." She was pregnant and Austin wanted to make sure she took care of herself. "Go on. You need to take advantage of any quiet time you can get. After the baby comes, who knows when you'll be able to have time for yourself."

"There's a mountain of work left fo—"

"The firm won't fall apart overnight," Austin interjected. "I insist that you go home and put your feet up."

Pam smiled. "Thank you."

His eyes burned with weariness, prompting him to press his hands over them.

Another hour passed before Austin gave in to his exhaustion, headed home and fell into bed.

He opened his eyes and checked the time. It was barely eight o'clock. He'd slept for almost two hours.

Austin went to the bedroom and stripped before stepping into the shower. Bowing his head, he let the water flow over his back.

A short time later he was dressed and in the kitchen making a dinner salad. Austin felt much better than he had earlier.

The telephone rang.

"Hello, sweetheart," he said.

"Are you busy?" Bree inquired.

"No, I left the office at five and came straight home to get some sleep. I was exhausted, babe."

"It was a rough day for me, as well."

"If you don't mind, I'm just going to stay in tonight," Austin stated. "I have court tomorrow morning."

"That's fine. It'll probably be an early night for me, too."

"Where are you?" he asked.

"I'm on my way home. I had to meet with a support group and it had just ended when I called you."

He stifled a yawn. "How about I come by your place tomorrow after I leave work?"

"I'll see you then," Bree said. "Get some rest."

Austin glanced down at the salad and sighed.

"The place smells delicious," Bree said when she entered the house.

She strolled through the tan-painted door that led into a warm kitchen, where Sara, wearing a flour-covered apron, was pulling a tray out of the oven.

"Hey, sugar. You home earlier than I expected," she said, setting the tray on a cooling rack. "Emery wanted some peanut butter cookies. I followed your recipe to the letter."

Bree set two large grocery bags on the counter. "Everything you bake comes out wonderful. I'm sure the cookies are fine."

Arms folded, Sara leaned against the counter. "We haven't talked about this sudden vacation of yours yet."

"Where's Emery?"

"He's in his room playing on that iPad."

"Austin is Emery's biological father," Bree announced.

Sara's mouth opened in surprise. *"What you say?"*

"I was just as shocked. Then I panicked. That's why I left town. Miss Sara, I didn't know what else to do."

She began putting away the groceries.

"You know that man loves you and Emery."

Bree nodded. "I believe that. I just don't like the way he manipulated me." She picked up the bag of apples and placed them in the fruit bowl. "Don't get me wrong. I understand why he did it."

"I know a good man when I see one," Sara said. "You have a good one, sugar. Focus on what's most important here. A man that loves you and your son. That don't come every day."

Bree helped herself to a freshly baked cookie.

"They're too brown, don't you think?" Sara asked. "They'll be dry."

"Miss Sara, this is *delicious*. They're perfect."

"Thanks, sugar. I'm glad you're enjoying them."

Putting away a loaf of bread in the pantry, Bree said, "He asked me to marry him, and I turned him down."

Sara gasped in surprise. "Now, why did you do a fool thing like that? That man loves you."

"I felt like he was mostly asking because he didn't want to lose Emery." Bree paused a moment, then said, "I was angry then. But after everything that's happened, I still love him."

She put away the canned goods.

"Does this mean that you two are working things out?"

Biting her lip, Bree gave a slight nod. "Right now we're waiting for the results of the paternity test so that Emery's birth certificate can be amended. Emery will become a DuGrandpre."

"If you'd go on and marry that man—you'll also be a DuGrandpre, sugar. One big happy family."

"We're taking it one day at a time, Miss Sara."

"What are you and Emery doing for Thanksgiving? You're welcome to come with me to my sister's house in Columbia."

"We're actually going to have dinner with Austin's family."

"That's great," Sara said. "I didn't feel too good about leaving y'all here alone."

Bree embraced the woman. "Miss Sara, you don't have to worry about me and Emery."

"Well, I do worry about you. You're like a daughter to me."

They hugged.

"I'd better get out of the way. I'm sure Austin will be here soon."

"He's not coming by tonight," Bree stated. "I think the drive back from Georgia yesterday wore him out. He's tired. I could hear it in his voice." She reached into the refrigerator for a bottle of water. "Truth is, I'm exhausted and all I want to do is crawl into my bed and sleep."

"I'll get out your hair then, sugar. I put a plate of food in there for you."

Bree walked Sara to the front door.

She was tired and felt a bit sleep-deprived, but she wanted to spend some quality time with Emery.

"Hey, sweetie," Bree said as she entered his room. "Are you ready for some cookies and milk?"

"Mommy…" He rushed over to her, wrapping his arms around her legs." Bree felt the tenseness leave her body and she became more animated. Emery was just the fuel she needed to recharge.

* * *

The following Thursday they spent Thanksgiving with Etienne and Eleanor and the rest of the family. Austin and Bree decided to wait on telling the rest of his family until after the results of the paternity test came back. After settling Emery at the children's table, Austin and Bree navigated into the dining room, where the others had gathered.

He pulled out a chair for her.

After she was seated, Austin sat down in the empty one beside her. He didn't say anything as he listened to the easy camaraderie between his family.

Etienne blessed the food.

"Amen," they all said in unison.

Austin handed her a plate of hot yeast rolls. "Aunt Rochelle made these from scratch. I have to warn you—you can't eat just one."

"I'll try and restrain myself," Bree responded with a chuckle. "I intend to leave some room for dessert."

Surrounded by the chatter of family, Austin's thoughts landed on his mother. He couldn't help but wonder how she was faring on this day. For many years, it was just the two of them and a few close family members during the holidays.

"Are you okay?"

He could feel the heat of Bree's penetrating gaze on him and glanced over at her. "I was just thinking about my mom."

"Have you spoken to her?"

"I called her earlier but she was at work. I'll call her after we leave here." Austin gave her a tiny smile before returning his attention to his plate.

He reached for the macaroni and cheese and spooned some onto his plate. Austin then picked up the platter piled high with ham, and placed a couple of thin slices on his plate.

Bree reached over, squeezing his hand.

After the entrée and before dessert was served, Etienne stood up to make a toast.

Austin excused himself moments later to check on Emery. He found the children laughing and teasing each other.

Emery spotted him and waved. "I have fun."

"Finish up your corn, buddy."

"Okay…"

"Did he eat all of his food?" Bree asked when Austin returned to his seat.

"He's finishing off his corn now."

That evening when they returned to Bree's house, he helped Emery get into his pajamas.

"Au'tin, I can do it," he fussed.

"Okay," he said. "I was only trying to help you, but I see that you're a big boy."

Emery grinned. "I'm big boy, Au'tin."

He heard footsteps and looked up to see Bree enter the bedroom. "He dressed himself," Austin told her.

"I'm so proud of you, sweetie."

"Me, too, Mommy."

They stayed in the bedroom with Emery until he fell asleep, and then tiptoed into the hallway.

Austin wrapped an arm around her. "I'm in the mood for a movie. How about you?"

"It's my turn to pick what we watch."

"No, it's not," he countered. "You picked that last movie, which was boring. It's my turn."

Bree turned to face him. "I'll be your best friend if you let me choose."

"That only works with Emery."

She laughed. "Hey, it was worth a shot."

In the family room, Austin placed a call to his mother, but didn't get an answer. He left a message for her.

He returned his attention to Bree and the movie they were about to watch.

"You still can't reach your mom?"

He shook his head. "I'm going to try her again when I leave here. If I can't get her then… I'm flying to Dallas to find out what's going on."

Irene called him back an hour later.

"Mom, where have you been?" he asked.

"I was out with a friend. Honey, I'm fine."

He reached over and gave Bree's hand a gentle squeeze. "I'm glad you're okay."

She snuggled against him.

Austin talked to his mother another ten minutes, then hung up.

"Now that we know your mom's okay, we can focus on each other."

He kissed her.

"You're welcome to stay here tonight," Bree said.

He normally spent the night whenever Emery wasn't home. "I need to get an early start on Christmas shopping. I'm actually going to the mall when I leave here."

"You're a brave soul," she responded, walking him to the door. "I don't have the energy to fight through the crowds. In fact, I'm making most of my purchases online."

Bree released a small moan when Austin's mouth drifted across hers, and for a moment she softened in his arms, her fingers trembling against his chest.

Austin pulled away and looked down at her tenderly. "I love you so much." As his lips touched hers once more, it was like oxygen to a fire that had been smoldering for years, but now blazed into a raging wildfire.

Desire overtaking them, Austin and Bree retreated to her bedroom, where he freed her of all clothing.

Bree couldn't hold back a shiver at the torrent of sensation pouring through her.

He paused, concern evident on his face. "Are you cold?"

"No," she murmured. "Everything is perfect."

Bree reached for his face, drawing him closer to her, and kissing him fiercely.

Austin groaned and responded with the same hunger, his mouth tangling with hers, his hands exploring her curves. He clutched at her, pressing close even as Bree pulled him closer still.

It wasn't enough for either of them.

Heart racing, breath ragged, he couldn't think of anything other than being with this amazing woman—his soul mate.

Mail in one hand and a shopping bag filled with wrapped gifts in the other, Austin was looking forward to spending his first Christmas with Bree and Emery. He dropped the gifts near a stack of presents, then scanned through the stack of envelopes in his other hand. He read the label of the large manila one.

Austin tore open the envelope and pulled out the single sheet of paper. He unfolded it, and stared down at the results. Sitting in his stomach was suddenly a boulder, stony and painful. It pressed his lungs until he couldn't breathe. "Dear Lord…" he uttered. "How could this be?"

His temper flared and curses fell from his mouth. *Jasmine.* Apparently, she had been cheating on him.

It wasn't something he'd ever considered. Although it certainly explained a lot. She started to change during the last six months or so, leading to their breakup.

He still had her phone number, although he'd meant to

throw it away. Austin squeezed his eyes shut, as if willing back further tears.

"Hello."

"Jasmine, we need to talk." He spat out the words contemptuously.

"Okay."

"I need the truth from you about Emery."

He heard a soft gasp.

"W-what are y-you talking about? What *truth*?"

"I'm not in the mood for games," he stated sharply. "I know where Emery is and I know that his blood type does not match mine. There is no way he can be my son."

His words were met with silence.

"Jasmine…" he prompted.

"I'm here."

"When I saw you a few months back, why didn't you set the record straight?" Clenching his teeth, Austin was furious.

"That's why I wanted to meet for dinner, but then you called me and you were so angry… I just couldn't."

"You didn't think I'd find out?"

"I guess I hoped you wouldn't. That's the real reason I left town with Cheryl. I was scared that the baby might not be yours."

"Who is that boy's father?"

"This guy I met one night at the club. We'd had a fight and you wouldn't return my calls, so I got drunk and had a one-night stand. To be honest, I don't remember much about the guy—not even his name. I think it was William…don't think I ever got his last name. I was ashamed and I just wanted to forget that night." She paused a moment, then said, "If I was sure it was your child—I never would've left, Austin. You are the only man I've ever loved. I couldn't risk you finding out that the child you thought was yours was actually someone else's."

"Which is exactly what happened."

"You found Emery?"

"Yes."

"Is he happy?"

"He is," Austin confirmed, his voice cold and exact.

"I'm glad."

"Thank you for telling me the truth, Jasmine."

"I'm so sor—"

"Save it," he interjected vehemently. "I'm beginning to realize that I never really knew you. I don't know how you can face yourself in a mirror."

She was crying.

"You did the right thing by giving him up," he replied with contempt that forbade any further argument.

Austin ended the call and blocked her number. He knew her well enough to know that she would try to reach out to him again.

He crept down the hall like a ghost to the room he was decorating for Emery, and hovered in the doorway.

It had all been a waste of time, money and energy because he didn't have a son. The thought was like a punch in the gut to him.

Austin's eyes grew wet with unshed tears.

He picked up the football and held it close to his aching heart.

Austin dropped down to the floor, his mind releasing all the dreams he'd had for his son—all the things he was looking forward to doing—tee ball, basketball, swimming…football when Emery was older… Everything crashed down all around him. His breath came raggedly in impotent anger and he bristled with indignation.

His cell phone rang.

He glanced down at it.

It was Bree.

Austin couldn't talk to her right now. His thoughts were racing dangerously. He couldn't talk to anyone.

Chapter 21

Austin didn't go to work the next day. He stayed in the condo, wrapped in a cocoon of anguish until he figured Bree had left the office and was on her way home.

"Hey, I was getting worried about you," she said when he arrived at her door. "You haven't returned any of my calls."

"I'm sorry," Austin responded. "I just got the results of the paternity test."

She smiled. "That's wonderful. Now you can have your name placed on the birth certificate."

Austin sank down in a nearby chair. "Actually, I can't."

"I'm not sure I understand."

"Emery is *not* my son." He felt an acute sense of loss in just saying the words. "Jasmine was cheating on me and I had no idea. Now that I think about it—I guess this is why she was in such a hurry to leave town. She knew the baby wasn't mine."

His face showed no reaction, which scared her most of all. It was like someone had turned off a switch. It had to be shock. "Austin, I'm so sorry."

Tears in his eyes, he shook his head. "All this time... Bree, I love that little boy."

Austin's features filled with so much emotion that his look almost brought tears to her eyes.

"I'm so sorry." Bree tilted up his chin. "Let me help you."

He pulled her down until she sat on his lap, while the chair leaned back with a resonant creak. Bree's hands fell instinctively over his shoulders, and wordlessly he looped his hands around her hips, holding her close. "What can I do to lessen the pain?"

"Just this," Austin whispered.

She wanted to ask, but didn't want to force him to talk if he wasn't ready. Bree kissed his cheek. "Hon, everything is going to be okay."

Austin gestured for her to get up and rose to his feet. "I've gotta get out of here," he said.

"Don't leave," Bree blurted. "Please, Austin, I've never seen you like this. In your frame of mind, I'll worry about you driving."

"I'll be fine."

"Austin..."

He shook his head. "I have to go. I'm sorry."

Bree's throat closed as she watched him walk away. Shoulders squared, back straight, his dark suit, a shadow of pain clinging to him.

She continued to watch until he drove away.

Her heart ached for the man she loved. She had never met his ex-girlfriend, but imagined she was nothing but a manipulative witch. Who else would play with someone's feelings like this?

He had been looking forward to his first Christmas with Emery and now this... Bree wished that the results had not come until after the holidays. It was then she fully understood why Austin delayed giving her the news about Emery. He was trying to protect her in the same way he wanted to protect him.

Regardless of what the test results said, Austin was a father to Emery. Having the same blood did not necessarily make a person family. Bree knew this from firsthand experience.

She would give him some time to deal with the shock, but she wasn't going to let him stay in this space. They were going to celebrate Christmas as a family. Bree wasn't going to accept anything less. This time she would be the one fighting for her family.

"Bree called me," Jordin stated when he opened the front door. "She thought you might need some company."

Austin stepped aside to let her enter. His sense of loss was beyond tears.

They sat down in the living room.

After a moment he uttered, "You didn't have to come all the way over here, Jordin. I'm fine."

"I don't believe you."

He met her gaze. "I feel like a fool," Austin said after a moment, shaking his head regretfully.

"*Why?* You had no idea that you'd been given wrong information. Jasmine's friend brought all this to you."

"I'm sure she was only going by what she was told. Cheryl wasn't a messy person."

"I find that surprising that she didn't know Emery wasn't your child," Jordin said. "Especially since she was Jasmine's best friend."

Austin considered her words. "I guess you're right. I hadn't thought about it that way."

"You told me that the last time you saw Jasmine, she wanted to talk to you."

"Yeah," he responded. "Over dinner."

"Maybe that's why Jasmine wanted to meet you that night," Jordin suggested. "Maybe she was going to tell you the truth. She had to know that you wouldn't just walk away from your son without a fight."

"Sis, it wouldn't have mattered because I wouldn't have believed her. She's a big liar." Austin released a long sigh, clasped his hands together and stared down at them.

Jordin shook her head. "I really don't understand women like her. One thing I know for sure is that Bree loves you, Austin. So does Emery. It's not too late for the two of you to become a family."

"I'm still working to regain her trust. Things are good between us, but I don't think she's ready to accept my marriage proposal."

"You proposed to her?"

He nodded. "When we were in Georgia, but she turned me down."

Jordin smiled. "She was upset then. I'm sure you don't have to worry about that now. Unless you decide to walk away."

His eyes filled with tears. "I have no claim to Emery."

"He may not be of your blood, but you've acted like a father to that boy...how can you abandon him now?"

"I don't know what to do."

"Do what you planned, Austin. *Be Emery's father.* You love Bree and you love that child."

"I do love them."

"Then you can't give up on them."

"I think Bree's given up on me," he responded. "She values honesty above all things and she feels I wasn't truthful with her. Jordin, I have to accept my part in all this and it's cost me a great deal."

A lone tear slipped down his cheek.

"I don't believe that," Jordin murmured as she embraced him. "Bree still loves you."

"I never knew love could hurt this much."

Jordin walked into the kitchen and made him a cup of tea. She brought the mug to him.

"Thank you, sis."

"I know it doesn't feel like it right now, but everything is going to work out between you and Bree. You're not going to lose your family."

Austin sipped the hot liquid. "I love them both more than my own life, sis. There was so much I wanted to do with that boy."

"And you can still do those things. Does finding out that he's not your son change your heart?"

Austin shook his head. "No."

"Then go to Bree," Jordin advised. "Let her know that you still want to be Emery's father and her husband."

Bree did not rest well. Her thoughts all night had been consumed with Austin and the pain he was going through.

After breakfast, she called to check on him. "How are you?"

"Still a bit numb," he responded.

"You know how you always tell me that things are going to work out fine," Bree began. "Well, you have to believe that this is going to be okay."

"Yeah," was his response.

"Are you going to the office today?"

"Yeah," he answered. "I need to keep busy."

"Honey, I hate the hurt I hear in your voice," Bree said. "I'm so sorry."

"Don't worry about me. I'll be fine."

She didn't believe his words any more than Austin believed them. She knew he was trying not to fall apart with her.

"I need to get going," he said. "I'll talk to you later."

Bree decided she was going to surprise Austin by taking him to lunch. She had to do something to cheer him up. *I need to remind him of how important he is to Emery.*

She walked through the Broad Street entrance of the building that housed the law firm a few minutes after 1 p.m. Bree knew that Austin never went to lunch before then.

She called him from the reception area. "Hey, I'm here."

"This is a surprise."

"I'd like to take you to lunch."

"Would you now..." he murmured.

Bree smiled. He almost sounded like his old self. "You probably need to eat something. I'm pretty sure you haven't left your office much since you got here."

"Sometimes I forget how well you know me. I'll be right out."

Minutes later he strode through a door. She met him halfway. "Hey, handsome."

"Where are we going?" Austin asked.

"Wherever you'd like to go."

They walked out of the building.

Out the corner of her eye, Bree saw a young woman getting out of a black town car. She wouldn't have paid her any mind, but Austin had a violent moment of reaction to seeing the woman, which she recognized as anger.

The woman was eyeing her, curiosity coloring her expression.

He stopped walking as she neared and asked, "Jasmine, why did you come here?"

Bree felt a thread of apprehension. What was Emery's biological mother doing in Charleston? She glanced up at Austin.

His expression was clouded with fury.

"I came to see you because I didn't like the way we ended our conversation. I'd like to speak to you *alone*."

"I'm not going anywhere," Bree stated.

"And you are *who*?" she asked, looking down her nose. "Actually, it doesn't even matter. This has nothing to do with you."

"That's where you're wrong," Austin replied sharply, taking Bree's hand in his own. "This is Emery's mother."

Jasmine's expression was one of pure shock. She tried to recover but was failing miserably. "You're dating the w-woman who *adopted* my s-son."

Austin's lips thinned to a furious scowl. "Our relationship is not your business."

"Does she know everything?"

Austin nodded. "Yes, she does. We don't have any secrets between us."

"Would you like to see a picture of Emery?" Bree interjected.

Jasmine's eyes filled with tears. "Yes."

She handed her a photo.

"He looks very happy and loved." Jasmine gave Bree a small smile. "Thank you for taking such good care of my son."

"I love him. I can't see my life without Emery in it."

"You were made to be a mother," Jasmine stated. "I don't have those maternal instincts. I'm sure you must think I'm a horrible person."

"It takes courage to acknowledge something like that. You shouldn't hang your head in shame. You did an incredible thing—you gave your son a chance to be raised by someone who desperately wanted to be a mother, but couldn't otherwise."

"Are you planning to tell him that he's adopted?"

Bree nodded. "I want to be honest with Emery. When he's old enough to understand, I'll tell him." She glanced over at Austin before asking, "Do you want me to tell him about you?"

Jasmine shook her head. "I'd rather you didn't. I think it'll do more harm than good. Will he be able to find out my name?"

Austin shook his head. "His birth certificate reflects Bree's name. The original one with your name has been sealed. The only reason I had a copy was because Cheryl gave it to me."

"He's better off not knowing anything about me," Jasmine said. "Austin, you may not be his father by blood, but you are the one I would've chosen. Emery's very fortunate to have you both."

"He's also lucky to have had a mother who loved him enough to give him up," Bree stated.

"I guess it's time I head to my hotel."

"You're staying in town?" Austin asked.

"My husband's performing in Savannah tomorrow night. I came a day early so that I could talk to you. I'll be leaving in the morning."

Jasmine walked back to her waiting car and got inside. They watched her drive away.

"Go on and say it," Austin said as they neared her car. "I know you have something to say."

"I can't really see the two of you together. She didn't strike me as your type. She's materialistic. I could tell from her wedding ring, the designer clothes...she loves a certain type of lifestyle."

"I guess that's why we didn't work out. I prefer to save my money."

"She loves Emery, though."

"*You really believe that?*"

Bree nodded. "Not everyone is cut out for motherhood. Jasmine recognized this about herself and she did what was best for him."

"I thought all women were born with maternal instincts."

"That belief is a myth," Bree stated. "There are women who find the idea of motherhood exciting, but find that having to commit eighteen years to raising a child frightening. While women's bodies are designed to carry children, it doesn't make them mothers. In grad school, I wrote a paper on this topic. Women like Jasmine value freedom and independence over the responsibility of being a mother."

"I guess I hadn't looked at it from that perspective."

They walked into the restaurant.

Once they were seated, Bree stated, "She's still in love with you."

Austin looked up from his menu. "I don't return those feelings."

"You still feel betrayed, though."

"Are you analyzing me?"

"No, I don't have to—I can see the pain in your expression."

"Everything you and I have gone through could've been avoided if she'd just told me the truth."

"I'm glad she didn't," Bree said, "because we wouldn't have met."

"Maybe we would have," Austin countered. "My family is here and you're my sister's best friend. I believe our meeting was inevitable."

The waiter came to take their orders.

While they waited for the food to arrive, Bree said, "I hope that you're still planning to spend Christmas Eve with us. You should be there when Emery opens his presents."

"I am."

"Good," Bree stated. "It will do you both some good."

He smiled. "I believe you're right. It's just something about that little boy that makes my world a much better place."

"Emery asked me if he had a daddy."

"What did you tell him?"

"I told him yes and that he'd meet him very soon." Bree took Austin's hand. "I want you to consider adopting Emery. Then he will truly be *our* son. We can tell him Christmas Eve."

"I see you've given this a lot of thought."

"I know you love Emery. I see it every time you look at him. I hear it when you talk about him. He is the son of your heart. It was the same for me when I saw him for the first time."

"We're going to have a wonderful Christmas," Austin said. "I believe this year we will all be getting everything we want."

Bree nodded in agreement. "You're looking more like yourself now."

"I have you to thank for this early gift. *I have a son.*"

"A beautiful little boy."

Austin shook his head. "He's handsome. Girls are beautiful."

"A mother has a right to call her son whatever she wants."

He smiled. "I guess I stand corrected."

Chapter 22

The rainy night in Charleston was a perfect one for staying inside and enjoying a quiet dinner. Soft, contemporary jazz floated throughout the house accompanied by the soft patter of raindrops on the balcony.

"I've never had sushi before," Austin said, "but I'm going to keep an open mind."

"You've never tried a California roll?"

"No. Just never had a desire to try them."

"I ordered a variety for you to try," Bree announced.

"I can tell you now, if it's not cooked—I'm not sure how I'm going to like it, but what do you recommend?"

"How about the empire roll for starters? It's spicy salmon with shrimp tempura, cucumber, avocado and their house sauce."

Austin sampled it. He found the texture interesting, but not offensive. "It's not bad. Not bad at all."

She smiled.

"This is delicious, actually."

Bree pointed to another plate. "Now try this one. It's a spicy tuna roll."

Austin tried it, then said, "I'm not crazy about this one."

She grinned. "Wait until you try the baked king crab roll. I'm pretty sure you're going to love it."

Bree was right. "Okay, I think this might be my favorite."

He glanced over at her plate. "What are you eating?"

"It's called a rainbow roll. Would you like to try some?"

"I'll pass. I think I'm going to stick to the king crab roll."

Bree had ordered deep fried chicken cooked with egg and onion and served over rice as their main entrée.

After they finished their meal, Austin and Bree settled down in the living room.

He pulled her toward him and kissed her. Heat sparked in the pit of his stomach and ignited into an overwhelming desire.

Austin kissed her a second time; his tongue traced the soft fullness of Bree's lips.

She gave herself freely to her passion, matching him kiss for kiss.

"When will Emery be back?" he asked. Jordin had taken him to the movies and to visit with Amya and Kai.

Bree glanced at the clock. "In an hour."

Austin grinned. "That gives us enough time…"

"Is that all you think about?"

He heard the teasing in her tone. "I know you want me as much as I want you." Pulling her close, Austin kissed her; the touch of her lips on his was a delicious sensation.

"I love holding you like this," Austin whispered. He bent his head, kissing her neck.

Bree returned his kisses with reckless abandon.

He stepped away from her as if he was about to speak, but he couldn't take his eyes off her. He just stood there looking at the woman he loved.

She breathed lightly between parted lips. She didn't say a word, but Austin could see her desire in her gaze.

He helped her undress right there in the middle of the family room.

No words were spoken from their lips; they communicated only through their hearts and their passion.

A fire blazing and Christmas lights twinkling, Emery stood between Austin and Bree as they placed the ornament he'd made on the Christmas tree. The air was scented with spruce and spices from cinnamon-studded oranges.

Clad in a pair of Hulk pajamas, Emery announced, "Santa comin' tonight."

When that cute little boy looked up at him with big, adoring eyes and a sweet smile, Austin wanted to be the best man he could possibly be.

"I know. I bet he's bringing you a lot of presents."

"Mommy say I was a good boy."

"That's what Santa looks for—good boys and girls."

Bree sank onto the sofa by the Christmas tree while Austin put their son to bed.

"Austin, I love watching you with Emery. You were made to be a father."

He sat on the rug in front of the fire. "I still feel like he's a part of me—that he's mine."

"I never had a real family, Austin. I don't know who my father was, and I don't want my son ever feeling the way I did. He needs you. I need you."

"I need you, too," Austin responded.

"I want you to know that I'd like to adopt again. I don't want Emery to be an only child."

He smiled. "We can adopt as many children as you want, babe. But first, there's something I think we need to do."

"What's that?"

"Get married. You turned me down the first time, but I'm going to put my pride aside and ask again." Austin bent down on one knee. "Bree, will you do me the honor of becoming my wife?"

He pulled a black velvet ring box out of his pocket and opened it, revealing a cushion-cut diamond surrounded by emeralds. Beside it was a smaller ring, a simple white gold band.

"That's for Emery," Austin announced. "I'm committing myself to be the best husband and father possible. Now, I just need an answer if you can stop crying long enough."

Bree felt her throat tighten with emotion. "Y-yes," she managed between tears.

She handed a gift to Austin. "I want you to open this tonight."

"Right now?"

Bree nodded.

Inside was a framed photo of him and Emery. They were both sleeping."

"You *are* his father," Bree murmured. "In every way that matters."

He grinned at her. "Always. Merry Christmas, babe."

"Merry Christmas."

Austin pulled her down to the rug with him and his mouth again found hers.

He was the right man, and the man she loved and would love forever.

The fire crackled and the Christmas lights seemed to twinkle even more brightly.

Bree smiled, feeling her grandmother's presence, and her love.

* * *

Bree woke up to find Austin staring at her. "How long have you been up?"

"For about an hour. Merry Christmas, babe."

"Merry Christmas, Austin." She sat up in bed, pulling the covers up to hide her nakedness. Her gaze traveled to the ring on her left hand. "I feel like this is all a wonderful dream."

"It's real. We're getting married."

Bree exhaled a long sigh of contentment. "I'm really happy."

"I'm glad." He propped himself up against a stack of pillows. "I don't know about you, but I'd like to get married as soon as possible. I don't want to deprive you of your dream wedding, though."

"I had a big wedding the first time and it was mostly Caleb's family. I had friends there, but no one outside of my foster parents. I'd like a pass on that this time around. I'm good with having the justice of the peace marry us."

"How about a small, intimate ceremony with just family?"

"Don't have any."

She glimpsed a shadow of disappointment in his eyes. "How about this…we get married and then have a really nice reception for family and friends."

"That's fine."

She studied his face. "Are you sure you're okay with this?"

"I don't care how we do it—I just want to marry you."

"Then let's plan a trip to Hawaii for the three of us," Bree said. "Unless you'd rather not take Emery. We can get married on the beach at sunset."

"No, Emery has to be there when we officially start our lives together," Austin stated. "I've never been to Hawaii."

"Neither have I, but I've always wanted to go there. I think it's the perfect place for me to become your wife."

Bree eased out of bed. "I'd better shower and get dressed. There's no telling when Emery will wake up."

"Mind if I join you?"

She smiled. "I thought you'd never ask."

Austin glanced at the clock on the nightstand. It was a few minutes past 7 a.m.

By eight o'clock, they were in the kitchen preparing breakfast.

Bree was in the middle of making scrambled eggs while he was on sausage duty.

He heard the patter of tiny feet and said, "Merry Christmas, buddy. Breakfast will be ready in a couple of minutes."

"Open presents?"

Bree planted a kiss on his forehead. "After breakfast, sweetie."

"I want juice pleeze."

"There's a cup on the table waiting for you." She scooped up eggs and put them on a plate laden with two sausage links. Austin added a piece of toast before Bree carried it over to Emery.

Austin followed with plates for him and Bree.

"Did you sleep here?" Emery asked while rubbing his eyes.

Austin smiled as he sat down. "I did."

"Why didn't you sleep in my room with me?" Emery placed a forkful of scrambled eggs into his mouth.

Bree chuckled as she dropped down in the seat facing Austin.

"Did you sleep with Mommy?"

She turned to look at Austin, curious to see how he was going to respond.

"Yes."

"Daddies sleep with mommies," Emery announced. He got out of his chair and walked around the table to where Austin sat. "Are you my daddy?"

He picked up the little boy. "What do you think?"

Nodding, Emery touched his cheek. "Can I call you Daddy?"

"It would make me very happy to hear you call me Daddy," Austin exclaimed with intense pleasure. "I love you so much."

"Love you, too, Daddy."

Bree's smile broadened in approval as she gloried in the shared moment between father and son.

After breakfast, it was time to open the presents.

Emery sat on the floor surrounded by more toys than Bree had seen anywhere outside a toy store. Austin was busy putting together a railroad set and train.

She looked on, both hands resting on the head of a stuffed brown teddy bear nearly three feet high, a gift to her from Emery. Jordin had purchased it for him to give to her, and Bree loved it.

"This is the best Christmas I've ever had," she told Austin.

He met her gaze. "For me, as well. Spending it with you and Emery… I couldn't ask for anything more."

"I want it to always be this way. I want this to be *our* tradition. I know your family's big on holidays, but I like the intimacy of it being just the three of us."

"We can do that," Austin said. "I promise."

Jazz floated slowly around them.

With Emery asleep in bed, Austin came out of the kitchen with two champagne flutes. He handed one to Bree. "I propose a toast."

She smiled and held up hers, as well. "To what, handsome?"

"You."

She chuckled.

"To me?"

"Yes, to you and to me. In a couple of months, you're going to be my wife. Most of our relationship has been fun."

"Yes," she said as their glasses clinked. "It's been fun."

Austin placed his glass down and studied her. "You are so beautiful, Bree. Sometimes I can't believe you're so much a part of my life."

"You've become very important to me. I've never been loved by anyone the way you love me and Emery." Bree walked over to the fireplace.

"This has been a beautiful day, Austin. Everything's been fabulous."

He smiled at her. "Glad you approve."

"I do. Now the thing is...you have to do this every Christmas. It has to be special every year."

"I can do that."

Bree placed her head on his chest as Austin tightened his arms around her.

Moments later she lifted her eyes to his.

As if on cue, they moved closer.

"Want to dance?" Austin asked.

"I'd love to."

They moved to the music slowly.

Non-rushed.

Their bodies swayed to the rhythm, speaking a language of love.

No words were needed.

* * *

The day after New Year's, Bree invited Jordin to lunch.

"Hey, what's going on?" Jordin asked. "You sounded really cryptic on the phone."

Bree waited until her friend was seated before holding up her left hand.

Jordin's mouth dropped open in her surprise. "Oh, my goodness! Girl, that ring is *gorgeous*. You and Austin are engaged."

"Yes."

"I'm so excited for you."

"No more excited than I am," Bree responded with a grin. "I'm so looking forward to being married again."

Jordin nodded in understanding. "So, when did Austin propose?"

"It happened Christmas Eve. We each opened one present and this was mine. We're planning to get married in Hawaii." Bree paused a moment before continuing. "He even bought a ring for Emery."

"How sweet is that?" Jordin murmured softly.

"It brought tears to my eyes."

Have you and Austin thought about a date yet?"

Bree gave a slight nod. "It's going to be in February."

"That's next month. How are you going to plan a wedding so fast?"

"It's just going to be the three of us," she responded. "We want an intimate ceremony."

Jordin's smile disappeared. "Really?"

Bree nodded. "I've already had the big wedding. I'm really not interested in having another one."

"I can't believe we're going to miss out on seeing you get married, but I do understand."

"We haven't told anyone about the engagement," Jordin said. "You're the only one who knows right now."

"Do you plan on telling the family?"

"Yes. We just haven't decided when." Bree laid down her fork. "How do you think your father's going to take the news that we want to get married without the family?"

"He'll be disappointed, but I don't think Dad's the one you really have to worry about—how will Irene feel about it?"

"I'm going to let Austin deal with his mother."

"Wise woman," Jordin said with a chuckle.

"I'm so glad that everything has worked out between you and my brother. I know that he really does love you."

"I know he does," Bree responded. "He's shown me in so many ways. Jordin, when I was in all that pain while we were in Georgia—Austin never left my side. He and his mother took such good care of me and Emery."

"I wish I could've been there for you. How has it been for you since the surgery?" Jordin picked up a French fry and stuck it into her mouth.

"I haven't been in nearly as much pain," she responded, "I still have some, but it's bearable. The treatments are helping."

Jordin signaled for the check. "This is my treat."

They left the restaurant minutes later.

"Girl, congratulations again."

They embraced.

"Thank you," Bree murmured. "We do plan on having a reception here in Charleston after we get back from Hawaii. We'll celebrate as a family."

"I just want you and Austin to be happy."

Chapter 23

The wedding went off without a hitch on Valentine's Day, the weather pleasantly warm on the beach. The vows were made, the rings exchanged and the marriage sealed with a kiss.

Back in Charleston, Austin unlocked the front door to Bree's house, then picked her up and carried her over the threshold.

"Welcome home, Mrs. DuGrandpre."

Emery laughed as if it was the funniest thing he'd ever seen. "You carry Mommy."

"One day when you get married, you'll do the same thing," Austin told his son.

"Surprise..." echoed all around the room.

Bree eyed the members of the DuGrandpre family, then looked over at Austin. "What did you do?"

"Trust me, sweetheart. This is to appease my mother, who was very upset that we didn't have a wedding."

"Should I be scared?"

He laughed. "Emery is our secret weapon."

"I can't believe your mother is actually going to be in the same room as your father and stepmother."

Austin nodded. "It might be a good idea to keep them on opposite sides of the room."

"She just arrived," Bree announced, peeking out the window. "She just got out of the taxi."

He met his mother at the door. "I'm glad you agreed to come."

"I'm not gonna miss the celebration of my only child's marriage. Even though he didn't invite me to the wedding."

"We wanted it to just be the three of us, Mom. Bree doesn't have family, and that's why she didn't want anything big. So, can you forgive me?"

Irene embraced him. "Of course."

Bree spotted Sara and went over to talk to her, but caught sight of Etienne and Eleanor coming through the front door. Her gaze strayed to Austin, who appeared to be searching for his mother.

Irene had seen them enter and was headed straight toward them.

"What's your mother doing?" Bree whispered when she rushed over to Austin.

"I don't know."

He watched as Irene greeted his father with a hug, then she embraced Eleanor. The three talked for a few minutes. His mother glanced over at him and smiled before she moved on to greet the next guest.

Dinner was a more elaborate affair. The caterers had transformed the dining room, adding to the wedding decorations and producing crystal, silver, champagne, wine, hors d'oeuvres and seafood salad, salmon, baby rack of lamb and a bouquet of fresh vegetables. Dessert was a three-layer wedding cake.

Bree was drawn into a conversation with Amya, Kai

and Emery. She bit back her laughter as they talked about Barbie being able to beat up Spider-Man.

"Barbie can't fight 'cause she a girl," Emery said. "Boys fight…not girls."

Kai looked over at her and said, "Girls can fight…can't they, Bree?"

She nodded. "There's Super Girl, Wonder Woman… lots of girls are superheroes."

"But Mommy…not Barbie."

"So tell us about the wedding," Eleanor said after the wedding cake was served.

"We waited until sunset to get married," Austin said. "Emery and I stood on the beach under an arch decorated with this gauzy fabric and vibrant red flowers, waiting for my bride. She showed up, dressed in a strapless satin gown with flowers in her hair and looking stunning. I kept thinking to myself that I was a blessed man to have this terrific woman by my side."

"I'm the one who won the lottery," Bree said. "Austin is a wonderful man and a great father."

He kissed her.

The room erupted in applause.

She glanced over at Jordin and crossed the room. Bree sat down, saying, "Hon, you don't look like you're feeling well."

"I'm a little nauseated," she admitted. "Ethan wanted me to stay home, but I wasn't about to miss this. I'm so happy for you and Austin."

She eyed her sister-in-law. "Are you pregnant?"

"Yes, but we haven't made the announcement yet," Jordin said in a low voice. "We'll tell everyone at the family dinner next weekend."

"Congratulations, sweetie."

The two women embraced.

"Do you want some crackers or something to settle your stomach?" Bree offered.

"Please…"

She left and returned minutes later with the crackers and a glass of ginger ale. "Here you go. If you need to lie down for a bit, you can go into the guest room."

Jordin gave her a grateful smile. "Thanks."

"Just go to the kitchen if you need more."

Bree found her husband and joined him for the cutting of the cake.

Several hours later, after everyone had gone home, she and Austin retired to their room.

Emery had gone with Ryker and Garland for the weekend.

"Thank you for today," Bree told him when he came out of the bathroom.

He climbed into bed with her.

Bree rearranged her pillows before settling back against them. "I saw your mom and dad talking."

"It's been a long time coming. I hope they were able to finally have closure." Austin rearranged his pillows.

"Jadin's boyfriend sure is racking up frequent flyer miles," Bree commented. "Maybe he should just move back to Charleston."

"He loves working with his uncle in Los Angeles, but from what I understand, Michael's been in love with my sister for years. I know she's tried to end it with him a couple of times, but he refuses to give up on her."

"Do you think they'll work everything out?" Bree inquired.

"Yes," Austin said with certainty.

"How can you be so sure?"

"I can feel Michael's determination…all I can say is that my sister better watch out. That man is determined to have a life with her." He pulled Bree into his arms. "Enough about our family. It's time to concentrate on us."

"I love the way you think."

Austin kissed Bree, and planned on doing a whole lot more.

"You're home."

Austin embraced his wife. "Sounds like you missed me."

"What are you talking about? We've been married for six months now," she said. "And honey, I can't wait for you to leave so I can have some time to myself."

He laughed. "Is that why you're always waiting for me at the door?"

Bree gave him a playful punch to the arm. "You make me sound like a puppy."

"You're definitely not a pup, my beautiful and sexy wife."

"Don't try to clean it up now."

He kissed her. "I'm going to take a quick shower. I'll be down by the time dinner's ready."

Austin went upstairs while Bree navigated to the kitchen to check on the baked ziti.

She removed it from the oven and sat it on the stove, then called for her son. "Emery, it's time for dinner. Wash your hands, sweetie."

"'Kay…" was his response.

They sat down to dinner fifteen minutes later.

"I'll clean up," Austin said when they finished eating.

"Hon, I don't mind—"

He cut her off by saying, "Bree, you give Emery his bath and I'll take care of the kitchen." Lowering his voice, he added with a grin, "I'll meet you in the bedroom."

"A man with a plan…"

"These came today," Bree announced when he walked out of the kitchen. "Although it's merely a formality."

"What is it?"

"The final decree of Emery's adoption papers."

Now the little boy was officially what he'd always been in Austin's heart—his son.

Later that evening as they readied for bed, Bree said, "Honey, I know we've been talking about adopting another child…"

Austin met her gaze. "Have you changed your mind?" He was looking forward to expanding their family.

"No, I haven't changed my mind," Bree responded. "But we may want to put it off for a year or so."

"Why?"

"Because we're going to have a baby." She placed his hand to her belly.

Bree immediately saw surprise leap into Austin's eyes.

"I thought you couldn't have children."

"Apparently, the laparoscopic surgery removed enough endometrial tissue to give us this chance of conceiving naturally…" She slapped his arm. "Stop grinning like that. You didn't do this by yourself, you know."

"We were meant to be a family. This proves it." He kissed her. "I love you so much."

With a whoop of joy, Austin lifted her high into the air, twirling her round and round.

* * * * *

LET'S TALK
Romance

For exclusive extracts, competitions and special offers, find us online:

MILLS & BOON

THE HEART OF ROMANCE

A ROMANCE FOR EVERY READER

MODERN

Prepare to be swept off your feet by sophisticated, sexy and seductive heroes, in some of the world's most glamourous and roma... locations, where power and passion collide.

HISTORICAL

Escape with historical heroes from time gone by. Whether your passi... for wicked Regency Rakes, muscled Vikings or rugged Highlanders, ... the romance of the past.

MEDICAL

Set your pulse racing with dedicated, delectable doctors in the high-... sure world of medicine, where emotions run high and passion, comf... love are the best medicine.

True Love

Celebrate true love with tender stories of heartfelt romance, from th... rush of falling in love to the joy a new baby can bring, and a focus ... emotional heart of a relationship.

Desire

Indulge in secrets and scandal, intense drama and plenty of sizzling action with powerful and passionate heroes who have it all: wealth, s... good looks…everything but the right woman.

HEROES

Experience all the excitement of a gripping thriller, with an intense ... mance at its heart. Resourceful, true-to-life women and strong, fearl... face danger and desire - a killer combination!

To see which titles are coming soon, please visit

millsandboon.co.uk/nextmonth